Where There's Muck

Catherine Robinson has taught English and drama in schools and colleges for more than three decades, and is currently teaching at Stonyhurst College, Lancashire. She lives with her husband in Lancashire, where she has always lived, and where (when not teaching or writing) she has raised a son, farmed a small flock of Derbyshire Gritstone sheep, and bred horses. Her debut novel, *Forging On*, was longlisted for the Comedy Women in Print Prize 2019.

Also by Catherine Robinson

Forging On

Where There's Muck

CATHERINE ROBINSON

ORION

An Orion paperback

First published in Great Britain in 2021
by Orion Fiction
an imprint of The Orion Publishing Group Ltd
Carmelite House, 50 Victoria Embankment
London EC4Y 0DZ

An Hachette UK company

1 3 5 7 9 10 8 6 4 2

A CIP catalogue record for this book
is available from the British Library.

ISBN (Mass Market Paperback) 978 1 4091 9993 9
ISBN (eBook) 978 1 4091 9994 6

Typeset by Deltatype Ltd, Birkenhead, Merseyside

Printed in Great Britain by Clays Ltd, Elcograf S.p.A.

www.orionbooks.co.uk

In memory of Pippa
1974 – 2019

POST CARD

Port Elizabeth September 2nd 2016

_Arrived safely in P.E. – which
is more than can be said for the
bloody car which still hasn't
arrived in Durban. Staying with
my dad for a few weeks until we
can get sorted – I'll give you the
address when we've got one. Hope
you guys are coping without me!_
      Dirk.
_P.S: The blue over the buildings in
the photo is sky._

_Professional Western Farriers
148 Hathersage Rd
Hathersage
North Yorkshire
FL9 0JJ
UK_

Chapter 1

I'd been working for Stanley Lampitt DipWCF for over a year. His forge was only fifteen miles from my home, but until I became an apprentice farrier, I'd never been to Hathersage. It is a relic of the Industrial Revolution, nestled in the valley between the Scorthwaite and Eckersley fells. Its solid millstone grit terraces, repurposed mills and empty warehouses line its main road and gradually give onto post-war semis and larger 'villas' with names like 'The Limes' and 'Sunny Bower'. It was from one of these, built on the promise of sustained manufacturing, that Stanley Lampitt plied his trade. Its garage had become a forge and its interior a parody of opulence. Ewan and I called it Bling Manor.

I'd passed my first set of farriery exams and Stanley had finally decided I was ready to nail a shoe to a hoof. I'd bloomed with pride when he told me. Nailing a horseshoe onto a hoof is real farriery. I'd pictured myself bent double with a hammer in my hand and wreathed in smoke – but now, with the book open on my lap and the shire horse twenty feet away, eels were tumbling in my guts. 'You'll be reyt wi' a shire,' Stanley had said. 'Stevie Wonder could shoe one o'them wi' a knife and fork.' Pedley, who owned the horse, was on the other side of the window now, tapping on the face of his watch, but the presence of Lucky, Stanley's psychopathic Jack Russell terrier, meant that a safe van-exit needed our full synchronicity and I was still checking a diagram of the internal structures of the foot. 'Give us a bastard minute!' Stanley advised, but Pedley opened the van door.

Before fresh air had fluttered through the gap, Lucky was in flight. I made a grab for her that sent *Hickman's Farriery (Second Edition)* up in a flapping flurry, but I might as well have grabbed for a Polaris missile. Pedley clamped her with his foot. Lucky swung a crocodile snap. Pedley hopped. Lucky squirmed then she scooted off in a blur of clockwork legs, her line as straight as a second hand. 'Don't just stand there!' Stanley yelled at me over the booming of Pedley's chained Rottweiler. 'Go on!'

Sheep were beginning to scatter. I set off, a bulldog after a greyhound. My only hope was the gate – it might slow her down – but a strut was broken and she flew the gap like a paper plane.

She'd locked onto two sheep apart from the flock. They darted, panicked, unsteady, desperate for the safety of numbers. The others had bunched in the corner of two dry-stone walls, their flanks heaving like racehorses'. Lucky dived at them now, snarling and yapping. A ewe ran at her with its head down. Lucky leapt back; stump tail still thrashing. Sheep wove and threaded, knotting to a clump. Lucky dropped a play bow. She yapped. She bounced in to the bunch and grabbed a mouthful of fleece. She ran in leaping circles with it, thrilled at her treasure. I picked up a stone. If it was play she wanted, I could play.

'Lucky!' I yelled, then again with more playful enthusiasm. 'Lucky! What's this?' I tossed it skyward. She glanced back at the sheep. 'Lucky!' I threw the stone up again and caught it with a downward sweep. I was shocked when she bounded the tussocks towards me, fleece flying from her teeth like a flag. I grabbed it for a game of tug-o-war, and when my left hand was on the fleece, my right scooped her into my arms. She squirmed and wriggled, slithering in my grip. She wouldn't fall for that trick again.

She was still barking in frustration at the receding sheep when I closed the field gate behind us. 'It wants shooting, does that!' Old Pedley was raging, his crimson face inches from Stanley's.

'What do you think it were going to do, Joe?' Stanley was looking on the little dog, now shaking with fury in the crook of my arm. 'Drag one up a bastard tree and eat it?' The tuft of fleece was still poking through Lucky's teeth making it look like she'd tried that already.

I handed Stanley the quivering terrier. He turned to put her back in the van and her head gyroscoped to keep her eyes on the sheep.

'I'll be ringing Michael Morrison next time my horses want shoeing,' Pedley said. Michael Morrison was my mother's farrier and Stanley's 'frenemy'. He irritated Stanley by securing all the lucrative veterinary work. He was no more qualified than Stanley, but he had the quiet blandness of a geography teacher and his even temper meant the vets preferred working with him.

Stanley turned back, the dog still in his arms. 'I've been shoeing for you for twenty year, Joe!'

'Aye, well,' Pedley grunted, 'Michael Morrison won't turn up an hour late wi' a savage dog in his van!'

'Come on,' Stanley pleaded. 'I can leave t'dog at home next time.' Lucky strained upwards to lick Stanley's face.

'You should o' left t'dog at home *this* time,' Pedley muttered.

Stanley's sigh rattled with the metal as he dragged open the van door and shoved a grinning Lucky onto the passenger seat. We unpacked the van through a six-inch crack and as Stanley bent to drag out a rasp, he whispered in my ear, 'I'll be doing the nailing on today.'

I halted the foot stand on its journey to the floor. 'I've been psyching myself up to this!'

'I've no chance o' keeping his business if you lame his bastard horse – have I?' he hissed.

'I've been reading up!'

He dropped the rasp into the pocket of his chaps, 'You can shoe one o' Sylvia's.'

'They're ponies!'

'She thinks the sun shines out of your arse!'

'You said Stevie Wonder could shoe a shire with a knife and fork!'

But Stanley wouldn't budge.

I watched with my hands in my pockets whilst he shod two shires with hoof walls as wide as Hadrian's, and sulked.

Pedley was grudgingly paying up when a machine-gun volley of barking fired from the van. Lucky's front feet were on the window, her stump tail was thrashing, and her ears had pricked to Toblerone triangles. A ewe had appeared behind the gate. Pedley pointed to the dog and shook his head in sad confirmation that we wouldn't be coming back.

She was still ping-ponging round the cab when we climbed back in. Stanley bared his teeth at her, growled at her and flung himself behind the steering wheel. I grabbed her collar and gathered the dog to my lap. Stanley slammed the van into gear and hit the accelerator so hard that Lucky shot straight into the footwell.

Chapter 2

The Best Van growled up Scorthwaite Fell, past yellow speckled gorse bushes and sheep splashed pastures. Lucky's ears triangulated as she gazed on the marshmallow softness of the grazing ewes. I covered her eyes and watched a line of numbered fell runners processing the edge of the road. 'Throstleden Show's on,' Stanley observed. I nodded. Set on the first Friday and Saturday of September, Throstleden Show marks the end of Throstledale's summer. My grandad once won the 'Victoria Sandwich Baked by a Gentleman' prize. The trophy's still in his cabinet. Throstleden Show hosts one of the biggest fell runs in the north of England. If I'd not been working, I'd have been watching my girlfriend, Millie, jumping her horse there.

I'd met Emilia Slater B.Vet. Med. MRCVS, six months ago, when she'd been treating a horse on Richard Jennings' racing yard. With Ewan's encouragement, I'd found the courage to ask her out. She'd joined me at Ewan's 'graduation' party and we'd discovered shared passions for horses, Ed Sheeran and the wild Yorkshire Dales. What were the chances of finding the one girl in Yorkshire who also thought a Sunday fell walk in the drenching rain was exhilarating? We'd climbed Pen-y-ghent in the snow and swum in Malham Tarn in the evening sunshine. We'd flown birds of prey in Settle, walked hand in hand round Skipton horse trials and drunk champagne on Scarborough sands. I could no longer imagine a future without Millie in it, but she was three years older than me and my career was in catch-up. Ewan had been the other apprentice then, but now he was a qualified farrier. If he'd been at Pedley's, he might have persuaded Stanley to let me nail on.

I turned to the passenger window. We passed two more stringy runners striding out with even paces. Stanley watched their steady, swinging rhythm. 'Your mum's on this year isn't she?' he said. He was glancing in his wing mirror as he spoke. 'Do you fancy watching her?'

I'd seen Mumma's demonstration a hundred times. 'I fancy watching Millie,' I said. He slid me a knowing look. 'She's jumping her horse!'

Millie had rescued The Onion from death. She'd been called out to euthanise the racehorse by his trainer, Richard Jennings, because his claustrophobia meant he fretted in a stable and in-jured himself in a wagon. Jennings had been sheepish when she arrived. 'Bad show all round,' he'd said and wished there was another way. All the time Millie was drawing up the first of the two euthanising drugs, Jennings was detailing the damage the horse had done. 'The other owners don't like it either, you see. I had to withdraw Lady Rebel when we got to Musselburgh; she'd been injured by this fellow in the wagon.' He pushed his hands through his fair hair. 'I can't even shut his stable door,' he went on. 'There's just a chain across, or he damn near kicks the thing off its hinges.'

The Onion was on the floor now, flat on his side with his umber coat gleaming in the sunshine. 'He's only five,' Richard added, 'and a lovely natured horse in every other way.' Millie was drawing the second drug into her syringe; the drug that stops the heart. She found the stop watch on her phone – timing is crucial – knelt by the prone racehorse and sought with her hand for a vein. The animal was warm, muscled and throbbing with life. She looked on his shining coat, his athletes' tone, his dancers' limbs and she withdrew her hand. 'Everything all right?' Jennings had asked her, but she had been unable to shift her eyes from the sleeping example of youthful, equine perfection.

'Can I have him?' she'd asked at last. Richard Jennings had been taken aback. The horse didn't belong to him, he was acting on owners' instructions; he'd need to make a phone call. Meanwhile, Millie had made a phone call of her own – to me. 'Do you think your mum would lend me her small wagon? I've driven one before… ' She omitted to mention that The Onion was inclined to trash them, but even if she had, I suspect my mother would have lent it to her; they're equally soft about horses.

Richard Jennings came back, beaming, Millie paid him a pound to keep the transaction official and my mother drove over to collect him herself. He'd still been heavily sedated, so the wagon survived unscathed on the fifteen minute journey to Mossthwaite Farm. As she drove, Mumma had devised a rehabilitation programme and Millie had agreed to livery the horse with us, at Mossthwaite.

This was Onion's first un-sedated trip in a wagon since then (he'd lost his definite article with his racing career). 'What about this afternoon's work?' I asked.

Stanley swung the van into a U-turn. 'Ewan'll cope.'

'Should I ring him?'

'Should you buggery. He'll kick off.'

My teeth slid over my bottom lip.

'Listen,' Stanley said, reaching down to switch on the radio, 'I've had a shit morning of it, and Monday's set to be shitter.' He selected third gear for the steepest slope of the fell road. 'If I fancy an afternoon at Throstleden Show. I'm my own boss and I'm entitled to it.'

I fished out my phone to ring Millie with the good news, but there were no bars showing on my screen.

We dropped into the cupped palm of Throstledale and pulled onto a cow-pasture car-park. We were nestled in a bowl of fells which lap and fold like rumpled silk. Lucky bounced up at the window. I clipped on her lead and Stanley clamped her jaw. 'Bloody behave yourself!' he warned her. She jumped down and trotted beside me. The line of fell runners were distant matchstick men, sketched on a crisp piebald tablecloth. I shaded my eyes to watch them process Throstle Rise like ants. Stanley bought a programme.

In the main ring, handlers in white coats were walking backwards to show off mild mannered cows on white ropes. They were 'Dairy Heifers in Calf; not more than three years old'.

'You know who'd have loved this?' I remarked, then I answered my own question. 'Dirk.'

'He would,' Stanley agreed. 'He loved owt proper English.' Dirk had spent nearly a year working with us, before returning to his native South Africa with his Spanish wife, Maria. They'd lived at Stanley's and we'd become close, so I was surprised by his lengthy silence.

'Have you heard how he's getting on?' I asked, but before Stanley could answer me, a man at my side pointed to Stanley's dog.

'Is this your sheep killer, Stan?' He was as gnarled as an oak log, with a face wider than it was long, and sandwiched between flat cap and anorak.

'Bloody hell, Seth,' Stanley shot. 'Have you been on t'bastard tom-tom drums all mornin'?'

'I can sort it out for you, if you want.'

'How?' Stanley asked and Seth tapped his nose. Stanley shifted and looked down on his dog. 'I'll have a think about it.'

'It'll never look at another yow.' The man beside him winked, his ancient chin was resting on his sheep crook. 'Not once Seth's sorted it.'

'Aye, but how will Seth sort it? I don't want t'RSPCA on us.'

'Oh, give o'er,' Seth scoffed. 'I've sorted hundreds out wi' no bother.' Stanley looked dubious.

Throstleden Show was still a forum for farmers to sow gossip, broker deals and view one another's livestock. Stanley chewed the fat and I took out my phone again. Millie didn't answer.

Stanley followed me past the vintage tractors, the craft tent and the horticulture display. We were heading towards the showjumping ring. Stanley couldn't pass the hog roast though. We were waiting in the queue and my eyes were on the matchstick fell runners silhouetted on the sky, when a punch in the kidneys buckled me over. 'Have you no sodding horses to shoe?'

I looked into Jay's grinning face. 'Have you no sodding horses to ride?'

He answered by holding up a bandaged paw. 'Trapped it in a car door.'

I winced. 'How's tricks at Mervyn's?'

'Shite,' he said cheerfully. 'Half a dozen injured horses, unpaid training fees, and I've just weighed in at eleven stone two.'

'You won't be wanting one o' these, then?' Stanley said to him as he handed me a dripping pork sandwich.

Jay shook his head. 'There's a bit o' good news though – Mervyn's selling Anvil Head to Richard Jennings!'

There was no need to ask why Mervyn Slack was selling Anvil Head; the racehorse was useless. The mystery was why Jennings was buying it.

The public address system crackled to life. *'Over in ring two now, we have local lad Aiden Buttershaw, in the final of the sheep shearing contest.'*

Stanley nudged me. 'We'll have to have a look at this,' he said, pork rind flapping on his chin.

'What about the showjumping.' I was looking in the other direction.

'It'll be two minutes,' he said, striding towards ring two.

'Do you know him?' I asked as we passed the Methodist tea tent.

'Course I do! There's only three families in Throstleden: The Holdens, The Buttershaws and the Holden-Buttershaws.'

We snaked like sidewinders between the Barbour jackets and the Le Chameau wellies and I glimpsed cages and cages of crooning, strutting, scaly fowl through a gaping tent flap and shuddered. I loathed the things. The shearers were being introduced: *'He's retired now, is Aidan, but he still dreams about sheep – don't you, Aiden?'* A cockerel hollered. I lifted Lucky up, so I could pass the poultry tent more quickly.

Seth Holden was in the middle of the sheep ring, flanked by two muscular men in vest tops and shearing shoes. He was holding the microphone like it was an unwanted lollipop. Suddenly, two gimmer lambs shot through a shutter. The shearers snatched them up and sat them like babies. Motors buzzed and Seth shouted, *'Hey up! Look at Tom go! He's up its neck already – and down the side he comes! Oh, Aiden's got a wriggler! Go on, Aiden! Peel it! Talk to it! Don't leave any danglers!'*

'Come on, Aiden!' Stanley shouted over the cheering.

'Tom's goin' for it now! He wants that eighty quid! Aiden's catching him though! Fast and clean – down the last side he comes! Oh, and he's done it!' Aiden had released his ewe lamb and Stanley raised his fist like Che Guevara. *'The local lad's done it! Twenty-seven point four seconds!'*

'Right,' I said to Stanley. 'Showjumping,' but just as I spoke, Stanley cocked his ear to the announcer. She was introducing Lizzie Harker and her 'Amazing Dancing Horses'.

'Surely you want to see this!'

'I see it every day!' I reminded him.

'Well, I want to see it,' Stanley said.

The familiar sound track of Ravel's *Boléro* had started and the announcer had moved on to Mumma's marketing spiel: *'Lizzie's skills are in demand all over the country, helping with difficult and dangerous horses. She's worked for the RSPCA, for Sheikh Mohammed Al' Amiry and for two Olympic show jumpers ...'*

'Come on!' Stanley ordered. 'T'showjumping's on all after-noon!'

I sighed and trudged behind him past the W.I. tent and the bouncy castle.

Mumma's four saddle-less, bridle-less mares were trotting, prancing and, head-tossing behind her. She looked younger in the main ring than her fifty-two years. The crowd clapped her entrance and my mother flicked her 'wand'. One horse – Ocean, I think – broke from the herd and began trotting a large left-hand circle. Another went out, right. Then a third trotted left and Phoenix went right. When four horses were weaving a reel, the music changed to a Highland Fling and the crowd spluttered a mesmerised applause. My mother bewildered audiences like a sorcerer. The horses followed her dance steps, lay flat and cantered figures of eight. After twenty minutes, they bowed on her command and the crowd blasted their appreciation.

Stanley turned from the rail. 'That's bloody impressive, is that.' It was, if you didn't see the day-to-day, step-by-step, methodical grind that led to it.

'Right,' I said, lifting Lucky from the tangle of legs. 'Showjumping.' Stanley didn't move. 'Come on!'

'I fancy t'beer tent,' he said. I rolled my eyes. I should have left him at the hog roast stand. He tossed me the van's keys then headed towards the laughing crowd who were grasping plastic glasses by the open flap.

I arrived at the showjumping ring just as a leggy bay gelding was leaving it: Onion. I sighed and set off towards Onion's receding tail. 'Millie!' She twisted in the saddle and resisted in the reins. It's difficult to kiss someone who's sitting on a sixteen hand high thoroughbred, but using her stoop and my tiptoe, we managed an awkward nose bash.

'Three down,' she grinned. She was genuinely pleased. All she'd wanted was for Onion to travel calmly – which, thanks to Mumma's expertise, he'd done.

I followed Onion's loping stride to the wagon park, where I hugged my mother, untacked the horse and helped load him. Once he was happily munching hay in a space no wider than his flanks, Millie and I strolled off to enjoy Throstleden Show. 'Just think,' she said, with one hand holding an ice cream cone and the other swinging my arm, 'when you've your own farriery business and I've my own veterinary practice, we can take a Friday off whenever we want.'

'You're getting ahead of yourself, aren't you?' I laughed and kissed her on the nose. We stopped to admire a pair of Gloucester Old Spots and I remembered Ewan. He'd be just about starting on his third polo pony.

Lesotho September 18th 2016

We're taking a few days in the Drakensbergs. We've seen klipspringer, eland, wildebeest and a Cape vulture today. Didn't I tell you that the mountains look like teeth, Will?

Phones work both ways, you know guys!

Dirk.

Professional Western Farriers
148 Hathersage Rd
Hathersage
North Yorkshire
_FL9 0JJ_
_UK_

Chapter 3

Stanley emerged into the forge wearing a neat grey suit. I'd never seen him dress like that before. His pale blue tie had horseshoes all over it, his shoes were polished to onyx and he was carrying a pale blue envelope file. (Why he was carrying a file was a mystery to me, unless its content had the reading age of a CBeebies magazine. The travelling family he'd been born into had barely sent him to school.) 'Is he still sulking?' Stanley asked me with a flick of his head. Ewan glanced up from the box of horseshoes he was sorting through, then looked away again. Stanley sighed, 'Ewan! You still had half a dozen to shoe!'

'*We* still had half a dozen to shoe!'

Stanley switched the file he was carrying to his other hand. 'You did a day's work; you got paid for a day's work!'

Ewan swung round. '*You* didn't do a day's work though, did you!'

'It's *my* bastard business!'

'It's not his!' Ewan's shaking finger was pointing at me.

'I didn't have a choice!'

'I'll bet you didn't complain though!' He turned back to Stanley. 'You wouldn't have left Dirk with a yard full o' polo ponies to shoe!'

'Oh, for pity's sake!' Stanley raged. 'Dirk's a grown man and a qualified farrier!'

Ewan chucked the shoe he'd been holding back at the box. 'I'll always be the fucking apprentice to you, won't I!'

The clatter had set Lucky yapping. 'I've got DipWCF after my name now! Remember?'

'Well bloody act like it!' Stanley shouted. He turned to me. 'Come on, Posh Lad.'

I trailed him towards my Astra.

'And I hope she takes you for every penny!' Ewan bawled after us.

Stanley stopped in the doorway of the forge and looked back over his shoulder. 'You might just want to think that one through, Dolloper.'

I was taking Stanley to the final hearing of his divorce case. His ex-wife, Lynne, had upped sticks with Fucking Gary (repetition had registered it in my brain as his forename and surname) and Stanley's teenage children, Jonathan and Katie. I struggled to imagine him as a family man. 'He wasn't,' had been Ewan's response. 'That's why she pissed off with Fucking Gary.'

Ewan had liked Lynne. The mystery to him was why she'd married Stanley in the first place. Now, Lynne was demanding half the value of Bling Manor; she had the children and they needed security.

I clicked open the passenger door of my car and Stanley stepped in. 'Thanks for this,' he said. 'The van would have shit me suit up, and I could hardly cry poverty if I turned up in my Porsche, could I?'

I started the engine. 'How long do you think you'll be?'

'Depends how much of a fight my brief puts up.'

I pulled into the traffic snaking Hathersage Road.

'Surely Lynne can't make you sell your premises then expect you to stump up for her every month?' Stanley was silent. 'It'd be like cutting your throat then expecting you to be a blood donor.' I crawled the car to a halt at the pelican crossing.

'You've never met Lynne, have you?' I shook my head and he didn't speak again until I'd pulled into a parking bay outside the family court; a grand building, hewn from millstone grit when Fowlden was rich from wool.

Stanley rearranged the file on his knee. 'Tell Ewan to mind what he's doing wi' that dark bay mare,' he said. 'Mervyn's aiming it at Aintree.' I nodded, and Stanley stabbed a finger at me. 'And I want every brass farthing you two take today. Comprendo?'

'Course.'

He let his seat belt seethe into its anchor. 'And make sure you get that two eighty he owes me from last week.'

'We will.'

He lifted the file off his knee. 'And don't try putting refits on and pocketing the difference, because I'll ask him. I'm not having Lynne robbin' me out o' one pocket and you robbin' me out the bastard other.'

'We don't rob you,' I said.

Stanley's movements had stopped and his deadpan face was looking straight at me. 'I know full well you pocket the money for the trims you do.'

'It's one or two trims,' I admitted, in a voice that implied he was being unreasonable.

'And you keep your tips!'

'They're *our* tips!'

'And there's that client Ewan's taken on at Scorthwaite and said nowt about.' I swivelled my head. *How did he know about that?* 'And there's one at Fowlden he thinks I don't know about an' all.' He gripped the door handle. 'So I want every bastard penny off you two this morning.'

I'd turned away but I felt Stanley freeze. I followed his gaze to a slight, well dressed woman walking up the building's broad steps. Her sleek dark hair was bobbed and she was wearing a knee-length pencil skirt in a dogtooth check. Her red high heeled shoes matched her fitted scarlet jacket and she was gripping a black leather shoulder bag to her hip. 'Hey up.' She turned the vast brass doorknob on the double oak doors and as she turned sideways, glimpsed Stanley. She swung her head quickly away and the action bounced her gleaming black hair off her collar like she was in a shampoo advert. I'd expected Lynne to be homely and wholesome, like Mandy his current love interest; this woman looked sophisticated.

'Right,' Stanley announced when she clicked into the building on high heels. 'I'll get a taxi back,' then he turned and stuck his head through the Astra's open window. 'And leave the dog at home.'

'Why?'

'Why? You've a short bastard memory, haven't you?'

'We're only at Mervyn's.'

'I've enough on my plate,' he said, 'wi'out frettin' o'er what my dog's savaging while my back's turned,' then he turned for the building with a world-weary tread. I remembered Lynne's sharp, snappy steps and worried for him.

Lucky was on the centre seat of the van. 'Stanley says she's to stay at home,' I told Ewan, but he fired the engine.

'We're only at Mervyn's.'

'I'm just telling you what he said.' He was already pulling the van off the drive.

'He won't know any different if we get her back by dinner.' I felt uneasy, but I didn't want another row with Ewan. Lucky had jumped onto my knee and I looked at her thrashing stump tail.

'We'd better make sure we're back then.' Ewan didn't answer. In fact he said nothing between Bling Manor and Fowlden traffic lights. I tried to thaw the chill. 'I thought we might have heard something from Dirk.' Ewan said nothing. He changed gear and pulled away from the lights. 'Have you heard from him?'

'Nope.'

That was the end of our conversation. I'd tried a few more openers as I started the fire at Mervyn Slack's racing yard, but he was obviously still too peeved for chit-chat. I ended up chatting to the head lad, Jay, instead. Whilst I was removing worn shoes from a sleek bay colt, Ewan was beating the palm of his hand with a rasp. Suddenly he found his voice. 'Cesar Millan here,' he said, 'lets Stanley's dog worry sheep – then he gets the afternoon off!'

'It wasn't *off*,' I corrected him. 'I had to go to Throstleden Show!'

'Which is where you'd have gone if you'd had the afternoon off!'

'Not with Stanley, I wouldn't!'

Jay broke into our bickering. 'You want to get Seth Holden on to that dog. He sorted my uncle's German Shepherd.'

Ruudi, the conditional jockey walked in and Ewan wagged his rasp at him. 'I was getting punsed round Jennings' yard while he was suppin' beer at Throstleden Show.'

I put my hands on my hips. 'Are you going to shoe this horse, or what?'

Ewan flung a pair of shoes on the coals and the routine of the racing yard ticked on around our silence.

The next horse in was a nervy creature, sensitive. I reassured it with a stroke down its shoulder as Ewan applied his nippers. No one spoke. Ruudi rode a rangy grey down the centre aisle of the American barn. Ewan reached his tongs into the fire and took out a glowing shoe. He dunked it in a bucket of water and snatched up the horse's leg. The horse jerked its head; it flattened its ears. It reminded him that horses are nature's mood barometer and I saw his chest expand with a calming breath. I took a handful of nails, stood beside him and handed him one. He banged it in with certainty. The horse tugged nervily, but Ewan talked to it. He banged in another nail. Then another. I made mock conversation with myself: *'How did Millie get on with her new horse, Will? She had three down, thanks, Ewan, but she wasn't bothered. Did you see her jump it? No, I just missed it, but I caught up with her afterwards.'* Ewan slid me a wry look. 'And for your information, I never went near the beer tent.'

Ewan took another nail from me. He tapped the nail as the dragon-thunder of an engine roared behind the wall. The colt's flanks fluttered; its shoulders twitched. It was wild-eyed, ready for the dragon. The floor under us throbbed. The horse reared. Ewan backstepped to safety. There was a flat crack. Ewan's phone had hit the concrete. In the next second, a hoof was on it. Ewan yelled. His phone crunched. Its insides spread outside its own edges and oozed over the concrete. I moved towards the horse's shoulder, eyes down. My hand crept up and took the horse's rope. The mechanical chug and sob receded and, but for the agitated breathing of the colt, the shoeing bay was still. Ewan gathered up the brittle fragments of his iPhone 5 from the floor. He stared at them. 'Fuck,' he said.

'That'll be a hundred and forty,' I told Jay twenty minutes later. 'And Stanley said to remind you about the two eighty Mervyn owes him from last week.'

'Not to mention the four hundred quid for a new phone,' Ewan said, cutting his eyes at the fragments now resting on the anvil.

Jay grimaced. 'How's that happened?'

'Some berk started a tractor on t'other side o' t'wall.'

'Ah,' Jay said. 'Mervyn must have taken his digger up the fields.' We stared, waiting for the cash. Jay stared back. 'He hasn't given it to me.'

'Can't you ring him?' I asked.

'He'll not hear it on t'digger.'

'Try!' I suggested, but Jay had sandwiched himself between the two horses we'd shod and begun walking them away.

Ewan turned to me. 'You'd better ring him!'

'I've lost half my contacts – remember!'

'Well, I can't bloody ring him, can I?' We stared at the jumble of glass and metal that had been his phone. 'We'll have to stop on t'lane. You can run up t'fields to him.' I glanced at my watch.

'We've got to get the dog back!'

Ewan wiped a hand over his mouth. 'Shit.'

'We're in shit either way,' I observed and I picked up the foot stand with Stanley's words clanging in my ears like a ringing anvil: *Leave the dog at home.*

We drove down the lane. Mervyn's digger hoved onto the horizon. It was rumbling over the far edge of the field, its bucket up, in mock salute. Ewan didn't stop. When we reached the junction with the moor road, I lifted Lucky to my face. 'We,' I confided in her velvet ear, 'are in deep shit.'

We were halfway down Bling Manor's drive with the dog trotting beside us, when I glanced Stanley's shape through the side window of the house. The shit was even deeper than I'd realised. I'd expected to get bollocked for coming back empty handed; now I'd get bollocked for taking the dog as well. I nudged Ewan and pointed. The three of us froze. I examined our options: we could breeze in, all nonchalant, like I'd forgotten what he'd said about Lucky – or we could take her to The Fleece and buy some time. 'The Fleece,' Ewan said, scooping the dog up. It would only delay the inevitable, but at least we'd have hot pies in us.

Chapter 4

I set Lucky down and she trotted into The Fleece on paws that bounced like mattresses. Her tail was up, her ears were triangles and her eyes were twinkles of delight. 'Eee!' Bob Entwistle exclaimed from his seat by the window that might as well have been his plinth. 'That's a little bonny 'un!'

Lucky wagged her tail in acknowledgement and lolled him a doggy grin. 'Come 'ere, then!' Bob commanded and Lucky scuttered over the carpet to meet her admirer. 'Best dogs I ever had, Jack Russells,' Bob stated as he scooped her onto his lap. 'Full 'o character.'

'I didn't know you'd had dogs,' I said.

Bob scrunched up his eyes to protect them from Lucky's tongue, lathering his face. 'Oh, aye! Cracker were nineteen when he died two year since.' He'd forced the dog back onto his lap where she was wriggling and wagging. 'What do you call it?'

'Lucky,' I said.

Trevor chuckled and looked up from the pint glass he was drying. 'Which is a bit of a bloody joke, seeing as how it belongs to Stanley Lampitt.'

I collected our two half pints from the bar and carried them towards Bob and Lucky. 'Is it all right with his hens?' Bob asked.

'Oh, aye,' Ewan nodded, lifting his lips from the froth of his beer. 'It's sheep it's no good with.'

'You little beggar!' Bob laughed. He'd taken the terrier's

jaw in his hand and was wagging it in admonition. 'He wants to get it to Seth Holden.'

Bob looked down on the grinning, tricoloured bundle of pelt on his lap and scrubbed her ears. 'What a little fauce 'un, eh?'

'We weren't supposed to fetch her out wi' us,' I confessed, as I leant back to receive a meat and potato pie. 'But we felt sorry for her.'

'I'd have her.'

Ewan looked up from his meat and potato pie. 'You?'

'Aye. It'd get me out and about,' Bob said. 'We'd go for a walk of a morning and then I'd fetch her in here of an afternoon.'

'It's an idea,' Ewan said, handing her a crust of potato pie.

'I want to run a pub!' Trevor shouted, his tea-towelled arm in a beer glass up to the wrist. 'Not a bloody care-home-cum-doggie-crèche!'

Stanley was back in his work clothes and sipping coffee at the breakfast bar when we made our planned stroll into Bling Manor's kitchen. Walking was proving trickier than I'd expected. Jauntiness implied innocence, but it might irritate him; so might guilty slouching. I couldn't find a mid-way walk. Stanley looked up. 'You know damn well you weren't supposed to take that dog with you.'

'She's been no bother,' Ewan said brightly.

'And I want four hundred and twenty notes off you.'

'Ah,' Ewan said. Like me, he'd expected a longer rant about the dog. 'Mervyn were up t'fields.'

'So?' Stanley demanded.

'So, he weren't there to pay us.'

'He has a bastard phone!'

'He can't hear it on t'digger.'

Stanley rounded on me. 'I told you!' He was pointing with a shaking finger. 'I wanted every penny this morning.'

Ewan went into full Gallic shrug. 'What could we do?'

'You could have walked up the bastard fields!'

'He were miles off!'

Stanley's glance darted between us. His arms were dangling like a gorilla's. 'If you're taking the piss …'

'As if we'd pocket four hundred and twenty quid!' I cut in.

Stanley pressed his circled fingertips on his forehead and grunted. It was close to acknowledgement.

'It looks like you've had a tough morning. Me and Ewan'll manage at Scorthwaite,' but Stanley was standing up.

'It'll take my mind off shit,' he said, and whistled for the dog.

'I thought we weren't taking the dog,' Ewan said.

'That were before you filled it wi' meat and potato pie in t'pub – and don't say you haven't, cos I know you will have! I don't want to come back to dog shit on t'mat.'

I'd thought dogs were supposed to be sensitive but Lucky wasn't reading the situation well at all. Her tail-wagging cheeriness was putting herself – and us – in peril. The second the van door opened she launched herself onto Ewan's lap and put her front feet on the dash-board. Stanley fired the engine.

Layer upon layer of cloud was skittering over Scorthwaite moor. I shifted in my seat. Sitting was proving as tricky as walking had been. Stanley didn't put the radio on. Should I chat, like nothing was wrong? Or should I let Stanley's mood melt the windows?

We passed Scorthwaite's Norman church and the delicatessen, then crawled quietly towards the traffic lights. Lucky spotted two dachshunds on a split lead toddling out of the post office. She grew three centimetres. She followed them with her eyes. She lifted a paw and let it dangle. *Please, no*, I thought. *Please don't start today*. Ewan passed her to me so I could turn her the other way, but her head was like a gyrocompass. The dachshunds drew level with the van. Lucky leapt back to Ewan's knee, threw herself at the window and began a baying and scrabbling that bounced the van's skin. 'Shut up!' Stanley bellowed. Then at Ewan, 'Shut the fucking dog up!' But Lucky's throat was open and her bark was bouncing her off her feet. Ewan managed to clamp her snout, but she was twisting and thrashing like a captured crocodile. The van still rang with her fury. She freed herself. The yapping upped by decibels. She banged herself on the window. The dachshunds' insouciance was infuriating. 'I'm in the wrong bastard lane, now!' Ewan tried covering Lucky's eyes but she ducked and swivelled like a snake. 'Four bastard years, you've let that dog create havoc in this van! Four bastard years!' Stanley accused Ewan. The dachshunds were receding, and having successfully shrunk them, Lucky was spacing out her barks. 'It should be a pleasure to take out, should that dog, but no. It's either ripping into sheep or else it's making my bastard ear drums bleed.'

We were approaching the next traffic lights and Stanley was craning and glancing for a gap in the traffic. He flicked on his indicator but no one gave him quarter. With one last glimpse in his wing mirror he slammed down a gear and swerved into the path of a blue BMW. It mounted the pavement to avoid a collision.

Ewan sucked in air. 'Jesus, Stanley!'

I glanced to my left. I couldn't hear the words spewing from the BMW driver's mouth, but each one was contorting his face and forking his fingers.

'He's not happy,' Ewan remarked, but Stanley was already accelerating away.

I hoped the BMW would turn left at the lights, but the roar of an engine flicked my eyes to the right. There it was, in Stanley's wing mirror; a blue BMW, growing in size. It drew level with The Old Van and stayed there. The driver's face was more purple than red now and spit was flecking his window. 'He's telling you to pull over,' I told Stanley.

'He can fuck off,' Stanley stated.

'He looks pissed off.'

'Don't look at him then!'

We rounded a bend in the road and Stanley slowed for the approaching roundabout. Suddenly, the BMW sliced across us. Stanley roared like an animal. The anvil, gas bottle and forge fought against the brakes. Lucky hit the dash-board. A bucket of used shoes slammed into the bulkhead. The van was still rocking when the driver's door was whipped open. 'Please!' Ewan begged the BMW driver. 'Just go away ...' but the BMW driver was hollering that he would knock Stanley's fucking head off. 'Seriously,' Ewan was pleading. 'He's an animal. Just go!' But the be-suited BMW driver banged on the side of The Old Van with his fist.

'Get out!' he yelled at Stanley. 'Or I'll fucking drag you out!'

Stanley gripped the steering wheel like a body builder psyching himself up for a lift. He inhaled a deep lungful of air. I was already wondering whether they'd send Stanley to an open prison, or lock him up with the burglars and the arsonists when Stanley burst out. His feet slapped the tarmac and he grabbed the driver by the lapels. A car behind us honked its horn. Lucky was barking furiously. Stanley lifted the man off his feet. His legs were kicking above the tarmac. Stanley started walking. He walked between the stationary cars. The man was calling him a psychopath, a lunatic, a madman. Stanley stopped at the central reservation. He dropped him on the metal crash barrier and pushed down. The BMW driver's arse slid between the two halves of the crash barrier until it was settled among the weeds. Stanley brushed his palms together, acknowledged the patience of the other drivers and walked to his vehicle, his padded shirt filling with the wind. He thumped onto the driver's seat, wiped his face with the rag that was meant for the windscreen and fired the engine. Behind us the BMW driver was shouting like a toddler who'd fallen down the toilet.

We'd driven another mile before Ewan spoke. 'I take it the court hearing didn't go so well, then?'

POST CARD

Port Elizabeth October 8th 2016

My new address is: 194 Wavecrest Drive, Bluewater Bay, Port Elizabeth. S.A. 60021.

My Hilux finally arrived – and there's Yorkshire mud in the footwell! Never thought I'd miss the place.

It would be really good to hear from you guys!

Dirk.

Professional Western Farriers
148 Hathersage Rd
Hathersage
North Yorkshire
FL9 0JJ
UK

Chapter 5

We'd shod big footed cobs and Clydesdales with hoof walls wider than those of nuclear bunkers and still I hadn't nailed on. Lucky was miserable too. Every time we came to stage four of the van-exit strategy (fling terrier over seat), a tail of rope flew with her so I could tie her up when the rear doors opened. Two attempts at escape this week had nearly hanged her from the door handle.

We'd just finished at Chris the Donkey Man's, and Stanley was barely settled behind the wheel of The Old Van, when his phone rang. I reached for it. 'If it's a funny looking number, don't answer it,' he commanded. 'I keep getting 'em.'

'It's Moneybags,' I said and flicked it to speakerphone.

'Joe Pedley's after me shoeing for him, Stan.' Stanley found second gear. 'But I don't like taking your business off you.' I felt Stanley's hackles rise. He stared at his phone as we rumbled down the rutted lane. 'So I thought I'd do you a swap.' Stanley's eyes narrowed in suspicion. 'How do you fancy taking Julie Thornton's warmblood mare on? It gets done regular and it's more on your patch than mine.'

Stanley's voice came out as a dull monotone, 'What's to do wi' it, Michael?'

'Nothing!' Moneybags laughed. 'I'm trying to be fair.'

Stanley ran his tongue round his teeth. 'Why *this* horse though, Michael?' We'd reached the junction with the road. 'You must have dozens you could swap me.'

'I said it's more on your patch than mine.' Stanley's stubborn silence called out Moneybags' conscience. 'Okay, it can be a bit tricky, but you've Lizzie Harker's lad with you, haven't you?' I threw my hands up in furious despair. At least once a week I had to remind Stanley that horse whispering isn't an inherited skill – but Stanley was already agreeing to the swap.

The Old Van was soon rattling down the wooded lane towards Sylvia's yard. Sylvia's ponies were her reason to get up in the morning; they were all her care and all her conversation. Stanley cranked on the handbrake. 'Right,' he said. 'Have you got your book with you?' He usually whipped the book out of my hands and told me nobody had ever learnt bugger all about shoeing horses from a book. I nodded. 'You might want to refresh your memory while we unpack.' I stared at him as he opened the driver's door.

'Does that mean ...?'

'You're nailing on,' he said, turning to me with the door handle in his hand. 'And don't let on it's your first time.'

Spiders were crawling in my belly when I fished the book from the door pocket. Welsh ponies leave less margin for error than shires or warmbloods. I opened *Hickman's Farriery* at a diagram of the internal structures of the foot and narrowed my eyes as if I could slice it onto my retina.

Three minutes later, I stepped onto the cobbles and toe-tapped a shiny conker. I stooped for it, turned it in my palm and watched the woody jewel gleam. I wished on its nutty smoothness and slipped it in my pocket.

Sylvia was smiling. 'There's Teddy and Willow to trim and Poppy needs shoes.'

Ewan set to work on Teddy and with no hint at his plans, Stanley instructed me to remove Poppy's shoes. I bent under the pony's tight round belly and a woodpecker tick-tocking on a nearby tree mocked the sound of my heartbeat. Soon the pony's shoes were off and her feet were prepared. It was now Stanley claimed to be parched. 'I could murder a brew, Sylvia love.'

Only when she'd slipped from sight did Stanley regard the sole of Poppy's small, smooth fore-foot, still dusted with the desiccated coconut of rasped horn. 'Right,' he said quietly. 'Do *not* tap a nail unless I'm standing o'er you – comprendo?' I nodded. Stanley placed a nail in my hand, 'And *listen* to the foot.' My brow must have puckered. Stanley took a nerve settling breath. 'Do they teach you nowt at that college? *Listen* to the noise of the nail going in.' Was this another piss-take? I glanced at Ewan, but he was examining the surface of Teddy's left hind.

Stanley handed me the nailing-on hammer. I took it. To me it was a coronation sceptre. I grasped Poppy's foot between my knees. The hoof wall was narrow; a blunt pencil line, not the jumbo felt-tip marker of Pedley's shires. I lined up the first nail. 'Right. Bang it,' Stanley hissed. I banged. 'Like a farrier, not like a fucking fairy!' I banged it again. 'That's what you want to hear!' he confirmed. Reassured, I found a rhythm.

I was on my third nail when Sylvia returned with a pot of tea and three slabs of home-made parkin. She put down her tray. 'You'll mind what you're doing, won't you, love?' I could hear the concern in her voice. I was relieved when Ewan spoke.

'I believe you did well at Throstleden Show.'

Sylvia beamed. 'Did you see us?'

'No,' Ewan answered, brightly. 'But these two might have. They were there, supping beer and chit-chattin' wi' clients – weren't you, Stanley?'

Stanley caught the conversation and deflected its trajectory. 'Did you get a trophy, Sylvia?'

She was thrilled at his sudden interest. 'I did! I'll fetch it out,' and grinning she headed for the house again.

With Sylvia out of the way, I found my rhythm again. This shoeing malarkey was turning out to be easier than it looked. I was hammering happily when Stanley suddenly shouted out, 'Whoa!' His voice had blundered through the beats but I'd hit the hoof again before he grabbed my wrist. 'Did you not hear it?' He grabbed the hammer, flipped it and whipped a nail out.

'Hear what?' The nail tinkled to the floor. It was L-shaped.

'The bastard noise change!' He sucked a steadying breath between his teeth then handed me a new nail. He stood beside me now; a slab of check-shirted judgement. 'Go on.' I gave the nail a belt – then another – and another – then Stanley snatched the hammer again. 'For fuck's sake, lad!'

Sylvia had been grinning as she made her way back with the trophy but her brow creased with concern. 'Is there a problem?'

'Just a bent a nail,' Stanley smiled. He took over the work though, and Ewan took on the role of best supporting actor. He pored over the gaudy, gilt, oversized trophy that Sylvia had won for best in-hand barren Welsh mare and kept her talking till Stanley hammered the last nail home with six strong, certain blows.

'Do you think I pricked it?' I asked once we were in the van.

'We'll soon find out,' Stanley rumbled, finding first gear. 'But next time you hear the note change, don't give it another knock to see if you're right – eh?' I dragged my teeth over my lip. I hadn't heard the note change.

I folded my fingers around the glassy cool of the conker. When the van stopped at Bling Manor, I took back my arm, cursed my childish superstition and lobbed it with the force of Liam Plunkett. I watched it arc against the pewter sky, hit the tarmac of Hathersage Road and get splattered by a Nissan Navara.

POST CARD

<u>*Port Elizabeth October 12th 2016*</u>

Have you lot been wiped off the face of the fucking earth?
*   Text me ffs! Or ring me! Or pick up when I ring you – eh? 08240543546.*
*   Dirk*

Professional Western Farriers
148 Hathersage Rd
Hathersage
North Yorkshire
FL9 0JJ
UK

Chapter 6

S tanley's phone buzzed. My heart knocked on my breast-bone. It must be Sylvia. It had to be Sylvia. Stanley squirmed in the driver's seat, drew it from his pocket and thrust it at me. I looked at it. Not Sylvia. 'Jay,' I breathed and put it to my ear. 'You couldn't pick me up, could you?' Why wasn't Jay at Mervyn's yard, waiting for us?

'We're not a bastard taxi service!' Stanley bellowed over the whirr and thunk of the windscreen wipers.

'I'm only on Tattersall Street,' Jay explained. 'It's nearly on your way!'

Stanley grumbled but when we drove through Fowlden's traffic lights he swung a right at the paper shop. Lucky stretched and stood, aware we'd deviated from our usual route. The Old Van laboured its way up the steep incline and the higher it climbed, the milkier mustered the mist. Through the gauzy air, I made out a police car slewed across the upper part of the street. Stanley leant forward and Ewan wiped the cloudy windscreen with the sleeve of his jacket. Lucky, who had a nose for trouble, had adopted her Jack Russell driving position: hind feet on Ewan's thighs; front feet on the dash-board. Was that Mervyn's blue wagon behind the police car? I squinnied into the drizzle. It was. It was angled across the road. As the scene slid into focus, I saw that its windscreen was shattered to a cataract-white. A semi-circle of sodden pedestrians was standing beside it in a pulsing blue light. Stanley dropped the struggling van down a gear. It gave us time to study the tableau.

Ewan leant over my lap for a better view. 'What the actual fuck ... ?' he breathed. Then a flap of floral curtain flicked the scene to sense. Mervyn's eighteen tonne Lambourne racehorse transporter was embedded in the wall of 42 Tattersall Street. The stone blocks of the terraced house, solid for a century, had folded round the grille of Mervyn's six-horse wagon. Jay was standing on the edge of the crowd, the only one of them staring outwards. Stanley signalled for him to walk round the corner. '*I'm on Tattersall Street ...*' he muttered, mockingly. He turned The Old Van into Havelock Street and pulled on the handbrake. The back doors thunked open. 'You've left some up, you know,' Stanley said to his rear-view mirror. 'And number forty-four still has its roof on.'

'Piss off,' Jay muttered as he climbed in. Stanley found first gear and pulled away from the kerb. I turned. Jay was squatting between the forge and the anvil with his head in his hands. Water was dripping off his dark coils of hair.

'So,' Stanley ventured; he was wiping the misty windscreen with his forearm, 'did number forty-two swerve at you, or what?' Jay took a long time to answer.

'I wasn't even in it! I was in my gran's. I saw it pass her window.' He paused. 'I thought *Fuck! Somebody's nicking the wagon!*' The throb of the windscreen wipers pulsed the silence. 'Then there was this massive bang.' Those of us in the front looked at one another. 'It was only when I looked out, I saw it was empty. If them at number forty-two hadn't rung 999, I might have got away with it.'

Ewan gave me his *what the fuck* face and Stanley took a bicep-shaking grip on the steering wheel.

'Jay, lad,' he said, 'you've just knocked half their fucking house down.' Jay's groan harmonised with the van's labouring engine. The swish and sob of windscreen wipers filled the van. The roofs of Mervyn Slack's racing yard floated into view above the grey moor.

The Old Van's wheels sizzled on the tarmac as it turned

right. It bounced through the puddles of Mervyn's lane, then pulled on to the car-park. Lucky's body stiffened. She knew what came next. Stanley grinned a sharkish grin at Ewan. 'We can't,' Ewan said, horror mixing with his glee. Lucky was trembling on my lap. Their delay was encouraging her fantasies. Her top lip had curled and she was baring zig-zag incisors.

'There's nowhere else to chuck her.' Her tremors of blood lust were rhythmic now.

'Oh, come on!' I pleaded. 'He's in shock already.'

'Are you going to take one for the team, then?' Stanley asked. Lucky was growling now. I shook my head and Stanley began the familiar countdown.

Jay must have been mired in his own misery. He never asked why we were counting aloud. On the shout of 'Five,' a Jack Russell terrier flew over the centre seat at him and we piled out.

A grenade thrown in couldn't have exploded more furiously. A gnashing biting devil-dog was loose in the metal box. Bashings, barkings and guttural growls were rattling the van. Stanley rolled against the side in laughter. Cries of 'get off me' and a 'you mental fucker' were interspersed with yelps of pain. Ewan was calling Stanley a rotten bastard but he was laughing just as hard. I dashed for the van's back doors. Stanley grabbed my wrist to savour one last yelp of agony from Jay, then he let me go.

When Jay dropped out, he was wounded, dazed and clutching his hand. Lucky was standing in her butchery, tail wagging, tongue lolling, jaws grinning. Jay sucked blood off his hand, bewildered and complained that the dog was a fucking psycho. 'Oh, give o'er whining,' Stanley laughed. 'That's nowt to what Mervyn's going to do to you.' It was the first time I'd seen Stanley thoroughly enjoying himself since the court hearing.

I was keen to build on his good mood. 'Do you remember when you did that to Dirk?'

'Aye,' Stanley chuckled. 'He didn't give a bugger, did he? He just strode out o' t'van dangling t'dog by t'scruff.'

'Have you heard from him?'

'I've had a postcard or two.'

'You never said!'

'They're in t'drawer.' There was no point in asking Stanley what they said. He struggled to read a road sign. I told myself I'd read them when I was back at Bling Manor.

There were two horses waiting in the shoeing bay, so Stanley bent under Tamarind, Ewan bent under Windy Day and despite his guilt, his shock and his wounds, Jay collected Vet-Wrap from the tack room to tend a gelding's over-reach injury.

He'd been gone ten minutes when Mervyn came shuffling down the aisle of the barn. His tweed cap was pulled low, his Barbour jacket was lashed with baling twine and his wellies were caked in mud. 'I told that wastrel Jay he'd to be back before you turned up,' he grumbled.

'He's here!' Stanley announced, then he lodged three nails between his lips. Mervyn craned and twisted to see the car-park. 'I didn't hear t'wagon.' He looked back at Stanley. 'He did get Enville Lad to Richard Jennings, didn't he?'

Behind him, Jay had stepped from a stable. He froze. Stanley took the nails from between his lips. 'Mervyn's wondering where t'wagon is,' he grinned. Mervyn turned to see Jay staring at him with bin-lid eyes.

'Fowlden!' he spat.

'Fowlden?' Mervyn asked. 'What's it doing in Fowlden?'

Jay's eyes were darting an S.O.S. 'It's had a bump,' he managed.

Mervyn snatched his cap from his head. 'Oh, bloody hell! What've you bumped?'

Jay couldn't seem to find the word, but Stanley could. 'A house.'

'A *house?*' Mervyn turned a circle on the spot. 'How could you miss a fucking *house?*' Jay was explaining that he'd not been driving, but Stanley spoke over him, 'He didn't miss it. He hit it.' He was enjoying his joke.

Mervyn wasn't listening though. 'It's not like it's a fucking bollard!' he raged. Jay insisted that it could have been worse; that no one was injured; that he'd unloaded the horse; that he'd just nipped to his gran's.

Mervyn froze. 'You did put the handbrake on, didn't you, Jay?' Jay stared back at him. Mervyn closed his eyes.

'Oh,' Stanley breathed. 'That'd put you in the shit with the insurers!'

'Where is it?' Mervyn demanded.

'Tattersall Street.'

'There's about two thirds of it on Tattersall Street,' Stanley clarified. 'The rest of it is in number forty-two.'

Mervyn covered his face.

Jay had the pose of one who's just had a bucket of water dropped on him. 'What do you want me to do, Mervyn?'

'Start on the afternoon feeds!' Mervyn blasted. Jay hurried away and Mervyn turned to follow him.

'It'll be a hundred and fifty for this afternoon!' Stanley said quickly, and Mervyn threw up his hands.

'There's a time and a bloody place, Stanley! You've just seen how I'm fixed!' and he stormed down the aisle of the barn.

In the van on the way home, Stanley was quiet. 'Must be hunting,' Ewan said, pointing to a kestrel that was riding the thermals on dithering wings. It was the sort of *look at the moo cows* effort a mother might make to distract a glum toddler. Stanley glanced, then glanced away. 'What's up wi' you?' Ewan dared at last. 'I thought you were enjoying the shitstorm?'

Stanley filled his body with air then shuffled his grip on the steering wheel. 'I think the shitstorm's heading our way.' Ewan and I exchanged a look. 'Mervyn Slack is forty per cent of our business! If he goes under, we go with him!' So much for his schadenfreude.

'He used to be a footballer, though, didn't he?' Ewan said.

'They still played with pigs' bladders when he was a foot-baller!'

I tightened my grip on Lucky's chest. 'He has a couple of good horses though.'

'You need more than a couple out of eighty,' Stanley observed. 'And it doesn't inspire owners when the place looks like a scrapyard.'

POST CARD

Port Elizabeth October 20th 2016

*Stanley – will you pick up your
fucking phone, man! I've massive
news for you!*
    Dirk.

*Professional Western Farriers
148 Hathersage Rd
Hathersage
North Yorkshire
FL9 0JJ
UK*

Chapter 7

I was leaning over The Old Van's passenger seat writing an appointment in the diary when I sensed Richard Jennings beside me. I backed out of The Old Van and greeted him. His hands were trapped in his pockets and he was chewing on his lip. He was too well bred to dive straight into his question but after a few mild pleasantries, he arrived at it.

'Did you ever ride Enville Lad?' He meant Anvil Head. His heavy hunter head was what had regularly plunged him to the ground on landing, so no one at Mervyn's yard had given the horse his racing name.

'I've ridden upsides him,' I said.

Jennings pulled on his bottom lip. 'It's just – we're having a few issues ...'

I tried to be diplomatic. 'You've bought him as a flat runner, haven't you?'

Jennings was nodding. 'I have – but the horse can't bally gallop.'

Stanley guffawed. 'It can't bally jump either!'

'I'll give him a bit longer,' Jennings sighed. 'The change of environment might have unsettled him.'

'Then what?' Stanley asked. He was standing by the forge, arms folded, waiting for a shoe to heat up. 'Pedigree Chum?'

Jennings smiled tightly, 'I hope we're in a more enlightened age,' then he turned to me, 'How's young Millie getting on with The Onion?' I was explaining his former racehorse's rehabilitation when we were interrupted by Stanley's phone.

My guts tightened again, he fished it from his jeans pocket, checked that it wasn't a PPI enquiry and put it to his ear.

'Yes, Sylvia, love.' I felt sick. 'Oh, deary me.' My hand crept up to my mouth but my nausea was shot through with the relief of a captured fugitive. 'Don't you worry, love. I should think it'll be easy sorted. I'll send t'lad round later,' then he swiped the screen and pocketed the phone. 'Get that shoe off Poppy on your way home.'

I looked over my shoulder, then remembered that Ewan was on another job. 'Me?' My thumb was on my chest.

'Of course you! It's your shit. You can sort it!'

The rain had stopped but the boughs were spilling fat drops. Sylvia was waiting, under the dripping eaves of the stables. 'Your girlfriend's been,' she said, before I'd even closed the car door. I didn't know why she'd even rung the vet. This was a post-shoeing lameness; anyone with any sense would have rung their farrier. I reminded myself to smile and picked through the puddles of Sylvia's yard.

Sylvia watched me closely as I lifted Poppy's foot and worked the shoe off. Twice I had to ask her to shift her shadow. Eventually, I dropped the shoe on the cobbles and wiped the foot clean. 'She should be okay in a day or so,' I said, maintaining my brittle cheeriness. 'Just give us a ring and we'll pop the shoe back on.' Sylvia nodded briskly. There had been no tea and parkin today.

I drove up Sylvia's puddled lane under the folding formations of blowing clouds, cursing Sylvia, cursing Stanley and cursing my own ineptitude. They parted to reveal a nail-paring of crescent moon above Eckersley moor.

I rang Ewan. 'It was crippled.'

'It'll heal fast,' he said. 'Unless it's set an infection up.'

I blew out a deep breath. 'It can't do permanent damage though, can it?'

'Unlikely,' Ewan said.

'But possible?'

'Only very rarely.' I flung my head against the head rest. Ewan snorted a laugh into the silence. 'Oh, get a grip, Will! Every farrier lames a horse at some point!'

'Tell Sylvia that.'

I rang Millie and thanked her for not dropping me in it. 'What the hell did you shoe it with, Will? An axe?'

We were facing another day of drops wriggling down shirt backs, numb thighs and cold feet. Even Lucky was fed up; she was curled on Ewan's knee and refusing to seek out sodden sheep at the roadside. Rain sloshed the screen between wiper sweeps. The Old Van climbed into the cloud of Loddenden Top. Slick grey tarmac took us past the quarry and the clay pigeon range until we began our meandering descent into Lodden Vale. The geometric fields, usually felt-tipped in emerald on the valley floor, were khaki today. The steep fell road swept down, unbounded by walls or hedges. In the valley, the river was almost at the arch of the humpbacked bridge. Stanley followed the road then at the sign of a jumping horse, he swung a left between well-spaced modern bungalows. A paved drive guided us onto a clean stable yard. Stanley pulled on the handbrake and Julie Thornton dashed out of the bungalow holding a tea towel over her head. A damp tabby cat shot past her and into the house. 'Belinda's in the field!' she shouted.

Stanley groaned. If this had been Joan Mitchell's cob or Christopher Clegg's donkey, he would have driven away, but Mervyn owed him hundreds, he'd lost Pedley's custom and the court ruling was looking expensive. 'The thing is, love,' Stanley began, 'we like 'em dry for shoeing. It blunts us tools if their feet are wet.'

Julie Thornton looked surprised. 'Oh,' she said. 'I thought I was doing you a favour. Michael Morrison always wanted her out before he shod her, so she could run some energy off.' Ewan wiped his hands over his face in the style of Oliver Hardy. Stanley's suspicions of Moneybags Morrison's motive had been vindicated.

'Fetch her in then,' he sighed.

Julie blanched. 'Me?' Stanley nodded patiently. 'Michael said you'd have a horse whisperer with you.' It was my turn to sigh. 'Neither of us could catch her last time.'

Stanley blew breath to his cheeks so they puffed like a hamster's. 'We'll have one go,' he said, 'but I can't chase it round all afternoon. We've other jobs on.'

Julie looked satisfied. 'I'll put the kettle on,' she said, 'warm us all up a bit.'

I turned to where a grey mare was crouched against the drizzle on an acre of mud. Stanley collected our spare head-collar from the van. 'Go on then,' he said, dangling it. 'Do your stuff.'

Wet denim pressed on my thighs with every step. The back of my damp sock was rubbing between my heel and my boot. I only looked up when I reached the gate. Cold drizzle speckled my skin.

There was a concrete square just inside the field gate, and beyond that, mud; sloppings of it. It would be quicker and cleaner if the mare would come to me. I lowered my eyes, positioned myself at an unthreatening forty-five degrees and called her name. Belinda didn't even look up. Resigned, but not surprised, I stepped past a battered galvanised bucket onto what looked like a solid patch of earth – but I sank up to my ankles. I pistoned my boots against the suck of sludge, waded two further strides then called the horse again. Nothing. Not even an ear flick. I would have to cross the mud. I cast about for an earthy clod. I'd plotted my next two steps when Stanley shouted from the gate. I looked up.

Belinda was thundering at me through the mud. Her ears were back, her teeth were bared and her neck was stretched like a dragon's. I tugged at my right foot. It didn't budge.

'Leave your boot!' Stanley shouted.

I'd have to unlace it! I was six sucking strides from the concrete slab. I heaved at my boot again. Belinda was getting bigger. Stanley was rattling the gate. His eyes were darting between the mare and the latch.

'It's okay,' I shouted back. 'She'll stop.' But Belinda was bearing down. The mud burbled then spat out my boot. Belinda was cinematic size now. Mud splats were rising and falling around her in a slo-mo kaleidoscope of black. I stepped to a clod. Stanley flung open the gate. I leapt to the concrete. The mare was suddenly keeling like a torpedoed gunship. She must have lost her footing. Stanley's heel touched the concrete. It slipped. His feet flew skyward. The mare was tipping and Stanley was still going up. The mare slapped the soil with her side. Stanley was dropping like a plank. His arms flailed. Mud was falling and flopping on the mare's fallen flanks. He landed on his back, half on the concrete. A steel bucket in his hand clanged. The bucket sang then settled to silence. The horse was motionless. So was Stanley.

Heaving moments passed.

'Stanley?'

He blinked.

'Are you all right?' I held out my hand. He took it and hauled himself to a sitting position. Side by side, we gazed on the grounded gunship that had been a warmblood mare. Her white coat was lying in tiny wet triangles.

A whisper from behind us broke our trance. 'Tell me,' it said, 'that you didn't hit it with that.' I turned to see Ewan pointing at the galvanised bucket still in Stanley's hand.

Stanley raised the bucket to eye level and stared at it. 'I must have swung it.'

'Swung it?'

'To protect myself!'

'Oh, very professional that, Stanley.' Ewan unhooked the

bucket from Stanley's limp hand and we stared down on the mare. 'And how are you planning to explain this one?'

'I never touched her bastard horse,' Stanley muttered. 'I was going to pretend there was food in it.'

The horse heaved a heavy sigh.

'Thank fuck for that,' Ewan breathed.

The mare drew up her legs. She sat, dazed. She gave a grunt then staggered to her feet. Stanley backed off a pace, but I could see that Belinda was only dimly aware of our presence. Cautiously, I took a step towards her. Belinda stood, blinking. I slid the lead rope over her neck and waited. Gently I eased the headcollar over her nose. I reached for the head piece. Belinda took in her surroundings. I buckled it. Belinda seemed not to disapprove. I waited for her breaths to settle, then Belinda ambled bedside me, as tame as a Bridlington donkey.

Julie was setting down a tray of tea and biscuits in the barn. She looked at Belinda, lolling in on a loose rope and grinned. 'Well, well, well!' she said. 'Michael Morrison said you were the experts!'

'Oh, it's just experience,' Stanley shrugged, dismissing his muddy clothes as a slip.

Belinda stood like a table whilst we shod her with her clean side to Julie. When Julie returned the tray to the kitchen, Ewan and I swilled the mud off her dirty side. When she'd clopped back to her stable as calm as one of Pedley's shires, Stanley accepted a generous tip and took a repeat booking without a flicker of embarrassment.

'You'll have to knock a few unconscious at Mervyn's,' Ewan said, once we were in the van. 'We'll get through 'em a lot faster.'

'I never touched that horse,' Stanley growled.

Ewan turned to me. 'The dent in that bucket was in the shape of a horse's head.'

I burst into laughter. 'Remember when Dirk trussed one of

Mervyn's up like a Christmas turkey?' We chuckled fondly at the memory.

'Has Dirk not rung you, Stan?' Ewan asked.

'He will,' Stanley said, swinging the steering wheel, 'when he wants summat.'

And then I remembered; I'd still not read his postcards.

Chapter 8

Clouds were still seething on the hilltops the following morning; roiling and rolling, hiding then revealing the fells, which crumpled under their soggy weight. We stepped from the van onto Jennings' yard and Stanley's eyes followed his daughter, Pippa Jennings. It was hard to resist it; she was wearing knee length black boots, second skin jodhpurs and swinging her hair. She knew she was being watched, but she preferred lapping up admiration to acknowledging it – so I called to her. She tossed her head in a way she'd never do alone, and feigned surprise. 'Oh, hi,' she said with a mini Mexican wave of her gloved fingers. How had I ever fallen for her artifice?

Her father was leading two horses towards us, a leggy grey and a gormless looking bay with loppy ears. I took the bay's lead rope and scrubbed the white star at his forelock. 'Hiya, mate,' I said. 'How are you settling in?'

Jennings answered for the horse. 'Not great,' he said. He was rubbing his chin. 'Did he have a knack of dropping his shoulder when he was at Mervyn's?' I shrugged. Anvil Head had decanted plenty of jockeys, but I couldn't say exactly how. The horse stooped to nibble at my hair. 'I don't suppose you'd fancy schooling him? He knows you.'

'No, he bloody wouldn't,' Stanley answered from behind the van door. 'He's no bastard use to me wi' a broken collar bone.'

I'd barely ridden at all since dating Millie. Her long hours, on-call shifts and commitment to Onion limited our available hours and I didn't want to limit them further by schooling racehorses on a trainer's schedule.

Jennings placed his palm on the horse's neck. 'He's not looking fast enough.' He smoothed his satin pelt. 'But I'd like to give him a chance to prove me wrong.'

'Will that lass o' yours not ride him?' Stanley asked, but Jennings was already shaking his head.

'Too busy with the dressage, these days.' What I think he meant was that Pippa didn't fancy a broken collar bone either.

Anvil Head stood patiently, occasionally mouthing his lead rope whilst he was shod with lighter shoes. His hoof wall made Poppy's look like The Great Wall of China but Stanley lined up and drove home each nail with utter precision. As if to underline my ineptitude, Stanley chatted as he worked, describing the devastation Mervyn's wagon had wrought on Tattersall Street.

'All done?' Zach, the head lad, asked as I untied the soggy lead rope. I handed Anvil Head over and as he crossed the yard the horse tripped on a cobble. Zach flung out his free arm and called to us over his shoulder, 'How the hell's it supposed to gallop if it can't even walk?'

Stanley meanwhile was standing by The Old Van, tool-box in hand and attempting to protect his interests by persuading Jennings to take Mervyn's horses to the races, but Jennings was ahead of him. 'I'm taking one of his up to Hexham next week,' he said.

The damp had crawled through my every vein; it seemed to soften my bones. 'Are we going to Mervyn's, or what?' Ewan demanded, stamping his feet to bring the blood back. It was a measure of how chilled through Stanley's hands were that he blew on them and threw the van keys to Ewan.

The Old Van grumbled out of Hathersage. Stanley had spread himself over a seat and a half and was far less tolerant of Lucky's stiletto claws on his thighs than Ewan was. I lifted her onto my lap. Stanley was still breathing on his fingers, so

I took his ringing phone off the dash-board. 'It's an unknown number,' I said.

Stanley grumbled about nuisance calls. 'There's one keeps coming up that doesn't even look like a proper number!'

'It'll be foreign,' I said. 'I've been getting some.'

'Knock it off,' he instructed. I silenced it and plonked the phone back on the dash. 'That tight-fisted, miserly, stingy-arsed shite had better pay up today,' Stanley chuntered as he whacked the heating up. I kept a firm hold on Lucky's collar and Ewan soothed us with John Legend's 'All of Me'.

The singed autumn shades of Scorthwaite Fell soon filled the windscreen. The bulges and arcs of the overlapping hills folded before me. The nearest were green, then buff, golden and brown against a soft grey sky, and as Ewan sang about 'curves and edges' and 'perfect imperfections', it all made sense. A tractor had striped the buff with parallel tyre tracks and surrounding dry-stone walls were crumbling like teeth. By the time we'd turned down Mervyn's rutted lane all three of us were belting it out, and Lucky was howling a counterpoint. I was silently thanking Ewan for the change in mood when Stanley burst out. 'Bloody hell! Look o'er yonder! Have t'bastard moles mutated?' Mervyn's paddock was piled with earth mounds the size of family saloons. A digger, its arm raised over the destruction was standing to attention between them.

Ewan swung The Old Van onto the car-park, then backed it to the barn doors for a dry unpacking. I waited until Lucky had been contained and rumbled the sliding barn doors aside. Mervyn began waddling away at a speed that rocked his walk. 'Oi!' Stanley shouted. 'Where are you beggaring off to, Mervyn Slack?'

'Stanley,' Mervyn said, like he'd only just noticed us.

'I hope you're going to be stumping six hundred quid up.'

'Ah.' He took his cap off. 'The thing is, Stanley, it turns out I've a bit of a cash flow problem.'

'Funny, that!' Stanley answered. 'Cos, I've bloody got one an' all!'

'I should have it by t'end o' t'month.'

'I'll shoe your horses at t'end of the month then,' Stanley answered.

Mervyn took a breath. 'You know how I'm fixed wi' t'wagon, Stanley ...' his voice petered out. He drew two fingers down the bridge of his nose. 'If you could cut me a bit o'slack ...' The hoof clops of a horse broke the brewing silence.

'Silent Shannon!' Ruudi announced.

Mervyn scrambled his wits. 'You know I'm aiming this at the Grand National,' he said. 'I can't train it if it has no shoes on.' Stanley was still eyeballing him. 'It could win at Hexham next week.'

Stanley held his gaze then took the lead rope from Ruudi. Without taking his eyes off Mervyn he pointed at the horse. 'This is the only one I'm doing,' he said.

Mervyn didn't argue. 'I'll be on t'digger,' he said, then he walked away with the gait of one following a coffin.

'What's he doing wi' that digger?' Stanley asked Ruudi when Mervyn was out of sight. 'He's made a right mess o' that field.'

'He dig for treacle,' Ruudi answered. Stanley and I crossed nonplussed looks.

'Ruudi,' I asked, 'do you know what treacle is?'

Ruudi shrugged as he walked away. 'Is what he say!'

'Well, let's hope he strikes it,' Stanley remarked. 'Or we'll all be up treacle creek.'

We'd finished the afternoon early so Stanley commanded a swift one in The Fleece. I'd rather have gone home; Millie was finishing early – but Stanley's look reminded me I was still on his time.

I set the drinks on the little round table, then grabbed it. Stanley was going through a fumbling, body-slapping, panto-mime of finding his ringing phone which had rocked the table and was slopping the beer. 'Yes, Flower!' A long explanation was being issued on the other end. 'Aye ... aye ...' We studied Stanley's intent face. 'It's reyt, Flower. We'll see to it in t'mornin'.' He agreed with speaker again, then hung up. 'That was your lass,' he said, shoving his phone in his jeans pocket.

'Millie?'

'Aye. She's had to go back to Sylvia's this morning. Abscess.' I nursed my head with my hands. He turned to Ewan, who was lowering his half pint to the table. 'You'll have to sort it.'

Ewan's half pint stopped in mid-air, 'I can't. I'm at the Maharaja's in the morning!'

'I'll do the Maharaja's.'

'Aw, come on, Stan! You know I look forward to the Maharaja's!'

'Well, I can't send Butcher Bill to Sylvia's again, can I?'

Ewan put his glass on the table and sighed. '*He's* not going to the Maharaja's wi' you, then!'

'Take him wi' you, if you want.'

'I will,' Ewan stated. 'He's not getting to eat khari biscuits and drink out o' china while I'm sorting his fuck-up out.'

'I am still here!' I reminded them.

Millie was grooming Onion when I arrived home. Despite the horse hide, stacked hay and droppings at her feet, she still smelt like Millie when I kissed her. 'How bad is it then, this abscess?'

'I couldn't get at it,' she said. 'I've given her some painkillers till morning.' She caught my look. 'It's not your fault!'

'I gave her the nail bind,' I reminded her.

'Most of 'em resolve in twenty-four hours! It's just bad luck.' I stroked Onion's velvet nose and he squirmed his top lip. 'Anyway,' she added, 'they're nagging me about next month's on-call rota, so I need to know what you're doing for your twenty-first.'

'I've told you,' I said. 'Grandad's doing a cocktail party.'

She paused in her grooming. 'Is that it?'

'Millie,' I said. 'If Stanley gets wind of my twenty-first birthday, I'll end up wrapped in cling film and propped on the roundabout under Fowlden viaduct.'

'He wouldn't do that,' she chuckled.

'They did it to Ruudi!'

She cracked into laughter and leant her arms on Onion's gleaming back.

'I'll settle for a civilised evening with my Grandad and my loathsome cousin, thanks.' She was still cackling when I walked out of the barn with my wheelbarrow.

Birch, beech and ash boughs ticked on The Old Van's paint-work. When Ewan and I emerged from the wooded track, Sylvia peered into the van. 'No Stanley?'

'He has another job on,' Ewan smiled. 'But, I'm fully quali-fied.' Lucky was yapping at her through the window.

'I have a friend who uses Michael Morrison,' Sylvia said. '*He* always comes himself.' Neither of us answered. We were concentrating on our van exiting routine. 'Poor dog!' Sylvia exclaimed when I launched Lucky over the seat.

'It's that or get bitten,' Ewan answered. Sylvia tutted and was shaking her head as we followed her towards Poppy's stable. Then Ewan stood back as she led her crippled pony into the daylight. It was worse than before but Ewan's face gave nothing away. He picked up the mare's left fore-foot, looked at it closely and smiled as he put the hoof back on the cobbles. 'We'll have that right in no time, Sylvia. Why don't you go and make us a brew?'

She dithered. 'I've not baked,' she said.

'We could still murder a brew.' Ewan winked, and Sylvia sighed. She shuffled off, towards the house and I passed Ewan the hoof knife.

'This,' he said quietly, 'is going to bleed like a stuck pig.'

He worked furiously, sweating at the effort. After five

minutes there was still no sign of pus and the hole in the sole was widening and deepening. I glanced anxiously at the house. Two brews weren't going to take her much longer. 'Got it,' Ewan hissed, relieved. A tiny black speck had appeared in the white horn. Sylvia emerged from the kitchen doorway. Another cut and the pus oozed out. The pony heaved a deep sigh. So did Ewan. I was feeling grateful that there had been no blood, then a crimson oozing blossomed on the sole of the foot. 'Told you,' Ewan said. By the time Sylvia had put the tea-tray on the stone mounting block, the pony's foot was dripping gore onto the cobble-stones.

'Oh my God!' Sylvia heaved, covering her eyes.

'It's fine!' Ewan answered. 'It means I'm down to healthy tissue.' Blood was puddling between the sets. 'She'll be right now, I promise you.' Sylvia's hand was on her mouth now but under her laser gaze Ewan flushed out the hole. He put Poppy's foot down and walked the pony two nearly sound strides. 'See,' he said, 'a few days poulticing and it'll be ready for a shoe.' Sylvia's smile was feathery and fleeting. She wasn't convinced.

Back at the forge Stanley was stuffing his face with the Maharaja's khari biscuits. He held out the tin and Ewan took a handful. 'Sorted?' Stanley asked through the crumbs. Ewan nodded. 'Have you plugged it?' Ewan nodded again, his mouth full of khari biscuit. 'Did she kick off?'

I answered for him. 'Yep. And she complained about us chucking Lucky over the seat.'

Stanley wiped a sleeve over his mouth. 'What did you chuck her over t'seat for?'

'You know – getting out of the van.'

'There's no need to chuck her!' he said, lifting his Jack Russell off the floor and nestling her protectively on his lap.

'We always chuck her!'

'No, we bloody don't!'

'*You* chuck her!' I was nearly shouting now.

'I have *never* chucked this dog. I send her.'

'What? Like you never hit that grey mare with a galvanised bucket?' Ewan asked, handing me a khari biscuit.

Stanley stood up. 'You can both piss off,' and he strode out, with the dog under his arm. Our laughter sprayed khari crumbs all over the forge.

Arrive. Saturday. Manchester:
17.20. (flight: IB3692.)
See you soon.

Chapter 9

The wet October had been hunted out by a wild November. Clouds were piled on Loddenden Top, layer upon layer, in nameless shades of grey. Slanting sleet was slicing off Eckersley moor and wind was rattling the forge roof and screeching down the chimneys. It was only just after eight o'clock, but both forges were lit and wraiths of Stanley's breath were mingling with the cold air. Stanley was stripped to the waist and stoking the coal. Ewan was rattling through steel rods on the floor. 'You started early,' I remarked to them as I walked in.

'Couldn't sleep,' Stanley said, settling the tongs. A gust of wind flattened the guttering flames. 'I thought we'd do a bit o' forging, given t'weather.' I groaned. 'You've an exam in three weeks unless you've forgotten, Posh Lad!'

I hadn't forgotten, but I'd rather have shod in a typhoon than stand over a forge.

Stanley was an instinctive blacksmith, but he had no patience for instruction. What I'd learnt about forging, I'd learnt from Ewan, who observed with a keener eye and instructed with greater enthusiasm.

Stanley clapped his hands together. 'Right, then! A graduated heart-bar!'

Ewan laughed out loud. 'He won't even have to make a graduated heart-bar for his finals!'

'And what about when he's working on his own – eh?'

'He'd buy one!' Ewan answered.

Stanley ignored him. Forging, to Stanley, is a skill; an art form, a conferrer of nobility. My grandad thinks of cricket in exactly the same way. Stanley was soon lost in the rhythmic banging of metal. His biceps were throbbing, his eyes were narrow, and his shoulder was rising and falling in a sea-rhythm. The shoe he wanted was far beyond my ability, but I crouched on the floor and drew out a steel bar. Stanley was absorbed. He held up his horseshoe in the tongs, studied it and returned it to the flames. He stoked, he poked, he wiped his brow with a sooty forearm and then set to pummelling again. His wife and his money worries and his sheep-savaging dog, had all melted in the heat of the forge. When his steel had been coaxed, moulded and persuaded, Stanley squinted along its section, turned it 360 degrees then, satisfied with his work, he sizzled it in a bucket of water. What emerged with a magician's flourish was a graduated heart-bar shoe.

In the hissing of the water and the shuffling of the coal, Stanley's self had seemed to return to him. 'There you are see,' he said, like he'd buttered a slice of bread. 'It's not hard, is it?' I stared at the mystery of the graduated heart-bar shoe. Forging, to me, was as wondrous as alchemy.

I cut through my length of steel, dropped it in the fire, willed it to co-operate and watched. It seemed to be heating unevenly so I raked some hotter coals towards it. 'Leave it alone!' Stanley snapped. 'It's not a bastard barbecue!' I put the rake down and watched as one end of the steel bar glowed orange and the other flattened to grey. I glanced at Stanley then shoved it with my tongs. 'Brew up!' he ordered. 'That'll stop you messing with it!' I was glad to walk away. I wiped the draining board and opened the tea caddy. Empty. 'Get some from t'kitchen,' Stanley ordered.

I stood in Bling Manor's gleaming kitchen and stared at the bank of cupboards. I opened one. Tins. I closed it. I opened another. Plates. The next handle I pulled opened a drawer. I found myself looking at a picture of the Drakensberg mountains. Dirk's postcards! There were more lying on a stack of tea towels. I scanned them as I walked back to the forge. 'From Dirk,' I announced handing one to Ewan.

'Where's the bastard tea-bags?' Stanley demanded. I ignored his question.

'He's been trying to ring us!'

Stanley flung his arms out. 'If you want a job doing … !' He flung his tongs on the workbench and stormed off to find some tea-bags. Ewan and I tapped Dirk's number into our phones and cursed Stanley's illiteracy.

'He's such a berk,' Ewan muttered, flicking his eyes at Stanley's back. 'This'll be that dodgy number he's been ignoring.'

I'd barely pressed 'save contact' when Stanley's voice rattled the forge roof. He was clattering down Bling Manor's back steps using a box of tea-bags as a rain hat. 'Get your bastard steel off t'fire!' I dropped the teaspoon and ran. 'Bloody hell, lad! You'll be pouring it on t'bastard anvil!' I fangled it out of the embers.

Whilst Stanley brewed up, I laboured over that graduated heart-bar. Long after they'd finished their brews, I was heating, hammering, heating again. After it had been back on the fire two dozen times, Stanley suggested I aim for something, 'Just roughly in the shape of a bastard hoof.' By lunchtime I was sweating, aching and frustrated. Stanley lifted my shoe with his pritchel. 'What's that supposed to fit?' he asked at last. 'A fucking moose?'

'Do you want me to give him a hand with it?' Ewan laughed.

'Nowt'll help him,' Stanley said. 'Bar a visit from Rumple–bastard–stiltskin.' Wordlessly, Ewan threw my heart-bar shoe into the fire and stood over it. 'Have you still got that racing programme on your phone, Posh Lad?' Stanley asked from the rack of shelves. My eyes were still on the fire.

'You can only watch it if you've placed a bet.'

'Put a couple o' quid on that 'oss o' Mervyn's then.'

'You put a couple of quid on it!'

Stanley dropped a box of shoes on the workbench, 'I've already got six hundred smackers on it – remember?' I looked at him. 'Mervyn only pays his bill if it wins!'

'You're not paying me enough to back horses, just so you can watch 'em race,' I said.

'I'm paying you far too fucking much to lame 'em!' he shot back.

'*I* wanted to start on Pedley's shire horse!' I reminded him.

'Oh! For fuck's sake!' Ewan shouted, slamming a two-pound coin on the workbench. 'Put that on the bastard horse!' Stanley looked at it and slunk away to the sink. I slid the money into my jeans pocket, opened the app and looked for Silent Shannon's name.

'It's a hundred to one,' I said.

'It's two quid,' Ewan answered, dead pan.

'The favourite's at nine to two,' I cautioned, looking at the screen.

'Just put it on!' Ewan said, taking the shoe from the fire.

At 1.30 p.m., my iPhone was propped on the workbench and we were crowded round it. I slid up the volume and a chipmunk voice told us they were '*under starters orders, and away in this two-mile, four-furlong novices chase ...*' I fixed my eyes on the screen. 'That's it,' I said, pointing to a jockey in blue and white. Ewan's shoulder was pressed against mine and Stanley's head was over my other.

Silent Shannon jumped the first smoothly, matching the pace of the leader. The favourite missed his stride at the third fence and Silent Shannon soared the jump beside him. Stanley roared his encouragement. The favourite made up lost ground, forcing Silent Shannon into third. I was watching far more intensely than Ewan's two-pound stake deserved. Silent Shannon held her position over the next four plain fences, but when they set out on the second circuit the two leaders pulled away.

Silent Shannon looked beaten. She laboured for three strides, then she went with them!

Ewan nudged me. Stanley growled in his throat. Maybe Baby was leading by a length from the favourite, Captain Caper. Silent Shannon was half a length behind them. Stanley's breaths in my ear were short, rhythmic. The field was in two groups of three. Silent Shannon was battling bravely in the group nearest the camera. The favourite clattered another jump. Silent Shannon was in second place! 'Go on!' I shouted. 'Go on!' As if the horse could hear us, Silent Shannon started gaining ground. Ewan was bellowing now, 'Run, you bugger! Run!' Stride by stride, Silent Shannon was advancing. Ruudi, on her back, was driving like the devil, all hands and heels. Silent Shannon kept on coming. Two strides before the winning post and she was level. Six feet more of turf and Silent Shannon would certainly win! Her neck was at full stretch. She passed the post.

'A nose!' I shouted. 'She had it by a nose!'

Ewan punched the air. 'Two hundred smackers!'

'I'll hold Mervyn to this,' Stanley said, lifting his weight off the workbench. I was relieved when a ribbon of confirmation unwound across the bottom of the screen, *First, number six, Silent Shannon: Second, number two, Maybe Baby: Third, number four, Captain Caper.*

Ewan picked up his hammer and broke into song, *'I wouldn't have to work hard, daidle deedle daidle daidle daidle deedle dum.'* He danced past the anvil. *'Lord who made the lion and the lamb, You decreed I should be what I am, Would it spoil some vast, eternal plan, If I were a wealthy man?'*

Chapter 10

I blundered bleary eyed into the kitchen to the sound of Alexa playing 'Twenty-One Today'. 'Happy Birthday, darling,' Mumma smiled. She stood up from the table and hugged me; she was still wearing her dressing gown. Dad looked up from his coffee, and dropped a key on the table. My eyes locked on to the Land Rover fob. When I looked up again, he was grinning back at me.

'We thought you were ready for a grown-up vehicle.'

I'd had posters of Land Rovers on my bedroom wall once, and a toy one on my windowsill, but I'd nudged the idea of owning one ahead of me. It was to be another trapping of my life as a farrier, along with my own part-bred Irish hunter and a Frank Rigel hoof paring knife.

'Come on,' Dad said, standing up. 'It's in the old barn.' I followed him onto the farmyard, past the barn where fifteen horses were standing round a hay feeder in clouds of their own breath, past the arena and on to the curved gravel track that led through the fields to the old stone barn that housed our tractor and the quad. Dad unlocked the vast padlock and drew on the heavy metal chain that lashed together the solid wooden doors. They trundled back like theatre curtains to show a short-wheel-base, green Defender 90. It was staring at me through the grin of its black grille. 'Go on,' Dad urged. I fished the key from my pocket and opened the driver's door. It felt satisfyingly industrial. I slid onto the black vinyl seat. The dials and knobs in front of me were simple and mechanical. My dad stuck his head in. 'Well?'

'I love it,' I told him.

'Hardly space age,' he said, patting the bonnet. 'But if it makes you happy ...' I turned the key and the engine roared, honest and simple. 'See you at the house,' Dad said and closed the car door.

I rode the unfamiliar clutch and nursed the car to the farmyard. Mumma was dressed now and her hair was whipping across her face as she stood at the kitchen door. I parked it by the kitchen window, stepped onto the flags and hugged her for a second time.

'Thanks, Mumma.'

I laughed through a daft birthday greeting on my phone from Millie, then tinkered with the car radio and adjusted the heat settings. It was the sight of Hathersage, topped by a ceiling of grey cloud that reminded me I was swanking my shiny new Land Rover into Stanley's life of falling takings, estranged children and an adverse court order. I cleared my throat, adjusted my grip on the steering wheel and wiped the smile off my face.

I slid my birthday present to a hissing halt in the gutter of Hathersage Road to find stark proof of Stanley's predicament parked right in front of me. His Porsche had a sign in its back window: *37,000m £27,000.* Stanley was beside it, his big arms folded over his lumberjack shirt. 'Birthday present?' he asked, looking up as I climbed from the Land Rover.

'How did you know?'

'Dolloper.'

I sighed. 'I'm not having a party, so you've wasted any ideas you've been cooking up between you.'

'You *are* having a bastard party,' Stanley grinned, all sharkish.

'I'm not,' I reiterated, heading for the forge. Stanley was following me.

'It's all sorted.'

'You'll be on your own then!'

'Have you heard yourself? You big babby!' We'd arrived at the forge. 'He says he's not coming to his own party,' Stanley told Ewan.

'I don't want wrapping in cling film and standing under Fowlden viaduct!'

'As if we'd do that!' Ewan answered. I rolled my eyes; I knew what they were capable of.

'That's been done!' Stanley explained.

'We were thinking Hathersage traffic lights,' Ewan added, and the pair of them doubled up in laughter.

I turned away. 'You can both fuck off.'

'Oh, come on!' Stanley was attempting wounded now. 'I've bought you a cake!'

'And a tub of axle grease,' Ewan added and they creased again like a pair of schoolboy pranksters.

'Your lass is coming!' Stanley stated. I stared at him.

'Millie knows?'

'I rung her.' He was smug. He waved an arm at Ewan. 'And his lass is coming.'

I looked at Ewan now. 'All the way from Lincolnshire?'

Ewan was nodding. 'She's getting off work early.' I was beaten.

Stanley must have seen it in my face because he rubbed his hands. 'And I've a surprise planned!'

I wagged a finger at him. 'I'm warning you, Stanley …'

'What?' he appealed. 'I'm allowed to surprise you on your birthday, aren't I?'

'Not if it involves axle grease!' Stanley chuckled and scrubbed my scalp. I didn't feel entirely confident about what he had in store for me, but I consoled myself that he wouldn't go too far over the top if Millie and Jade were there. I joined Ewan in swinging boxes into the van. Stanley set up a chorus of 'Twenty-One Today' and Ewan joined in with gusto.

We climbed into The Old Van and Ewan slammed the door. Stanley pointed through the windscreen at his Porsche. 'I thought I'd arrived when I got that car,' he said. He stared at it. 'Every Porsche engine is hand-built, you know.' He'd told me that a dozen times, but I pretended it was news. 'She will have her pound of flesh though, won't she, Lynne?' He started the engine and pulled The Old Van past the shiny new vehicle I had arrived in.

Chapter 11

Millie arrived at Bling Manor at six o'clock with a change of clothes for me. I went upstairs to shower in the marble cubicle that wouldn't have been out of place in the palace of the Sultan of Brunei. When I came downstairs again a newly scrubbed Stanley and Ewan were in the kitchen and Jade had joined them. She wished me a happy birthday and kissed me on the cheek. The absence of cling film, crowds and axle grease was already consoling, but the arrival of Mandy was all the consolation I needed; she'd stand no nonsense.

Stanley's 'girlfriend' (she was fifty, if she was a day,) ran a hairdresser's salon in Fowlden, but she'd been brought up on a sheep farm in Throstleden and had a Yorkshire woman's liking for the pure unvarnished truth. 'Hey up, William lad,' she said, and when I went in for a welcoming peck on her cheek she grappled me close with her sturdy arms. 'Happy birthday, love.' Once she'd wriggled out of her quilted coat, she handed me a Marks and Spencer's bag. 'You can tek it back if you don't like it. I won't be offended.' It was a surprisingly inoffensive turquoise polo shirt. I thanked her and Ewan looked up from where he was arranging candles on a supermarket sponge cake and admired it. Then he slid a gift-wrapped packet across the workbench. I started unpicking the Sellotape from what was obviously a book. I slid it from its wrapping and found myself looking at A.P McCoy's autobiography.

'Thanks!' I was genuinely pleased. It had been signed on the flyleaf from Ewan and Jade. 'I've been meaning to read this.'

'Well, you like all that shit, don't you,' Ewan said, looking away before I could become more effusive.

Stanley nodded at me from over a cauldron of spitting sauce. 'There's a six pack o' Yorkshire Blonde in t'fridge. You can take it home with you.' I thanked him and he wiped his sweating brow with the red gingham tea towel that had been draped on his left shoulder. 'And get a couple more out of the fridge – and whatever the lasses want.' I heard a calming in-breath from Millie and swung back the left-hand door of a fridge that was big enough to store bodies in. Lucky belted in from the living room with a tennis ball in her mouth and Mandy bounced it on the kitchen tiles for her. 'Don't play wi' t'dog in here!'

'I like homes,' she said. 'Not show houses.' I cracked open Stanley's can and placed it at his elbow whilst it was still hissing.

'Get one for Millie!' he ordered as if I'd been ungallant.

'I'm driving,' she said, peering into Stanley's pan. 'Should I chop some salad?'

'We're having spag bol,' he explained, as if it were a contradiction.

I looked into the pot. 'Bloody hell,' I said. 'How many are you feeding?' He laboured his wooden spoon through the thick sauce. 'I hope you've not asked all that lot from Mervyn's yard.'

'I do own a bastard freezer,' he grunted then he pointed to the fridge and addressed Millie, 'There might be a bit o' cucumber if you want some, love,' he looked at Mandy. 'And you can set t'table.'

'Why can't we have it on our knees?' Ewan asked.

I heard Mandy chuckle. 'It'd suit me!' Stanley dropped a fistful of dried spaghetti into a pan then busied himself with the knobs on the hob.

'Is there anything I can do?' I asked.

'Sit down,' Jade ordered. 'It's your birthday.' I sat at the dining room table and looked through the French windows at the inky sky. Stanley walked in polishing a wine glass. He put it down and decided to fetch a tablecloth. Millie brought the salad bowl. Mandy dumped a handful of knives and forks. A car engine died outside. Was someone else coming? A distant car door slammed. I snapped a look at Stanley. His triumphant grin was as wide as the crescent moon. I slid back the French windows and a woman's voice drifted up the drive, '... too old now to drive like a crazy man!' Sense dropped into its pocket with the clunk of a potted pool ball.

I leapt down the back steps. A gorilla sized slab of South African was striding up them with a rucksack in his arms. Lucky shot past my legs and fired at him like a missile. Man and rucksack were in my hug. 'Happy Birthday!' Dirk laughed. I let him go.

Lucky was circling him now; her stump tail a thrashing rudder.

'Hey! Dolloper!' He was grinning at Ewan who was striding down the steps behind me. Dirk crushed Ewan in a shoulder clinch and whilst Ewan demonstrated his new phone as explanation for his silence. Lucky planted her front paws on Dirk's shins. He bent to pet her and Jade went in for a hug on his other side. Millie stood back all the while, her eyes smiling. She and Mandy didn't know Dirk like we did.

Stanley was watching from the patio in his stockinged feet; his arms were folded smugly over his belly, 'I told the lad I had a surprise for him.' Dirk walked up the steps as Maria arrived at the foot of them, dragging a wheeled suitcase. Stanley looked up. 'Bloody 'ell, love,' he said. 'There's no need to ask if you've any news!' Maria looked exhausted. She had leant on the handle of the suitcase and the curve of her belly beach-balled through her open coat. 'When's it due?' Stanley descended the steps. He kissed her left cheek, staggered clumsily in for another and took the suitcase. I congratulated Maria, Millie shook her hand and I expressed my surprise that they were here at all. 'I want to have baby in Madrid,' she explained, like it was local.

'We had to break the flight somewhere,' Dirk explained, then he took my cheeks between his thumb and forefinger. 'And as it was your birthday ... !'

'Thanks,' I grinned. 'It's good to see you.'

Stanley returned with another suitcase and Dirk took Maria's arm to help her up the steps. When he reached the top, the two senior farriers embraced like reunited silverback gorillas. 'It's good to see you, man,' Dirk said, and Stanley walked to where Maria had dropped herself into a wet garden chair.

'That,' she stated, 'was the worst fifteen hours of my life.'

'You've another tomorrow,' Stanley reminded her, but Maria was shaking her head.

'You'll be fine when you've had a rest,' Dirk assured her with a squeeze of her hand. 'It's a lot shorter.'

Once the luggage was in the kitchen, Maria had dried off her coat and Stanley had opened a bottle of wine, he led us to the dining room. There, he glooped strings of spaghetti onto plates and Mandy followed them with dollops of Bolognese sauce.

Dirk glugged out the wine and Maria dipped into the pocket of her coat and presented me with an envelope. 'Is just money,' she apologised. 'Is difficult when we were travelling ...'

'It's perfect,' I interrupted, and kissed her cheek.

'He likes money,' Stanley confirmed.

Between mouthfuls of Bolognese sauce, Dirk described their lives in South Africa and Mandy became animated. 'It's different all together in a hot climate, in't it? I'll bet you damn near live outside! I'll bet you're in and out o' that pool ...' She turned to Maria. 'You'll have been the same in Spain, won't you? It'll all have been paseos and vino tinto on the terrace,' she sighed wistfully.

Maria said nothing. She looked exhausted.

'You must be dying to see your mum and dad,' Millie said to her.

Maria looked up from her plate, her eyes like a cow's. 'If I can manage flight …'

Dirk slapped a hand on her knee. 'Course you'll manage the flight!' but Maria was shaking her head. A tear splashed onto the linen tablecloth. It struck between spatters of Bolognese sauce. Jade handed her a paper napkin. 'We can't delay it, Cookie,' Dirk said. 'You're at the limit for flying.' Maria slashed at her eyes with the heels of her hands and apologised.

'She's just tired,' Dirk explained.

'Go to bed if you want to, love. We aren't bothered,' Mandy suggested, but Maria shook her head and apologised.

Stanley steered the conversation to his savage terrier and drew some welcome laughs at the tales of Belinda and my incompetence at an anvil. I served up a Viennetta, as beyond the French windows the sky dimmed to indigo. After a chorus of 'Happy Birthday' and the lighting of twenty-one candles, Maria finally lumbered towards the stairs. I realised that she'd stayed up for my sake. It was odd to watch her gracelessness. Maria had been quick and lithe.

Dirk glugged more wine into glasses. 'Sorry about Maria,' he said, when she'd gone. 'She's a bit … you know.' We didn't, but Stanley reassured him with a flap of his hand.

'Not much of a birthday party for you, huh?'

'It beats being wrapped in cling film and plonked under the viaduct,' I said and Dirk guffawed his wine out in an explosion of remembrance.

We sipped wine in silence, Millie began clearing the table and above us, floorboards creaked.

'Leave it, Flower,' Stanley commanded Millie. 'I'll do it in t'mornin'.'

Millie picked up an empty wine bottle and looked at Stanley over imaginary spectacles. 'I don't think you will,' she predicted and she went on collecting plates. Mandy stood to help her.

Dirk was lost in thought. 'She was keen to get back to South Africa last summer. We have a great life out there, then suddenly, she wants to have the baby in Madrid.'

Mandy nodded her sympathy. 'I wanted to be near my mum when our Kelsey were born.'

Stanley narrowed his eyes. 'You were. She were only in Pudsey!'

'I know!' Mandy snapped. 'I'm just saying.'

Dirk swirled the wine in the bowl of his glass and stared at it. 'She really struggled on that flight. Her legs swelled up.'

'She'll feel better when she's had a rest,' Stanley said. 'And it's only a couple of hours to Spain.' Dirk took a mouthful of wine and savoured it,

'She's been talking about *moving* to Spain.' He was staring at his glass now. 'I can't even speak Spanish.'

'There you are!' Mandy said, vindicated. 'I moved to Pudsey!'

I looked at Millie and she supressed a smile. I was relieved there'd been no axle grease but the party was becoming maudlin, so in the language of glances I'd first learnt from Ewan I suggested we leave. Millie stood up. I thanked Stanley for his party, told Dirk I'd see him in the morning and accepted two slices of Tesco birthday cake wrapped in kitchen roll from Stanley.

'You got off lightly, there,' Millie mused as we wove through Hathersage's darkened streets. I agreed with her. Stanley had replaced an axle grease stunt with Dirk's surprise homecoming – but Maria hadn't quite been with his programme.

'I hope Maria's all right,' I said. 'Dirk looked worried.'

'She'll have to be,' Millie answered. 'Airlines won't take you after thirty-four weeks.'

The white lights of the street lamps seemed to loop into chains, like the pearls in the photo of Grandma on Grandad's wall. Millie drove on, past Eckersley's shuttered shops and past the wrought iron railings of its deserted municipal park.

Showers of ovine eyes glinted in the headlights as we started the moorland climb. A ewe stood grudgingly from where she'd been dozing on the tarmac. I stared through the passenger window at the moor, glowering black beside me. The brass-button sparkle of randomly sewn on lights was pricking out the distant farmhouses. Eventually, the crest of the moor shook out the twinkling lamps of Loddenden before us, like a magician's tablecloth. They rolled and undulated like a tide. I wondered at the unseen lives, the secret loves and the unspoken losses tumbling beyond the spangle of the sodium lights and put my hand on Millie's hand where it was resting on the gearstick.

Chapter 12

Dirk's hire car was parked on Stanley's drive; its boot and rear door were open. 'What time are they off?' I asked Ewan who was rattling about in his tool-box.

'They should have gone,' he answered. 'But Maria's still in bed.' I raised my eyebrows. Maria usually bustled through life with the efficiency of a war-time matron. Ewan shrugged, fished his paring knife from his tool-box and ran his finger across the blade. Stanley strolled in.

'If you're sharpening that, you can do mine an' all.' Ewan rolled his eyes, but he lifted Stanley's tool-box onto the bench.

'What's up with Maria?' I asked Stanley.

'Big legs,' he answered. 'Dirk's ringing round for a later flight.' Ewan had started up the linisher and I began stocking The Old Van with racehorse shoes. When the job was done, I dropped onto the passenger seat and took out my phone. 'Thanks very much for the detour,' I typed. 'Hope all goes well.'

Stanley thumped onto the driver's seat. The van bounced. Ewan piled in on the other side and Lucky launched herself through the diminishing wedge of daylight and landed on Ewan's lap just as the door slammed behind her. 'I was leaving that at home! Stanley complained as the engine sputtered to start. 'It's not like there's nobody in!'

Mervyn was waiting for us on the car park with a grin on his face and a wodge of notes in his hand. He doled twelve fifty-pound notes into Stanley's palm. 'I told you it'd win!' he said. 'I hope you had summat on it!'

'This'll do me,' Stanley answered, folding the notes.

Mervyn winked at me. 'How much did you make, Posh Lad?'

'Nothing,' I admitted.

'Nothing?' Mervyn repeated. 'You won't get them odds again.'

'I made a half an iPhone 7 on it,' Ewan bragged, waggling his new phone in the beam of the barn's skylight.

'So, are you back in the black, then?' Stanley quizzed Mervyn as Ruudi passed us with the morning's first horse.

'It'll take more than one win,' he admitted. 'But it's helped.'

'It'll win a few more, will that,' Ewan predicted as we followed Ruudi in, but Mervyn was shaking his head.

'It'll be doing bugger all else now it's qualified for t'National,' he said. 'We don't want t'andicapper taking notice.'

'You're serious, then?' I asked. 'About the Grand National?'

'Too right,' Mervyn answered. 'I'm building some Aintree fences to practise o'er.'

'Is that what you're doing wi' t'digger?' Stanley asked him. Mervyn hit the side of his nose with a forefinger then stabbed it at Stanley.

'Never you mind what I'm doin' wi' that digger.' I was clenching up the first horse and Ewan had started on the second when Stanley's phone rang. He narrowed his eyes at the peculiar number. 'Dirk?' Ewan reminded him. Stanley answered. His half of the conversation was a series of grunts. I recognised sympathetic, reassuring, disappointed and resigned grunts. He finished off with, 'Aye, aye. I'll see you in a bit.' He hung up and looked at us. 'He's had her to t'doctor's,' he said. 'Looks like this babby'll be born a Yorkshireman.'

I groaned my sympathy. 'What's up with her?'

Stanley was shaking his head. 'Summat to do with her ears.' I looked at Ewan for help, but he was shaking his head too.

We shod another two, then Stanley walked to the house

for the further three hundred pounds owing for the morning's work – but Mervyn had disappeared like a moorland mist. Back at the van, Stanley cursed himself for not getting it earlier. He took out his phone again and rang Mervyn. He waited with it to his ear, drumming on the van's roof with his fingers, then he glanced at his watch and sighed.

'Ring *me*!' Ewan demanded.

Stanley slid him a disdainful glance. 'Why? You're standing there!'

'Oh, go on!' Ewan pleaded. 'Nobody's rung me on it yet!' I rolled my eyes, took out my phone and rang him. A male voice choir filled Ewan's hand *'Rollin' … Rollin' … Rollin'.'* It was 'Rawhide!' Ewan grinned and killed the call. Stanley was not amused. He looked at his watch again.

My phone was still in my hand. 'Should I ring Jay?' I suggested.

Stanley took a deep breath. 'Go on. It's worth a go.'

Jay picked up after two rings. 'Where are you?' he asked in a voice so shaky I already knew I wouldn't be mentioning the money.

'On the car-park. Why? What's up?' The world around me stilled to a freeze frame as I took in what he was saying. 'Get the first aid kit!' I ordered Stanley. With the phone still at my ear, I ran. My feet slapped the ground like wet leather. I blasted onto the middle yard to see Jay on the step of a red tractor with his right foot resting on his knee and his left hand clutching his foot. The bloody tissue beside him made it look like he'd had a nose bleed; but my eyes had registered the mutilated welly on the floor. His face slackened in relief.

'I tried to ring Mervyn,' he said. Stanley was at my side now, panting.

'Tell me about it,' Stanley snarled.

'The front loader's dropped on his foot,' I said.

Stanley drew air between his clenched teeth and handed me

the first aid kit. I rummaged through bottles of Burneze and tubes of Germolene. Jay was whitening by the second.

Ewan was next on the scene. He took in the situation and crouched beside Jay, who gingerly lifted a reddened sock. It had been pressed over the place where a toe had once been. Ewan pushed his lips together. Bile surged in my stomach. Wordlessly, Ewan reached for a bottle and trickled TCP on the raspberry puree where a toe had been. I heard Jay's sharp snatch of breath. Ewan wadded the wound and, as he made jokes about two-toed sloths and killer front loaders, he wound the foot in Vet-Wrap, then addressed the dead-legged zombie who was retching over a drain.

'Stanley!' Stanley answered with a gut heaving surge. 'Get one of the lads to take you home. We need the van.'

Stanley nodded.

Between us, we staggered Jay to The Old Van where Lucky licked Stanley's vomity lips. Stanley handed over the keys and Jay passed me the crisp packet he'd been clutching in his free hand. I looked in it, then snapped it shut again.

'Jesus!'

Ewan laughed out loud.

'They say you should keep them,' Jay explained.

'On ice!' I gasped. 'You're supposed to pack them with ice.'

'I only had a crisp bag.'

'Salt preserves, bacon,' Ewan mused. 'You never know.'

Two hours later, Ewan and I walked back into the forge. Only Lucky greeted us. Stanley was heating up a straight bar shoe and Dirk was perched on a plastic chair with a mug in his hands. Stanley looked up. 'How did he get on?'

'They couldn't sew it back.'

'Shit day all round,' Dirk mused.

'You're still here then,' I remarked.

Dirk didn't look up. 'No. I'm in fucking Madrid.'

'In a beltin' mood an' all!' Ewan exclaimed. 'Must be all the sunshine.'

'Sorry, man.' He took a gulp from his mug. 'Doc said she's not flying anywhere.'

'I don't know why you're so miserable,' Stanley said as he lifted the shoe from the fire. 'Geoff Boycott's a Yorkshireman.'

'And Sean Bean,' Ewan added.

'And David Hockney,' I said.

'I mean, bloody hell, it could o' been a lot worse.' Stanley dropped the shoe on the anvil and nodded at the forge wall. 'Another fourteen mile that way and the poor little begger would be a Lancastrian.' Ewan sucked his teeth at the thought and Stanley tapped the shoe with his hammer.

'Her dad says he'll pay for us to go Eurostar.'

'There you are then!' Stanley said, between hammer taps.

Maria had appeared in the doorway of the forge. She was wearing a coat over her dressing gown. 'I have suspected pre-eclampsia!'

'You'll be reyt, after a rest!' Stanley assured her.

'Estanley! I'm a nurse!' she reminded him. 'It might need for baby to come early.'

Stanley straightened. 'You'll be reyt if it does! I were calving when I were nine!'

Maria rolled her eyes and Stanley turned to Dirk. 'It's legs that are t'problem. A babby has half as many.'

'How were you calving?' Ewan demanded. 'You can't stand t'sight o' blood!'

'I can't stand t'sight o' severed body parts!' Stanley clarified.

Ewan slunk towards the sink and Stanley held up the finished straight bar shoe. 'What's that for?' I fixed my eyes on the fluorescent strip above me and mentally scoured my revision notes. 'Come on, Einstein!'

'Hoof cracks; hoof avulsions, lacerations, severe medial/ lateral, anterior/posterior imbalance; hoof distortions; chronic laminitis; keratoma, or post-surgical support.'

Dirk let out a whistle and Stanley pointed the pritchel at Ewan. 'You, Dolloper, could o' done wi' sleepin' wi' a vet an' all.'

Chapter 13

Saturday was the night of my family's celebrations at Grandad's. I hadn't been looking forward to this shared birthday party with Piers. Piers is my younger cousin by a week, and our grandad is about the only thing we have in common.

Grandad's parties had been thrilling, once; Mumma in high heels and sparkles, Dad in a dinner jacket, exotic sounding snacks on silver platters and a bran tub for me and Piers. Piers and I had spent one party when we were six, sipping from unattended champagne flutes and had ended up fighting. I'd punch him now, if I could still get away with it.

Millie looked classy in flowing wide legged trousers and a high-necked top and I proudly introduced her to my great aunts and great uncles. Her profession somehow mitigated their disappointment at my own trade. Eventually I found myself face to face with Piers. He was wearing a dinner suit printed all over with skulls. I decided not to remark on it and hoped Millie wouldn't either; I'd warned her he was a tool. 'How's the erm … stonemasoning?' he asked.

'Farriery.'

'Yah?' It sounded like a question – but then, so did everything else Piers said. He shuffled his weight from his right foot to his left.

'On your own?' I asked, as the loveliest woman in the room folded her hand over mine. (Uncle Charles and Aunty Caroline had chattered non-stop about Piers' girlfriend at Grandad's summer barbecue. They had been especially animated by her family's country estate in Norfolk.)

'Yah,' he explained. ''Fraid Cressida's in the Cayman Islands.' He sipped his champagne. 'Family commitments.' My eyes had fixed on a crease in the floral curtains behind him. 'You must be Millie, yah?'

'Yes,' she smiled, holding out her hand. 'Nice suit.'

He missed her irony and fingered his lapel. 'Thanks, yah. I like to mix things up a bit.' Warmed by her interest, he went on. 'Did Grandad say you're a medic?'

'A vet.'

'Ah.'

He absently swilled his champagne dregs.

'What do you do?' Millie asked. I'd already told her, but she was playing the game.

'Cambridge. Trinity.' He followed it with a long list of options for the following year, which included, opening a gallery, trekking in the Himalayas and forming a property management company. By this time I'd begun counting the repeats of the roses in the curtains.

Grandad approached with the champagne bottle. 'Good to see you two getting on at last.' He was doubtless referencing the bite marks, wailings and fistfuls of hair littering his memories of the preceding years. 'Hard to believe you're twenty-one.' Champagne glugged out until it fizzed over the rim of my glass and onto the carpet. I licked my fingers. 'Actually, boys, I'd like a word with you both.'

Piers glanced up from his phone. 'Sounds ominous.' We were rarely included in the same sentence, let alone the same invitation.

'Not at all,' Grandad smiled. 'It's to your advantage.'

Piers pocketed his phone. 'I can come now if you want.' His eyes slid to me.

'Yeah,' I shrugged. 'Fine.'

'Jolly good,' Grandad said and when he'd emptied his

champagne bottle into the glasses of the chattering guests, we followed him from the hum of the dining room to the muffled quiet of the breakfast room.

It was a grand house with its long windows and tapestry sofas, but it was a faded one now; an old man's house. I pulled out a pine chair and sat opposite Grandad at the table. Piers sat beside me. Grandad splayed his gnarled fingers on the lace tablecloth and spoke to his knuckles. 'As you know, boys, your grandma left you an inheritance.' His eyes drifted to the wall beside us where the familiar photograph of a laughing sparkly-eyed lady in wide-brimmed hat and a pearl necklace held his attention for a moment. To me, it was as if restraining that hat in a breeze had been the only action of my grandmother's life. A breath lifted Grandad's ribcage then stirred the leaves of the peace lily between us. His liver spotted hands reached across the table and rested; one on mine, one on Piers'. He let the clock tick. 'She thought the world of you boys.' Prickles of discomfort were bristling my skin. I felt Piers shift in his seat. 'Anyway,' he withdrew his hands. 'I took the liberty of investing your inheritances, so you'll each be getting a tidy sum.'

'Exactly how tidy?' Piers asked.

Grandad sat back in his chair. 'This isn't for travelling the world with, Piers, or buying fast cars.' I bit the inside of my cheek. 'Your generation won't be retiring at fifty on generous pensions, or have the NHS to replace your dodgy knees.' I was nodding. 'This money is for your futures.' The clock ticked on. 'You might want to think about buying property, or shares.'

'It's our money, though,' Piers insisted. 'You can't tell us how to spend it.'

'I can't,' Grandad agreed. 'But I'd like you to consider it carefully.'

'So how much am I considering?' Piers asked.

Grandad's glance took in both of us. He was rolling his left hand softly around the fingers of his right, 'You'll each inherit just over two hundred and twenty thousand pounds.'

I couldn't breathe. I couldn't even blink.

'Wow!' Piers whispered, moving his head slowly from side to side. He reached for his champagne glass. 'Wow.' He took a swig from his glass, clattered his chair and stood up. 'Wait till I tell Cressida.' He was dragging his phone from his pocket as he left the room.

'It's what your Grandma wanted,' Grandad answered, looking at the picture of my decades dead grandmother. My eyes drifted with his to the photograph. My head had gone to sponge.

'What was she like?' I asked, and Grandad smiled at me. I could see his yellow teeth right up to the gum line.

'She was wonderful,' he said. 'I miss her every day.'

I hugged Grandad my thanks and headed back to the dining room. Millie was perched on the sofa next to Great-Aunt Margaret, distantly diagnosing her bichon frise. Piers had opened another bottle of champagne and was being back-slapped by Uncle Charles – as if he'd achieved something. Dad grinned at me from across the room. Mumma sidled up, oddly tall on her four-inch heels. 'You're very lucky,' she said quietly. I nodded, tight-lipped; still trying to set the information in the jumbled jigsaw of myself. I'd jumped from hand-to-mouth apprentice to 4x4 driving man of substance in a matter of a week, and I'd done nothing to deserve it. 'Think of it as an insurance policy,' she added.

Grandad's CD player began blasting 'Happy Birthday' and Piers was standing by our two-tier cake, wielding a cake slice.

'Is everything okay?' Millie asked, under the singalong.

I squeezed her hand. 'I'll tell you later.'

'Go on!' she urged, shoving my shoulder. 'Don't let Piers steal the limelight!'

I walked towards him, fantasising about places I'd like to stick a cake slice.

Chapter 14

The practical examination was the last one of my December block release and I'd spent every free minute of the preceding fortnight practising in Stratford college's state-of-the-art forge. When two agriculture students 'borrowed' a tractor to transport us to the pub, I was familiarising myself with the gas forge. When my fellow farriers challenged the farmers to a fist fight behind the refectory, I was practising a plain stamp hind shoe. When Danny Pugh used a fallen tree to catapult a brick through Dave Hodgkinson's office window, I was forging a three-quarter fullered.

Dave Hodkinson FWCF looked round the forge. 'You've each been allocated a shoeing bay,' he said. 'So as soon as you find your name, turn on your gas forge.' My palms were sweating and my mouth tasted of cardboard. I went in search of my forge. It was the middle one of a row of five. I stood beside it. Exam nerves had set ice flowing through my innards. Five horses were led in: a Dartmoor pony, followed by a fifteen hand appaloosa, then a fourteen hand cob and two thoroughbreds. *Not the cob*, I chanted inwardly, *please God, anything but the cob.* I was far more used to making shoes for thoroughbreds. The girl with the cob headed for me. The ice seemed to form a block in my belly. I managed a courteous smile at the girl who tied the horse loosely in my shoeing bay. I smoothed its silken coat, stood quietly at its shoulder and waited for Dave Hodgkinson's next instruction. He gave us his confidence boosting smile before he spoke. 'Right, lads, you've got two hours to make a front pair of three-quarter fullered shoes for the horse you've been presented with.' I'd practised three-quarter fullereds. They were straightforward. The belly ice started melting. 'You can start as soon as you're ready.'

Gas! I suddenly remembered Dave Hodgkinson's instruction. *Turn on your gas forge.* I fired up the forge in panic, then I looked at the cob's feet. They were round. They'd take a good bit of metal. I picked up a front foot and measured it. Six inches across; I'd need to add one and a half inches to that. Or should it be one and three-quarter inches? I gripped my chin. Or was one and three-quarter inches for a hind foot? I scoured my memory. Perhaps *three-quarters* was in my head because I was making a *three-quarter* fullered? Think, I told myself. I stared at the brick wall on the other side of the forge. I could feel sweat seeping at the bridge of my nose. A low roar of gas was humming in the cavernous hall. It sounded like a headache. I looked round. They were cutting metal. I looked back at the cob's feet. The forge was filling with the clang and clatter of steel. My instinct had been one and a half. I pushed the metal under the guillotine. I suddenly felt more confident. It was one and a half. I cut it.

The unwanted length of metal dropped to the concrete with a clang. I glanced at it. Should I have gone for one and three quarters? I looked at the length behind the blade. It was done now. There was no point worrying about it. I fed the metal into the forge and went to adjust the height of the anvil. I pulled a peg. It didn't move. I wiped my hands on my jeans and pulled again. Not a twitch. I tried another peg. It was rusted. I took out my pliers. I gripped the peg and yanked it. The anvil tottered. I lurched to catch it but its weight crashed it to the concrete. My horse skittered. Candidates looked up. I cringed an apology and righted the anvil gingerly. Dave Hodgkinson had crept across to me. He was carrying another anvil stand. I thanked him in a whisper and he helped me set it to the right height.

The metal was co-operating. It was glowing an even irides-cent. Relieved, I fished it from the forge. I set it on the anvil and picked up my hammer. The hot steel itself seemed to coax my blow. It was showing me the shape of a hoof. Very soon, I had a shoe. It looked good; round and regular. I impaled it on my pritchel and dunked it in cooling water. I lifted up the cob's foot and approached it with the shoe. I froze. It was too small. I could see it a metre away. A pulse started to bump in my throat. I looked at Dave Hodgkinson in his tweed waistcoat and brass chained pocket watch. I hesitated a moment longer then I flung the shoe in the pail of water and returned to the pile of steel.

When Dave Hodgkinson called the end of the exam, I'd made one shoe. One. My knees buckled. The clank and rattle of discarded tools jarred beyond the thud of my blood. I dropped to a crouch. One shoe.

I usually enjoyed the train journey home. I liked the views onto back yards and lorry parks. I liked the unreeling motorways and the slow crumpling of counties into the Pennine foothills – but every time I imagined telling Stanley that I'd failed my practical exam my eyes blurred and the windows blinged with a kaleidoscope of sparkling Christmas trees. It wasn't even like it was my first failure. I'd flunked my A levels, I'd lamed a pony, I was useless in the forge and now I'd failed my forging exam. I shuffled in my seat. The coarse pile of the upholstery shifted with my skin. I rang Millie. I stared at the prickly blue plush of the empty seat opposite me and relayed the entire cock-up, disaster by disaster. I could hear her breath in my ear when I'd finished. 'Didn't Ewan fail one?' He had – then he'd gone on to get the best marks in the country in his finals. 'Ring him,' she advised. 'See how he thinks you should handle it.'

The second I hung up, my phone rang. I glanced at it, Stanley again. I'd already ignored three calls from him. I picked up.

'All done then?'

'Yeah.'

'What did you have to make?'

'A three-quarter fullered.'

'Piece o'piss!' he chuckled. Then he turned to what concerned him most. 'Dolloper's doing a turn at Cribbs' Social t'weekend before Christmas; I thought we'd cheer him on. Do you fancy it? We could make it our Christmas do.' (Our Christmas 'do' the year before had been at the hunt ball – another sign of Stanley's reduced circumstances.)

'Okay, yeah.'

'Fetch your lass.' Stanley ordered, then in a surprising flash of sensitivity he asked, 'Are you a'reyt, Posh Lad? You're quiet.'

'Just knackered,' I lied, but it satisfied him. He wished me a good night, and hung up.

I waited whilst the spangling lights of a nameless northern town had split and fractured in the raindrops on the carriage window, then I slid my finger over Ewan's name on my phone.

Ewan listened sympathetically, but when he spoke it was decisive, 'Don't tell him.'

'He'll get my report,' I reminded him.

'Not till after Christmas, he won't.'

I chewed on my lip. He had a good point. 'Have you been busy?'

'Dead,' Ewan answered. 'Dirk's helped out once or twice, but only cos he's bored.' It wasn't unusual for business to be slack in winter, but it wouldn't be helping Stanley's mood.

'How's Maria?'

'She's at the hospital every day, for check-ups.'

'I googled pre-eclampsia,' I told him. 'Turns out, it has nothing to do with ears.'

'Or clamps,' Ewan added. 'But don't tell Stanley that either – eh?'

Chapter 15

Dad had persuaded me to see his financial advisor, Frank. Frank was an earnest little man, with a liking for brightly coloured ties. He greeted Dad at the door of Lower Mossthwaite Farm, then strolled on into the kitchen, set his briefcase on the table and chatted about the weather as he took out his files and papers. Mumma offered him a coffee and whilst she waited for the kettle to boil, he asked her about her business, and reminded her of what she could offset against tax. Mumma set steaming mugs and a carrot cake on the table, thanked him absently for his advice and walked off. Dad pulled up a chair and sat down.

Frank ran his fingers down columns and outlined the pros and cons of different portfolios whilst I lurched between cold fury and steaming embarrassment. Dad was discussing *my* money as if it were his own. It had been withheld until I was an adult, and here he was, treating me like I was still a child! When I made an enquiry about ethical investments, Dad interrupted with his view that as all profits took pressure off the welfare state, they were therefore all ethical. At that point, I sat back, folded my arms and let them talk about my two hundred and twenty-one thousand, one hundred and sixty pounds as if it had nothing to do with me.

When they'd made decisions about where to invest it, what funds should be available to me immediately and how long to lock it in for, Frank handed me a pen. I looked at it, stood up and told them I needed time to think.

It made me look 'churlish, arrogant and rude,' apparently.

Later that night, I used Ewan's name as a password and as Millie and I walked through the swing doors of Cribbs Social Club, I felt my secrets were poking through my skin.

'What's up?' Millie asked as we handed our coats to the cloakroom attendant.

I shook my head. 'Dad, Stanley, a failed exam, unearned privileges ...'

She leaned in. 'Will, what you've just been handed will take me seven years to earn. Be grateful.'

'I am!' I spoke in a stage whisper. 'And if Stanley finishes me, I'll need it.'

She rolled her eyes. 'Why would he finish you?'

'I've just failed my forging exam.'

'Ewan failed one!'

'Stanley wasn't skint then.'

She shook her head. 'You've been about as much fun as a septic ulcer since you came back from Warwickshire.' She quickened her pace and I followed her past an artificial Christmas tree into a dance hall with an orange carpet and paintwork the colour of nicotine.

The room had sticky table tops, polystyrene ceiling tiles, and an ancient cigarette machine. Foil decorations swooped from the corners to a pendant glitter ball which was disintegrating with age. Half a dozen women were adding sandwiches, and sausage rolls to a row of trestle tables, and at the bar, two of the drinkers sported Stetsons. Dirk was there too, and for once, his cowboy boots didn't look out of place. Across the room I could see Maria sitting beside Stanley. It was a few weeks since I'd seen her and I thought she looked a bit better. Stanley was in conversation with a stranger who was leaning over his shoulder. We wove through little girls in leggings and sequinned tops who were nicking Smarties from the fairy cakes and little boys in jeans who were knee sliding on the dance-floor and arrived at his side.

'Nah,' he was saying. 'It'd be no good for you, Neil. Your Michelle'd never get in it.'

'It's not for Michelle!' Neil argued, but Stanley wasn't listening.

'You want a nice 4x4 wi' room for her wheelchair.' Neil was still protesting but Stanley was shaking his head. 'It wouldn't be fair to sell it to you, Neil.'

'Hiya, love.' It was Mandy, Stanley's girlfriend. She leant round Stanley to greet us and was dragging out a chair for Millie. 'Sit yourself here, love.'

Jade, Ewan's farrier girlfriend, had stood up too. She kissed Millie, then me, then nodded at the trestle table. 'Have you seen that cake?' she said, pointing at a chocolate gateau and sweeping the drapes of her swinging dress aside to sit. Stanley who'd abandoned Neil, to his disappointment, puffed out his cheeks and pointed his elbows in a covert pantomime of obesity. I punched his shoulder.

'A'reyt, Will?' It was Ewan's brother, Lee. He and his father, Steve, had arrived with a tray of drinks. Dirk was behind them. They doled them out and Mandy complained that it was fucking December and fished the ice from her gin and tonic with her fingers.

The lights dimmed. A compere took the stage. He was portly and florid and wearing a V-necked jumper, but when he threw back his right arm he spoke in the tones of a gameshow host. 'Put your hands together now for Cribbs' very own answer to Michael Bublé!'

Lee let rip a whistle. Whistling, clapping and table banging filled the hall, then a rumble of male voices tumbled into, *'Rollin'! Rollin'! Rollin'!'* Now I understood Ewan's ringtone. Ewan was crossing the stage. He was dapper in his rat-pack suit and tie. His shoulders were squared, his stride certain and by the time he was at the microphone, half the room was bellowing 'Rawhide!' Ewan took the mic. He claimed the song. He was on home turf. His easy finger clicking drifted him into

'The Girl from Ipanema', then 'Thinking Out Loud'. I watched his first set with fascination and a broad smile. Forge Ewan was mischievous and practical; stage Ewan was slick and confident.

When he returned to our table, it was through wolf whistles and applause. He pulled out a chair and Mandy fired a question at him, 'Have you ever thought of working on the cruise ships?'

'No, he bastard hasn't!' Stanley shot back.

She didn't even acknowledge Stanley. 'You want to wait while *he* qualifies,' she was pointing at me. 'then you want to get yourself on t'cruise ships.' Ewan swigged at his pint. He wasn't looking at her. 'You'd get to see all over. I went all round t'Caribbean and t'Greek islands, I went round t'Mediterranean. I danced wi' Roger Moore ...' Stanley's eyes were darting round the table like wasps at a barbecue but Mandy's memories were sailing on. 'Venice is lovely. I loved Venice.'

'Has somebody dropped summat in her bastard drink?' Stanley interrupted.

'Venice and St Lucia. They were my favourites.' She turned to Stanley. 'We should go on a cruise sometime, you know.'

'Go on a cruise?' His face had crumpled in incomprehension. 'By t'time Lynne's done wi' me I won't be able to go on a bastard bus!'

Mandy took a sip of her gin. 'Best years of my life,' she said, dreamily. 'Then somewhere between Kos and Istanbul, Neville came in t'salon for a short back 'n' sides, and the rest – as they say – is history. You want to do it while you're young enough, love,' She'd snapped herself back to Cribbs Social Club. Stanley's eyes were like pint glass bottoms. He raised his beer to his lips. 'How many of them have you had?' He stopped the glass on its journey.

'It's Christmas.'

'I don't want you getting lairy.' She turned to me. 'He gets lairy after he's had a few.' In my experience, he fell over and passed out. 'Make that your last,' she ordered.

'Yes my Flower,' he said, in a voice that told her he had no such intention.

'And get some grub down you to soak it up,' she suggested. 'They've opened t'buffet.' Then she turned to Ewan. 'Think on what I said,' she winked, 'you won't regret it.' Stanley took her by the elbow, keen to separate her from Ewan. 'And you're certainly good enough.'

I watched them go. Stanley's concern at the thought of Ewan leaving his employ had been clear. If he planned to save money on wages, they wouldn't be Ewan's.

Mention of the buffet had lifted Jade and Dirk to their feet too. Millie, who was in mid-conversation with Jade, followed. That left just me, Maria and Ewan at the table. I put my pint glass on its beer mat and told Maria I thought she was looking better. I wanted to say, *Well done, Ewan* or *I enjoyed that*, but the words sounded cringy in my head, so I left them there. Ewan's talent seemed limitless to me. I was still working on a way to express my admiration when two girls sat in the empty seats at our table. One was wearing a black tourniquet, partially unzipped at the front, the other was in a snake-print bikini top and denim shorts. She slewed herself across the table and spoke to Ewan. 'Our Courtney says you work with horses. I love horses, me.'

Courtney was twisting a lock of blonde hair round her finger, but her eyes were on Ewan. 'We thought you were mint.'

Ewan nodded his thanks.

'Are you gonna get us a drink?' Snake Girl asked.

'No,' Ewan said. Maria laughed and I looked up, surprised by what seemed to be his bad manners but Snake Girl shimmied her way behind his chair and poured her arms all over his chest. I glanced towards Jade, who was concentrating on the buffet table across the dance-floor. Ewan brought his pint to his lips as if Snake Girl wasn't there. Undeterred, she finished her groping then slithered her denim clad rear to his lap.

Stanley returned, took the sight in then dumped a plate of

turkey sandwiches on the table. 'Our lasses'll be wanting their chairs back,' he said, loudly.

'I'm not taking a chair up,' Snake Girl pouted, so Stanley tried another tack.

'See that big girl o'er yon,' he was pointing at Jade, who still had her back to us at the buffet table. 'That's his girlfriend.'

Snake Girl snorted. 'Time he upgraded to a thin lass then, in't it?'

In following Stanley's finger, I noticed that we were being approached by a Neanderthal man and a human Smeg fridge. Their arms were folded over their ice-white T-shirts and both were dressed in leather biker jackets. I nudged him. Stanley turned his bulk towards the on-coming menace. 'Don't worry about them two,' he scoffed. 'Their dad thinks he's a hard man an' all. They couldn't knock skin off a rice puddin' between 'em.'

'Hey up, lads,' he remarked, when they arrived at our table. 'You look very nice, lads. Did your mother dress you?'

Neanderthal looked past him.

Smeg fridge said, 'Piss off, Lampitt.'

Neanderthal yanked Snake Girl off Ewan's lap. She teetered on her heels and smashed into the table with her hip. Maria caught it before it hit her baby bump. Ewan crossed his legs.

'What's goin' off?' Mandy asked, pushing between them and plonking her plate down.

Smeg hitched a thumb at Courtney who jumped up and teetered to his side. 'You!' he said to Ewan in a voice that wobbled the table. 'Will be singing fucking soprano, if you touch our lasses again.'

Ewan sniggered at him.

'I mean it, Grimshaw.'

'It were nowt to do wi' 'im,' Stanley clarified as he folded a turkey sandwich into a brick-sized bite. 'It's them lasses o' yours. You want to keep 'em on leads.'

Smeg slammed his fist straight into Stanley's face. Maria

struggled to her feet. Stanley fell backwards, flinging his sandwich to slam his hand over his nose. Ewan was on his feet now. Blood was blossoming through Stanley's fingers. Maria tended to him. Ewan punched Smeg in the belly. The whole of Cribbs estate, where Ewan had been born and raised, was suddenly standing. *'Feyt, feyt, feyt!'* rang over rhythmic clapping. Lee was legging it from the bar. It was as if I'd just flicked to another channel.

A moon-faced thug ran in and up-ended our table. Beer, butties and black forest gateau flew, spun then splattered on the carpet. I punched him. Me! In the belly. He buckled, but he slammed an upper cut into my jaw as he dropped. Teeth smashed into my tongue. My whole head rattled. The fight had fanned way beyond our table now. Pork pies were flying. Arcs of beer were spangling the glitter ball. I wrapped my legs round Moon Face's legs. He staggered and clattered into a chair. I grabbed his sweatshirt and spun him. He ricocheted off Maria and sent her staggering, then his weight dropped him like lumber. Dirk left off swinging a bloke by his tie, to drag his wife from harm's way, but his opponent recovered and jumped on his back. The room was shouting, clapping, stamping. I swung a kick at him, but Lee, who was grappling with Neanderthal, crashed backwards into me. I fell. When I scrambled up again, it was into a rotavator of fists. Cheekbone, eye socket and nose took blows, but Moon Face's windmilling arms had lurched him forward. I grabbed the back of his neck and pushed down. All around me was rattling and grunting. Dirk had thrown off his assailant and now had him pinned to the wall. Moon Face leg-locked me and I was struggling to breathe through blood, but I'd landed more punches than ever before in my life. This felt like victory.

Enough now lads! Come on! The PA system had crackled to life. *Think o' the babby Jesus!* A turkey drumstick struck my shoulder. *Come on, now! We've paid young Grimshaw for two sets!* Moon Face loosened his leg lock. I straightened up and his outstretched hand was in front of me. I looked at it. Did he want me to shake his hand? He thrust the hand nearer. I expected a trick – but I took it. Over by the wall, Dirk was patting his adversary on the back.

Meanwhile, 'Rawhide' had started up over the devastation. I looked up to see Ewan peeling half a sandwich from his elbow. A red circle was shining on his cheekbone and his shoulders were beaded with beer, but he leapt to a jog and headed for the stage. *'Give him a big round of applause now – and hope they've left him some teeth in! Ewan Grimshaw, ladies and gentlemen!'* The room cheered him with double its former fervour. Neanderthal put his fingers to his lips and ripped a searing whistle, like his girlfriend hadn't just been sitting on Ewan's knee. Moon Face whooped his appreciation and Snake Girl was clapping wildly.

Stanley was sitting with his head back and pinching the bridge of his nose. His shirt looked like a slaughter-man's apron. Jade had righted our table. Stanley cut his eyes at me, 'I didn't think you had it in you!' he said in a stuffed up voice. The seed of a smile stiffened my swelling nose. 'You couldn't knock a fly off a window twelve months since.'

'Sorry – are we supposed to be impressed?' Millie asked. She had appeared from nowhere, like the shark in *Jaws* with a white faced Maria by the elbow.

Lee grinned and pointed at me. 'He'd have been meat paste last year.'

Millie was shaking her head. 'And you think it's some sort of joke? A thirty-eight weeks pregnant woman has just been knocked flat.'

'No!' Lee insisted. 'Not that bit, but your fella landed a good few fists!' He mimed a quick flurry of boxing moves to make his point. Millie brushed smashed sausage roll from her lamé skirt.

'Tell that unreconstructed ape on the dance-floor that I'm taking his wife home.' This silent Maria was unfamiliar. She should have been screeching at Dirk in slicing Spanglish syllables. She should have been prodding his shoulder and scalding his face with her close-up fury. Dirk seemed unaware. He was skipping and shimmying on the beer slicked dance-floor with the rest of the recovered Cribbs crowd. Millie snatched her bag from the back of her chair and flung it on her shoulder. 'This,' she announced in a voice sharp enough to cut glass, 'is not my idea of a night out.'

'Loosen up.' Lee laughed. 'It were just a friendly bust up!' But Millie's heels were clacking across the dance-floor. Maria walked behind her, her steps ticking on the tacky parquet. I watched as the swing doors slammed behind them.

Steve slapped another pint in front of me. 'Well!' he said. 'That livened things up!'

Chapter 16

It was Saturday afternoon before I'd recovered enough to ring Millie. When she didn't pick up, I grovelled by voice message. I wondered where she could be. I didn't remember her saying she was on call. I tried again an hour later – and again there was no answer. Mumma was with a client and Dad had sunk two glasses of Malbec with his lunch so I'd hoped Millie would take me to collect my car; it was still at Cribbs Social Club. When her phone was still ringing out at four o'clock, I rang Ewan.

'It's at Stanley's, mate,' he told me. 'Our Lee's got third party so he took it.'

'How?' I asked. 'He didn't have the keys.' Ewan's bark of a laugh reminded me it was a daft question. Not only was Lee a mechanic, he'd been brought up on Cribbs estate where hot wiring a car is learnt between telling the time and tying your shoelaces. 'Tell him thanks – I think.'

'You're all right. It wouldn't have had wheels on it if it'd stayed on Cribbs all night. It'll be reyt at Stanley's till Monday, though. Can't it wait?'

'And how will I get there on Monday?' Ewan groaned so that the phone crackled in my ear.

'I'll be half an hour.'

I waited for Ewan at the top of the drive and half an hour later I clambered in to The Old Van beside him. 'Thanks, mate,' I said. 'I'd have asked Millie to take me, but she's not picking up.'

'Still pissed off with you, then?'

'Looks like it.' We drove in silence between bleak black hedgerows. I turned to Ewan. 'How did she and Maria get home? Do you know?' It was the first time I'd considered it.

'Taxi.'

That would have meant a taxi to Stanley's with Maria, and then on to Eckersley, with Millie. The grey ribbon of road unwound under The Old Van's wheels. The moor was pewter; even the sheep seemed subdued. I craned and twisted as we drove through Eckersley. A light was on in Millie's flat – but she left a light on when she went out. 'Do you want to stop?' Ewan asked, noting my gaze.

'Nah,' I said. I didn't want Ewan to witness my rejection.

He drew the van to a halt just behind my Land Rover which was parked half on the broad pavement to the left of Bling Manor's drive. I thanked him and he would have driven off again had Lucky not scooted from the drive and straight out in front of the van. I scooped her up and Stanley appeared at the top of the drive red faced, flustered, and shouting her name.

'You should shut the gate!' I said.

'And you should shut your mouth,' he snapped, snatching the dog back, 'when you don't know what's going on!' I passed Lucky to him and he shoved her down the drive with his foot under her tail, so she ran on two legs. He turned and waved his free hand at Ewan who was checking the traffic in The Old Van's wing mirror. When he failed to get his attention, Stanley ran to the bonnet and banged his fist on the van. Ewan swung round and Stanley ordered him out. Ewan wound down the window.

'Why? What's up?'

'Never mind why! It's my fucking van!'

Behind us, an engine roared. Stanley swung his attention to Bling Manor's drive. Dirk was in the driver's seat of The Best Van and Maria was beside him with a bag on her lap. Stanley had set off down the drive. Ewan jumped from the van and followed him.

'Stanley! Are you going to tell me what's going on?'

'T'babby!' he shouted. 'She's havin' t'babby and he's sent his hire car back!' He waved his arms. 'Dirk! You're not insured on it!' Dirk revved the engine. 'I can take us in t'Old Van now!' but Dirk had hit the gas. I threw myself against the hedge at the top of the drive. The Best Van spewed a spume of carbon monoxide. It screeched past Stanley who'd pinned himself against the wall of the house. It swung sharp left – straight into the back of Stanley's Porsche.

The boom segued through a crash, a clatter and a tinkle and left Stanley's co-joined vehicles in a pool of shattered glass. Stanley walked to the top of the drive. His hands were on his bald head and his eyes were as round as the Porsche's empty indicator sockets. Lucky scuttered to the bottom of the garden; she knew Stanley as well as the rest of us. Ewan, at my side now, folded his arms. 'Well, that's fucked t'job.'

Maria stepped from The Best Van. She'd seemed a ghost of herself since they'd arrived in England. She'd been ill, then I'd disappeared to Warwickshire and then she'd been whisked away by Millie. Now, on the rim of childbirth she was in full corporal technicolour again.

She strode to Ewan, and slapped out her flat palm. 'Keys.' No one messed with Maria when she acted like this; not Dirk, not Stanley and certainly not Ewan. He fished in his jeans and handed them over.

'You can't drive yourself, Maria!' he reasoned.

'He,' she was pointing at Dirk, who had stepped from The Best Van and was clutching his pelt of hair with one hand, 'will kill us.' Maria had already opened The Old Van's door and was heaving herself up.

'Stanley!' Ewan pleaded, arms outstretched. 'You're not going to let her drive herself!' but Stanley was transfixed by his co-joined vehicles. 'Dirk!' Ewan pleaded. Dirk snapped back to his senses and ran towards The Old Van, but Maria slammed the door and locked it from inside.

'Let me in, you stupid mare!'

'Peas off!' she answered and then she folded in a wince.

'Maria! Don't be bloody ridiculous!' He was pulling on the door handle. Maria's eyes were closed.

'I want to have baby in hospital!'

'You can't drive when you're in labour!' The contraction washed over her and she set to rattling the seat controls.

Stanley's hand was on Dirk's shoulder. He spun Dirk away and shouted at the glass. 'You won't slide that seat forward. It's broke!' She stopped rattling. She was wedged behind the steering wheel even though her feet must be short of the pedals. 'What if I drive you?' There was a second's pause, then Maria unlocked the door and shuffled to the middle seat.

'You are bloody idiot ass well,' she remarked to Stanley. Dirk was on the passenger side now. Maria unlocked the door and he piled in.

He slunk a look at Stanley. 'Sorry about your Porsche, mate.'

'And me bastard van.'

'And your bastard van.'

Stanley turned the ignition key, stuck his head out of the window and spoke to Ewan.

'Tell your daft brother to come and sort the van out,' he instructed Ewan. 'And make sure he keeps his bastard hands off my Porsche – comprendo?' and The Old Van pulled away from the kerb.

Carlos Jaime Ramirez-Koetzee!
December 24th 2016
3.5 kg.
Mother and baby fine.
Father traumatised.

Chapter 17

My failed exam and the taut mood between me and my dad following the meeting had punched Christmas in the guts, but Millie's departure knocked it dead. She didn't answer my calls. She didn't reply to my texts. On Christmas morning I lurked about the stable yard, stuffing hay nets and checking water buckets, hoping she'd arrive to tend to Onion. My guts leapt with hope when my phone pinged – but it was a picture of a puckered face over the cocoon of a white waffle blanket. I couldn't even be bothered to reply with a good wish, so I just sent a heart. Eventually, Mumma tacked Onion up. Millie wasn't coming. I heard the click and swill of my throat and walked indoors again to stare at the little square box I'd wrapped in Christmas paper.

Christmas had been fun when I was little; the last door on the advent calendar, a bran tub, then midnight mass and rushing home before Father Christmas. Today, would be drinks at Grandad's with remote aunts and alien cousins, then Mumma grappling a dead turkey and Grandad complaining that we never used the dining room.

Millie and I had planned to go to Wetherby races on Boxing Day but when Boxing Day arrived, I was too restless even to watch it on the telly.

Hathersage was still slumbering under a soft blanket of valley mist when I wove my way to work on the day after Boxing Day. Eckersley moor in my windscreen was backlit by a rising sun;

its white rays were veiling the hillside like a caul. Ewan had taken a few more days holiday, but at least work would distract me from thinking about Millie and stop Dad asking me if I'd thought any more about what Frank had said.

I'd hoped Dirk would be joining us, but despite Bling Manor's kitchen being piled high with boxes depicting cherubic infants, packs of disposable nappies, and parcels wrapped in blue stork paper, he was off to buy 'essentials' for Maria and Carlos.

'Essentials?' Stanley asked. He was tolerating the defilement of his granite worktops surprisingly well. 'There's even a bastard rugby ball in among that lot.'

'That's his Christmas present,' Dirk explained.

'What're you buying now then? His bastard school uniform?'

Dirk took out a list. 'Sterilising tablets, nail scissors, changing mat, *baberos* ...' he looked up. 'What's a *baberos*?'

'Don't look at me,' Stanley said. 'Jonathan and Katie never had any *baberos*.'

'Congratulations, anyway,' I said, penetrating Dirk's concentration. He looked up from his list.

'Ja. Thanks, man.'

'*Baberos*,' Stanley muttered, heading towards the forge. 'T'last babby born at this time o' year got plonked in a bastard hay rack. I'll bet it never had any *baberos*.'

I was tapping *baberos* into my phone as I walked.

'Bibs!' I cried.

'There you are then,' Stanley remarked. 'It weren't gold, frankincense and a packet o' bibs.' I wanted to run back and tell Dirk but Stanley ordered me to pack the bastard van.

Frost was sparkling on dry-stone walls, roadside hawthorn berries glinted like rubies and sparsely scattered ewes were seeking grass between glistening boulders. Such a morning would have lifted my mood but added to Millie's Christmas silence was my knowledge that, Sylvia's pony still wasn't back in work. 'I would have taken her to the winter championships,' she complained when we arrived at her yard. 'But that hole your lad dug in her foot hasn't even closed up.'

Stanley lifted the pony's foot. 'I'll tell you what I could do, Sylvia. I could use my anti-bacterial nails on it.' I looked at him, interested. 'They're a bit dearer than the others, but they're made of germ repellent steel.' He turned to me. 'Go and get one of them anti-bacterial nails out the van to show Sylvia.' My depression hadn't stopped me registering his tone.

A year before, I'd have panicked, asked him where they were or claimed I'd not seen them, but I walked coolly to the van, opened a box of ordinary nails, took one out and handed it to Stanley. Stanley took the head of the nail between a thumb and forefinger and held it in front of Sylvia's eyes. He turned it in the watery sunshine. 'Can you see how it's not shining t'same as it should?' She stared, mesmerised. 'That's because there's an anti-bacterial agent in it; it dulls t'steel.' She was nodding, convinced it was unlike any nail she'd ever clapped her eyes on. Stanley handed it back to me and I dropped it in the box. 'T'thing is though, Sylvia ... they're dear.'

'Oh, that doesn't matter!' she said.

But Stanley was sucking his teeth. 'They're two pound apiece!' He'd said it as if it were the budget deficit.

'Put them in all four feet,' she said with an indulgent wave of her hand.

'Are you sure, Sylvia?'

'Whatever it takes!' She was smiling when she led her pony back to its stable.

Stanley was smiling when he climbed into the van.

'How do you sleep at night?' I asked from the seat beside him.

'What do you mean? I've just made a client very happy.' He started the engine.

'You've just scammed a client out of forty-eight quid!' Stanley was smirking, so I turned away and watched the sugared woodland slip past the window in shades of white, black and brown. I turned back to him when we were on the main road. 'And what happens when she asks Ewan for anti-bacterial nails?'

'I shall make sure t'van's well stocked with them,' he chuckled, then he let go of the steering wheel and rubbed his hands. 'And all her friends'll want 'em when she's been to t'winter championships!'

We arrived back at Bling Manor and Stanley inserted The Old Van between the Porsche and the Poshmobile as he was now calling my Land Rover. A pot-bellied man in a navy-blue sweatshirt was peering in at the windows of the battered Porsche. Stanley ratcheted on The Old Van's handbrake. 'Cheeky bastard!' He was out of the van and marching towards the man before I could reason with him.

The Porsche viewer lowered his hand from where it had been shading the reflection on the glass and stepped back, smiling. 'Is this yours?'

'What's it to you?' Stanley demanded.

'I'd heard it had taken a bit of a smack. If you'll talk about the price, I might be interested in buying it.'

'Well, keep your bastard hands off it till you're sure.' The viewer drew his neck back a ratchet.

'I have a body shop, you see.'

'Good for you.'

The viewer folded his arms. 'Are you selling this car or not?'

Stanley folded his. 'I don't know. Am I?'

'Not with that attitude, you're not, mate!'

Stanley threw his hands wide. 'There you are then!'

'Who else do you think you'll sell a stoved-in Porsche to?'

'What's that to do wi' you?'

The man shook his head. 'Un–be–bloody–lievable,' he said. Then he swung his belly in the direction of the road and strode away wondering what had just happened to him. Stanley watched him go. I joined him on the pavement.

'You might want to work on your sales technique,' I advised, whilst Stanley wiped the viewer's breathy marks off the Porsche's passenger window.

'I wouldn't sell it to the likes of him, even if it weren't wrecked.' He was buffing the car's wing with his sleeve. It was the nearest thing to actually polishing a turd that I'd witnessed in real life. 'He's even marked it with his hand, look.' I watched him for a few more seconds, amazed, then Stanley looked up. 'He'd have offered me next to nowt anyway.'

'You didn't give him the chance.'

'Come on,' he sighed. 'Let's have a swift half.'

The first person we saw in The Fleece, was the Porsche viewer. He was recounting Stanley's sales pitch to Trevor, who looked up. 'Your Porsche's still up for sale, i'n't it, Stanley – or are you getting it fixed first?'

'Why?' Stanley demanded on his way to the bar. 'Do you want to buy it?'

Trevor chuckled as he dripped the last droplets of ale into the foaming pint he was pulling. 'Folk'll have to start supping a lot more ale before I can buy a Porsche! Even a smashed one!'

'It has a bloody sign on it!' the Porsche viewer pointed out to Stanley, exasperated.

'I have Barbour on my jacket,' Stanley swaggered. 'But it dun't make me a bastard hairdresser, does it?' He strode towards a window table, pleased with his joke.

Our afternoon jobs were at Mervyn's and, unusually, he was waiting to greet us. 'What about that then?' he gloated as he rocked down the aisle between the stalls, his boots caked in mud. He was referring to Silent Shannon's win at Wetherby on Boxing Day – which I'd missed. It hadn't been decisive – she'd been carrying extra weight, but she'd put in a late run and stolen it at the winning post, just like before.

'So, will you be paying me today, then?' Stanley quipped.

'You always get your money,' Mervyn answered.

Stanley looked round the van's back door. 'Are you in a parallel bastard universe?'

'Since when have you not had your money?'

Stanley pointed his rasp at him. 'Since you've been paying for a terraced house and a racehorse wagon!'

'So,' I asked, diverting the conversation. 'Is that Shannon's last race before the National?'

'Might be,' Mervyn answered.

I nodded towards his muddy boots. 'Have you been building your Aintree fences?'

'They've been built for weeks,' he said, pointing towards the gallops. 'You want to go and have a look at my Becher's.'

'So what are you doing on the other side of the lane, then?'

Mervyn's face darkened. 'Never you mind, what I'm doing on the other side o' the lane,' he said, and he stalked out.

'What do you reckon he's digging for?' I asked Stanley as we waited for the coals to heat.

'He'll be diggin' his bastard grave if he doesn't stump up today,' Stanley predicted.

Chapter 18

I arrived at work to see an envelope with the crest of Stratford College franked in its top right-hand corner. Stanley had left it on the workbench. 'That'll be your exam results,' he said. I gave the envelope a wide berth, headed for the kettle and played for time. 'Are they home then, Maria and the baby?'

'Aye,' Stanley answered. 'And it has a set o' lungs on it. I'm bog-eyed.' He turned to me. 'Go on, then. Get it opened.' My mouth had dried and I could feel sweat on my top lip. I hadn't been optimistic about Stanley's reaction to my failure even before I'd known he was sleep deprived.

'Do you want a brew?' I asked, but Stanley was shaking his head.

'I've had one.'

'When are they flying to Spain?'

'Tomorrow. Are you going to open that envelope or have I to do it?'

'The thing is,' I said, under the gush of the cold water tap. 'My forging exam didn't go that well ...'

Stanley stopped broddling the coal. His eyes narrowed. 'I thought you'd forged a decent shoe ... ?'

'I did. One.' I chewed on my top lip. 'I cut the steel too short.' Tea leapt from Stanley's mug.

'You did what!' He snatched the envelope off the bench. His eyes were slits now. 'Forty-one per cent!' He slapped me about the ears with the flapping paper. Dissatisfied with the result, he dropped the paper and repeated the action with the flat of his hand. I covered my ear and crouched to pick up the paper.

'I got ninety-six for the theory – look!'

'And how many bastard nails does that bang in?' He walked to the steel pile, pulled out a rod and flung it on the work-bench. It bounced and clattered, shaking a finished shoe to the edge and dithering the tea in Stanley's mug. 'Cut that for a six and a quarter inch fore!'

'I know *now*!' but Stanley's look impelled me towards the steel cutter.

'I was forging bastard door hinges at fourteen!' (It had been a hoof pick last time and it would be a Ford Cortina by next week.) 'Do you know how many shoes Dolloper had made for his exhibition board at your stage?' I concentrated on cutting the steel. 'Six!' The steel clanged to the floor. 'Six! And *he's* a bastard dolloper!' He picked up the length of steel, held it against the measuring stick on the bench and a grudging rumble rattled from his throat.

Our first job was at the Maharaja's; he doesn't celebrate Christmas or drink alcohol, but he gave us a belated crate of Indian beer to go with the six pack of Budweiser Julie Thornton had donated the day before Christmas Eve. Stanley was jolly with the Maharaja, and patient with his Arabian horses – but he spoke to me only to bark instructions.

He drove us to Richard Jennings' against a cheesy sound-track of festive singalongs through villages decked like Blackpool seafront, and every now and then he'd let go of the steering wheel and cast his palms skyward as if praying for an explanation of how I could have been so stupid.

Pippa Jennings' warmblood had cast a shoe and a pair of hurdlers needed shoeing for the Catterick meeting. 'You're not taking Anvil Head to Catterick, then?' I asked Richard Jennings as I took a warm mince pie from the plate he was holding out.

He shook his head. 'He's not really doing much, to be honest.'

Stanley straightened from under the horse he was shoeing. 'You know, if it can't gallop, and it can't jump – you might want to consider whether it's in t'right career.'

Jennings wiped crumbs from his tweed field jacket. 'It's bred for the job.'

'You're not always like your mam and dad though, are you?' Stanley reasoned. 'His dad's a ...' he was indicating me to illustrate his point, '... what is he?'

'A barrister ...' I said.

'A barrister. But this pillock can't even measure a length o' bastard steel.' This was not the time to plead my case. I tried to move the conversation on a bit.

'My mother works with horses,' I said. 'I inherited that.'

'Of course,' Jennings remembered. 'Lizzie Harker. Would she have room for Enville Lad?'

I shrugged, 'She might – but if it can't gallop and it can't jump ...'

Jennings was holding up his hand, 'I know, Will, I know – but if she could train it for a career outside racing ...'

'Like what?' Stanley interrupted. 'Pulling a bastard cart?'

Jennings tugged at his bottom lip. 'I might nip up to Mervyn's this afternoon; pick his brains about the horse.'

Stanley's phone interrupted us. He listened then held it out. 'It's Julie Thornton, for you.'

'For me?'

He nodded

'Why does she want me?'

'I'm not a bastard clairvoyant, am I?' Stanley snapped. I took the phone cautiously.

'William, love,' she started. 'Millie's had a bit of an incident with Belinda.' A white explosion detonated in my head. An incident? What was an incident? 'She says you have the spare keys to her car.' I did. They were still on my keyring. 'She wants

109

you to pick it up for her.' Why couldn't she drive? Confusion, fear and hope were crowding at my throat, constricting my voice to a squeak.

'Where is she?'

'A & E. Nothing serious.'

I found my farrier's voice. 'I'll come now.' I hadn't considered how I'd get there, or how I'd get back, or how I'd deal with Stanley going off like Krakatoa again. I hung up and was explaining at a gabble when Stanley sighed and groped for his car keys.

'Get in the bastard van before I change my mind.' It was a shock. 'Is it all right if I come back to finish this job off?' he asked Jennings.

'No problem,' Jennings smiled, ever genial, and as I packed the van, Stanley spoke into his phone. 'You know that few days rest you were having, Dolloper? You've had 'em.'

I heard *and a happy fucking Christmas to you too,* then Stanley held the phone from his ear as the hard syllables of Ewan's rant transformed to electronic sibilants. 'It's an emergency, Dolloper. Posh Lad's lass has been rushed to hospital.' A chastened silence followed. 'So, you'll have to make a start at Mervyn's, while I finish up at Jennings'.'

'And how the fuck am I going to get there? You've got the only van.' Stanley slapped the heel of his hand to head.

'Jade's here,' I whispered and Stanley gave me the silent nod.

'I thought your lass was here?'

'She's not brought her bloody tools with her!'

'She'll have brought a bloody car though! Get to your Lee's garage and get t'tools out o' t'Best Van!' Ewan groaned. He'd been rumbled.

'Thanks,' I said as I slid in The Old Van beside Stanley.

'Self-interest,' he said. 'You've had a face on you like a slapped arse since Christmas.'

I couldn't make conversation on the journey. My blood

felt bubbly. I was running scenarios, testing possibilities and interrogating motives. No thought finished its trajectory before another one had pinged in and deflected it. Stanley seemed to have forgotten he was mad with me. He flicked Radio 2 on. The Old Van rumbled towards the moor road and a peregrine falcon crossed our rectangle of windscreen; its feet were crayoned in yellow and its screech of triumph rolled down the moorland slopes. I hoped it was right.

'I believe your mare's been attacking vets,' Stanley chuckled as he climbed from The Old Van at Julie Thornton's.

'I should have had her sedated really,' Julie admitted, 'but it's a dear do.'

'What happened?' I asked.

'She swung her head with the gag in.' I winced. Millie must have been carrying out a dental check. The steel speculum is like mouth armour. It would have knocked Millie flat. 'She was out cold for a few seconds, so I thought she should get checked over.'

'Where is the madam?' Stanley asked.

'At A & E.'

'No!' he chuckled. 'I mean Belinda! It's a sensitive mare is that.'

'Oh, she's in her stable. I didn't dare touch her when I saw the mood she was in.'

'It'll have upset her,' Stanley surmised.

'Do you want me to turn her out for you?' he offered.

'Oh, would you?' Julie said, her eyes pleading. 'She terrifies me when she gets like this.'

We followed Julie into the barn where the great grey mare was munching on hay. It was hard to believe she'd so recently committed ABH. Stanley ran a hand down her face. Was he checking that the galvanised bucket had left no lasting mark? 'Have they been upsetting you?' he asked the mare. 'Looking at your teeth,' I reached out too, but Belinda's ears shot back and her neck snapped round. I stepped away.

'I'll just go and get Millie's car,' I said, and I walked on, through the barn.

There it was; the ten-year-old black Vectra. I unlocked it, climbed in and pushed back the seat. It smelt of Millie. I took in a long draught of her perfume. There was a woollen scarf on the passenger seat. I picked it up, pressed it to my nose and put it down again. This must mean something, surely? I adjusted the seat, connected my phone to her Bluetooth and dared to dial her number. For the first time in four days it connected. 'Millie?' She didn't answer me but I could hear her breathing. 'How are you?' White noise susurrated. It fizzed. It lisped in my ear. 'I've got your car.'

'Thanks.'

'Are you okay?'

'Yes. I've a heck of a lump though.'

I managed a mild laugh. 'You should have doped it.'

'I know that now.' We'd run out of words again. The electric breath of the airwaves fuelled the hush.

'Where do you want me to leave your keys?'

'Just keep them,' she said.

An air bubble lifted in me. It floated. 'Are you sure?' The taut silence sang.

'I've missed you.'

'I've missed you,' I said. 'I was a complete berk.'

Her laugh was soft. 'We can agree on that.' I could see her smile.

'It's just with my dad blagging my head and my exam on my mind ...' I paused. 'I should have acted like a grown up.'

'You should.'

'Should I pop round later?' I asked. 'I can fetch your Christmas present.'

'I'll text you,' she said. 'If they discharge me.'

I topped Eckersley Fell in Millie's car. The hedgerows

112

glittered, the sky glowed cornflower blue and in my rear-view mirror I could see Stanley's mouth opening and closing to what was probably Status Quo.

'Is it back on then?' Stanley asked when I stepped into The Old Van with a smile on my face.

'Could be,' I said.

'I bloody hope so,' he said. Stanley had never fathomed why it had been off; to him, splattering Moon Face across Cribbs' dance-floor had been my finest hour. 'I might get some bastard conversation out of you.' He turned down Status Quo. 'I've just been on t'phone to Moneybags Morrison about you.' A masonry fall of horrific possibilities avalanched in my head. He dragged on the handbrake at traffic lights. 'He sorted Ewan's forging out for him.'

'I didn't fail on forging,' I reminded him. 'It was measurement,' but he went on, like I hadn't spoken.

'So, you're working with him for a week, starting on Monday.' I banged my skull onto the headrest. 'Don't be so bastard dramatic!' he said. 'There's nowt wrong wi' Moneybags!'

According to Ewan there was, and I knew who I believed.

We finished off at Jennings' in double quick time and when we arrived at Mervyn's, Ewan was waiting on the spot where Mervyn Slack's Lambourne racehorse transporter used to park. Jade was at his side in a pair of Ewan's overalls that wouldn't quite fasten over her ampleness. Stanley wound down the window. 'How is she?' Ewan asked.

'Who?'

'Millie!'

'Oh, she's reyt,' Stanley answered with a flap of his hand. 'Just a bump on the head.'

Ewan glared at Stanley and then shouted at me, 'I thought it was an emergency!'

'It could have been,' I said. 'I didn't know till I spoke to her.'

'So, is it back on then?' Jade asked as I grabbed Lucky's jaw.

'Looks like it,' Stanley answered stepping onto the gravel. 'That's what a knock on the head's done for her.'

'And how's Maria?' Jade enquired.

'Grand,' Stanley answered, and Jade's long *ahhhh* ... made us all look at her.

'Anyway,' Stanley said to Ewan, 'never mind babbies and his bastard love life! You should have your arse in the air!'

'It's bloody chaos in there!' Ewan explained. 'Nobody knows what needs shoeing – and if they do, they can't find it.'

'So, have you shod owt?'

'One.'

'And has he stumped up?'

'No.'

'That's it!' Stanley roared, slapping the van roof. 'We're not knocking another bastard nail in for Mervyn Slack until I see the colour of his money! Where is he?'

'Dunno,' Ewan answered.

'He'll be on that bastard digger.' Stanley's lips were set like a lizard's. He bounced back in The Old Van and fired the engine. Ewan and Jade climbed into her Fiesta and followed us.

Chapter 19

As Stanley had guessed, Mervyn's digger was moving in squirts across a field as blasted as Passchendaele. Stanley, at the wheel of The Old Van, jerked his head right, then, without a word, he hit the brakes. The combined weight of anvil, gas cylinder, forge, stock, two farriers and a dog hiccupped the van violently on its axle. My seat belt locked. My head banged the side window and Lucky hit the floor. I heard Jade's car lurch to a stop and skin the lane behind us. 'Brakes are all right then,' I said, rubbing my temple but Stanley had already flung the door open.

He blasted from the van, vaulted the dry-stone wall and was belting across the wasteland. In the distance, the digger juddered on. Its bucket clattered into the earth, the sward crumpled and the turf split and surrendered. Stanley stopped. He was right in front of the gnarling machine. Its arm lifted again and Stanley stepped under it. In The Best Van's wing mirror, I could see the panic on Ewan's face. The digger's arm swung right and unfolded its limp wrist. Ewan was shaking his head. Earth and stones rumbled to the ground. The arm swung left and Stanley arched backwards to save his eyebrows. 'Jesus,' I breathed. The bucket crunched into earth. Fear met helplessness somewhere in my guts. Ewan had seen it too, he leapt from Jade's car. I was out of the van a millisecond behind him. I stumbled over the blasted heath with the cold paralysis of nightmares slowing my limbs. I was yelling for Mervyn's attention and Jade, horrified, was yelling for Ewan's. Lucky was bouncing and yapping beside us; this was as thrilling as a sheep chase. The digger's arm was pitching back again.

Ewan juddered to a teetering halt at the edge of the crater. 'Stanley!' he yelled. 'Get out of the way!' I stopped beside him, a lurching puppet.

'Stanley!' The digger's bucket was teetering over Stanley's head, but Stanley just folded his arms.

'Mi money!' he shouted at Mervyn.

'Get out of the bloody way!' Mervyn bellowed back through the digger's open window. The bucket clanked and swung.

'Oh, you're a reyt hard man, aren't you, wi' a forty-ton digger on your side!'

Mervyn jerked his thumb. 'Bugger off out the fuckin' 'ole!' He managed to say it without parting his teeth.

'Mi money!' Stanley repeated. The digger rumbled on but it didn't move. 'You're wrecking your own bastard business here, as well as mine, you berk!' The digger growled.

'You know nowt about my business!' Mervyn shouted. 'So piss off before I drop this lot on your 'ead!'

'I know about land!' Stanley shouted back. 'And I'll bet you've not kept the top-soil separate, have you?' The digger's rumbling engine was the only reply. 'It'll be at least eight hundred quid to reseed this paddock!' Mervyn took his head back into the cab. 'And you'll have to level it and roll it first.' He released his grip on the wheel. 'And have you thought about the hay you won't get off it? What's that going to cost you, eh?' Mervyn had taken on the shape of a punctured lilo crumpled on the seat of the digger. Suddenly, the digger's engine died. 'So, are you going to get out o' there then, and tell me what the fuck's going on?' We waited. The wind whipped across the moor. Then, Mervyn stepped on to the digger's caterpillar track. He dropped onto the mud with a splat and Stanley clambered out of the crater.

*

Five minutes later, Lucky was back in the van, and the three of us were trailing Stanley and Mervyn into the farmhouse. Jade punched Ewan in the shoulder. 'That, Grimshaw, was bloody stupid!'

'Tell Stanley! He's the one who stood to get killed!'

Jade was exasperated. 'You're not his keeper, though!' Ewan throbbed an unexpected chuckle. 'What's funny?' she demanded.

'I was imagining if Dirk had been with us!'

I laughed at the thought. 'He'd have been swinging from that bucket!'

'He's a bloody legend,' Ewan mused. Jade stopped dead on the lane. We turned to see her stock still with her arms folded across her bosom. 'What's up?'

'Listen to yourselves! You're making a joke out of what could have killed you!'

'It's how we roll,' Ewan appealed with outstretched arms.

She flapped her hand at him. 'I'm going for a bath,' she stated. 'You can make your own way home.'

We reached Mervyn's stone farmhouse and as I passed through the door frame of the kitchen I saw the slab of Stanley, stock still in front of me. His eyes were cast upwards like an unlikely plaster saint's. I followed them to the drying rack above the Aga. I blinked. Banknotes were swaying in the rising heat. Mervyn, who'd pulled out a chair, was tracking my gaze. 'They're still damp!' he said, as if to deter my interest.

'Why the fuck were they wet?' Ewan demanded. Coal shuffled in the grate. Mervyn took his flat cap off and settled it on his lap. The mantel clock ticked.

'I've been looking for some money I buried a few years since.'

'Thank fuck for that,' Stanley breathed. 'I thought you were printing your own.'

'I wish I knew how,' Mervyn laughed, joylessly.

'You *buried* money?' Ewan asked. I waited. I'd thought I'd

misheard Mervyn but he nodded his answer. Ewan spread his hands. 'Why?'

'Have you never heard of Northern Rock?' I exchanged glances with Ewan. I'd heard of Northern Soul. 'Banks!' Mervyn shouted. 'I don't trust banks!' Still no one said anything. 'Anyway, I've found a few notes.' He, waved at the soggy fifties swaying over the Aga. 'But that's all.'

Stanley's eyes drifted back to the line of banknotes, 'I'm not bothered about 'em being damp,' he said.

Mervyn was shaking his head. 'It's money, money, money wi' you, in't it?' but he hoisted himself from the kitchen arm-chair and stripped a red note from its peg.

'You owe me two more o' them,' Stanley stated. Mervyn snatched two more fifties and pushed them into Stanley's open hand. Stanley didn't close it. 'And how many more am I doing this week?'

'I don't know,' Mervyn said, turning away.

'I want paying up front.' Mervyn reached for the washing line and dragged down six more notes. Stanley pocketed them. 'And I'm telling you, it's a bastard shambles since you sacked Jay.'

'What can I do?' Mervyn pleaded. 'I've advertised.'

'You could get him back!' Ewan suggested.

'He's working on his uncle's dairy farm,' Mervyn answered. I knew the place. Jay had pointed it out to me once; it wasn't half a mile from Bling Manor.

We arrived back mid-afternoon to see a family of five exam-ining the crumbling Porsche. The father was scrutinising the damage and a yummy mummy was a few feet away on her mobile phone, a Mulberry handbag dangling from her arm. Two children were peering in at the windows. 'Oi!' Stanley shouted dropping from the cab of The Best Van. 'Get your bloody hands off that car!' Undeterred, the father approached Stanley with a smile. 'Dean Almond,' the man said, handing him a card. 'Almond's Car Repairs and Sales, Fowlden.' Stanley looked right past him. 'I was just passing.'

'Get your bloody kids off my car before I tan their bastard arses!'

Dean smiled. 'I can make you an offer on this, if you're interested.'

'Bugger off,' Stanley growled, with a wave of his hand. The children had stood back from the car, so he turned and walked down his drive, muttering about chancers and vultures. Dean Almond watched him from a puddle of his own puzzlement. Ewan explained Stanley's behaviour with a screwing finger at his temple as he passed.

Stanley was still raging when we walked into the forge. 'No bugger was interested in that car when it was in one piece! They're like bastard hyenas!'

I'd been looking at my phone. 'She's been discharged,' I announced. 'Can I go?'

Stanley threw his arms wide. 'I said I'd put their Ikea cot up!'

'You'll manage on your own,' I assured him. 'There'll be pictures.'

'And we've both got girls to sweeten up,' Ewan added.

'Oh, go on, then,' Stanley sighed.

Ewan double-checked, 'So, I can resume my Christmas holidays?'

'Aye,' Stanley grouched. 'Get off with you.' We headed for my Land Rover with synchronised steps before Stanley could despair at the Ikea instructions.

Millie's mane of hair had been tamed to copper coils by the shower, and when she stepped back from my hug, her eyes were sparkling like fairy lights. I had to brush my eyes quickly too and then I laughed at myself and she laughed. She looked tired.

'How are you?'

'I'm fine,' she answered. 'They've given me a list of symptoms to watch out for and told me not to be on my own tonight.'

I answered her with a wry twinkle, 'Good job I'm here, then!'

I followed her to the kitchen-cum-living room of her cosy flat above the veterinary surgery and commented on the neat little Christmas tree sprouting from the breakfast bar. 'I've borrowed it from the waiting room,' she chuckled. 'I thought we could have our Christmas tonight.' She poured two glasses of red wine from an open bottle that had been breathing on the radiator shelf and curled herself on the sheepskin rug. I sat beside her with my back against the sofa and my feet on the hearth of the faux fire.

'Something smells nice.'

'Turkey and cranberry ready meal,' she grinned. 'Half price.' She took a sip of her wine. 'And Father Christmas has left something here for you too.' She slid her hand under the sofa and came out with a box covered in ribbons and flying reindeer. 'Go on,' she urged with a rattle of the box. The reindeer flew back to reveal a Parrot hands-free car kit. 'To bring your Land Rover into the twenty-first century!' I thanked her with a kiss on the nose.

It was my turn. I dipped into my pocket then I pressed a little gold wrapped gift box into her hand. The upward flash of her eyes held just a glint of panic. I gave her no clue except my smile, so she looked back at the present.

She opened it slowly, peeling back the Sellotape a strip at a time, then she lifted the lid of the navy-blue box and laughed. She was looking down on a coiled, plaited loop. 'It's made of Onion's tail hair,' I said.

She slipped it on her wrist. 'I love it!'

'Were you preparing a speech?' I grinned.

She lifted her eyebrows. 'It does look like a ring box, Will.'

'And what would you have said, in this speech?' Her hand

crept across the carpet and folded over mine, her shoulder nested in my clavicle.

'I would have said ...' she paused, weighing her words. 'That you need to finish your apprenticeship and I need to save some more money ... but ...'

'But?'

'But these past few days have shown me that I can't picture a future without you in it.' I kissed her copper hair.

'And you're always in the future that I picture.' This Christmas wasn't turning out to be too bad after all.

Chapter 20

I parked my Land Rover on the gravel behind Buckthwaite Hall and looked at the sandstone archway which announced *Michael Morrison; Farrier and Artisan Blacksmith* in wrought iron. I reminded myself that this was only for a week. I reminded myself that Ewan had spent a week with Moneybags Morrison. It still felt like a prelude to a future I didn't want, though. I opened the door and dropped to the limestone chippings.

I walked under the archway and found myself in a stone flagged corridor between the iron railings of Victorian loose boxes. The three on my left had been knocked through to create a state-of-the-art forge. On my right two were still intact and the third had a desk, a chair and two filing cabinets in it. Moneybags was sitting at a computer, undermining the image of ye olde village blacksmith of yore created by his sign. He swivelled on his office chair, swept off his glasses and grinned a row of even teeth at me, then he stood and offered me his hand. 'How are you, Will?'

'I'm fine thanks,' I said, remembering to smile. 'Impressive forge.' My eyes had glided to an open staircase which led to a glassed-in mezzanine. Gym equipment was visible through the glass.

'It was derelict when I bought it,' he said. 'I did it up from scratch.' I nodded my approval. 'Come in.' He was gesturing towards the open door of the office. I followed him. 'Your mum says you're enjoying working with Stanley.' His tone implied some surprise.

'I am,' I said. 'I just need a bit of help with my forging.'

'Aye,' Moneybags smiled, returning to his chair. 'Ewan did an' all.' Irrational defensiveness flashed in me like a firecracker. Stanley's sense for hot steel belonged in Viking mythology – he just couldn't teach it. 'I'd have taken you on myself if I hadn't had Daniel working for me at the time. He's qualified now though.'

I changed the subject. 'Is that a gym upstairs?'

Moneybags had returned to his computer. 'It is,' he said. 'There's a shower room an' all. A bit fancier than Stanley's garage, eh? You've to look after yourself in this job.' I studied him whilst he gazed at his spreadsheet. His neatly parted dark hair was greying at the temples and half-moon glasses were perched on his nose. He was a different species from the be-jeaned gorilla I was used to working with. He interrupted my thoughts by nodding at a sealed polythene bag on his desk. 'You can be putting your kit on while I finish off here,' he said. 'Make yourself look like one of the team.'

What team? I thought. *There are two of us.* Anyway, I wasn't one of his *team*. I was on Stanley's *team*. I thanked him politely and opened the bag. I found myself looking at a black polo shirt. Moneybags was wearing an identical one. It was embroidered with a rearing yellow horse and the words *Michael Morrison; Farrier and Artisan Blacksmith.* 'There's a matching fleece in that cabinet,' he added.

The cabinet held a collection of fleeces, polo shirts and black socks. How many farriers did he think he was employing? I dragged off my sweatshirt and pulled on the polo shirt. By the time I was zipping up the fleece, Moneybags had logged off his PC and was pushing his arm into his own fleece jacket. 'Oh, very smart,' he grinned at me, then he fished in the bottom drawer of his desk and handed me a duster and a tin of shoe polish. I looked at them. 'Boots,' he commanded. I looked down. My boots were grey with mud and encrusted with stalks of dry straw. They spent their days in shitty stables and muddy gateways. He must have read the incomprehension in my eyes. 'It's to do with respect,' he explained. 'The same applies to a vehicle. A farrier should run the smartest vehicle he can afford so he drives onto a yard looking like a professional outfit.' I could feel my teeth clenching. He'd bumped into us on yards often enough to know what Stanley drove. 'So while you're working with me, you'll be cleaning your boots every night and treating your chaps wi' saddle soap.' My jaw had clamped tight and I rubbed at my mud-caked boots. 'If you do that, not only will you look smart, but your kit'll last you. It's police horses this morning, so we can't turn up looking like a pair o' farm hands. Discipline, you see; same as in the police force, same as in a monastery.' What the hell was he talking about monasteries for? I snapped the lid on the shoe polish tin. 'Right!' Moneybags announced, slapping his hands on his thighs. 'What will you be loading up for five seventeen-hand hunter types?' I dropped the duster and the tin in the drawer.

'Size fours?'

'With … ?'

'Road nails?'

'He's taught you that much then.' I felt my teeth slide over my bottom lip.

We set out for Wakefield in Moneybags' green Land Rover Discovery Commercial with John Humphreys' grilling of a dithering politician as our entertainment. It made for uncomfortable listening, so I looked at the landscape. The road was grey. The sky was grey. The hedges were black. They'd be listening to Chris Evans now in The Best Van. Or Stanley might have put a Status Quo CD on. I watched a kestrel swoop and twist.

'How is Stanley these days?' Moneybags asked, as if he could read my mind.

'He's all right,' I shrugged.

'Is Ewan still working for him?' Rows of goblet shaped trees lined the road, their bare arms seemed to be stretched up in supplication.

'Yeah.'

'Full time?' Mousy stone walls unreeled past the window.

'Yeah.'

'Word is, he's been having it rough.' I ignored him. 'With his divorce, I mean.' I grunted and Moneybags turned his attention to the news. I watched as the morning sun plated an unfamiliar moor in gold and the underside of slate grey clouds glowed nail-polish pink.

My phone pinged a message. It was the sixth picture of a baby – this time with aviator glasses covering his face:

> Carlos the jet setter off to Madrid. See you when we get back.

I rolled my eyes and slid the phone back into my pocket.

Moneybags pulled up his vehicle between a horse walker and a row of smart wooden loose boxes. He was greeted as 'Mister Morrison'. Four neat grooms led four saintly police horses onto the yard. I tied one up. At the word *give* from its groom, each horse raised its next foot. I removed their worn shoes in half the time it usually took me.

'He works with the bloke who shoes every nut job in Yorkshire,' Moneybags explained to them, laughing.

'We do a couple of racing yards,' I qualified, and complimented a groom on her horses' manners. 'Where do you source them?' I asked.

'Anywhere and everywhere,' she said. 'In fact, we're looking for another if you hear of anything suitable.' Moneybags snorted, as if the idea of me knowing a sane horse were ridiculous. 'Sixteen-two or above, mare or gelding, good in traffic.'

Moneybags shaped and nailed the steel. I clenched up, and three hours later, we were back in the Discovery. No one had offered us so much as a brew. By the time we'd driven back to some dismal Radio 4 drama about the First World War, I was gagging for one. I scanned the forge for a kettle. I watched Moneybags walk to the draining board and pick up a mug. (*If you think it's expensive to hire a good farrier, try hiring a bad one,* it said.) I followed him with my eyes but he thrust the oh-so-funny mug under the water cooler's spigot. 'Where do you keep the kettle?' I asked.

He looked at me like I'd asked him where he kept his semi-automatic machine gun. 'I don't agree with caffeine.'

I stared at him. 'You mean, you've a gym, a shower, a mini fridge, and a water cooler – but no kettle?'

'If you want a brew, you'll have to fetch a flask.'

Silently cursing Ewan for failing to tell me there was no kettle, I picked up a mug (*Keep Calm and Call your Farrier*) and shoved it under the spigot. From the corner of my eye, I saw Moneybags knock back his water. 'I'll be back in twenty minutes,' he said and disappeared through an invisible door in the glass wall.

Distant whale music was accompanying my glum eating of soggy tuna sandwiches when Ewan's name lit up my phone. I swept my thumb over the screen. 'You could have told me there was no bastard kettle!' I shouted.

Ewan was already laughing. 'Sorry, I forgot.'

'And tea tastes like shit out of a flask.'

'It's a smart forge, though – eh?'

I grunted. There was no pleasure in a smart forge that didn't have a kettle.

'He did it all himself, you know?'

I grunted again.

'He's a proper craftsman, Moneybags. It needed gutting. Plastering, rewiring, the lot.'

'I know. He said.'

'I'll bet he never told you about the boiler though, did he?'

'What about the boiler?'

'He couldn't sort the boiler, so he asked a mate o' Stanley's to fix it for him.' I reached out and touched the radiator behind Moneybags' desk. It was warm. 'Stanley's mate tells him it's fucked, only Moneybags won't have it, cos Jesus has told him to buy this barn.'

I stopped chewing. 'You what?'

'Oh! He's big into Jesus, is Moneybags. Has he not mentioned it?' I lowered my sandwich. 'Anyway, Moneybags asks Stanley's mate to come back in a week or two, and in the meantime Moneybags and his mates from t'church come up to t'barn and pray over t'boiler.'

'Are you for real?'

'Night after night, for hours and hours at a time, on their knees round t'boiler.' I took a bite of tuna sandwich. 'Anyway, after a fortnight, Moneybags tells Stanley's mate he can come back and have another look at it. So, he drives all t'way back up to t'barn, he takes t'front off t'boiler, he has a good poke about in it – and do you know what?' Ewan's voice had turned breathy with wonder.

'What?' I breathed.

'It were still fucked!' He'd cracked up laughing. 'He had to buy a new boiler.'

I flung what was left of my tuna butty in its Tupperware box. 'You're a pillock,' I said.

'I take it he's not there?' Ewan chuckled.

'He's listening to whale music.'

'He'll be meditating,' Ewan corrected me, and I groaned. 'Don't knock it!' Ewan laughed. 'Stanley could do wi' meditating now and then.' The thought blasted a snort from me. 'Or starting on the whacky baccy – or summat.'

'Bad, is he?'

'Bad? He's thrown a rasp at my head, threatened Ruudi with an 'ammer and nearly turned The Old Van over!'

'What was Ruudi doing?'

'Prattling – like Ruudi does. I've a full fucking week of this coming!'

The whale music stopped.

'Gotta go!' Ewan said, and told me to count my bloody blessings.

Moneybags was calm when he returned to the forge. He ate what looked like a frogspawn salad and drank another mug of water. After he'd washed his mug, then washed and dried his hands, he asked me what I thought my problems with forging were.

I shrugged, 'I just find it hard.'

'Forging is just heating, holding and hammering,' he said. 'Let's start with heating.'

He was a patient and meticulous teacher. That afternoon, he let me heat and reheat thin steel and thick steel. He let me play with different temperatures and settings until, in the end, I could use his gas forge.

Tuesday's lesson was holding. 'If you can't hold it, you can't hit it!' he said. He watched me closely; he changed my grip on the hammer and he showed me how to use the different clamps, vices and tongs. He lavished praise on Ewan's instinctive skills. 'There's wrought iron railings and weathervanes in that lad,' he said.

By Thursday we'd got as far as *hammering*. He let me try out 40lb and 48lb soft face and flat hammers until I understood the effects of each on metal. 'You won't hit straight if your hammer shaft's lower than your anvil face,' he insisted. He made me wear eye protection; not the health-and-safety props of Bling Manor, but the sort they have at college that you can actually see through.

By the end of the week I'd had photographs of Carlos on the plane, Carlos between two sixty-year-old strangers on a wooden framed sofa, Carlos in a pram on the Plaza Major

– and Moneybags had made no mention of Jesus. We parted on a friendly handshake. 'You've nothing to worry about,' he said. 'You'll walk that exam.'

Chapter 21

I awoke, on Saturday morning to the rattle of a horse trailer. It wasn't an unusual alarm clock. Mumma regularly had horses arrive for schooling, so I turned over. I heard Mumma greeting the arrival, but the answering voice was what made me push the duvet away from my ears. A rattle of metal told me the ramp had hit the hard standing, and then there was the voice again. I swung my legs out of bed, stepped two strides to the window and curled back the curtain. I was right. Standing by the trailer was Richard Jennings. After two thundering clumps, a large, lop eared head lumbered into the day light. An oversized bay thoroughbred was walking down the front ramp. It stumbled as it stepped off. Anvil Head.

On Monday, I walked past the decomposing Porsche, and Lucky celebrated my return to Bling Manor by shaking a tea towel to death. I challenged her for it but she shot through the forge's open door and continued to rag it in a puddle. I left her to it and strolled towards my slogan-free, tea-stained mug. Ewan took over the battle for the tea towel. He won it and dropped the cloth on the draining board. We should have had dengue fever, by rights.

'A'reyt, Posh Lad?' Stanley enquired as he walked into the forge. 'Has he sorted you out or are your shoes still like fucking cake forks?'

'He's sorted me out,' I said. I described my week with

Moneybags Morrison and Stanley seemed delighted that I'd loathed it. 'Have I missed anything?' I asked.

Stanley rubbed his belly. 'Nah, not really.' He accepted a mug from Ewan. 'Dirk's gone to Madrid wi' t'babby ...'

'Which gives him a fighting chance of not getting done for GBH,' Ewan said, jerking his thumb at Stanley.

'I wasn't getting any bastard sleep!' Stanley pleaded in his defence.

Ewan spread his hands. 'And what about when they come back? I needed fucking riot gear till Wednesday.'

'They'll not be stopping,' Stanley said. 'They'll be packing their kit up and going back to South Africa.' He took a drink from his mug. 'Them anti-bacterial nails worked a treat on Sylvia's pony. She's thrilled to bits wi' 'em.'

'She'll dream up another problem,' Ewan predicted.

'I thought you might have sorted your Porsche out,' I said.

'Dirk's paying for it,' Stanley explained. 'He's waiting for his dad to wire him the money.'

'Our Lee could have been getting on with it!' Ewan said.

Stanley pointed a threatening finger at him. 'Your brother is going nowhere near that Porsche, Dolloper. Comprendo?' Ewan shook his head and sipped his tea. Stanley threw down the last dregs of his tea and stood up. 'Right,' he said, pointing at Ewan, 'You can get off to Tracy Prichard's – and take the dog.' Lucky shot out of her basket, ears up.

'There's wall to wall bloody sheep up at Tracy Prichard's!' Ewan reminded him.

'There's no sheep in t'bastard van are there!' Stanley said.

'There's no sheep in your bastard van, either!' Ewan argued.

'We can't take her,' Stanley pointed out. 'We're doin' Belinda and I can only deal wi' one psychopath at once.'

'Leave her here then!'

Stanley shook his head at Ewan. 'You're one rotten bastard,' he said. He looked at the hopeful terrier. 'In your basket, Lucky.' Lucky slunk back, ears down, tail tucked.

Ewan stared at the dog for a second. 'Oh, come on!' he ordered her. She leapt up like she'd been play acting and trotted beside his slump with her stump tail thrashing merrily.

Stanley swiped a finger across his ringing phone. 'Hello!' He made it sound like a threat. 'It's been sold.' He dashed the phone from his ear, killed the call and banged it down. I was shaking my head. 'What?' he demanded. 'I can't sell it in that state can I?' He picked up his tool-box. 'Anyway, it's not a lass's car, isn't a Porsche.'

The Best Van hardly deserved its name any more. Lee had replaced the white bonnet with a navy blue one. *('I'd have sprayed it, but you said you wanted it back quick.')* He'd replaced the smashed headlight with a crosshatched lens which gave the illusion of an eye patch. *('You can't get the plain lenses any more.')* and his inexpert straightening of the side panel gave it the look of an egg carton. *('I never said I was a panel beater.')* Stanley dropped into the driver's seat. 'He's not touching my bastard Porsche,' he repeated.

There was no sign of Julie Thornton. A tabby cat was cleaning itself on the stone mounting block and two milk bottles were waiting on the doorstep. Stanley walked to the barn to look for her and I began unloading the van. A few seconds later, he was walking back out of the barn. He shrugged at me and headed for the house. By the time I'd unloaded the anvil, the foot stand and the tool-boxes, Stanley was rapping at Julie's back door for a second time. 'The downstairs curtains are shut.' I wondered if he'd got the day wrong, so I opened the diary. No, there it was, a picture of a horse with devil horns at nine o'clock.

'Try ringing her,' I suggested. He dabbed at the screen of his iPhone and seconds later we heard the distant peeps of a mobile phone – then I saw it, lighting up the kitchen window ledge. 'Could she still be in bed?' I asked. Stanley depressed the door handle. It opened. He looked at me, puzzled.

He put his head round the door. 'Hello?' He walked in. 'Hello, Julie?' I waited. 'It's like the bastard *Marie Celeste*,' he called back. 'There's half a supped brew on t'table.'

'Did you check the hay loft?' I asked, but Stanley had disappeared deeper into the house.

I strode across the yard. I stood inside the barn's open doors. I listened. There was a sudden crack. It snatched the breath from me – then a wood pigeon flapped from a rafter. I breathed again.

In front of me was the wash bay, its hose-pipe coiled like a serpent. To my right were feed barrels, stacks of straw, bales of haylage and the ladder to the hay loft. To my left were two internal stables, one empty, the other framing Belinda's pig-eyed face. The mare's ears were plastered to her skull and she was throwing her head up and down in warning. 'Calm down,' I told her. 'I'm not coming any closer.' I tilted back my head and looked up at the hay loft. 'Julie!'

'Oh, thank God!' The voice was fragile, but it wasn't in the hay loft. Something rustled. Boots scraped.

I walked towards the stables. 'Where are you?'

'I'm in here!' I dared to crane past the mare's vast shoulder. Behind the horse, Julie Thornton was uncurling to a standing position. She was festooned in straw and looking dazed. I took another step towards the stable but Belinda detonated at both ends. Her neck shot out, her teeth flashed, her tail thrashed and one back leg blasted backwards. Julie flung herself against the stable's back wall. 'I can't get out,' she said in a breathless, splintering voice.

'Don't panic,' I said. 'I'll get Stanley.'

Stanley listened with his head on one side, then strode into the barn like the sheriff in a 1940s western, his mouth curled in amusement. 'Nah then, missus,' he was addressing the horse, 'I've come to open hostage negotiations.' He rooted in his pocket and came out with a polo mint. Belinda stretched her neck for the mint, but Stanley closed his fist on it. 'I think we'll talk first,' he said, reaching for the nearby headcollar. He slipped it over her nose, flicked the headpiece behind her ears, buckled it and gave her the mint. He unbolted the stable door, Belinda clopped into the body of the barn and a horror movie zombie staggered out behind her. 'By bloody hell, Julie, how long 'ave you been in there?' Julie just shook her head; she seemed incapable of speech.

Stanley turned to me. 'See she's all right and I'll make a start on Belinda.'

Julie zombie-walked to the house and I followed, unsure of how much to assist her. Once in the kitchen she pushed her hands through her hair and spoke to me. 'I'll be all right,' she said. 'I just need a shower.'

'Should I make you a brew?' Working with Stanley had taught me the value of a brew.

She nodded. 'I could murder one.'

I brewed up, then stared through the kitchen window. Through the open doors of the barn, I saw Stanley tie Belinda up and begin removing her shoes. The rapport between them was unfathomable. When Julie re-emerged, she smelt floral and was wearing a fluffy dressing gown. I handed her an Emma Bridgewater mug. 'How long were you trapped for?' I asked.

'Eleven hours,' she said, staring into her mug of tea. 'Howard's working in Dubai.' I was afraid she'd burst into tears if I sympathised, so for a long while, the only sound was the rhythmic dripping of the kitchen tap. 'Thank God you were booked in.'

'We'd been shouting.'

'I must have nodded off.' I sipped my tea. 'There's no point in Stanley shoeing that horse.' She cupped her mug in both hands and took a drink. The threads of her thoughts weren't easy to trace.

'You might feel better when your husband's back,' I suggested, but Julie was shaking her head.

'Enough's enough,' she said. 'You'd better go and tell Stanley not to shoe her.'

I rested my mug on the counter. 'Only if you're sure?'

She nodded, desperation cracking the fatigue on her face.

Out in the yard, Stanley was already heating the shoes. 'Nay bloody 'ell,' he said, as he put his tongs down. 'Not another.' He walked to the kitchen door and addressed Julie from the doorstep. 'Why don't you have a think about it, love? I can come back next week if you change your mind.'

'No. It's really kind of you, Stanley, but I've made my mind up.' She was gripping her mug so tightly that her knuckles were white. 'She's no pleasure to own and she's too dangerous to sell.' I flicked a look at Stanley. Was she saying what I thought she was saying?

'Why don't you just turn her away for a week or two?' Stanley suggested. 'I'll rug her up and put her in t'paddock for you. She could be a different mare after a rest,' but Julie was grim.

'I've tried that before.'

Stanley turned to me. 'What about your mother?' He'd said it quietly, but Julie heard him.

She flapped her hand. 'I've had trainers to her, I've had behaviourists to her, I've had vets to her. I've even had an animal communicator!' She took a deep breath and stood up. 'There comes a point where you've to admit defeat.' She drained her brew. 'Now, if you don't mind, gentlemen, I'm going to bed.'

With no further instructions, we went in search of a rug. Stanley rugged Belinda, smoothed her silver mane with his hands and talked to her all the way out to the paddock. 'You might just have gone too far this time, lady,' he told her, before he let her go.

We watched her canter over her acre of mud with easy elastic strides, then Stanley pressed his hands on his skull. 'It could be a lovely mare, could that,' he said. 'What a bloody shame.'

Chapter 22

There was one other farrier in Stratford College's forge. We exchanged nervous nods. The first horse through the door was a chestnut Arab. I greeted it with a hand on its shoulder and I thanked the gods of iron and fire that it wasn't a round footed cob. Dave Hodgkinson spoke, 'Plain stamp; front pair. You've an hour.'

I smiled and fired up the gas forge. I pulled down the safety goggles and I didn't feel like I was under water. There were no eels in my belly when I drew the second plain stamp shoe from the fire. It sizzled in water, changed from red to grey and fitted the shape of the Arab's foot like its own hoof horn.

Millie cooked me a celebratory meal that night; it was premature, and she was on call, but I felt like celebrating. We were curled on her sofa when she broke the news: 'Julie Thornton's asked me to book Bill Cotham.' I sighed and swilled my wine so it filmed the sides of the glass in pink. 'You know what my worst fear is?' I looked at her. 'That Belinda will move her head when there's a gun to her skull.'

I winced at the thought. 'Can't you do it with Somulose?' but Millie was already shaking her head.

'Julie won't hear of it. She's old school.'

I looked at her over the rim of my glass. 'She'd stand still for Stanley.' Millie looked sceptical. 'I don't know what it is, but the horse behaves for him.'

'Do you think he'd hold her?'

'He'll have nothing else to do, the rate he's losing clients.' The consequences of my quip rolled over me and I looked past the open curtains to the dark boil of clouds over Scorthwaite moor. 'Besides, he likes playing the big man, doesn't he?'

She looked at me. The candlelight was flashing her eyes. 'You're not still worried about your job?'

I slapped her knee; tonight was supposed to be a celebration. 'Nah! I've just aced this exam, haven't I? I'll ask my mum about Belinda. She might have some ideas.'

We plotted how we'd pitch it to Mumma as we loaded the dishwasher. We decided that I'd invite Millie to Sunday lunch and we'd edge it into conversation.

Neither of us slept well when Millie was on call, and at two in the morning her buzzing mobile snapped me into wakefulness. Millie's questioning was precise. 'Is she eating?'

The silence of the bedroom magnified the tinny voice on the other end of the line. 'Not since tea-time.' I was half asleep, but I recognised it.

'Surely, this can wait till morning,' I whispered. Her silent agreement was ironic and resigned.

'Is she sweating or stamping or kicking her flanks?'

'Stamping,' came the tinny response. Millie sighed.

'I'll be with you in twenty minutes.'

My groan rattled the bed head against the wall. 'I thought you said it could wait.'

'I dare say it can, but I won't know unless I go, will I?' I worried about her dead-of-night call-outs with a car full of drugs, so I blinked my gritty eyes and hauled my carcass off the mattress.

We crested the moor and the lights of Eckersley blinked beneath us. The stars above the town sparkled between galaxies of swirling astral dust and I was lost in sleepy reverence for the universe. I drifted off again. Suddenly, G-force pinned me to the seat. Grit spun under the tyres and stones spat at the bodywork. We screeched to a cobble striping stop and my chest banged against the seat belt. 'Sorry,' Millie laughed as my head re-bounced off the headrest. 'If I don't drive in like The Stig, she thinks I'm not taking it seriously.'

Sylvia was jogging towards us, her face blanched by the floodlights. I couldn't make sense from her jabbering, but I trudged behind them to a stable. Sylvia continued to gabble through the opening of the stable door and Millie's application of her stethoscope. Millie listened to Poppy's gut and the cold night nudged me nearer to consciousness. I needed to distract Sylvia so Millie could concentrate. 'I hear Willow did well at the winter championships,' I said, but for once Sylva didn't seem interested in crowing about her ponies' successes.

'It's just one thing after another,' she told Millie, who'd started loading a syringe, then Sylvia stopped her with a hand on her wrist. 'I hope that's an antibacterial needle?' Millie kept on working; she rubbed the mare's neck where she planned to jab.

'It's a sterilised needle,' she answered between teeth that were gripped on the needle cover.

'No, I mean the metal itself,' Millie found the vein, stabbed it and plunged the syringe in a movement so fluid the pony hadn't even noticed she'd been injected. 'Stanley Lampitt shoes her with antibacterial nails.' Millie was stretching on a long latex glove, but the look she slid me from under her eyelashes was pure condemnation. Within a minute, Poppy had relaxed and was picking at her hay net. Millie assured Sylvia there was no sign of impaction, but that she'd ring her in the morning. Sylvia settled herself in the straw beside her pony and left us to make our way back to the car. She had no intention of leaving the animal's side.

'So, what are these *antibacterial nails,* then?' Millie asked when we were back in the Vectra. An owl passed in front of the windscreen. I pointed to it in a bid to distract her. 'Well?'

'You know what she's like,' I explained. 'They shut her up.'

Millie bashed the car into gear. 'I know what *he's* like! He's like a slimy snake-oil salesman!' My eyes searched the indigo sky for the owl. 'He's not the only professional working with that horse, and if we can't trust one another ...'

I zoned her out. Midnight call-outs did this to her – and there was no point protesting that Stanley's odd white lie might keep me in a job. The odd intrusive sentence that floated over the engine noise suggested her lecture was about quackery and the setting up of unrealistic client expectations.

Back at the flat, we stared at the ceiling, waiting for the next emergency call – which never came. At first light. Millie pulled on her jodhpurs. Either she'd forgotten she'd been annoyed or she'd recognised her rant as the fuddled dead-of-night impatience that it was. We chatted over tea and toast, she fulfilled her promise to Sylvia, then we set off towards Lower Mossthwaite Farm. Millie drove behind the Land Rover in her drug packed Vectra in readiness for another call-out.

On the last downhill slope of the familiar road, I approached a horse and rider. I slowed the Land Rover right down. The single-track road is narrow with high hedges on both sides and they were coming to a left-hand bend. I realised from the horse's long white hind stocking that it was Anvil Head with Mumma in the saddle. Mumma raised her hand in thanks to the unknown driver – then I heard the deep throaty throttle of motorbikes. A bubble burst where my heart should be. Anvil Head was new to the roads. Mumma had him out early to avoid the traffic. He was a fit thoroughbred, straight out of training. He might bolt; he might spin; he might put himself across their path. He might rear; he might dive into the hedge. Every scenario risked my mother; some risked both of them. The bikes blasted into my wing mirror's view. I lowered my window. I signalled for them to slow down. The orange bike rider ignored me, the blue showed me his middle finger and screamed past. Anvil Head was on the bend. Mumma must have heard them, but the horse strode on. Mumma sat tall. The orange bike leant into the bend, its wheel was not a metre from the horse's hoof. It roared as the biker hit the throttle. Anvil Head tossed his mane. The blue bike shaved six inches from the orange's arc on the road. Anvil Head skipped a step; Mumma's shoulder brushed the hedge and the bikes were gone. She reached down, patted the horse's neck and Anvil Head clopped on.

I passed horse and rider slowly and turned down the track leading to Lower Mossthwaite Farm. Millie parked her car behind mine. 'What idiots,' she said, staring after the long gone scrambler bikes. 'It's a good job your mum was on a steady one.' Onion whickered at Millie from the fence, so she turned her attention to him.

Anvil Head plonked onto the yard. It was odd to see him tacked up like an ordinary riding horse in a conventional saddle and bridle. Mumma flicked her feet from the stirrups and jumped down. 'I'm impressed,' I said.

'He's utterly unflappable,' she smiled, pulling one of his long ears through her hand. Having witnessed his failure on two racing yards I suspected his sanguinity was just another expression of his idleness. 'He'll make someone a lovely hack.'

Once Anvil Head was back in the field, Mumma joined Millie in the school, where she encouraged her to thread Onion through narrow spaces between the jump wings. That horse too was beginning to look like he'd never had an issue.

Three hours later we were settled round the kitchen table in front of roast chicken and three tureens of vegetables. I deflected a couple of questions about ISAs and ignored Dad's remark about expecting his money to work for him so he turned to Millie and asked her about her work. She answered politely but crept the conversation to where we wanted it to be. 'It's such a shame,' she said as she pronged a carrot. 'I've been asked to put another healthy horse to sleep next week.'

'Oh, here we go,' Dad quipped, scooping green beans onto his plate. 'Bring out your dead; they see you and my wife coming!'

Millie wasn't deflected. 'It's a 16.2 Grade A show jumper – but it's aggressive.'

'To people?' Mumma asked, with her fork poised before her mouth.

Millie nodded. 'I don't know what it's like with horses; it's kept on its own.'

'Does it get turned out?'

'As much as she can. She doesn't have much grazing.'

Mumma was shaking her head. 'What's she feeding it?'

'Oats, I should think,' Millie said. 'It's in work, and she's old fashioned.'

Mumma sighed. 'What do they expect when they feed grazers on grain, keep herd-animals alone, and confine plains animals to twelve by twelve boxes.' She took a sip of her water. 'Tell her to turn it away with company for six months, then start again.' Mumma glanced up to find both of us looking at her. 'Oh, no! If it were mid-summer, I could – but cramming an unknown quantity into my barn now could be a disaster.' We kept on staring at her.

Dad looked up from his plate. 'This isn't the horse that put you in hospital is it, Millie?' Millie's rueful silence answered his question. 'You can't expect Lizzie to take on dangerous horses …'

'I'm not worried about the danger,' Mumma interrupted.

'I am!' Dad said.

A silence fell on the table. Mumma was torn between standing up to Dad and taking on a horse she'd no room for. Dad was annoyed and Millie had seen the dusty cogs behind the gilded face of our middle-class family.

POST CARD

Madrid January 14th 2017
Dear Stanley (and boys),

It is so good to be home! Carlos has met all his family, including his great-great aunty Pilar who is 93!

Today, my parents are looking after him so I can show Dirk my city. (Royal Palace, El Ritiro, Plaza Major). Tomorrow, the Velazquez in The Prado. My parents love to babysit. They say thank you for all you have done. I hope you are all behaving as well as Carlos. See you soon.

Maria (and Dirk and Carlos).

Stanley, Ewan and Will
148 Hathersage Rd
Hathersage
North Yorkshire
FL9 0JJ
UK

Chapter 23

I hadn't heard from Jay since before Christmas so I was pleased when his name flashed up on my phone. It was usually another picture of a baby and I was running out of responses. 'Jay! How's tricks?' His answer seemed to come through a sponge. 'Sorry, mate, it's a bad line.' I listened again. Was he asking my whereabouts. 'At the forge. Why?'

'*Bith off a kitsh,*' was what I heard.

'Bit of a bitch?'

'*Ficth*'

'Bit of a fix?'

His next words were drowned by Stanley's deep groan. 'Don't tell me he's lost another bastard body part!'

'Sorry, Jay. You'll have to say that again.' I listened hard, then I covered the mouthpiece. 'I think he's injured. He sounds bad, Stanley.'

Stanley threw his arms wide. 'Why's he ringing you, for fuck's sake? Does he think we're the bastard paramedics?'

I put my mouth back to the phone. 'Are you on your own, Jay?' I couldn't make any sense of his answer. I turned back to Stanley and covered the phone. 'The farm's only two minutes away, Stan.'

'Does no bugger else work on it?'

'What if he's bleeding to death?' Stanley lifted the earpiece of Ewan's headphone and bellowed into his ear. 'Dolloper! Van!'

Ewan looked puzzled. 'I thought we were forging this morning?'

'Just get in the van.' We'd need Ewan's level head if Stanley was as useless as last time. 'We should have a bastard blue light on this,' Stanley chuntered as he climbed into The Old Van.

We drove the half mile through the new housing estate to Willow Mount Farm and the first thing I saw when I stepped from the van was a brown man-shape slumped against a wall in a brown puddle. Ewan walked towards it. 'You'll not fight for t'chocolate fountain again, will you?'

'What happened?' I asked him.

'Thell in the thlurry,' Jay explained through a jammy rip. 'Cow kicked ny teef ou'.' I looked to where a heifer was standing up to her belly in the vat of bovine diarrhoea.

'Come on,' Ewan said, taking Jay's arm. 'We'd better get you looked at.'

'He's not getting in my van,' Stanley stated.

'Your van's a shithole anyway!'

'There's no actual shit in it though!'

Jay was still dripping, shoulders bowed. Ewan was holding him by the elbow and staring at Stanley. Stanley folded his arms. I tried to break the deadlock.

'Is there anywhere to hose him off?'

The whites of Jay's eyes flashed in panic. 'Ish thucking Thebruary!' Beads of chocolate were dripping from his hair.

'Is there any warm water, anywhere?'

Jay pointed to the milking parlour.

'I'll get a bucket,' Ewan said, and he walked off. Jay leant against the wall of the cow byre.

'How did you end up in the slurry?' I asked.

'I wash moving t'cows,' Jay explained, through letterbox lips. 'But one kanicked and thell in. I went to in strak it uk to t'tractor – but it kicked me off t'ledge.'

'Shit,' I breathed. (Slurry pits can be twelve feet deep in it.)

'Den de vugger kicked me in the gov.' He pointed to the swelling red rip of his mouth.

Ewan was on his way back with a bucket, a flannel and a pair of overalls. 'I found these,' he said. Jay dunked the flannel in the bucket and dabbed at his face. He winced as he uncovered a deep gash on his top lip. A bloodied nose and a scarlet cheekbone emerged, like numbers appearing on a scratch card. Ewan helped him to his feet. He unpeeled Jay's shit-soaked overalls and Jay stepped into the stolen ones.

On account of Jay's injuries, he was allocated my seat and I was bundled in the back with half a hundredweight of stuff that would crush me on sudden braking.

We'd gone two miles down the dual carriageway when Jay suddenly shouted out: 'Ny overalls!' He pressed his hand to his forehead. 'Ny uncle Gryan'll find 'em!'

Stanley tightened his grip on the steering wheel. 'Jay, lad, your Uncle Brian is going to find his cow in the fucking slurry pit – unless it's dropped off the ledge – in which case he'll find it at muck spreadin'!' Jay buried his head in his hands and I began to understand the limitations of his employment opportunities.

Perhaps it was a hygiene issue, but the triage nurse admitted Jay immediately. We left him to get the bus home.

Chapter 24

'Your lass,' Stanley said, pointing at his phone like she was in it. 'She wants a hand wi' Belinda this mornin'.'

'You're gonna need more than a galvanised bucket this time,' Ewan quipped, but Stanley didn't laugh. Neither did I.

'Get up to Donkey Man's,' he ordered Ewan. 'And take the dog with you.'

'Piss off!' Ewan shouted over his shoulder. 'I'll have enough to contend with, with his killer llama!' The van door slammed. Stanley groaned and whistled for the dog.

'Come on,' he said to me, with a flick of the head. 'Time to be a big boy.'

William Cotham and Sons. Collection and Disposal of Fallen Stock. The sight of the words on the steel-bodied knacker wagon tightened my throat. We contained Lucky and escaped the cab. The heavy air enfolded me like a wet sheet. No birds were singing that morning and the flagstones were gleaming with damp. Julie murmured a subdued greeting and Millie, at her side, shot me a tight smile. Bill Cotham unfolded his arms. 'Are we ready now, love?' It was a gentle enquiry. A kinder, milder deliverer of death than Bill Cotham, you couldn't hope to meet. Julie stooped for the battered galvanised bucket at her feet and turned towards the muddy paddock.

Belinda was munching contentedly on a heap of hay, oblivious that it was her last meal. Julie shook the bucket. Its dull rumble carried easily in the damp air and Belinda looked up, ears pricked. She cantered towards Julie, but stopped at the sight of a headcollar. Julie dipped into the bucket and came up with an apple. I was starting to grasp how the bucket might have conspired in the flooring of Belinda. The horse giraffed her neck and took it with outstretched lips. Julie reached for another apple, this time holding it closer to her body so Belinda had to walk a step. As Belinda's teeth touched the apple, Julie reached forward with the headcollar. Belinda dodged, dropped the apple and bolted, strafing Julie with mud.

She was cantering through the sludge now, her nose high, her tail arched, churning the air with mud and snorts. Stanley had been watching. He set off towards the paddock. Julie swiped a clod of earth from her face. Belinda stopped at the far end of the paddock. She was staring back at us, her breath swirling like dragon smoke. 'It's a bonny horse,' Bill Cotham remarked at my shoulder. 'What's to do wi' it?' We looked at the graceful grey mare, wreathed in clouds of her own breath.

'Temperament problems,' Millie answered.

Stanley had arrived at Julie's side. We watched as he dipped his hand in the galvanised bucket and came out with an apple.

'Has she tried Lizzie Harker?' Bill Cotham asked Millie.

Millie nodded. 'She's full up.'

Stanley's eyes were on Belinda's and his apple was out-stretched. In short, his approach was the opposite of what Lizzie Harker would have advised, but Belinda lowered her head. She took the apple and she accepted the headcollar from him.

'It looks mannerly enough, there,' Bill remarked. Belinda was nuzzling Stanley for another apple.

'Don't be fooled,' Millie said. 'It's put me in hospital.'

Stanley was scrubbing the fur between Belinda's eyes. He walked to the end of her lead rope and led her slowly across the mud and through the gate to where, in a few minutes, her body could be winched into the knackers' wagon.

Bill was holding the bolt gun; a grim weapon: black, square-barrelled and almost as long as his forearm. He turned to Julie, 'Are you sure about this, love?'

'She's had chance after chance,' Julie answered him; there was a catch in her voice.

Bill walked to Belinda's side. Her nose was still in the bucket. Distracted by the apples, she only flattened her ears at him. He spoke softly to the horse and rubbed the gun over her face, so its final touch wouldn't distress her. She lashed her tail. Slowly, he lifted the gun to her head.

Death was Millie's weekly work. She dispatched racehorse casualties at Wetherby, she delivered stillborn lambs on hill farms and put down geriatric family pets in the surgery – but she lowered her eyes. I turned my back. The only sound was the crunch on crunch of apple – then Bill's voice. 'There are folk who specialise in problem horses, you know, love.'

Julie's answer was sharp. 'Please don't make this harder!' I closed my eyes. I steeled myself for the shot. I waited. I slit a sideways glance at Millie. Her fists were balled. The metal of Belinda's headcollar clinked. Metal on metal. I tightened my jaw. I stiffened my shoulders.

'Don't, Bill!' It was Stanley's voice. I turned back. Millie's hand was sweeping over her face. Stanley was walking Belinda away. His hand was on her neck. The clop of her hooves overlaid his voice. 'Will you let me have her, Julie?' I stared at him. 'I'll take her away now, if I can borrow your trailer.'

'Yes,' her voice cracked like crockery. She was shell-shocked, drip-white. She should have been looking on her horse's corpse.

Millie and Julie worked quickly. They gathered Belinda's rugs, tack and feed barrels and before death could drag itself back to the yard, they piled them into The Old Van on top of the shoes, nails and the anvil. Julie took Bill's hand in both of hers and thanked him.

'Hey, I'd have had a bullet donkey's years since if you got

shot for being nowty,' he smiled. He climbed into his empty death wagon and was gone.

With no idea of how closely death had brushed her and an expectation of a day's show-jumping ahead, Belinda loaded calmly. I raised the tailgate and turned to Millie. The damp had frizzed her hair to a copper halo. She kissed me on the cheek, thanked Stanley, hugged Julie, and climbed into her car.

'I'll call you later,' she said, and closed the door.

I jumped into The Old Van's cab. From the driver's seat, Stanley waved at Julie. Julie waved back and walked to the house, smiling. She closed the door. We sat in the van.

'Where to now?' I asked.

Stanley turned to me. 'Do you want a horse?'

'No, I bloody don't!' I said. 'And certainly not this horse!' We stared at the snake of black tarmac that slithered between hedges on the other side of the gate. 'What are you going to do with her?'

He wiped a paw over his face. 'Fuck knows.' The van rocked softly.

'I thought you had a plan.'

'I hadn't time to make a bastard plan, had I!' He drummed the seat with his fingers. 'I can't just ask the 'ens to make a bit o'room in t'bastard chicken coop!'

'Why don't you ring Scorthwaite Livery; see if they have a free stable?'

Stanley twisted in his seat, the better to regard the idiot next to him. 'Have you heard yourself? I'm buying t'bastard dog food from Lidl! How can I afford livery fees?'

'Just temporary, I meant. Until we can come up with something.'

'And have you thought what that schizoid in t'trailer'll do to a pony mad kid wi' pigtails who happens to stroll past her stable?' He was right. Belinda didn't belong on a livery yard. 'What about your mum's?'

I was shaking my head. 'No chance.'

'Jennings?'

'You're forgetting his wife.' He rubbed the pads of his fingers over his pressed lips and stared once more into the grey morning.

The long silence seemed to tick – then Stanley grinned, sat up straight, and roared the van to life. 'Where are we going?' I asked.

'Watch and learn,' he winked, and we pulled off the yard.

Chapter 25

Low cloud was flapping across the windscreen like washing on a line and fog had faded out the daytime colours. Flashman Freddie's caravans only became visible when we crunched onto his car-park. Freddie looked up. He left the pile of logs he was chopping and strolled over to the horse trailer. He peered into it, then spoke at the van's window. 'Have you fetched me a wee present here, Stanley?'

Stanley glanced at the trailer like he'd forgotten he was towing it then wound down his window. 'Oh, you wouldn't be able to handle this one, Freddie.'

'Ach! Catch yourself on!' Freddie scoffed. 'There isn't a horse on God's green earth I couldn't handle.' Freddie was legendary in the traveller world for his knowledge of horses. When he wasn't serving time at Her Majesty's pleasure, he staged illegal trotting races on the Fowlden bypass.

Stanley was shaking his head determinedly. 'This 'oss were damn near shot for viciousness an hour since.'

'Is it yours?'

Stanley nodded. 'It is now. I'm on my way to Scorthwaite Livery wi' it.' I felt my brow crumple in confusion.

'How big?'

'Sixteen-two.'

'Let's have a proper look at it, then?' Stanley sighed, like it was a woeful inconvenience, then we contained Lucky – who'd not had a leg stretch all morning and was whiffing sheep on the air – and stepped out of the van. Stanley unlatched the trailer's jockey door, all the while warning Freddie to watch himself in a doom-laden voice. I could imagine Belinda's flat eared expression and thrashing tail threats when Freddie stepped in. After a few seconds he climbed out again. 'You could breed a nice foal out o' that one, Stanley,' but Stanley was shaking his head.

'Nah, I haven't the land, Freddie.'

'I have!' For a second, I thought I saw Stanley's plan – but then he confused me by resisting the suggestion.

'I dunno, Freddie. They've an indoor school at Scorthwaite. I fancied gettin' back in t'saddle again.' Now I *knew* he was lying.

'Ach! You'll never do it!' Freddie scoffed. 'Be honest with yourself!' Stanley said nothing. 'Oh! Come on, Stanley! We can run her with my stallion.' Stanley rubbed his jaw, as if considering the offer. 'I'll tell you what I'll do, Stanley, I'll not charge you for the livery and I'll take your first foal.'

Stanley cupped his chin. 'All t'foals after that are mine, though?'

'Aye.'

He seemed to consider it. 'Aye, go on then,' he conceded, like he was doing Freddie a big favour. Then he spat on his palm, held it out, and told me to fetch Belinda's lead rope.

I flung open The Old Van's rear doors. I was still questioning my own understanding of what had just happened, so I forgot that Lucky was in there. I grabbed but I might as well have grabbed for a fish. She'd launched herself from the heap of Belinda's rugs. I stuck my leg out but she feinted, darted right and accelerated past the trailer. I screeched her name, but Lucky was airborne now, launching herself off a dry-stone wall. Stanley was bawling his threats at the folding fog but Lucky was bouncing into it, joyous. Freddie looked bewildered. In the milkiness of the mist I could see the dense dots of his ewes drifting together; clumping like globules of fat. February: they'd be well in-lamb.

Lucky ran faster; more of an arrow than a ball now. Stanley turned on me. 'Are you just going to stand there?'

I flung my arms wide. 'How can I catch her!'

The sheep had clumped in a corner of a dry-stone wall, and Lucky was closing on them. Stanley cupped his hands at his mouth and bellowed her name again. Her thin yap was bouncing off the clouds. Freddie's face was as still as a paving stone. He turned towards the caravan. 'Where are you going?' Stanley demanded.

'For my gun,' Freddie answered. His stride was even and determined.

'Run!' Stanley shouted at me. I was already blasting across the car-park. I knew Lucky wouldn't come to my call, but I called anyway. I vaulted the wall and lumbered uphill. My foot caught stones that rolled and plunged behind me. Wet, spongy turf slowed me. I was breathing through grit. Lucky was in amongst the ewes. Her barking was less rhythmic now; more purposeful. The growls between her yaps were being gulped by the wind.

Freddie would be back by now. He'd be in the car-park with his loaded gun. He could be taking aim. I slogged on, labouring up the hill. Each breath scouring my throat. Ewes were spilling over a dry-stone wall, darting left, reeling circles. Lucky would have their fleece in her teeth. Trophies. Would Freddie shoot if I was in the way? I was on the steepest slope now. It was soggy, slippery, strewn with rocks. My throat was raw and skinless. Lucky was unhindered; as fluid as when she'd flung herself from the van. I gasped. My chest couldn't widen enough.

A shot. Its bang exploded off the flank of the moor. I'd flinched, but I looked up. Lucky was stone still, staring into the mist. Freddie's gun was at his shoulder; still pointed at the hillside. 'Lucky!' I yelled. Another shot blasted the skies. My ears sang with it. I folded; winced. Lucky's sheep-trance had been broken. 'Lucky,' I crooned, more softly. She looked at me. I crouched. I held out a hand, like it might be holding biscuit. She trotted towards me, ears down, tail low. She'd been fazed by the bangs. I bent and scooped her up. Lucky licked my face. She wriggled her snake-muscle body in delight. Behind me, ewes were scrambling back over the dry-stone wall.

I wondered, as I picked my way down the hillside with wobbling legs, if Flashman Freddie had aimed to miss me, or to miss Lucky, or if he was just a lousy shot. As I reached the bottom of the hill, I squared my shoulders, swung my hips and feigned a smile. 'No harm done!' I said when my feet were back on the chippings.

Freddie broke the barrel of his gun. 'We'll know that in a month.'

'You frightened the life out of me with those gun shots!' I said, all mock-chirpiness.

'If I'd been any closer,' Freddie scowled. 'I'd be handing you a shovel.'

Stanley's face was the colour of ash. 'It's not done that for months.'

Freddie thrust a forefinger at him. 'I'll tell you what, Stanley Lampitt, I won't miss next time.' He shouldered his gun. 'This time, I'll just have your mare off you.'

Stanley looked up. 'You what?'

'I'll have that mare off you for the inconvenience and the slipped lambs.'

'What slipped lambs?'

Freddie cut his eyes at him. 'There'll be slipped lambs.'

'I'll pay you for your slipped lambs!'

Flashman Freddie folded his arms. 'Your life's going to get very expensive, then isn't it, Stanley?'

'Depends how many they lose,' Stanley shrugged.

'I mean, on top of your livery bills at Scorthwaite, and the prices they'll charge for hay ...'

Stanley's mouth dropped open. 'I thought we'd just agreed ...'

'Why would I want you up here, visiting your horse with a sheep killer in your van?'

'I wouldn't ...'

'You say that now!' Freddie interrupted. 'Then you decide to call in on your way back from a job, then you get careless and the next thing I know ...'

'Do you think I want a bullet in my dog?'

'Take it or leave it,' Freddie smiled, and the shark's twist of the mouth told me he had seen straight through Stanley.

Stanley shook his head. 'Well,' he sighed, 'I had my own horse again for an hour and twenty minutes.'

If I'd not been in the van with him an hour and twenty minutes earlier, I might have thought he was disappointed.

I returned Lucky to the van and Freddie turned his attention to his new horse. Belinda played up to her billing. She launched herself down the ramp like a two-thousand-man army. Her ears were up, her tail was up, and her eyes were like bin lids. When Flashman Freddie dragged off her travelling rug, she whipped round. It was satisfying to see the would-be dog killer dive from her kicks and lashes.

With Stanley leading her, Belinda passaged to the wooden gate that opened onto fifty sheep-free acres of stone-walled moorland. She was snorting, barging and throwing in the odd leap. Freddie opened the gate. Stanley turned the mare to face him and slipped off her headcollar. She was pulling for freedom before it was unbuckled. She swung round, bucked and galloped away, ecstatic to be free of her lonely little patch of mud. She plunged, she squealed and she high-tailed it across the moor. Black trotters and coloured cobs lifted their heads in the distance and she slowed to a passage. 'I'll bet that can jump,' Freddie remarked.

'Grade A,' Stanley confirmed. 'If you can ever get on it.'

Belinda greeted the first cob, nose to nose, her neck arched. After a second of stillness she squealed and trotted a circle.

I wondered how long Belinda had lived without her own kind. By now a black trotter had joined them, its damp mane swinging in dreadlocks. There were more nose to nose, and nose to tail greetings, then the cluster exploded like a firework. They galloped to safety, then turned to regard one another. The other six horses had ceased grazing and were gazing, ears up, heads up. A rear and a plunge from Belinda set them galloping, and were it not for the airborne clods of mud, the Yorkshire moors could have been the Colorado prairie. They galloped into the mist, the thunder of their hooves bouncing off the clouds.

'They're bloody lovely animals, aren't they?' I turned to see a tall girl with long black hair standing beside me. I hadn't even seen her arrive. She was leaning on the mossy stone wall, her eyes locked on the diminishing rodeo.

Stanley noticed her for the first time too; he took his weight from the wall. 'Hey up, Rochelle, love. Are you a' reyt?'

'Aye,' she answered. 'Skint, but that's nowt new.'

He sympathised, then turned to me. 'Come on, Posh Lad. We'd better get this trailer back to Julie's.'

Freddie turned his eyes away from the horses. 'What did you want, anyway?'

Stanley looked blank. 'When?'

'Now.'

'Oh!' Stanley pretended a sudden memory – then he fell silent. 'Why did we call in, Posh Lad?'

Wild panic heated up somewhere near my middle. 'Proven!' I shouted. 'We wondered if you'd the right proven for a thoroughbred.'

Freddie's chin flicked, sceptically. 'Wouldn't you have been better calling at Mervyn's for that?'

'You're joking!' Stanley said, finding his stride. 'Mervyn doesn't know whether he's coming or going, he's that short staffed. You're lucky if he can find an 'oss, never mind a bag o' proven.'

Rochelle was already walking away but she stopped and turned back. 'I'm looking for a job.'

Freddie flapped a hand at her. 'Ach! You're too busy with the wee one!'

'I need the money, Dad!'

'Why? I won't see you short!'

'I know, but it'd be nice to pick up the tab for myself once in a while.' Embarrassment at my riches steamed in my stomach.

'Why don't you drop in and introduce yourself to Mervyn?' I said. 'It's only round the corner.'

'Good idea,' she smiled. 'I will,' and she walked away.

We waited until Belinda had settled to grazing on the periphery of the group, then we waved goodbye to Freddie and headed for the van.

'Well, you've off-loaded your mare,' I remarked quietly.

'Aye,' Stanley said. Lucky was curled like an ammonite on The Old Van's passenger seat.

'I think he was on to you though.'

'Happen.' He thumped onto the driver's seat. 'If that dog hadn't cocked it up for me, I could have had the best o' both worlds!' He'd raised his voice, like the dog could understand him. When she failed to blush, he shoved her into the footwell.

'Is it not time you rang Seth Holden?' I said. 'His cure can't be worse than a bullet in her.'

Chapter 26

Stanley pointed at a small stack of envelopes. The logo of Stratford College of Agriculture was emblazoned on the upper most one. 'You'd better open that.' My heart was filling my throat when I picked it up. Beneath it were a bank statement and a postcard with a picture of The Prado on the front. 'Go on.' I looked across the forge at Ewan who encouraged me with a nod. A zig-zag of paper sprang free of the envelope. My eyes scanned it; they snagged on a number. My shoulders fell in relief.

'Eighty-seven percent!' I said.

'I should fucking think so,' Stanley growled.

I had hoped for a bit more praise but Ewan was giving me a grinning thumbs up from across the forge. I handed Stanley the bank statement which he pushed in his pocket with a groan. Ewan picked up the postcard, skimmed it and dropped it on the bench. 'Well then?' Stanley pressed.

'She's glad to be home,' Ewan answered. 'She hopes we're behaving and her parents say thanks.'

'Does she say when they're coming back?'

Ewan shook his head. 'Just *See you soon*.'

Stanley groaned. 'My house looks like a branch o' bastard Mothercare.' He swept his keys from the workbench. 'Now,' he said. 'Let's get that dog in t'bastard van.'

The whiff of sheep had set Lucky a quiver before we'd even arrived at Seth Holden's. By the time we pulled onto the farmyard, she was thrashing in Stanley's grip like a salmon. Seth Holden shuffled his walking stick so it was vertical between his knees and nestled gnarled hands on it. 'It's a wick little beggar, is that, Stan.'

'Can you sort it?' Stanley asked, retrieving Lucky from where she was scrambling over his shoulder.

A few seconds had passed before Seth answered. 'I've never failed one yet.' Talking to Seth was like conversing over a satellite link. He shuffled his stick to his right hand and set off at the speed of a caterpillar. After four strides he looked over his shoulder. 'Gi' me ten minutes,' he said. I took in a long breath. Ten minutes of Seth-time could be days.

A field roller was rusting under a yew tree at the corner of the farmyard. I strolled towards it and sat with my feet in the surrounding bracken; in a few weeks it would uncurl in emerald coils, but for now it was brown winter sticks. The roller was wide enough for the three of us, so Ewan joined me. Stanley followed with Lucky straining at the leash, desperate to follow her nose to the sheep-scented fields.

The moorland grasses were still the winter colour of the Sahara. I gazed at them through the green frame of a yew's overhanging branches. A red car crawled the sweeping fell road beneath us. I ground my toe into the damp soil between the sticks of bracken and watched a robin dipping for insects in the gravel. Its beak was working but it was strutting on, busy, bustling, unconcerned. Its grey rump bobbing at every stab. Ewan snapped a twig in two and sighed. The robin stretched its red breast and leapt into flight. We waited. Ewan pulled out his iPhone7. 'I could find us a film on Netflix.' Lucky curled at Stanley's feet.

It was twenty-five minutes before Seth's sheep trailer crashed onto the cobbles behind a battered Land Rover. Its wheels stopped but the racket from the trailer rumbled on. Seth creaked from the cab. 'This gen'lly sorts 'em,' he announced, slamming the Land Rover's door. 'I've cured all sorts wi' this:

Doberman's, Alsatians, Alaskan Malamutes ...' he was having to shout over the banging from the trailer.

'Bloody hell, Seth,' Stanley bellowed. He was looking down at his little dog, all prick-eared and bright-eyed. 'It's only a six kilogram Jack Russell!' The trailer thundered and lurched. 'What've you fetched? A bastard rhino?'

Seth chuckled over the pounding and pummelling and pointed at Lucky. 'It's as keen as mustard is that. There's no point in playin' at it.'

Lucky's body was stiff, her tail was taut and her lead looked set to snap under the strain of her surges. She'd smelt sheep. The trailer rocked and boomed. Seth put his hand on the inspection door. 'Get it chucked in there, Stan!' Stanley stood stock still. 'Come on, Stan. It'll only finish up wi' a bullet in it if you don't.'

'He's right,' I said. I didn't need to remind him of Flashman Freddie. Stanley picked up his tiny terrier and walked towards the rumbling trailer. Tremors of murderous intent were rippling her body. Seth opened the trailer's inspection door. Lucky's eyes were bulging now. Stanley lowered her to the lip of the metal floor. Her feet scrabbled. 'Let her go!' Seth urged. Stanley unclipped her lead and Lucky shot through the gap.

The trailer blundered. Barking counterpointed bleating. Seth leant on his stick. There was a bash. 'It's a nowty beggar!' Seth smiled. The trailer walls rattled. Seth laughed! Metal banged. The trailer teetered on its axle.

Ewan stepped forward. 'I'm letting her out!'

Seth raised his hand. 'Just give it a few more minutes.' The trailer was see-sawing now as if building to a capsize.

'For God's sake!' Stanley pleaded. A screaming yelp pierced the trailer's metal walls. 'That's enough now.' He was striding towards the trailer

'Well, it's your dog,' Seth shrugged – but before he could open the inspection door, the trailer fell still and silent. Stanley looked at Seth. Seth snatched open the door and his shout of anguish echoed in the metal box. Ewan covered his face. Stanley pushed Seth away and reached in. His wail was pure pain. It hung like a howl in the air. He loved that dog. I closed my eyes. I didn't want to see a limp lump of bloodied dog flesh dangled in the day light. The only sound I could hear in my darkness was Seth's boots on the trailer's metal floor. I peeped through slatted fingers. Stanley was withdrawing his arm – and a writhing, seething knot of muscle snarled into view. Lucky was attached to his wrist by her teeth. I laughed in relief.

Dancing and grimacing, Stanley shook her off his main artery and clipped her lead. He put her on the cobbles and she rushed towards the trailer, like a child's pull-back toy. 'Come here you little bugger!' Stanley shouted, trying to hold the lead and his bleeding wrist. Seth backed out of the trailer. He was ashen. He pointed a shaking finger at Lucky, who hadn't finished her fight.

'It's a bloody psychopath is that.'

'Sorry,' Stanley said, dragging his panting maniac towards The Old Van. 'Will your tup be all right, Seth?' Pride was tingeing his sympathy.

'It's drawn blood! There's nowt else drawn blood on it! I've had Rhodesian Ridgebacks in there wi' it! Japanese Akitas!' Lucky was still swivelling her head towards the trailer and skidding her stubborn paws on the cobbles. 'Get it home,' Seth ordered with a flap of his hand. 'There's on'y a bullet'll cure yon.'

Lucky leapt to Ewan's knee in The Old Van. Stanley slammed the door. We looked at the terrier sitting up, all grinning jaws and lolling tongue and we burst into laughter.

Stanley turned the key and glanced at her from the driver's seat. 'You are one horrible little fucker,' he chuckled, and she licked his arm.

Chapter 27

Striding through the open doors of Mervyn's American barn was Rochelle, leading a racehorse. Her long thin legs were encased in shiny black boots, her pink jodhpurs were spangled on the pockets and her black hair was encircled by a pink tweed head-band. She lifted the arm of her silver Puffa jacket and waved at me. 'Who's that?' Ewan asked, his eyes were following her across the yard.

'Rochelle.'

'Rochelle who?'

I shrugged. What was Flashman Freddie even called?

'She knows you!'

'I'm just puttin' this on t'walker,' she bellowed and Ewan eyed me suspiciously.

In the shoeing bay, six horses' names were written on the chalk board and two were already waiting for us in the stalls. 'Bloody hell,' Stanley breathed. 'Have t'bastard fairies been?'

By the time we'd lit the forge and laid out our tools, Rochelle was on her way back down the aisle of the neatly swept American barn leading a different horse. It was sleek and shining and I noticed a tag on its headcollar: 14. Its stable rug was also marked 14. I looked around me and saw that numbered exercise sheets were draped over every stable door.

'This place is running nice and slick,' Stanley remarked to Mervyn with awe in his voice.

'Oh, Eva Braun, you mean?' He was handing over a wad of damp banknotes. Stanley pocketed them and Rochelle appeared at Mervyn's shoulder. She reached in his copious pocket, brought out a dandy brush and held it in front of his nose.

'I thought so,' she said.

Mervyn reddened like a naughty school boy. 'I ... I were on my way to put it back!'

'Back where?' He opened and closed his mouth. 'It's number 64,' she was speaking with the exhaustion of one who's been through this before. '0-35 down there. 36-70 up there!'

'Sorry, love.'

'What else is in your pocket?'

'Nowt.' But she'd already dipped into his other one. She brought out a snaffle bit.

'What's this off?'

Mervyn rubbed his bristly chin. 'Ummm ... I swapped it for a Dexter yesterday ...'

'Which horse?'

Mervyn bit his lip in concentration.

'No wonder nobody can ever find anything!' she said, pocketing it. 'And where's your phone?' He patted himself like a magician, and when a look of blank guilt had shrouded his face, she dropped her weight over one hip and pulled Mervyn's phone from her own pocket. 'In the feed bin.' Mervyn took it like a chastened child and Rochelle began striding away with her spoils.

'You needed her at beginnin' o' t'season, Mervyn.' Stanley grinned. Mervyn nodded grudgingly. 'You might have been running a few more in t'National.'

'I've to get one in t'National yet,' Mervyn said.

'I thought it had qualified?'

'I'm waitin' on t'ballot,' Mervyn explained. 'They can only run forty these days.'

Stanley picked up his hoof pullers. 'Does it have a chance?'

'They all have a chance.' Mervyn shrugged.

The soft boom of an igniting gas forge bumped the walls of

the shoeing bay and Stanley changed the subject. 'How are you getting' on wi' th'insurance?'

Mervyn was leaning on the partition. 'I've got a solicitor on it,' he said, and he might have told us more, but his phone rang. With much muttering and cursing he dragged it from his pocket, spilling with it a length of baling twine and a wrinkly carrot. 'HELLO!' he shouted.

Rochelle's voice snapped out of it. 'I'm just checking you still have it on you!'

'You only give it me back two minutes since!'

Rochelle cackled gleefully on the other end.

'She's bloody everywhere,' Mervyn chuntered, pocketing his phone.

Within minutes Rochelle had appeared with five mugs, a teapot and a packet of digestive biscuits. I couldn't remember the last time we'd had a brew at Mervyn's, and never from a teapot. She poured the tea, settled her neat, jodhpured arse on the edge of the anvil, cradled her mug and told us how well Belinda was faring. 'Every day, I just slip her headcollar on her, give her a carrot, then let her go again.'

'Let me see your hands,' Ewan said and Rochelle fanned out her long fingers for him. Ewan took the tips of them. 'Just checking you've not lost any,' he said and Rochelle giggled. When she took up his empty cup, she winked at him. Ewan reddened and looked away.

'So, she's Flashman Freddie's daughter?' Ewan asked, when she'd walked off with the empty cups.

'Aye,' Stanley confirmed, slapping his rasp against the palm of his hand for emphasis. 'And the bloke who fathered her two-year-old is still eatin' through a straw, so I wouldn't even go there, lad.'

'As if!' Ewan scoffed, somersaulting his own rasp and catching it by the handle.

Despite the tea break, Rochelle's efficiency meant we'd squared the morning's work away faster than usual. By twelve we were packing up the van. A racehorse transporter glided onto the yard. It was nothing like as flash as the one Jay had embedded in forty-two Tattersall Street, but it was only taking Mervyn's horses as far as Wetherby races. Punctual as a machine, Rochelle appeared at the doors of the American barn with a racehorse in a travelling rug; Ruudi was behind her with another one. The driver dropped from the cab, walked to the back of the wagon and began lowering the ramp. Stanley strolled to his side and struck up a conversation.

We'd stowed our tools, climbed in the van and slammed the door. Still Stanley and the driver were chatting. The horses thundered into the wagon, partitions were adjusted and the ramp raised. Ewan and I were debating whether to ditch our sandwiches in favour of a tray of chips from Effin Elsie's when Stanley waved a farewell and climbed into the driver's seat. 'What were all that about?' Ewan asked him.

Stanley fired the engine. 'I were quizzin' him about his transporting business.' Ewan and I exchanged a look; Stanley saw it. 'How long do you think I can keep this caper up – eh?' I wanted to check Ewan's reaction, but Stanley was staring at us. 'I'm nearly fifty!'

'You're all right though,' I told him.

'Am I buggery all right!' Stanley shot. 'I've had half my bastard guts out – or had you forgotten?' He let off the handbrake. 'My back's buggered, my knees creak like a pair o' rusty hinges and I've had more nails in me than Jesus o' Nazareth.' Stanley pulled the van onto the main road. 'I could do wi' a desk job.' I didn't dare look at Ewan. Like me he'd be remembering the unintelligible pictograms in the diary, the unread postcards from Dirk and ending up in Salterforth when we should have been in Saltaire.

Arrive Manchester Sunday: 16.20 IB3796.
See you soon!

Chapter 28

Lucky was in Ewan's arms. He was twisting his face from her lathering tongue and nodding towards a small metal cage on the kitchen floor. 'Look at what he's doing with her.'

'Why doesn't he just leave her in the forge if she can't come with us?' I asked.

'Because it's bloody perishing wi' no fire lit,' Stanley answered as he strolled in.

'Can't you just leave her loose in the house?'

'Aye – if I want me bastard kitchen redesigning.'

'She wouldn't do that.'

'Two chewed chair legs and the bitten corner of a carousel unit say she would!' She'd launched herself from Ewan's arms and was now propped on my calves with her stump tail thrashing. Stanley put his phone away and scooped her up. Strides from the cage, Lucky stiffened. Stanley quickened. She swung and snapped at him. Stanley slung her in and slammed the door. Lucky's growls were bubbling at her throat. His fingers found the latch. Lucky's teeth were gnashing on his knuckles. The cage clattered like a waterfall of tumbling cutlery. Stanley swore and Lucky howled.

'You can't blame her!' Ewan said as Stanley stood up. 'How would you like being stuffed in cage?'

'It's a crate!' Stanley said, sucking his bloodied knuckles. 'And she'll get used to it.'

'You reckon?' he smirked. 'You said that about us getting out of the van.'

Lucky kept up her cage clattering fury until the kitchen door was closed. As Stanley turned the key, it became a desperate yelp then a pleading, screaming urgency. 'Surely we can take her to Jennings'?' I said.

'Start as you mean to go on,' Stanley stated. He pocketed the keys and we followed him down the steps. None of us spoke as we took up our usual positions in the van. Stanley started the engine, his lips a grim line of determination. By the time we pulled off the drive, Lucky was howling long plaintive wails of utter misery. I turned my head and looked at Stanley.

'She's brought it on herself,' he said and flicked on the CD player. Status Quo's 'Whatever You Want' bounced off the skin of the van. We'd got to the far side of Fowlden when he turned it down. 'How are you fixed on Saturday night?' I glanced at him. 'Dirk and Maria are picking up their stuff, so I thought we'd give them a send-off.'

'Awww ...' Ewan groaned. 'Jade'll be gutted. She's not seen the baby.'

'Neither have I,' I remarked. 'But I've seen more photos of it than I have of Donald Trump.'

'Tell her to come,' Stanley said, and Ewan took out his phone.

I opened the van door on the whooshing crash of dropping boughs. Jennings was gazing towards the woodland. 'There's a beech too close to the Victorian glass-house,' he explained.

All morning, the pulse and thrum of the chain-saw counterpointed our rasping and hammering. We'd shod a grey and a chestnut was almost finished when Richard's daughter, Pippa, appeared with a tray of tea and biscuits for us. Why wasn't she in a padded jacket like any sensible equestrian? Why wasn't her hair in a plait? I'd once lost sleep over her, but she seemed fake to me now, airbrushed. 'Not that one,' she said, peeling strands of hair from her lip gloss. 'That's Jay's.'

I looked up at her. 'Jay?' She nodded. 'Jay who used to work for Mervyn Slack?'

'Yes.' Jennings had come up behind me. 'He seems to have had a run of bad luck lately,' he said, lifting a mug from the tray, 'so I've given him a break.'

I was delighted at the change in Jay's luck. 'He's a good jockey.'

'Oh, he's not riding for me,' Jennings smiled. 'He's cutting down the tree.'

Stanley's biscuit came to a sudden halt on its way to his mouth. 'Is that him with the chain-saw?' Jennings nodded and dunked a biscuit. 'Are you off your head? If that lad loses any more body parts, he'll favour a bastard tortoise.'

'He seemed to know what he was doing,' Jennings assured us. 'He's done a course.' Jay had seemed to know what he was doing driving wagons, operating tractors and moving cows. 'He says, I won't even know he's been.'

I hadn't seen Jay since he'd left his front teeth on his Uncle Brian's dairy farm, so I offered to take his brew to him. Walking slowly, so as not to spill the tea I rounded the back of Jennings' Georgian mansion. With the east wind licking at my face I turned the corner of a laurel hedge, to be faced with the Palladian grandeur of Jennings' home. I paused to take it in and whilst I was gazing on its finials, pediments and symmetry, Stanley dropped out of a jog at my shoulder. 'How the other half lives – eh?' he said, taking in the mathematical proportions of the rear elevation of Jennings' home. 'I've just come for a nosey.' We walked on, Stanley gazing and craning at splendour beyond the scope of Bling Manor and the growl of the chain-saw growing louder.

The sandy path took us round the corner of the mansion to where a large tree was overhanging the kitchen garden wall. It was blocking the light from an impressive Victorian glass-house and brushing it when it stooped in the wind. Jay's orange safety helmet was visible near the top of the tree. He was wearing a face guard and ear protection, he was roped like a climber and his chain-saw was clipped to his safety harness. It all looked reassuringly professional. Jay's feet were braced on the tree trunk and a rope was taking his weight so that both his hands were free to work. The sound was of an oversized wasp as it chomped through branches; every now and then a bough whumfed its descent to the grass on the other side of the wall. Perhaps he'd found a job he was cut out for.

We passed through the open gate of the walled garden and called Jay's name but our voices couldn't penetrate his ear defenders. Stanley put his fingers to his lips and ripped a piercing whistle. Jay worked on. Stanley bent and picked up a broken branch. It was about the length of a ruler and the width of my forearm. He lobbed it with the strength of an Olympian. It hit Jay between the shoulder blades. Jay swung round – and his chain-saw sliced his safety rope. With his brace gone, Jay lurched backwards. He grabbed for the tree but the weight of the falling chain-saw was yanking him upside down. Thankfully, the motor cut, but that meant we heard Jay's anguished shouts as his bones banged on the branches. I crouched into my shoulders at the noise. Then his head hit a bough. It flipped him like a rag doll. Rope was licking and snagging behind him. It tangled with his chain-saw. *Thank God*, I breathed. His belly bounced on a branch. I was taking my hand from my face when he was bashing through the branches again! The gap was closing between his head and the wall. I covered my eyes. There came a splitting crash, a clattering rush, a groan. There were four faint clinks, and then silence.

I lowered my hand. Jay's head had exploded the glass-house roof. He was dangling upside down, six feet from a skull smash. His rope tail had swung round a branch, and tangled with his chain-saw. Branches were creaking above him. I watched him rotate a half circle above the flag floor. 'Hiya,' he said, and began rotating back again. 'Good job they've planted out, eh? Else I might have made a right mess.' I looked up at the hole in the glass-house roof, and at the chain-saw dangling from the branch of the battered tree, then down at the glass gravelled floor. 'It wouldn't do to fuck up entirely on my first tree surgeon job, would it?' I watched him turn; it was as mesmerising as a tropical fish tank. 'How come you two are here anyway?'

'We've fetched you a brew,' Stanley said.

Chapter 29

I'd agreed to help Stanley prepare Dirk's homecoming dinner but when I arrived at Bling Manor, Jade was frying chicken legs and Ewan was topping and tailing fresh shrimps. I looked over Jade's shoulder. 'I thought we were having spag bol.'

'So did Stanley,' she quipped. Stanley, who was leaning against the kitchen units with his arms folded, rolled his eyes. 'We're having paella.'

'He'll be sick o' pie-ella,' Stanley countered. 'He'll be ready for summat Yorkshire in him.'

The back door opened and in walked Mandy, flapping the rain off her umbrella and sprinkling the tiles with raindrops, Stanley groaned and went for a mop.

'How's spaghetti Bolognese Yorkshire?' Jade demanded.

'Spaghetti Bolannyessa,' Mandy pronounced before she'd even got her coat off. 'That's how they say it.'

'Here we go,' Stanley said, mopping the wet tiles, '"Travels wi' Mandy", Episode Three.'

'You want to broaden your horizons,' she told Stanley. 'There's more to life than Yorkshire.'

'It's God's own county,' Stanley asserted and Mandy tutted loudly.

'What can I do?' she asked Jade. Jade nodded at a translucent plastic bag on the work top. '

'You could slice those kiwi fruit.'

'Kiwi?' Stanley repeated. 'That's bloody New Zealand!' Mandy followed Jade's instructions whilst Lucky worked the floor between them like an anteater. The kiwi fruit were to top a crème pâtissière tart that I was instructed to take from the fridge, where it had been chilling beside a dish of homemade pâté.

Redundant in his own kitchen, Stanley lifted his weight off the units. 'Well,' he said, 'if I look hard enough, I might be able to find some cricket being played somewhere in the world.'

'If you're going in there, lay the table,' Jade ordered, like it was her house. Stanley fished a handful of cutlery from the drawer, and meekly did as he was told.

'Where did you learn to cook?' I asked Jade and she looked up from weighing rice.

'A book!' she said. Mandy reached into a Tesco bag she'd fetched and lifted out a bottle of Sauvignon Blanc. 'Here,' she said. 'Get that open. Oil the wheels while we work.'

Jade had us all so busy that by the time Dirk and Maria bustled through the French doors, I'd almost forgotten why we were cooking. Jade slipped off her apron and was easing little Carlos from Dirk's arms whilst still asking permission. I caught a glimpse of a cushion cheek and black hair as Jade swooped away with him, enraptured. 'Watch the pan,' she told Ewan without taking her eyes off the infant. Ewan cut short his greeting and picked up the wooden spoon. Lucky wagged and greeted, and Stanley emerged in his stockinged feet. He back-patted and kissed, and I noted that they'd arrived with far more luggage than they'd left with. I was releasing Maria from a homecoming hug when Millie arrived and added our wrapped gift to the pile of paraphernalia.

Despite Jade's preoccupation, we were soon at the dining room table before plates of French toast and pâté, and Carlos was back in his baby seat. 'So,' Stanley asked as he scraped a curl of butter on his toast. 'How long do I have the pleasure for?' Dirk looked at Maria. 'When's your flight booked for?' Stanley clarified. There was a beat of silence then they both spoke together.

'I'm booking it tomorrow ...'

'We haven't decided ...' They locked eyes again, and Dirk spoke alone.

'Maria wants us to move to Madrid.' The chink of knives on china and the crunch of French toast filled the dining room.

'Madrid,' Mandy repeated, dreamily. 'The Prado. The Grand Via.'

Stanley glared at her. 'She knows! She were born there!'

The baby niggled and Jade reached across and stroked his soft head.

'Carlos is Espanish,' Maria said without raising her eyes from her plate.

'He is also South African,' Dirk answered quietly, and I had a sense that this was the refrain of a well-rehearsed argument.

'What a choice though, eh?' Mandy mused, filling her glass. 'The plains and game of the Transvaal, or the culture and sophistication of Madrid.' She looked up. 'For me, it were Pudsey or else Bradford.'

Jade stood and began lifting empty plates from the table.

Millie tried to lighten the mood. 'What's for mains?'

'Paella,' Jade almost whispered, and Dirk's eyes rolled skywards. 'Sorry,' she added.

'No, no!' Maria answered. 'Is bery thoughtful.' Millie feigned interest in Carlos and Ewan scuttled to his feet to help Jade. The rest of us sat in silence.

Mandy tried to resuscitate the conversation. 'T'best paella I ever had were on a beach on t'Costa del Sol,' she said. 'T'prawns in it were this size,' and she demonstrated with her thumb and forefinger.

'Can we just drop it wi' "Round the World Wi' Mandy Ackroyd"?' Stanley asked, but his words rolled off Mandy like water off a duck's back. When the paella arrived, she enthused again. 'It looks good does this, love.'

Stanley took a mouthful. 'Aye, it is. She's a keeper, this one, Dolloper.' Ewan managed a weak smile but the awkwardness persisted. 'I knew she'd be a good cook!' Stanley went on. 'You on'y need to look at t'size of her to know that!' The awkwardness stretched. It shivered. Even Maria raised her head. 'What?' he protested through a mouthful of saffron rice. 'It's a compliment!'

'Well, let's hope you never insult her,' Millie quipped.

'I'm just saying, I can see what Ewan sees in her!' He turned to Jade. 'You're not offended, are you, love?' Jade looked as though she was still making her mind up.

'Ewan sees what the rest of us see,' Millie said. 'A beautiful, talented, independent woman who doesn't conform to stereotypes of femininity.'

'Aye,' Stanley agreed. 'And she's a belting cook who's good wi' t'babby.' He waved his fork at Ewan. 'You want to get a ring on that before it's somebody else who's guzzling her pie-ella down.'

Millie was slowly shaking her head.

'It's fair dos,' Jade said at last. 'I could do wi' droppin' a bit o' timber.'

Maria and Ewan rushed in quickly to tell her she looked lovely and Jade reached for a crust of bread to mop up her shrimp juices.

Maria filled the next silence with an explanation of how different regions have their own paella recipes, and Mandy helped her by describing a dish of suckling pig she'd eaten in Segovia.

Ewan shook his head. 'Is there anywhere you've not been, Mandy?'

'I've told you what you want to do,' she reminded him with a stab of her fork. 'Cruise ships.'

'And how many horses'll need shoeing on a cruise ship?' Stanley demanded of her.

She tapped the side of her nose. 'He can do more than shoe horses, this lad.'

I was relieved when Dirk finally moved the conversation on

to safe ground. 'Have you had an estimate on the Porsche?'

Stanley shook his head. 'I've not got round to it yet.'

Dirk speared a circle of squid and looked at Ewan. 'Would your Lee have a look at it for him?'

'No, he bloody wouldn't!' Stanley spat through a mouthful of chicken. 'Have you seen what he's done to t'Best Van!'

'You wanted it in a hurry!' Ewan protested. 'And you know our Lee won't rip you off.'

'Aye, and I know it'll look like a bastard bin wagon when I get it back.'

'I've a baby to pay for,' Dirk told him and Stanley said he should have thought of that before he jumped into The Best Van with no bastard insurance and Dirk reminded him that it had been a fucking emergency in case he hadn't noticed and Carlos started to cry.

Jade swept the child from the baby seat and insisted that Maria should finish her meal. She paced the floor until the baby's cries had softened to a snuffle and Maria complimented her baby-whispering and served up the crème pâtissière tart.

'You're selling the bloody thing anyway,' Dirk grumbled as he poured cream onto the gleaming confection on his plate.

'I'm selling a Porsche,' Stanley said. 'Not a cut-and-shut, welded up out o' biscuit tins and bits of a scrapped Leyland bus!'

Ewan rolled his eyes.

'If you tell him you don't want him to use bus parts in it, our Lee won't use bus parts.'

'I want white *Porsche* parts,' Stanley insisted. '*White.*'

'He'll do it!'

'Well,' Millie remarked as she steered the Vectra onto Eckersley moor twenty minutes later. 'I didn't expect that.'

'Neither did Stanley,' I said. 'In fact, I'd say the whole night went off the rails – again.' Millie giggled as she took a bend in the road. 'And what the heck's Dirk going to do in

Madrid?' Millie didn't answer me, and I gazed at the black moor. I couldn't imagine another job. No office décor would equal a purple carpet of heather fading into the backdrop of the fells; no warehouse muzak would bubble Dirk's ears like the wriggling trill of a skylark, and no strip-lit ceiling would swoop crows over him like wind-blown wrappers.

Chapter 30

The following morning, Stanley dragged the forge's only chair – the plastic sort you see in schools – towards him and slowly lowered his backside onto it. I thought he was hungover, but he wiped a hand over his ashen face, and signalled me to sit too. I lowered myself to a box of shoes that bore the imprint of my buttocks and waited; my throat thickening. After twenty seconds of silence that were more intrusive than hammer blows he spoke. 'The thing is, Posh Lad.' He wiped his hand over his chin so his bristles hissed. 'I've been having to rethink since I went to court.' The coals sucked on the fire and sang. 'What wi' Lynne taking me for every penny, Mervyn looking like he's goin' under and losing clients all o'er t'shop, I'm going to have to make some changes.'

I shifted on the box of shoes. Stanley straightened. He placed his hands on his knees as if bracing himself, then he met my eye. 'It turns out, Posh Lad, you're a luxury I can't afford.' I felt my stomach sink. A void was opening where my future used to be. I was watching it widen.

'I won't leave you high and dry,' Stanley was saying. 'I've been talking to Moneybags. He weren't thinking o' taking another apprentice on, but seein' as how he knows your mother and he thinks you're a nice lad ...' Stanley's words were lost in the wilderness of my shock. The only sound I was listening to was Lucky's snoring. Stanley looked down at his clasped hands. 'You know I'd keep you on if I could, Posh Lad.' I nodded. Black and yellow fleeces, buckwheat lunches and whale music were stuffing my imagination to suffocation. Tears were puddling under my lower lids.

Stanley swallowed. 'It's not how I saw it panning out.' He stood up. 'I'll put t'kettle on.' He took two strides and then stopped at my side and clasped my shoulder. 'We can still meet up in t'Fleece of a Friday.' I nodded and a tear struck my jeans with a flat slap. 'Give o'er,' Stanley said. 'Moneybags isn't that bad.' I slashed at my eyes with my fingers and Stanley scrubbed my hair.

Ewan bowled in. He looked at us and stopped in his tracks. 'What's up?' I couldn't answer.

Stanley put a hand back on my shoulder. 'He's going to be finishing his apprenticeship off wi' Michael Morrison.'

Ewan dropped his tool-box. 'Why?' He flung his glance between us in search of an answer. 'What's he done?'

'Nowt! I can't afford to pay him.'

'What? You can't even afford fuck all?' Ewan argued.

'He's a second year! He can't even *do* fuck all!' Stanley explained, then he remembered his contrition. 'I'm not doing this cos I want to, Dolloper. Wages are my biggest outlay.'

'Do you nick the steel then?'

Stanley's composure finally folded. 'You know shit all about it!' he shouted. 'And you'll be the next if you keep on giving me your fuckin' lip!' He was striding towards the house now, away from his guilt and his sadness.

Ewan bellowed after him. 'Go on then! Run away! Like you always do when you know you're wrong!'

'I'm going for piss!'

'I'd like to see how long your business'd last wi' out me!' Ewan turned to me. 'Are you all right, mate?'

'What do you think?' Bling Manor's back door slammed.

I rang my mother. 'You'll be fine with Michael Morrison,' she said. 'You'll learn a lot.' I'd wanted more understanding but Michael Morrison was her farrier, and she liked him. She and my dad had never approved of Stanley. They'd never said so, but I'd seen the looks that passed between them when I mentioned him. Stanley was, after all, an acquired taste.

Stanley was issuing instructions for our trip to Mervyn's when Dirk walked into the forge in his stockinged feet. 'I'll come!' he announced. 'Give me a minute to get some shoes on,' and whilst Stanley issued death threats to be carried out in the event that Lucky so much as sniffed fresh air, we piled into The Old Van. Dirk dashed down the back steps stuffing one arm into a Musto jacket. The Old Van lurched when he flung himself into the passenger seat. He slammed the door. 'Drive, man!' Ewan turned the key. 'Quick! Before Maria spots me!' The Old Van blundered into the traffic on Hathersage Road and Lucky crawled from my knee to Dirk's. She wagged her tail and circled until she found a spot to curl on. Dirk stroked her silken pelt. We wound silently out of Hathersage and through Fowlden. I knew why Ewan was quiet and I suspected Dirk was questioning his decision to do a runner. 'Look,' Ewan said in response to a sigh from me that rattled the passenger window. 'Another three years and you'll have DipWCF after your name, no matter who your boss is.' My eyes travelled to a kestrel as it rode the updraughts of the moor.

'You'll be fine,' Dirk said. I looked at him now. 'Stanley told me last night, when you'd gone,' he admitted guiltily. I barked a bitter laugh. 'He could hardly tell you in between insulting Jade and criticising Ewan's brother, could he?' The bird swooped a sharp arc, like a skater. 'How is Jade?' he asked.

'She's fine,' Ewan answered. 'She takes no notice of Stanley.'

'He's right, you know,' Dirk added. 'About her being a great girl.' Ewan's head jerked sideways.

'I know that.' The kestrel was hovering again, straining to hold its position in the sky. 'I don't need telling.' The kestrel plunged. I thought of a falling arrow.

Rochelle smirked as we survived our evacuation of the van. 'If that had been anybody else's Jack Russell, my dad would have shot it,' she said as Dirk attached Lucky's lead to the inside door handle.

'You're brave,' she said to Dirk.

He answered without looking at her. 'I've wrestled fucking crocodiles, lady. This luttle shut's no bother.'

Rochelle grunted. 'I'm used to working dogs. Not pets.'

'What's that spaniel then?' I challenged her. 'What does that do?'

'It's a sniffer dog,' she said. I laughed out loud at the thought. 'Anyway,' she said, holding out a hand to Dirk, 'I'm Rochelle, and I can't stand here all morning. They've all to go on the walker.'

'Looks like he works you hard!' Dirk answered, introducing himself.

Rochelle was appraising him from the cowboy boots up. 'Shame you're too big to ride for me.' Ewan chuckled. 'You're not though,' Rochelle said, pulling on her glove.

It was my turn to laugh. 'He's never so much as sat on a Bridlington donkey!'

She was holding Ewan's eye. 'I could teach you, if you want.'

'Never fancied it,' he said, looking at the stony surface of the car-park. '*He* rides though.'

I held up my ten fingers. 'Hey, I don't see enough of Millie as it is!'

'Suit yourself.' Rochelle walked two strides then looked over her shoulder at Ewan.

'I'll brew up in a bit.'

'Don't worry about it,' I said. 'We can see you're busy.'

'We have to keep the farriers happy!' She winked as she walked away.

I lit the forge and laid out the tools. Silent Shannon was already waiting in a stall. I looked at her; lean, ripped and almost in her full summer coat. 'That's a bugger,' I said to Ewan. 'The gallops frozen in the last few weeks before the Grand National,' but Ewan was still staring into the space Rochelle had left.

I passed a hand over Ewan's face. Ewan bent mechanically and picked up a foot. 'And don't prick this,' I said. Ewan's look swung at me like a scimitar. 'Well, you never know!' I protested. 'And it's aimed at the Grand National!'

There was a harrumph from behind me. 'If it runs.' I turned to see Mervyn, flat capped pulled low, his hands deep in the pockets of his greasy waxed jacket.

'When's the ballot?' I asked him. His eyes were rheumy with cold and a clear bead was balanced between his nostrils.

'Bugger the ballot,' he answered. 'How can I train with the gallops like rock?' He breathed on his hands.

'They'll all be in t'same boat though, won't they?' Ewan pointed out.

Mervyn paused in the blowing of his hands. 'Oh, aye, cos Lambourne's at 1,300 feet an' all in't it?'

'Can't you harrow the gallops?' I asked as Mervyn turned away.

'Wi' what? T'tractor's frozen up!'

'Before you go,' I called after him, 'Stanley says it'll be two hundred and ten for this morning's three.'

Mervyn rotated his upper body, slowly. 'I've already given him that.'

'Oh.' My eyes were still on his.

'He must have forgotten,' Mervyn said, and turned away again. I flashed a worried look at Ewan.

'Are you sure?' Ewan asked, pointedly. 'Because if you've got it wrong, we're the ones who'll cop it.'

Mervyn had progressed further down the aisle of the American barn but he turned round again. 'Course I'm bloody sure! I wouldn't forget two hundred and ten quid!'

'Neither would Stanley,' Ewan said, but Mervyn was striding away again, tightening his scarf in readiness for the unseasonal Siberian blast, 'Shit.' Ewan breathed.

Dirk slapped him between the shoulder blades. 'Don't worry, I'll back you up,' but Ewan was shaking his head.

'If Mervyn's going under, Stanley's going under with him.' Ewan pointed at Mervyn's receding back. 'That's forty per cent of Stanley's business.'

I was adding the information to the list of logical reasons that I was better off working for Moneybags when my phone rang. It was Stanley. 'I'll see you in The Fleece. Six o'clock,' he stated. 'Moneybags is coming.' It was a summons, not an invitation.

'Stanley,' I said before he could hang up. 'Mervyn says he's given you that two hundred and ten.'

'Has he buggery!' he bellowed. 'Put him on!'

'He's gone.' Stanley's sigh threatened my ear drum.

'I'll ring him.'

'He'll never pick up for Stanley,' Ewan said when I'd hung up.

Dirk grimaced and sucked air through a portcullis of teeth. 'Man, there's no way I'll be getting out tonight.'

'Perhaps you shouldn't have left her on her own this morning,' I said quietly, but Dirk was already answering.

'I swear if I hear any more about Madrid I'll beat myself to death with her fucking castanets.'

'How will you earn money?' Ewan asked.

'You tell me, man! I can't even speak the lingo!'

Moneybags Morrison was standing with Stanley at the bar of The Fleece. 'Bloody hell!' Stanley sneered at Ewan. 'Does he go to t'bog wi' you an' all?'

'Evening, Stanley,' Ewan smiled, like Stanley hadn't spoken. 'Evening, Michael.'

'I suppose you'll be wanting a half o' blonde?' Stanley said, jiggling the coins on his palm. We both nodded.

Moneybags turned to me. 'Aren't you driving?'

'Bloody 'ell, Michael, they can have a half!' Stanley insisted. 'I'll bet you take the bangs out o' Christmas crackers an' all, don't you?'

Moneybags lifted his lime and soda to his lips. 'I never think it's worth the risk.'

'What? Christmas crackers, or halves o' blonde?' Moneybags was silent. Stanley pocketed his change and Ewan chose this moment to tell him that Mervyn hadn't come back with the money. I saw Stanley's Adam's apple bounce. It was masterful timing from Ewan. 'No,' Stanley said, as if it hardly mattered. 'He didn't pick up.' He took a steadying gulp of his beer. 'I'll get it next time,' then turned to me. 'Michael says he'll take you on, as soon as t'paperwork's sorted.'

I grunted a subdued thanks and Moneybags reached for a bundle of A4 sheets that were at his elbow on the bar.

'I'd rather blacksmith, these days to be honest,' he said. 'Less risky; but seeing as I know your mother ...'

'Oh, Posh Lad's learnt a lot from his mother,' Stanley assured him. 'He'll be grand wi' your tricky ones,' but Moneybags wasn't listening.

'I've started my own website, you know: *www.hotncrafty.*' Ewan smirked behind his half-pint glass. 'You want to have a look at it. There's sconces, fancy door handles, weathervanes. I've had a few orders already.' Stanley pretended interest. I sipped at my beer and Ewan glazed over. Either Moneybags had bored him already with his projections for the effects of Brexit on the price of steel, or the horrors of life as Stanley's sole employee had started to play on his mind.

Moneybags drained his lime and soda and handed me the bundle of papers. 'I'll be off then,' he said. 'I'm looking forward to working with you.' He shook hands with Stanley, raised his hand to Ewan and headed for the doors. The pub itself seemed to drop its shoulders when he disappeared behind the etched glass.

'*Hot and Crafty*,' Ewan sneered as Moneybags' shape passed the window. 'It sounds like a pick-pocketing prostitute.' I snorted into my beer.

'Listen here, Dolloper,' Stanley said, mildly. 'We're going to have to get on with Moneybags if Posh Lad's workin' for him.'

'If Posh Lad's working for him,' Ewan observed. 'It's me and you that are going to have to get on.'

Chapter 31

The Old Van was winding its way down the grey ribbon of the fell road and Ewan was grunting into Stanley's mobile phone. He ended the call and dropped the phone back onto the dash-board. 'New client?' Stanley asked, hopefully.

'Nah.' Ewan was shaking his head. 'There's bloke coming to see your Porsche.' Stanley swung round. 'What? Now?'

'We'll be home in twenty minutes, won't we?'

'I wanted to get it fixed first!'

'Let *him* get it fixed!' Ewan advised. Stanley told him to mind his own bastard business, but his ire washed over Ewan as usual. He was watching roadside daffodils flatten in the back draught of the van.

Stanley pulled The Old Van to the kerb behind the battered Porsche. A man in a sharp navy-blue suit was examining the tailgate. At the slam of the van door he looked over his shoulder and I recognised him instantly. I elbowed Ewan. 'Oh, fuck,' Ewan breathed.

Stanley was striding towards him pocketing his keys. When he looked up a cryogenic blast swept Hathersage Road and both men froze. Rods of blue light were all but beaming from their eye sockets. Ewan lowered the van window. Stanley had gathered himself. 'Come for some more, have you?'

'You!' the other man said. He pointed at the Porsche's crumpled tailgate. 'I see you've had your comeuppance.'

Stanley took a step towards him. 'Have you though? Were

you stuck in t'middle o' t'A56 for long enough?' The man backed up a step.

'You're a bloody maniac.' He began hurrying towards his car which was parked in front of The Fleece. 'I'm phoning the police now I know where you live!' he shouted with his hand on the door of his BMW.

'You do that!' Stanley yelled back. 'In fact, I've a good mind to ring them myself!' The BMW's door slammed. 'Cos the police'll be very interested in your road rage!' It sped off.

Ewan stepped out of the van. 'You see!' Stanley finger-wagged him. 'That's why you shouldn't go making executive decisions!' It made no sense, but Stanley was already heading down Bling Manor's drive. Lucky came to meet him, bouncing and barking. It was only when Dirk and Maria acted as doggy day-care that I realised how much daily stress Lucky generated. I twisted that realisation into another positive of working for Moneybags Morrison. It was a conscious act of self-consolation.

Ewan and I had turned for the forge when Maria opened the back door of Bling Manor and called down the steps, 'Boyce!' she shouted. 'Espanish stew for you!'

Surely she was feeling better if she could make Espanish stew? I took one look at Ewan, another at my Tupperware tub of cheese and pickle sandwiches and turned right round.

The smell swam out through the kitchen door as I opened it and stepped into the comfort and condensation of the kitchen. Maria was dolloping ladle loads of smoky red stew into deep bowls. 'Is bery cold day,' she said without looking up. I took my bowl from her. Chicken legs were sprouting through thick tomato sauce and olives were breaking its surface. Ewan sat beside me looking dubious; he stirred his bowl a bit.

'What are these?' He was pushing at a green olive with his spoon.

'Yust leave what you not like,' she smiled. I took a mouthful to encourage him and before long, Ewan was shovelling down everything but the olives.

Dirk had grunted a greeting from the dining room where he was sitting in front of a laptop with his bowl beside him. Carlos was lying in a Moses basket on the table, waving stumpy arms and kicking his legs in excitement at an invisible show on the ceiling. 'I'm duty farrier at Scorthwaite this afternoon if you fancy a trip out,' Stanley shouted to him. He'd stopped eating to pull a chicken bone from his mouth.

'Sorry!' Dirk answered. 'I'm grounded.'

Stanley looked at Maria for an answer. 'He applying for jobs in Madrid.' That explained Maria's cheeriness.

'What can he do without Spanish?' I asked.

'Armed robber,' Stanley suggested. 'Prostitute.' Maria flicked his bald head with the tea towel.

'He have lessons,' she announced.

Through the open door, I saw Dirk push his hand through his pelt of fair hair. 'There's a job in an English restaurant,' he said, managing to weight his words with equal measures of information and exasperation, thereby satisfying both Maria and us.

'And security job at a nightclub,' Maria added.

'You'd need to talk for that,' I said but Dirk was shaking his head.

'I could just fold my arms and grunt.'

'And is this what you want?' I asked. Dirk spread his hands in a gesture of surrender and Ewan recognised it as a good time to repeat his question to Maria about the ingredients of the stew.

'Fetch t'paperwork,' Stanley said, as we climbed into the van, full of Spanish stew. 'We'll fill it in when we're slack.' It was still in my inside pocket. Duty farrier role isn't a two-man job, but Stanley was trying to be nice to me. Millie was competing Onion at Scorthwaite, and he knew that I'd want to watch her, so he dispatched a grumbling Ewan to shoe Lord Hathersage's hunters.

The smell of saddles, sweat and straw always surged adrenaline through me. It was the scent of competition. Mumma's borrowed three and half tonne wagon was empty on the car-park. Millie must be working Onion in, so I carried on towards the outdoor collecting ring. I must have competed against Millie back in the day; she'd ridden for Macclesfield Pony Club and I'd showjumped for Eckersley and District. I should look through the old photos; see if she's on any. A horse motorbiked the corner of the collecting ring; it soared the poles like a surface to air missile. A handsome grey was cantering round the outside with big, even paces. Its pink crystal browband glittered in the daylight and the rider's long dark plait swung against her shocking pink jacket. It met the fence on a stride, lifted its vast muscled shoulders, arced a perfect bascule and cantered away showing the red warning ribbon in its tail. It was then I saw Flashman Freddie on the opposite rail with a toddler in his arms. The grey was Belinda! He grinned and gave me a thumbs-up. I was following Belinda with my eyes when a bay horse passed so close that it blocked my view. It stopped right in front of me and the rider adjusted her girth. I was craning past it when she spoke. 'Hiya. I hoped Stanley might fetch you.'

'Millie!' I'd almost forgotten I'd been looking for her. I vaulted the rail and held Onion's head for her. She nodded towards Rochelle. 'That grey can jump.'

'That's Belinda!'

'No!' She peered more closely.

'It is! That's Flashman Freddie's daughter.' We watched as Belinda soared one metre thirty.

Millie let out a low whistle. 'Should I just go home?' I laughed, patted Onion's shoulder and reminded her it was all about the taking part. Millie picked up the reins again and I saw Stanley walking towards us with a tray of chips in his hand.

Before I had the chance to tell him who I'd seen, the tannoy crackled the announcement: *Next in is number 32, Rochelle West on Belinda.*

A half bitten chip came to rest between Stanley's teeth. He pulled it out. 'Our Belinda?'

I grinned my affirmation and we turned for the main arena. As we took up our seats a blur of pink and white rollicked in. Belinda flung out a hind leg in a joyous hint at a buck. The weekday crowd, made up mainly of riders, grooms, coaches and their associates rippled a laugh.

Belinda jumped the first with ease and expression. The second and third were no more of a problem. 'What's the prize money?' Stanley asked.

'Dunno,' I said. 'But Millie won't be seeing it.' Belinda cleared a wide oxer and cantered towards the first upright of the triple. She soared it.

'I could throttle that bastard Jack Russell,' Stanley remarked. We watched as Belinda met every fence on a stride, sliced metres off the corners and left all the jumps up.

'But you didn't really want a horse,' I reminded him.

'Missed chances,' he grunted. 'The story o' my bastard life.'

During a clatter of polite applause, Rochelle leant forward and patted the mare's neck. I accepted a chip from Stanley and followed him towards the collecting ring where he stopped in front of the mare he'd owned for an hour and twenty minutes and dipped in his pocket for a polo mint. 'Hey up,' he greeted the horse. 'How's my bonny lass?' Whilst Stanley rubbed the whorl of Belinda's forehead with the heel of his hand, I congratulated Rochelle, but she was looking past me.

'Is Ewan not with you?'

'Nah,' I said. 'He's had to go to Hathersage Hall.' Belinda pushed her big white head onto Stanley's upper arm and he was wrapping his arms about her neck when the tannoy called for the duty farrier to attend the secretary's tent. Stanley sighed, released his grip on Belinda's ear and handed me what was left of his chips. 'You stop here,' he said. 'It won't need two of us.' This really was a swan song of generosity. Rochelle gathered up her reins and walked to where her dad was standing with her daughter. From the corner of my eye I saw Onion clear the practice fence.

Back in the main arena, a fat chestnut lumbered a clear round. After a bay had knocked two down, the tannoy announced *Number 37, Emilia Baker and The Onion.* I was surprised at the bump of nerves that jolted me at the sound of Millie's name and I realised I'd be jumping the course with her.

I counted every stride and floated every airborne moment until Onion's trailing hind leg cost them four faults. I groaned, then I joined in the trickle of applause that overlaid their exit from the ring.

Meanwhile, Stanley had replaced a piebald's front shoe. 'Let's get that paperwork filled in, now your lass has jumped,' he said. I pulled the crumpled transfer form from my inside pocket and stared at it.

Flashman Freddie lowered himself to the bench beside me. He peeled the sticky paper from an ice lolly for his granddaughter and settled her on the bench. I pulled a pen from my back pocket. The ring was being prepared for the jump-off. The child squawked and banged her boots on the bench in fury at bits of paper stuck to her Mini Milk. Freddie ignored her. With my eyes on the transfer form, I registered the progress of the jump-off by the sounds from the scattered crowd. By the time Belinda cantered into the ring, the little girl was quiet. I put down my pen and watched. It was clear from her first stride she'd be the fastest; she just had to leave them up. Flashman Freddie leant forward. The toddler was more interested in her lolly. Her dark curls were mingling with the Mini Milk. Freddie held his breath as Belinda cantered to the first. She floated six inches above it and landed like a gazelle. When Belinda had cleared the last with ease, Flashman Freddie punched the air. Rochelle was doing the same to thin applause. Belinda bucked in triumph. 'You've a bloody good mare, there, Freddie,' Stanley observed.

'Aye,' Freddie countered. 'And you still have your little shit of a Jack Russell, so I'd call that fair.'

I leaned in to Freddie. 'Have you thought of putting her to Argento or Big Star?'

He drew back his neck and looked at me like I'd asked him for a kiss. 'I *have* a stallion; you've seen it.'

'I know that – but a foal off Big Star would be worth a mint.'

Flashman Freddie folded his arms. 'And, you know what, Posh Lad: it won't have clue about that and it'll wrap itself in wire and stick its legs down rabbit holes just the same as one off my stallion.' He held out his hand. 'Shaniqua!' but Shaniqua was dragging the strawberry Mini Milk through her hair, so he scooped her off the bench, took a Mini Milk in the ear, and headed for the collecting ring.

With very little ceremony, the top three horses were award-ed their rosettes. We looked on applauding, as Belinda can-tered her lap of honour. I stuffed the transfer paperwork in its pre-paid envelope and followed Stanley towards the Old Van. He cheered up slightly when he saw the tail lashing histrionics that Freddie and Rochelle were enduring beside their trailer. Shaniqua, was in her pushchair no more than six feet from Belinda's hooves, still absorbed in her Mini Milk.

'Well done, Rochelle!' I shouted. She raised a hand in acknowledgement, then made another attempt at fastening the Velcro on the mare's hind travel boot. 'Would she calm down if you held her for them?' I asked Stanley, but he hadn't stopped walking.

'It's not my bastard horse, is it?'

We stopped at the postbox in Fowlden and I held onto the

envelope for a second before letting it drop. It swooped, then settled with a feathery whoosh.

I really was going to Moneybags Morrison.

I arrived home that night to see a police car parked in the farmyard. Were they in there now, sipping tea from mugs and waiting for the witness to a road rage incident to come home? I took a steadying breath. I stepped from the car already formulating a script. I needed to make sure I informed them of the BMW driver's threatening behaviour before describing Stanley's assault. A horse passed the corner of the arena. Was that Mumma on it? I waited for it to pass again. Yes; it was Mumma. She wouldn't leave them sipping tea on their own. I walked up the slope to the arena.

Anvil Head was swinging along in an easy trot, and two police officers were leaning on the rails; one was wearing black jodhpurs. 'He's still a work in progress,' Mumma was saying, 'but nothing much fazes him.' The jodhpured officer buckled on her riding hat and Mumma asked Anvil Head for canter. It was an even, rhythmic, loping pace. 'Hiya, Will,' Mumma shouted. 'Throw your jacket at us!' I slipped it off, balled it up and next time she passed, I launched it at horse and rider. Anvil Head's loping canter did not break. Mumma asked him to trot, to walk, to halt. He stood; nose parallel with the vertical fence posts, like a show horse. She slid off.

The police officer had to lower the stirrup to mount. With another boost from Mumma, she was in the saddle. 'I can't believe he was a racehorse,' she said as she asked him to trot.

'Neither could Mervyn Slack or Richard Jennings,' I laughed. 'That's why he's here!' The police officer was competent rider. She put him through all three paces before pulling him up against the rail.

'What do you think?' she asked her colleague.

He was nodding. 'He seems solid enough, and he certainly looks the part.'

She slid off him and patted his neck. 'Would you have him back if he didn't make the grade?'

Mumma was nodding. 'I can rehome his type every day.' I found myself wishing I had the time for him.

Chapter 32

It was my last day as apprentice to Stanley Lampitt DipWCF. Curlicues of kettle steam were rising to the rafters and I followed them with my eyes to where the forge's metal chimney met the roof. I'd smashed a sledge-hammer through there once. I looked at the workbench; it was still dented from the devastation. I knew the shape of every soot mark over the fire and the line of the loop of the linisher flex where it obscured the kettle plug.

To mark the occasion, we headed for Peggy's café and a final breakfast sandwich. Peggy's farewell gift was an egg custard tart. 'Here you are, love; a bit o' summat to have wi' your dinner,' she said, folding over the top of a paper bag. The day that followed unfolded as a caricature of my apprenticeship.

By 10 a.m., Lucky had savaged a DPD driver, Ewan had backed The Old Van into a bollard and Stanley had heated the handles of Ewan's tongs in the fire and passed them to him as his revenge. It inflamed my wounds with nostalgia for the casual violence, careless driving and vicious terrier that had patterned my apprenticeship with Stanley.

Our second job was at Mervyn's. I noted, as we drove down the lane that his digger hadn't moved since the frosts. Its arm, resting on the mud of the cratered field, put me in mind of Rodin's *The Thinker*. It was, however, the only stillness at High Scorthwaite.

Silent Shannon had made the draw for the Grand National

and despite the frozen gallops, Mervyn had decided to run her. There was an excitement about the yard, a buzz. The secretary had booked the transporter and Rochelle was issuing orders to polish tack, pull manes and tails and wash travelling rugs. 'You're going to be on t'telly!' Stanley told the black mare as he tied her in the shoeing bay.

'So are your shoes!' Ewan reminded him. 'So make sure you do a smart job.' Stanley flung a mock cuff at his ear. 'What are we doing for lunch?' Ewan asked over hammer blows. 'Effin Elsie's?'

'What about The Fleece?' Stanley suggested.

'It's your call,' Ewan reminded me. 'What do you want to do?' I walked to the barn's open doors to where the gravel was piebald with a thin covering of snow. 'Well?' A million grated diamonds might have been cast on its skin.

'What about a picnic?'

Ewan looked up from under his horse. 'A picnic?'

'It's bloody perishing!' Stanley complained.

'Oh, come on,' I said. 'It's beautiful outside.' Ewan looked out on a tundra of dapples and ripples. The earth was puddled and patched with snow. The sky was china blue. The hawthorn hedge, a negative, white against the mottled moor.

'I'm up for it,' he grinned. 'Let's get some posh grub from Booths.'

'You're mad,' Stanley pronounced.

We finished shoeing. I patted Silent Shannon and told her to stay safe. Stanley took the money owing to him from a grudging Mervyn, and Ewan clapped Ruudi on the shoulders and advised him to come back alive.

Ruudi replied with a thumbs up. 'We win! You put plenty bet!'

'Yea, right,' Ewan laughed.

'What do you reckon?' Stanley asked as we walked away. 'Has it a chance?'

'Anything can win the National,' I said.

Stanley grunted and handed me a fifty-pound note. 'Get some nice picnic stuff wi' that,' he said.

We were standing by the chiller cabinets when a voice turned Ewan's head. 'You again, Grimshaw!' A twinkling Rochelle was pushing a sticky faced toddler in a shopping trolley. Ewan was suddenly pink about the gills. 'We're just buying some lunch,' he stuttered. I could see from Ewan's tongue-tied embarrassment that I'd have to take responsibility for the conversation. *(Have you finished for the day? Who usually minds Shaniqua for you? How do you fancy Ruudi's chances? Hasn't this weather been an unexpected set back? Has Mervyn managed to start the digger?)* Ewan had taken up a giggling game of Peepo with Shaniqua and Shaniqua was clapping her sticky hands in glee. As Rochelle answered my questions, she watched them with a coy twinkle. I wished them a good afternoon then lifted two packs of sushi from the refrigerated unit. 'Ewan!' I ordered. 'Go and pick up some drinks.' Shaniqua waved goodbye and Ewan stared at a row of Irn-Bru. I swiped eight cans of dandelion and burdock off the shelf and flung them into the trolley. Ewan remained in his trance whilst I paid for the picnic, packed a carrier bag and led the way back to The Old Van.

'Who's the kid's dad?' Ewan asked as I clattered the trolley into a row of others.

'I dunno.'

He pushed his hands into his pockets. 'Is he still on the scene?'

'I don't know that either!' He was about to form another question when he met my judging eye. 'Oh, don't be fucking ridiculous!' he barked. Dirk's re-hired Audi was gliding across the tarmac. I pointed at it. Dirk stepped onto the supermarket car-park with a slit-eyed Jack Russell dangling ignominiously from his fist. He held her at arm's length to avert the possibility of damage from delayed car-exit rage.

'Is this a fucking wind-up?' he asked in a cloud of his own breath.

'What?'

'What? A picnic when there's fucking snow on the ground!'

'It's lovely!' I answered.

'There's no way Maria would come,' he told me. 'Not even for you!'

Stanley stepped out of The Old Van. 'Babby'd bloody freeze in this,' he said, then he tossed the keys to Ewan who caught them in a knuckle banging fumble. 'Me n' Dirk'll follow you,' he explained, then he turned to Dirk. 'Chuck t'dog in t'van.'

'How come we get the dog?' Ewan grumbled, but Stanley was already laying out his plans.

'Light forge as soon as you park up, then we've a bit o' warmth.' I wasn't planning to picnic at the roadside like a pensioner.

It was 12.30 when Ewan pulled into a lay-by beside candelabras of sugared reeds. Lucky was wagging perkily on the end of a lead rope, thrilled to be let out of the van and we were halving the picnic when Dirk's Audi pulled in behind us. 'I thought I told you to get that bastard fire lit!' Stanley said, pulling Ewan's Peruvian hat down over his eyes.

'We're not stopping here,' Ewan said and, pushing his hat back up, he climbed the roadside barrier. 'Are you coming?'

I followed him down a hard, narrow path, between clumps of crunching tussocks. 'My dad used to fetch us here in the holidays,' he said as we approached a copse of spindly trees. In the secret centre of them, a glittering beck was weaving, luminous. I imagined Ewan and Lee dabbling in its brackish waters. I'd have been splashing in the pool of Grandad's Lanzarote villa when they were here. I watched the cold light flash off the water and dapple the solid soil with dabs of sunlight. I'd have swapped it for that swimming pool any day. I walked on and a scudding rumble turned my head. Dirk was stumble-running behind me to regain lost balance. He slid into Stanley.

'Whoa!' Stanley shouted as Dirk shouldered him. I side-stepped their trajectory as they lumbered past me. I lowered myself to a slab of millstone grit at the water's edge.

'Get off the table!' Ewan shouted. I'd violated an ancient Grimshaw custom. I stood quickly, I put two packets of sushi and a pack of smoked salmon on the 'table' and spread the carrier bag on the crispy grass. Ewan added dandelion and bird muck (in the ancient Grimshaw tongue), four vanilla slices and two bags of Doritos to the table. Stanley dipped into their carrier bag.

'Sit down,' I urged, like they were at my dinner table.

'I need to keep moving,' Dirk answered and reaching for the dog lead, he set off through the trees with a chicken leg.

'Me too,' Stanley said and he followed him at a jog.

Ewan blew on his fingers. 'To be fair,' he said. 'This is a bit eccentric.'

'More memorable than chips from Effin Elsie's though – eh?' I peeled back the cellophane on a packet of sushi and offered it to Ewan. He looked dubious but he took a maki roll.

'So,' he began, picking at the masago. 'Does Rochelle live with her mam and dad, or what?'

'How do I know?' I said. He dangled the masago over his mouth.

'How old is she?'

'Why don't you just give her a questionnaire?'

'Fucking hell!' he shouted, spitting out masago. 'That's shite!' His nose was crumpled and he was wiping his tongue with his sleeve. He stood, wiped the scatterings of rice from his sweatshirt and reached for his can of dandelion and bird muck.

'You're meant to put it all in your mouth at once!' I laughed, but he said he'd rather eat Stanley's shit, and opened a bag of Doritos. I watched the beck glinting in the watery sunlight. 'So, why all this interest in Rochelle?' Ewan swigged from the dandelion and bird muck can. He was staring at the slabs of farrier winding through the trees; Stanley in a tartan padded shirt and a hat with ear flaps; Dirk in a quilted nylon jacket and a beanie hat. Dirk stooped for a stick which blasted a barrage of barks from the lead-free Lucky. She reared and bounced until Dirk sent it clattering through the trees. 'Well?'

'I hope Lucky doesn't smell those sheep,' Ewan remarked nodding at a pom-pom flock of them, snuffling in the frosted grass beyond the wood.

'Have you forgotten about Jade?' I pressed him. 'You know, big lass, farrier, worships the ground you walk on.'

'Piss off,' Ewan said quietly.

'Who you see is your business …'

'Dead right,' he interrupted.

'But if you're going to mess Jade about …'

'How am I messing Jade about? I've asked a few questions.'

I took another mouthful of sushi. 'I just think you need to think about what you want.'

He looked straight at me. 'No shit, Sherlock.' A roar from Stanley turned my head

He'd broken off a lump of tree and was lumbering after Dirk with it.

'Just don't mess Jade about,' I urged quietly. Dirk was laughing and stumbling and apologising as he ran. Lucky's lust for violence had kept her interested in them and they blundered panting and chuckling into our clearing.

'A toast to Posh Lad,' Dirk said and stooped for the remaining cans of dandelion and bird muck. 'To your future.' It sounded sombre and final. Cans cracked and hissed.

'We'll still be mates,' I said. Dirk reached for a pork pie.

Stanley raised his can. 'To Friday nights in The Fleece!'

'I've got an interview in Madrid on Friday.' Dirk said, through pastry crumbs. 'English restaurant.' He looked as happy about it as I was to be working for Moneybags Morrison.

*

Ewan made sure he was never alone with me that afternoon and at five o'clock, my time as Stanley's apprentice was done. 'Well,' Stanley said as he wiped his blackened face on the cloth that served as tea towel, dish-cloth and manky rag, 'I didn't have high hopes, but you lasted longer than either Fetch-It or Fuck-Wit.'

'Thanks, Stanley,' I said, meeting his eye. 'For everything.'

He clapped me on the back. 'I think you'd have lasted the course if things had been better.'

'I know.'

'Anyway,' he said, dropping the rag back on the sink, 'I've taught you the essentials: you can look after yourself on Cribbs estate and you know how to sup a proper brew.' I nodded, though it would be a redundant skill at Moneybags'. Stanley groped in his pocket and pulled out a fat brown envelope. 'A bit o' summat extra,' he said then he gripped my upper arm with his free hand and squeezed it.

'Thanks,' I repeated, and Stanley gripped my other arm and dragged me to him in an awkward grapple. A hard lump bulged in my throat

'Bloody hell!' Ewan cut in. 'He's only going ten miles.' He banged Stanley away and clapped me in his own hug. 'See you in The Fleece on Friday!' he said.

I nodded. 'And think on what I said.'

Ewan took a deep breath. 'I'm doing nothing but think.'

Stanley narrowed his eyes. 'About what?'

'About how shite it's going to be!' Ewan barked. 'And that's my paring knife you've just dropped in your tool-box!'

Chapter 33

Moneybags Morrison's familiar wrought iron sign was swinging above the door and whale music was spilling into the barrel-vaulted entrance arch of the forge. I pushed the door. It swung freely. There was no sign of Moneybags but the fire was glowing and ironwork bees and beetles were basking on the workbench, each one intricately different. I picked up a newly forged flower. Its petals were open and grooved like a lily's. Seven fine fronds flowed from its centre, curling artfully and ending in stigmas. I turned it over; five sepals were cupping the petals as gently as a baby's hand. I put it down, carefully.

I walked towards the whale music. Behind the barn's internal glass wall, Moneybags was lying flat on his back. 'Michael?' I said. He raised a hand, but not his head. I walked back to the forge and examined the tools hanging neatly on the walls. There were some I'd never seen. I picked up an unfamiliar fork and turned it over. The whale music stopped. I put the fork back. I examined a Frank Rigel loop knife. It filled the palm of my hand and its smooth wooden handle felt like warm silk. 'I was just doing my morning meditation,' Moneybags explained from behind me. He looked down at my hand. 'I only use Frank Rigel's,' he said. 'Anything else is a false economy.' I put it down. A metal cupboard creaked as Moneybags opened it. Two black fleeces were hanging beside two bomber jackets. He reached in and handed me one of each. 'Welcome back,' he said. I put on the fleece and regarded myself in the glass wall. Moneybags Morrison's creature was looking back at me.

Moneybags assumed I was as needful of tuition in trimming, rasping and clenching as I had been in forging, so my work was sound tracked with his unnecessary instructions: *Make sure you've taken enough sole out: take all that toe off: don't leave them edges on: that heel nail doesn't want clenching too tight.* His clients never offered us brews and by lunchtime of the first day, I was dehydrated, head-pecked and bored. 'It'll be more interesting this afternoon,' he assured me. 'We'll be in t'forge.' I turned my back on him so I could roll my eyes.

The afternoons panned out much as they had during my week's placement, except there was less for me to do. I was fetcher, forge feeder and receptionist. 'Hello, Michael Morrison's workshop,' I said, for the fourth time. 'Just a minute, Mrs Callinicos, I'll fetch the diary.' I looked up to see Moneybags' sweat reddened face moving from side to side. He clicked then flicked his fingers at me so I passed him the handset.

'Alice,' he said. 'I'm afraid I'm not covering your area any more, love; I'm trying to focus my business south o' Throstleden … I know … I know. Just wait a minute.' He covered the handset and turned to me. 'Will Stanley go as far as Hoddlesborough?' I nodded; and he spoke into the phone again. 'Stanley Lampitt's taking on new clients, though,' he said, and when he passed me the phone again, I gave her his number. 'Pair of lunatic ex-racers,' Moneybags confided when I'd hung up – and I remembered his gift of Belinda.

Moneybags didn't even have drawings for the steel dragon-fly that was forming under his hammer blows. It was as if the angles, proportions and dimensions were known to the metal which flowed, twisted and curled by wizardry. By the end of the afternoon Moneybags was soot-blacked and sweat-slicked, but he'd crafted a steel dragonfly that looked like it would flit round the forge.

The next day was worse. We were at Lower Mossthwaite Farm. Home. My mother beamed widely when Moneybags' Land Rover Discovery drew onto on our yard with me in the passenger seat. (She'd worn the same grin when I'd read at Beaumont College's leaver's service.) As soon as Moneybags opened the door, she started with the parent stuff: *I hope he's behaving himself. He won't be pedalling his trike too near your forge today, will he?* Moneybags asked me to trim Phoenix. Mumma's face fell. 'Aren't you going to watch him, Michael?'

'I don't need watching,' I argued. 'I've been trimming for nearly six months!'

'He's all right to trim,' Moneybags assured her but she bent over Phoenix's foot and blocked my light just the same. I reminded myself she was a client, and said nothing. I came to a stubborn section of horn. I jerked my wrist and a crescent moon of sole arced a trajectory across the yard. Mumma sucked a sharp breath. Phoenix tossed her head. She tugged her foot from my grasp. I put down my paring knife. 'Mumma!' I said. 'You're making me self-conscious.'

'Sorry.'

'Stanley even lets me nail on!'

Michael looked up. 'Does he? He never said.'

Mumma walked a circle of the yard. Phoenix flicked her tail at a fly. I picked up her foot again.

'You've not done her left fore, you know?' Mumma remarked.

'I know! I'm rasping this one!' She apologised again, but she couldn't stop her eyes from darting to my work.

That afternoon Moneybags fashioned a spider; it was all high legs and small hooked mandibles. I stoked the fire for him and listened to the chirring crescendo of an ascending curlew. I strained to see it through the barn's open arch. The thaw had set in. Lambs that had dithered in the shelter of greasy fleeces were splitting their polyethene jerkins. Blue had blown from the sky and Stanley would be working under the vault of the stony clouds that had swept in from the west.

Turns out that 'be yourself' isn't such great advice after all! See ya all sooner than Maria would like!

Chapter 34

Aintree cameras had wandered into the crowd where scouse girls who'd mistaken it for Ascot were clinging to their pashminas. 'You used to buy bacon that looked like that, do you remember?' Trevor said. His eyes had drifted from the whipped ice-cream stout he was pulling, to the TV screen where goose fleshed girls were dithering in fascinators. There, the Liverpool turf was bright green, but the west wind was slicing straight at them off the Irish Sea.

'I'd forgotten that,' Stanley smiled. 'It had hairs on it sometimes, didn't it?'

The commentator thrust a mic at the blue lips of a chicken skinned lass who stooped off her teetering heels and yelled 'Aquilegia!' The girl next to her shouted 'Whipperting!' No one, it seemed, fancied Silent Shannon. The *Racing Post* had described her as 'a lightly raced long shot', and the *Mirror,* 'a game no-hoper better suited to soft ground'. I knew she could jump; she'd stay the trip and Ruudi Tamm was a talented jockey. I'd have ventured a tenner if she'd not lost that last week of training to the weather.

The double doors banged behind Dirk, who was strolling into the pub with his hands in his pockets. 'I didn't know you were back,' I said, and ordered us two pints of blonde. He rattled his change in his palm.

'Maria's not.' I must have looked alarmed. 'Aw, I couldn't stand another day with the in-laws, man.' Trevor slid a pint at me and Dirk handed over the money. I sipped enough beer to make the glass portable.

'I take it you didn't get the job then?'

Dirk was shaking his head. 'We should be back in South Africa by now!'

'So, what about your South African clients?'

'He's to keep Maria happy first,' Stanley said as he fell into step with us.

Dirk's sigh rattled the optics. 'She says she's looking for a job.'

'Ah, you'll be reyt,' Stanley assured him, ''Osses are 'osses – and you can work anywhere in the world wi' DipWCF after your name.'

'You mean anywhere there are horses.' He took a sip of his beer.

Ewan had been engrossed in the screen, but he suddenly looked at us. 'Is that true?'

'Is what true?' Dirk asked.

'That you can work anywhere in the world wi' DipWCF after your name.'

Dirk nodded, vaguely.

'So, I could work anywhere in the world?'

Dirk's shoulders lifted. '*Ja.*'

'You want to start in Yorkshire,' Stanley suggested. 'Save your bastard plane fare.' Ewan turned away. Stanley had done it again; the rope trick of logic.

On the screen, the runners were entering the paddock. Trevor upped the volume. The Saturday afternoon pub shifted and shuffled as the camera panned across Mervyn. His concession to the occasion had been the omission of the baling-twine belt from his waxed jacket. 'Hey up,' Ewan said as the camera settled on number fourteen, Silent Shannon. She was strolling round the paddock at an even pace, shoulders rippling, black coat gleaming, Rochelle at her side, matching her stride. 'She looks well,' Ewan added.

'So does the horse,' Stanley teased, and Ewan slid him a look of pure poison.

'Your shoes!' I shouted, pointing to the thinnest stripe of silver glinting against the ground.

Trevor turned the sound up again. '... Slack's lightly raced contender from over the Pennines ...' A supportive chunter rumbled the pub. '... remains to be seen if she'll get the trip ...' The camera slid on.

'You've ridden it, haven't you?' a Guinness drinker asked me. 'What do you reckon to it?'

'It was last year,' I said. 'It would have stood more of a chance if the gallops hadn't been frozen. I've only put a couple of quid on it.'

Ewan sipped at his pint.

'I've gone wi' Danny Cook's mount,' the Guinness drinker informed me.

A punter at his shoulder was shaking his head. 'Not worth backing a favourite in the National.'

'I have a system,' a little round gambler confided. The punter waited.

'Are you going to tell us?'

'I always back summat that come fourth last time out.' There was a pulse of silence.

'Why?' he was finally asked.

'Always have done,' he shrugged.

'And you've left your Lamborghini on Hathersage Road, have you?' The crowd laughed.

'I didn't say my system were any good.'

I turned to Ewan. 'Have you had a flutter?'

'Might have,' he smirked.

I hoped his beginner's luck hadn't skewed his good sense. 'You've not gone daft, have you?'

'Let's just say, I'll be buying more than an iPhone 7 if this comes in.'

I raised my eyebrows. 'How much more?' He took a sip of his blonde. 'Are we talking two iPhone 7s, or a house?'

'It's eighty to one,' Stanley reminded me. 'So two iPhone 7 is ...' his eyes read the ceiling for an answer. 'A ten pound stake.' For one so illiterate he was a swift arithmetician.

'What would I want with two more iPhone 7s?' Ewan asked.

'So you've done more?' I whispered.

'Chill,' Ewan answered quietly. 'I won't have to sell a kidney if it loses.' My stomach turned over for him, but the horses were gathering at the start. The camera shot down the course took me back to my own mounted throat-clenched view of the birch fences of the year before when I'd schooled the same mare over the same fences; moss against emerald; stripes on a ribbon. It was a year ago, but the feelings flushed my face again. The starter mounted the podium. The pub nudged and jumbled itself for views of the screen. They were off.

The rumble of hooves on the way to the first shook my ribs as if I was with them. I picked out Ruudi Tamm's yellow silk and fixed on it. 'Go on, Ruudi!' a punter shouted. The horses rose like a Mexican wave, Ruudi's silk cresting it somewhere around the middle. When the last horse's stride hit the turf, I breathed again; they were all safely over the first.

'That's mine,' the little round gambler said, pointing at the back marker. 'Running like a pig.'

The Guinness drinker turned to him. 'Was it fourth last time out?'

'Dunno,' he said. 'I used my other system.'

'What's that?'

'I back a mare.' Wafts of birch avalanched as they took the second. The pub breathed again.

'What's that to do wi' it?' Stanley asked him.

'It's a lass, in't it? So t'lads'll chase a lass.'

'They're geldings,' I pointed out.

'Oh,' he said. 'That's why it's at t'back.'

They cleared the third, and after four fences, forty horses

were still galloping with Silent Shannon somewhere in the middle. I wished Ruudi had taken her out wide. 'You'd have been better on that,' Ewan said, pointing to Ruudi's yellow cap. 'That's a mare.'

'Oh,' the clueless punter said. 'How do you know?' Before Ewan could answer the crowd was laughing.

'Bloody 'ell Dave, you've bigger problems than your betting system if he's to explain that!' Trevor said from behind the bar.

They were approaching Becher's Brook; a faller in front of her could bring her down – but Silent Shannon landed safely to a hiss of '*Yesss*' from Ewan. The canal turn was coming up. I remembered how my stirrups had clashed with Fintan's as I'd taken it straight. Angles crossed and heels clipped. I cringed. Three horses went down. Thirty-seven horses galloped on – and Silent Shannon was one of them! I'd found Ruudi's yellow cap again.

She crossed the Melling Road with only six horses in front of her. Two loose horses had ditched their jockeys and were making the most of their day out. Ruudi would have to watch them. Silent Shannon soared The Chair – but the favourite went down! A groan grumbled to my right. In the long run up to the seventeenth the crowd grew still. Silent Shannon moved up through the field, picking them off, one at a time.

Approaching Becher's for the second time, she was in third. 'Go on, lass,' Ewan whispered. She sailed it. She landed galloping and headed for the Foinavon fence in second place; a loose horse gave her a lead and she landed full of running. Horses were being pulled up behind her, rather than risk a tired jump at Valentines. There was only one horse in her way when she crossed the Melling Road again, and it looked to be flagging. I couldn't hear the commentary now for the roar of the pub. Silent Shannon jumped the next two fences with ease, just behind the leader and when they reached the Elbow, Ruudi pressed the accelerator.

With only one loose horse for company Silent Shannon sailed past her only opposition. No one in the pub was sitting on a chair; everyone was roaring. Some were walloping the air, two were standing on stools. Silent Shannon cantered past the winning post with twenty lengths to spare.

As the camera settled on Mervyn, the shouting stilled a bit. Trevor bellowed for silence. Mervyn was telling a presenter that this was a dream come true, and the presenter remarked that there were tears in Mervyn's eyes. Tears.

Ewan stuffed another pint in my hand.

'It was my turn,' I reminded him.

'This one,' he winked, 'is most definitely on me.'

'Go on,' I said. 'How much did you have on it?'

'A hundred,' he grinned.

'At eighty to one!' I'd nearly choked on my beer. 'That was bloody reckless!'

'That was bloody inspired,' he winked and then nudged me hard. Stanley was approaching.

'Have you won owt, Posh Lad?'

'Hundred and sixty quid,' I confessed.

'What've you won, Dolloper?'

'Enough to buy *three* more iPhones!' Ewan winked, raising his pint glass. 'If I want 'em!'

'Hey!' Dirk called across the bar, to Stanley. 'Your shoes just won the most famous horse race in the world!' and Stanley cheered himself.

Mervyn threw a party the following night. It was a rowdy affair, weaving in and out of the barns to the soundtrack of whatever iPhone a drunken jockey had last slotted in the speaker dock. Dirk was in the swing of it when we arrived, cowboy boots polished and smelling of aftershave. 'First night out since fatherhood!' he announced, snapping open another can. Mervyn was in a Barbour jacket with a zip and wearing the smile that hadn't dropped from his face since Aintree. He approached Stanley with a bundle of banknotes in his hand. 'This'll straighten us up,' he said and began counting the notes into his hand. I'd never seen him smile before when he was handing out money.

'Bloody hell,' Stanley rumbled. 'They're dry!'

'One ten, one twenty,' Mervyn concluded. 'Fresh from t'cash point.'

'Have you stopped using Scorthwaite moor as your safe deposit box, then?' Stanley asked, stuffing the notes into his best jeans.

Mervyn was shaking his head. 'I think that cash must o' rotted away,' he said. 'Still!' The grin was back on his face. 'Seeing as I've owned and trained a National winner, I can set t'paddock straight and chalk it up to experience.'

'And what about your wagon?'

'I can fix my wagon, I can rebuild a terraced house, and I'll still have change for a pie and a pint.'

'New jacket?' I asked.

'Aye,' Mervyn grinned. 'I went to Leeds today.'

By nine o' clock it was impossible to find a jockey or a groom capable of conversation. Ruudi was slumped between hay bales with a grin on his face and Fintan was blundering from guest to guest with a can in each hand, telling them how much he bloody loved them all and a wet-eyed Dirk was showing pictures of Carlos to strangers. Moneybags wouldn't cut me any slack for a hangover, and neither would Millie's boss, so we perched side by side on shaving bales, nursing our drinks. I scanned the revellers. 'Have you seen Ewan?'

Millie lifted her eyebrows and gestured with a thumb towards the feed room. It would be quieter in there, so I stood up. 'With Rochelle,' she explained. I sat down again. 'Come on,' she slid off the bales. 'Introduce me to a Grand National winner.'

Silent Shannon mooched to the fence and lowered her beautiful black head so I could scrub the white star under her forelock. She'd carried me safely round Aintree once and made me look like I could ride a bit. I pulled on her loppy ear and kissed her soft nose. 'You wouldn't think, would you,' Millie mused as she slipped her hand round my waist, 'that only yesterday, she'd run for four miles at thirty-miles-an-hour and jumped sixteen five-foot obstacles.' She reached up to the horse's neck with her free hand. 'She just looks like any other horse.' Rubicon too had wandered over to the fence. He earned a pat on the neck. He'd not won the Grand National, but he was an absolute gentleman to shoe.

By the time we'd wandered back to the barn, two of Millie's vet colleagues had turned up. They regaled us with tales of Mervyn's escapades over the years, including the acceptance of a microlight in lieu of training fees. 'He'd never so much as flown a kite,' Millie's boss was laughing, 'but he insisted on giving it a go! *I'll get the hang of it,* he kept saying.' There were tears in his eyes now. '*I'll get the hang of it!* Like it was a bike!' We waited until he'd caught his breath. 'The head lad had to disable the engine, or he wouldn't have lived to train a Grand National winner!'

'He's always been a nutter,' Millie's other colleague added. 'He was the same as a footballer,' and he recounted the famous headbutt in the match against Uruguay. Their tales entertained us and when I looked at my watch again it was five to midnight. I had a full day ahead with Moneybags and I'd promised to drive Ewan home.

Ewan though, was nowhere to be found. Neither was Rochelle.

Chapter 35

'Is something kicking off?' I asked the police groom. Two big bays were crossing the police stables' yard in breast plates and Perspex visors. Their riders were carrying shields.

She shook her head. 'Remounts,' she explained. 'They're broken to saddle but not fully trained as police horses.' I looked back at them. They were dopey looking war-horse types and one had a long white stocking. I smiled in recognition.

'How are they getting on?'

'Have a look if you want,' she said. 'They're going to put them through their paces now.' I glanced at Moneybags.

'Go on,' he said. 'Ten minutes.'

I entered the indoor school by the pedestrian door and I was suddenly in a fog. It took me a few seconds to realise that there was a smoke machine in the corner. The two horses walked in and a groom rumbled the barn door closed on its runners behind them so the horses were trapped in a haze of grey. I made out two more grooms standing against the back wall. The horses were walking calmly round the outside, side by side, trusting their riders to guide them. There was a count of three, then the grooms stooped and a cacophony ricocheted off the metal roof and boomed into the sand. They'd picked up metal bin lids and were banging them with batons. Anvil Head threw his neck high. The other horse bolted five strides. Anvil Head's quarters swung out, he jogged two paces but he kept moving towards the sound through the mist. The riders circled their horses until they had accepted the noise. It was

Anvil Head who led them back towards the lid-bangers. He hesitated, he backed a stride and then he agreed that he would pass them. I had already put my fingers in my ears but the horses were ignoring the racket. It was time for the lid-bangers to up their game. One banged harder whilst the other two reached in to a dustbin, now visible through the thinning fug. They began pelting the horses with tennis balls. There was a tail swish from Anvil Head and a spook from the other, but within seconds they were tolerating the onslaught, much like I had when I'd signed on with Stanley. I wondered if police horses could be happy in civilian life. Working with Stanley had taught me to discount so many stimuli that Moneybags' employ was sheer boredom.

The groom who'd been holding Moneybags' horse slipped in through the pedestrian door and stood at my shoulder. 'How are they doing?'

'Great,' I said, over the crashing of a bin lid. 'No spills.' The police officers were deflecting tennis balls off their riot shields. 'The one with the white stocking has barely turned a hair.'

'Elland,' she said. 'It's an ex-racehorse. It came with pink Wetherby's papers.'

A tennis ball hit the wall between our heads and I flinched.

As I walked back towards Moneybags, I played with Anvil Head's new name: *Elland*. It was noble. It was Yorkshire. It was no less than he deserved.

Moneybags was forging iron fish scales when the office phone rang. He looked up from the anvil and nodded at it. 'Michael Morrison's forge,' I said brightly. 'Will Harker speaking.'

'Will!' It was Lord Hathersage's familiar plumminess. 'Hoy ahh you?' As we exchanged courteous pleasantries my guts swilled with fear for Stanley's business. He'd shod for Lord Hathersage for twenty years; surely he wouldn't shift his loyalties. I handed the phone to Moneybags and listened to his grunts and agreements. With the phone to his ear he opened his diary, flicked a few pages and wrote.

'New client?' I fished when he'd hung up.

'No,' Moneybags said, 'I wouldn't fancy shoeing his thoroughbreds. He's after me doing a demonstration at his fête.' He looked round the forge. 'I could sell a few knick-knacks.' I cut another rod of steel for him and wondered why Lord Hathersage hadn't asked Stanley instead.

I arrived home that evening to find Dad with the *Daily Telegraph* open on the kitchen table. I wriggled out of my jacket. 'I can't believe you still buy a newspaper.' I flung my Land Rover's keys on the table. 'Think of the trees.'

He looked up. 'I can't believe you still drive a car that starts with a key.'

'Touché,' I conceded.

'And it'll be more greedy than my Audi.' He folded the paper. 'So, have you decided how to invest this inheritance of yours?' I shook my head. 'I'm sure there are lots of green projects, since you're suddenly the eco-warrior.'

'Do we have to do this now,' I sighed. 'I'm knackered.'

Dad was standing up. 'It never is the right time, though, is it, Will? And whilst it's resting in your savings account it's losing value.' I pushed my fingers through my hair. It had dropped discomfort on me, this inheritance. It had re-ordered priorities. It had shuffled responsibilities. It had shifted power. I didn't want to think about it.

'I'm going to get changed,' I said, and as I walked into the lobby I heard the crack of the *Telegraph* as it hit the table.

Wednesday was much like Tuesday, which had been much like Monday and yet again I was bent under a cob. A rumble was rolling in the distance. I looked to my left. Smoke from the shoe Moneybags was fitting was wraithing him in billows. I glanced up at the cob whose right fore I was holding. It was chomping on its hay. A faint vibration hummed in the bones of my feet. My cob snatched at his hay. A hiss overlaid the rumble. Moneybags' cob flicked its ears. Relax, I told myself. Keep working. The noise grew. It surged to the sound of a mechanical sea. Moneybags' cob attended the fly near his ear. The sea smashed. The 8.45 Leeds to London was thrashing its ribbon of reds and greys feet from us. I stood as it lashed past the chain link fence. The sound seethed to a sigh and its yellow scut disappeared into a silver sky. 'If you're going to stop every time a train goes past, we'll be here all morning,' Moneybags said.

'Sorry.'

'I've told you, I don't shoe spooky horses.'

No, I thought, remembering Belinda, again. *You bloody well don't, do you?* How was I supposed to improve if every second horse was a cob? I picked up the foot again. I've nothing against cobs. They are solid, safe animals who don't react to passing trains – but Stanley had me working on polo ponies, racehorses, driving horses, dray horses, Arabs and hunters.

The morning wore wordlessly on. Without Ewan pinging used nails off my backside or Radio Two's 'Top Tenuous' straining my brain power, I had time to percolate the problem of two hundred and twenty thousand unearned pounds that had slipped into my bank account. Ewan's life was simpler. I stood up. The sting of my jealousy and the rasp of my ingratitude had attacked simultaneously. I was not ungrateful for the money. My eyes were on Scorthwaite's heaving wind turbines, their arms churning with slow effort on the horizon. I was bewildered by it. I arched backward to ease my spine.

'Have you finished trimming them feet?' Moneybags demanded.

The knot of nostalgia I felt at the sight of The Best Van on Scorthwaite Livery Yard was twisted with resentment. I watched their slick containment of Lucky and then I strolled over. 'Hey up,' Stanley greeted me as I stepped out of Moneybags' Discovery Commercial.

'I thought you weren't fetching her out with you any more!'

'Dirk's back in Madrid,' Stanley groaned, then he pointed at Ewan. 'And he sulks if I leave her in her crate.'

'Cage,' Ewan corrected him.

'Has he told you what he'd said to Lord Hathersage?' I must have looked nonplussed. 'Go on,' Stanley urged Ewan. 'Tell him what you said to Lord Hathersage.' Lucky's hollow yapping was bouncing the van.

'You tell him,' Ewan shrugged. Stanley wagged his rasp between the two of them.

'We could have had a stand at Hathersage Hall's garden party.' I wasn't following him. 'He's fundraising, isn't he – for his new roof?'

'Is he?'

'*Is he?*' Ewan echoed me. 'He was on the visitor's car-park himself, with a collecting tin!'

I couldn't picture it. 'Lord Hathersage?'

'Lord Hathersage! If you and me rattle a tin in front of strangers, it's begging. If Lord Hathersage does it, it's fundraising – apparently.' The look he slid at Stanley implied it was an old conversation. Ten feet away, Moneybags was methodically unloading the Discovery. I knew I should be helping him.

'Anyway,' Stanley went on. 'He asks Dolloper here, if we fancy renting a stand at his fundraiser to show off a rural craft type o' thing.' He waved his rasp at Ewan. 'Go on. Tell him what you said to him!'

Ewan rolled his eyes. 'I didn't think you'd want to rent a stand. You're always skint!'

'He's the queen's bastard cousin!' Stanley shouted. 'It would have been an honour!' Ewan leant on the van. 'Go on! What did you say?'

Ewan folded his arms. 'I told him to pay for his own fucking roof.'

Stanley slapped a hand on his forehead. Hearing it a second time had extracted none of its shame. Moneybags, who was pretending not to listen had made a neat pile of our tools.

'I don't know why the fuck I sent you there on your own,' Stanley told Ewan and Ewan took his weight off the van.

'Stanley, if your roof leaked, would you expect Lord Hathersage to pay for it?'

Stanley dithered. Sense, snobbery and justice were bottle-necking in him. 'That's not the same!'

'What's the difference then?'

'He's bastard nobility!' Stanley blustered. Ewan barked his laughter and Stanley snatched up a tool-box. Moneybags quietly held out his hand.

'Wrong box, Stan.' Stanley handed it back. 'Sorry, Michael. How many are you doing this morning?'

'Half a dozen,' Stanley answered. 'Up on t'top yard.'

'I've only a couple to do,' Moneybags said and the two far-riers set off side by side. I suspected Moneybags wouldn't be admitting to the phone call he'd taken from Lord Hathersage.

Trapped in the van, Lucky was still barking at top pitch. 'Should I let her out for a minute?' I asked Ewan. Ewan scanned our surroundings.

'Go on,' he said. Like me, he must have concluded that the distant sheep were far enough away. I opened the passenger door and Lucky fired herself at me. She scrabbled at my jeans until I scooped her up and wilfully coated Moneybags' black livery in her adhesive white hairs. Lucky's taut little body thrashed and wriggled as she licked my face.

'Anyway,' I asked Ewan through the dog-lick latherings. 'Where the hell were you on Sunday night?'

'What do you mean?'

'I was supposed to be giving you a lift home after Mervyn's party.' Ewan set a foot stand on the concrete.

'Oh, yeah,' he said, like he'd only just remembered. 'It was a good do though, eh?'

'What the fuck are you playing at, Ewan?'

Ewan sighed. 'I was pissed; she was pissed.'

'So?'

'So, no harm done!'

'I hope not.' Ewan had turned away. 'Because Jade deserves better.'

'I know.'

'In fact, Rochelle deserves better!'

'Just give it a rest, Will.'

'You need to sort this.'

'I know.' Ewan turned away and started unscrewing the valve on the van's gas bottle. 'Shouldn't you be helping Moneybags?'

'I just want to know what's going through your head.' Ewan let his hands fall.

'I don't know.' I stared at him. 'I don't know what I want.' We stood in silence and he returned to the empty gas bottle. 'A "for sale" sign's gone up at Bling Manor.' I leant on the van and exhaled loudly. I remembered the pride Stanley had swelled with when he'd first shown me round that house. Bling Manor, as we'd christened it then, was an over-the-top parody of poor taste. It was vulgar – but it said: *look at me, Stanley Lampitt; born in a caravan, can't read or write, but I've made it.* Bling Manor had stood solid when his wife, his children and his health had deserted him. Who'd have thought I'd miss its marble staircase, shag-pile carpets and remote-controlled curtains? I looked at Stanley's distant slab of a back in a chequered shirt. He looked like a door, standing next to Moneybags.

'Where will you work from?'

'He says he'll rent a lock-up on Cribbs.' Ewan blew out his cheeks. 'There's no escape from fucking Cribbs for me, is there?'

I might have reminded him that qualified farriers can work anywhere in the world, but knowledge of my two hundred and twenty thousand pounds kept me quiet. Ewan was my friend, my mentor, my co-conspirator, but all our differences of family, wealth, education and life experience shone through in high-viz colours again.

'How's he been?' I asked.

'Grumpy,' Ewan said. 'It's not even a laugh now you've gone.' I lifted Lucky to my face for a final fuss. 'Where are you this afternoon?'

'The forge,' I groaned. 'Same as every afternoon. We'll be making a fucking caterpillar. Or a wrought iron frog to whale music.' Ewan burst out laughing. It was a relief to hear it. In the distance, I could see Moneybags tying up a piebald cob.

'I'd better go,' I said. 'See you in The Fleece on Friday.' I passed Lucky back to Ewan – but as he reached for her, an invisible line connecting her to the distant sheep was yanked. She swung like a salmon, slipped, scrambled from my hands and sprinted. Her diminishing dash of white flashed me back to the morning's passing train; it's imperative, its inevitability. Ewan had already gone after her, but he had no chance. Their gap grew with every stride. Fifty yards away, Stanley was already raging and arm flinging, so Ewan had to make it look like he was trying.

'How's it got out?' Stanley thundered on his way back to me. He turned back to Moneybags. 'They never listen to a bastard word I say!'

Lucky was streaking the rutted lane like a comet. Ewan was stumbling behind her, arms pumping, legs pistoning – then he was in the shape of a diver. I blinked. A second earlier he'd been a stick man cartoon, labouring against the muddy ground and now he was in flight. I blinked again and he was splayed; a beached starfish. Lucky was lashing on. One gate separated her from a moorland of sheep.

Moneybags was heading back towards us, his face furrowed. He looked over his shoulder. 'Ewan's not moving,' he observed.

'The lazy shite'd lie there all afternoon!' Stanley answered, then he cupped his hands round his mouth. 'I can see you, Dolloper!'

Moneybags was more concerned. 'Could he have hit his head?'

Stanley shoved his hands in his pockets. 'I'll hit his head if he doesn't get up. I'll kick his bastard arse an' all!'

I'd lost sight of Lucky. The land undulated beyond the gate. Logic told me she'd gone through it, but the sheep were grazing, unconcerned. Ewan drew himself to his knees. He crouched there on the wet ground. 'Get up!' Stanley ordered. 'You're not at Elland Park!' Like me, Ewan was scanning the hillside for Lucky.

A quad bike appeared on his left through a gap in the dry-stone wall. A border collie was at the axle and what could have been a white rag was dangling from the rider's left hand as he steered with his right. The border collie's interest in it and the rag's yelps of protest identified it for us. 'Is this is yours?' he asked, when the quad reached the end of the lane. Lucky was hanging by the scruff, her lips were stretched to a rictus grin and her eyes were dragged to slits. The dog showed no remorse when Stanley took her, only relief that her features had dropped back into place. 'It'll get itself shot, will that,' the farmer warned him, and Stanley, usually so quick with ripostes, just nodded, shoved his dog back in the van and worked on securing her firmly in there.

Ewan, meanwhile had been slogging his way back down the path. Stanley, with his head still in the van, blamed him for letting the dog out, for being too slow to catch her and for being too idle to stand up when he'd fallen – then he turned and saw him. Ewan was mud-caked from boot-lace to hair-root and holding his arms away from his body, like an ape. His face was totally expressionless. Stanley guffawed and spun him. Ewan's back was perfectly clean. His hoof pick was still poking from his pocket.

When Ewan had completed a circle, he spoke. 'I suppose you'll expect me to work like this?'

'You don't get t'afternoon off for being a fuckwit!' Stanley chuckled. A line of mud thickened at the corner of Ewan's mouth; it was the start of a smile.

Moneybags looked uncomfortable. 'Come on, then,' he said with a clap of his hands. 'Let's get these cobs shod then we can get back and finish that ladybird.'

'Whoopee fucking doo,' I mumbled. Ewan smirked through his mud pack and Moneybags pretended he hadn't heard me.

As Stanley and Ewan set off to shoe the hunters on the top yard, their mutual insults lodged like longing in my chest. I followed Moneybags and remembered the stories from my history books of men being dragged to their executions on hurdles.

All that afternoon, my hands hammered and stoked, and *what ifs* found a rhythm in the bang and bounce of my hammer. *What if* I invested in Stanley's business? The possibilities of my two hundred and twenty thousand pounds began curling and snaking about my head. Stanley might be able to keep Bling Manor; Ewan wouldn't have to work out of Cribbs; I'd escape Moneybags. The thoughts wrapped me round like smoke. My dad wouldn't be happy. Ewan might take some persuading – and I'd have to run it past Millie. I dunked a hot iron in water. Its sizzle could have come from my blood. I'd keep some cash back, so I'd still have a mortgage deposit.

Moneybags interrupted my thoughts. 'How's it looking?' he asked, peering over my shoulder.

'A lot better,' I told him. 'A lot, lot better.'

Chapter 36

I could have parked outside The Fleece on Friday, but habit had me pull on the handbrake at the top of Bling Manor's drive. More than forty-eight hours had passed since my epiphany in Moneybags' forge. I stood on the pavement and looked at the empty space which the crumpled Porsche had occupied, and then at the estate agent's board. Investing with Stanley still seemed like a good idea; Millie thought so too. I crossed the road, pushed on the etched glass of the pub's door and breathed the familiar smell of beer, wood and sticky carpet. Stanley was alone at the table nearest the dartboard. He raised his hand then pointed to half a pint of beer gleaming amber in the light. Two men in sweatshirts were playing darts and Bob Entwistle raised his brimming glass at me from a seat by the window.

'No Ewan?' I asked Stanley, as I lifted my half pint from the table and took a swig.

'He'll be a bit yet,' Stanley answered. 'He had six to do at Jennings'.' I winced. 'Turns out, you were more bastard use than I gave you credit for.'

The soft foam of my half pint feathered my lip. Was this my moment?

'Are you going to sit down, or what?' Stanley demanded. I glanced at Bob Entwistle. He had ears like Fylingdales' Early Warning System.

'Shall we sit outside?' He looked at the multi-coloured curtain of plastic strips stirring slightly in the doorway. 'Oh, come on,' I urged him. 'I've been in the forge all afternoon.'

What was laughingly referred to as the Beer Garden was a flagged yard, carpeted with tab ends and furnished with cheap white plastic chairs and tables, so I understood his hesitation.

Stanley unfolded himself and sighed. 'Tell t'Dolloper we're out t'back,' he instructed Bob, then he followed me across the tacky carpet towards a square of fading blue sky that hung above the back yard wall.

Stanley's plastic chair creaked and spread its legs. I swiped an empty crisp packet from the chair opposite, and sat. The spring sky was blooming lilac over Hathersage. It shaded to slate and then to the colour of an airman's jacket, incongruously lined with pink and peach. 'Are you likin' it any better wi' Moneybags, then?' Stanley asked me.

'It's great,' I answered. 'If you like making The Animals of Farthing fucking Wood out of metal.'

Stanley chortled. 'We've missed you, Posh Lad.'

Was this my moment?

'I notice your house is up for sale.'

Stanley stretched out so his chair looked close to splitting. 'End of an era,' he said, sadly.

I played my finger in the dribbles of beer that Stanley's pint had shed. 'Stanley, have you ever thought of taking on an investor?'

Stanley rubbed his sandpaper chin so the bristles crackled and rasped under his thumb. 'Who'd want to invest in a farriery business?'

'Another farrier ...' I said vaguely.

'I wouldn't want some know-all bastard farrier telling me what supplier to use.' He snapped to attention. 'Why? Has Moneybags said summat?'

'No,' I laughed. 'He's only interested in blacksmithing. He thinks they're dangerous if they flick their ears.'

'Who's said summat, then?'

'Nobody.'

He shook his head and picked up his pint. 'So what are you bletherin' on about an investor for, you daft bastard?'

'Because, I've inherited some money.'

Stanley gawped at me. 'You?'

I nodded.

'How much?'

'Enough to want to invest it.'

'In my business?'

'Possibly,' I shrugged, like I was Alan Sugar himself.

Stanley took a gulp of his pint. 'How would that work out, then?'

'I dunno. We'd have to think about it.' An amber moon was dangling over the folds of Scorthwaite moor. I watched it, half expecting it to drift off like a balloon.

'And where would that leave Dolloper?' He'd spoken my biggest worry.

I took a breath that lifted my shoulders. 'I don't know that either.' Stanley was uncharacteristically silent. I fixed my eyes on the thickening moon and he raised his pint glass to his lips again. 'If you think you might be interested,' I said quietly, 'I'll have a look at your books.'

Stanley's pint came to a halt on its way to the table. 'You'll do what?'

'I'll look at your books, so I can see how your business is doing.'

'You'll piss right off!' Stanley said.

'Oh, come on, Stanley! Any investor would want to look at your books,' I reasoned. He banged his glass down.

'You've bloody well worked for me!'

'What's that got to do with it?'

'You see what we take!'

'I don't see what you spend! I don't see the overheads!'

'Fuck off, you uppity little shit!' Indignation had stood Stanley up but the plastic chair had stuck to him and made him duck-arsed so he couldn't storm out. I dragged at the chair. It jerked free, staggering Stanley forwards. He saved himself on the wall of the pub.

'Stanley,' I pleaded, with a garden chair in my hand, 'will you at least think about it?' but he was already heading for the plastic fly curtain. 'I'll be investing that money *somewhere*!' I shouted after him. 'It might as well be with you!'

His answer was a backward flap of his hand as he wafted through the rainbow strips.

The sticky trickle of the settling fly curtain left me alone in The Fleece's back yard. It wasn't yet fully dark, but the one wall light was flickering with moths. I put the chair back on the carpet of tab ends and sat down on it. I was glad I'd not mentioned the idea to my dad.

Ewan breezed into the yard. He was glancing back over his shoulder. 'Was it something you said?' I pictured Stanley, sweeping past Ewan in the pub doorway.

'You know Stanley,' I said vaguely. 'It doesn't take much.'

Ewan looked round the dingy beer garden. 'You've not started smoking have you?'

'Ewan,' I said. 'It's a fucking miracle I've not started on smack.'

Ewan laughed. 'How have you upset him?'

'Oh, it was just an idea I had – but he didn't go for it.'

'Too right he didn't. He's left his pint.' I looked at Stanley's abandoned glass. 'Come on in,' Ewan said. 'It's getting chilly out here, and you can tell me about this idea.'

'No point,' I answered, standing up. 'It's not happening now.'

'Suit yourself,' he said. 'Mine's half a blonde.'

Chapter 37

There were perhaps fifteen horses in the collecting ring at Lofthouse on Sunday evening; some on the right rein, some on the left. A sixty-centimetre oxer had been set up and horses were peeling off at canter, jumping it and re-joining the herd. They were mostly bays and the riders were mostly girls in navy blue jackets, so I was struggling to identify Millie when a vast grey flank interrupted my vision like a shutter: Belinda, in a hot pink saddle cloth and brushing boots. Her ears were pricked, her head was down and her quarters were swinging as she headed towards the practice jump. She and Rochelle had distilled to a pinprick of focus. After three, three-beat footfalls, they were airborne. Belinda's heels showed me two shining shoes and she landed noiselessly. Rochelle sat a self-satisfied landing skip, lifted her hand and waved at me as she rode the corner. Her smile gleamed as brightly as Belinda's crystal browband, then she pointed to the opposite rail where Ewan was standing with Shaniqua in his arms. What the hell was he doing here? He raised his hand. I waved back at him but Onion was approaching the practice jump. Millie's navy jacket flashed its scarlet lining. Onion landed and cantered over to where I was standing by the gate. Millie reached down for the water bottle I was holding and took a swig.

'What do you think?' she asked.

Rochelle, who had stopped beside us, answered for me. 'You could do with having him rounder going in to a fence,' she said. Millie lowered her water bottle and looked at Rochelle.

'Only trying to help,' Rochelle grinned and walked Belinda towards the gate.

Millie followed her with narrowed eyes. 'She shouldn't even be competing at this level. It's a grade A mare.' I said nothing. 'Ewan's here with her, you know?'

I nodded.

'She's sucking him right in.' Applause pitter-pattered from the main arena and a chestnut warmblood trotted past us on its way from the ring.

'*Number fifteen, Rochelle West and Belinda,*' the tannoy announced. Ewan started walking towards the main arena with Shaniqua by the hand. I wished Millie good luck, and caught up with him. 'What're you doing here?' I asked.

'Grooming for Rochelle.'

'Why isn't her dad grooming for her?'

'How do I know?' We'd reached the arena and Ewan slid onto a seat and lifted Shaniqua onto his lap. 'Hey – you know that sniffer dog of Flashman Freddie's?' I nodded. 'It sniffs for banknotes.'

It was as if I'd swallowed ice. I turned to look at him. 'You've not told her what Mervyn's been digging for, have you?' Ewan spread his hands like he couldn't see the problem. I banged my forehead. 'Have you forgotten what her dad does for a living?' Belinda trotted into the ring. Shaniqua shrieked and pointed a finger at her mother.

'You're the one who insists that Flashman Freddie's all right.'

'All right for a criminal!' I exclaimed. 'All right for a bloke who shoots at people!'

Ewan indicated the toddler on his lap, as if she could under-stand me. 'He was shooting at the dog,' he said.

'You weren't there.' He turned his eyes back to Rochelle. 'Anyway, she won't tell her dad.'

'She'd better not,' I said. 'Because if Flashman Freddie finds out there's several grand buried on Scorthwaite moor, every traveller in England'll be up there with a shovel.' The bell rang and Belinda skipped over a blue and white vertical.

'She wants to go up and look for it on a clear night, so I've said I'll help her.' She cleared a green and white oxer.

'At *night*?'

'She doesn't want Mervyn knowing in case he starts asking about the dog.'

My head swung round. 'It's Mervyn's effing money!' My voice had lifted an octave.

'I know! Only that dog – it didn't start off as Flashman Freddie's.'

'You mean it's stolen?'

He watched Belinda fly the water jump. 'And she's worried it doesn't look good – him having a cash sniffing dog.' This was sounding dodgier and dodgier. Belinda soared a black and white double; its presence had barely impeded her canter. Shaniqua clapped her hands.

'And why *does* he have a cash sniffing dog?'

'To help his mates out, she said.'

'His criminal mates, you mean?' Ewan was silent. 'What's happening to you, Ewan? I feel like I don't know you!' Belinda landed clear and Ewan encouraged whooping and clapping from Shaniqua.

'If you're digging on Scorthwaite moor, I'm coming with you,' I said, folding my arms.

Ewan turned to face me. 'I can be trusted, you know.'

'Not at Mervyn's party, you couldn't.'

He stood up, and took Shaniqua's hand. 'We're just friends,' he said, then he reached into his jacket. 'Here. I nearly forgot.' He was handing me a thick, brown A4 envelope. There was nothing written on it; not even my name.

'What's this?'

'A fucking envelope!' he said. 'Stanley sent it,' then he turned away. I watched him disappear through the double doors, stooping to hold Shaniqua's hand, then I put my finger under the flap of the envelope and peered inside. Columns; numbers; lines. Stanley had seen sense! It was a start at least; a step towards my future; a step away from Moneybags Morrison and *The Animals of Farthing Wood*.

Millie and Onion cantered into the ring. I shook off other thoughts and leant forward in my seat. For ninety-seven point four seconds my anxiety could be smothered by concern for Millie's safety. I lifted with her at every jump. They went clear, albeit with less style than Belinda. I joined the thin applause then left the viewing gallery and crossed the lorry park to find them.

A battered trailer and Nissan Navarra were parked beside Mumma's borrowed wagon. I recognised them and groaned. Gifts of clairvoyance couldn't have served me better. The driver's door opened and Sylvia stepped from the Navarra. By the time I'd reached Onion's shoulder she was describing Poppy's latest ailment to Millie who was unsaddling Onion.

'... because foot problems can start in their mouth,' she was saying.

Millie was processing Sylvia's statement as she unbuckled Onion's bridle. 'Where have you heard that, Sylvia?'

'I read it on the internet.'

Millie took a steadying breath. 'The thing with the internet,' she explained, slipping off the bridle and sliding on Onion's headcollar, 'is that anyone can post anything. Did you check the references?'

'It made sense to me,' Sylvia insisted. 'She's had colic and she's had a foot abscess!'

'But have you actually seen any symptoms in her mouth?'

'Ah! – but there won't *be* any symptoms in her mouth!' Sylvia said. 'That's the point! It tracks through their bloodstream to their guts – where it causes colic – and to their feet, then they're lame!' It was like being trapped in the loop of a telephone answering system. I avoided Millie's eye as I took Onion's lead rope.

'She's sound now though, isn't she?' Millie said.

'I'd feel a lot better if you'd have a look in her mouth just the same.'

Millie explained that she didn't have her dental speculum with her, that the light was bad, that Sylvia should ring the practice for an appointment if she was concerned – but Sylvia was already opening up the trailer. 'It won't take you a minute,' she was saying. 'Just a quick look.'

Millie sighed and I led Onion up the ramp of Mumma's wagon. What was Sylvia doing here anyway? It's not like Poppy was a showjumper. Millie followed Sylvia up into the gloom of the trailer, and I could hear their murmurings as I secured Onion to his tie ring and hung up his hay net. By the time I joined them at the jockey door, Millie was withdrawing her hand from Poppy's mouth. 'There's no obvious sign of infection,' she was saying. 'But I can give you something to put in her drinking water, if you want.'

Sylvia brightened at the prospect of medicine. 'Oh! Do you have something with you?'

'Just by chance, I do,' Millie told her. It was news to me that Mumma's wagon was stocked with veterinary pharmaceuticals but I followed her to the cab.

'What's she even doing here?' I hissed.

'There was a showing clinic this afternoon, apparently – so she stayed on.' She reached into the cab and withdrew her outer jacket. She fished in its pocket and with mischief twinkling in her eyes, she took out a small cylindrical bottle; the sort used for blood samples. She checked over her shoulder and from the pocket of the driver's door, she took a bottle of Tropicana apple juice. Masked by the door, Millie carefully tipped the apple juice into the sample bottle. 'Stanley Lampitt might just know a thing or two,' she remarked as she secured the lid. She lifted a pen from the dash-board and turned to me. 'What do you think I should call it?'

I scoured my mind for half-forgotten Beaumont College

Latin. '*Malum Discordiae.*' She raised her eyes, remarked on the pointlessness of a public-school education and handed me the pen. I scrawled on the sticky label and seconds later she was instructing Sylvia to keep it in the fridge and add two to three drops daily to Poppy's drinking water. 'You shouldn't have any problem getting her to take it,' Millie assured her, smiling. 'It tastes of apple.'

Half way down the row of vehicles opposite, Ewan and Rochelle were strapping her floppy limbed daughter into a Land Rover's car seat. They looked like parents. 'Well done,' I called to Rochelle, with a wave. She withdrew her head from the Land Rover and waved back. 'Have a good weekend, Ewan!' I shouted. 'Are you off to see Jade?' He banged his head on the door frame and glared beams of fury at me.

Smirking, I climbed into the cab of Mumma's wagon and drew the brown envelope he'd given me from my inside pocket. 'What's that?' Millie asked from behind the steering wheel.

'That,' I answered, 'is day light.' She glanced at me. 'Stanley's accounts.'

'Well,' she grinned, easing Mumma's wagon out of its parking bay. 'That's good news all round. I was starting to think you'd never invest that money.'

'And I was starting to think you'd never jump a clear round.' She laughed out loud and punched me in the thigh. 'You did brilliantly,' I told her. 'And don't worry; I'll leave some money for a deposit on our house.' She glanced at me. 'We've our future to think about, haven't we?' At the junction with the road, Millie ratcheted on the handbrake, leant across and kissed me on the cheek.

'I'm glad you think so,' she said.

Maria's got a second interview. Hospital Universitario. Guess I'd better learn to use the washing machine.

Chapter 38

Stanley's accounts on the front seat seemed as heavy as a passenger. I pulled up on the pea gravel drive of Grandad's house and walked to the door of his imposing Edwardian detached. The black paint needed touching up and there was moss between the paving stones of the path; tell-tale signs, my dad said, that Grandad was 'letting things go'.

Grandad agreed. 'We pass this way but once,' he'd said, 'and I'd rather watch the cricket on Sky than paint the window frames.' It was because Grandad knew what really matters that I was showing him Stanley's accounts.

The heavy door swung back. I wiped my feet on the vestibule mat and pushed the glass door that led to the lobby. Wafts of steamed vegetables and furniture polish coddled me like a blanket. I stepped onto the swirled red carpet which Grandad refused to update ('*It's Axminster,*') and walked to the living room where he was sitting in a high backed wing chair with *The Times* folded open at the crossword page. 'What a lovely day,' he announced, clapping his hands on his knees and smiling broadly. 'Can I get you a drink?' Grandad never meant tea.

'Go on then,' I said. 'Just a small one though.' In the honey pine kitchen, he uncorked a bottle of Tempranillo and glugged two generous measures into crystal glasses. I took a sip.

'Have you eaten?' he asked. 'I've a freezer full of ready meals.' He was already rifling through them. 'There's lamb shank with mint sauce; Tex-Mex barbecued ribs; Moroccan chicken; fish pie ... What about the lamb shank? I've two of those.'

'I don't want to be any trouble, Grandad.'

He craned round the freezer door and looked me in the eye. 'You've not gone veggie, have you?'

'No,' I laughed.

'Then, how's putting two foil trays in the oven a trouble?' I had no answer. 'I get fed up of eating on my own,' he added. So, whilst Grandad put two lamb shanks in the oven, I walked to the adjoining breakfast room and laid Stanley's paperwork out on the table.

Grandad pulled out a chair and sat in front of the papers. 'Dad's been banging on about buying stocks and shares,' I said. 'But I think I'd rather invest in what I know.' Grandad nodded and fished his reading glasses from his shirt pocket.

I tried to read *The Times*, but I was distracted by his every quizzical eyebrow as Grandad scanned, flicked, ran his fingers down columns, cross referenced and rubbed his chin. In the end, I left him to it. I refilled his glass, plonked the plates on the table and eventually, dished up the lamb shanks. 'So, what do you think?'

'The sums are adding up,' he said, rubbing his chin. 'But more money seems to come in during the summer months.'

'That's farriery,' I told him.

He ran a lizard tongue over his lips. 'If it were me, I'd want a more predictable cash flow.' He turned a page. 'Are you expecting it to sustain three qualified farriers?'

'We could take more work on,' I told him. 'And we could expand into horse transport.' Grandad lifted one fuzzy eyebrow. 'But that's just an idea ... for the future ... possibly.'

Grandad balanced his knife and his fork on the edge of his plate and laced his fingers. 'Any investment's a risk, William, you do know that?' The drumbeat of my heart counterpointed the kitchen clock as I nodded. 'But, with the exception of last year ...'

'When he was ill,' I put in.

'Stanley's income looks to have been generally up over the last four years.' Grandad took a forkful of lamb. 'How much were you thinking of putting in?'

I was surprised to find a lump in my throat, and it wasn't from the meat. 'I don't know. I'd take your advice.'

Grandad pushed a bundle of green beans onto his fork. 'Have you considered your relationship with Stanley's other employee?' I bit down on my knuckle. My future relationship with Ewan was compelling me like Swaledales compel Lucky. I'd spent two years fitting in as apprentice farrier; two years dropping H's and going cold-turkey off Earl Grey. Two hundred and twenty thousand pounds could unmask me. Or would it mask me? *Be yourself*, Millie always urged. Who was that though? For two years I'd been finding new colours and corners in my character – but this inheritance had whitewashed me.

'I'll have to talk to him,' I answered.

By midnight we'd finished another bottle of Tempranillo, the carpet was strewn with Wisden's Cricketers' Almanacks, and I was wearing Grandad's spare pyjamas.

In my father's childhood bedroom, I switched off the bedside lamp. Headlight beams swept the ceiling. They sliced light across the void, then darkened it again. I could just suck it up, of course. I could pretend I didn't have the money, finish my apprenticeship with Moneybags then set up on my own in three years' time. I turned onto my side. That would put me in competition with Stanley, though – and with Ewan. They'd need their pay packets more than I would. I punched the pillow. My inheritance was the peripheral flicker of an exit light during a bad film. I wished I couldn't see it. It made me want to escape. I closed my eyes.

Ewan was sitting in an alcove of the trendy gastropub. He was on the edge of his seat thumb scrolling the screen of his mobile phone. He looked up when I neared his table. The sight of him was both welcoming and incongruous – like a pot of Yorkshire Tea in Lanzarote. 'I hope you've a good excuse for dragging me to this posy ponce-hole,' he said. I sat down in front of the half pint that he had waiting for me. The glass was cold and slippery. 'And I hope it isn't about Rochelle,' he said, 'because I've told you, we're just friends.'

'It isn't about Rochelle.'

'And even if we weren't, it'd be none of your fucking business.'

'It's not about Rochelle.'

Ewan took another sip of his beer. He replaced his glass on the beer mat and twisted it so its reflection wavered on the polished table top. 'What's it about then?'

I watched drops of condensation slide down my golden glass. 'I've inherited some money,' I said.

'Oh, aye?' Beer froth was moustaching his top lip, but he didn't wipe it off. He was trying to fathom out what this had to do with him.

I took a breath. 'I'm thinking of investing it in Stanley's business.'

Ewan lifted his eyebrows. 'It must be a fair few bob then?'

I hesitated. 'He'd be able to keep Bling Manor, and his Porsche – when he's fixed it – and I'd be able to come back.' He swiped the froth from his top lip with his sleeve and sat back against the padded hessian wall. 'Over the next couple of years, we could mop up Moneybags' farriery clients, and perhaps branch into racehorse transport, eventually ...'

'*We?*'

I stared at him.

'You mean *you*,' he said, plonking his glass down.

'I mean *us!*'

Ewan snorted a bitter laugh. 'Do you buggery! Your lot have been buying and selling my lot for generations – and here you are, at it again!'

I looked at my beer mat. 'I'm just buying into a business, Ewan.'

'Aye. A business that pays my wages. A business that decides if I buy or if I rent; if I eat or if I starve.' He might as well have rammed a pritchel between my ribs, but I tried to reason with him.

'That's how all businesses are! Somebody has to own them!'

'Bullshit.' I couldn't see how this was bullshit, but I knew that asking him to explain could result in a recitation of *Das Kapital*. 'It's just how your lot have engineered it.'

'My lot?'

'Public school boys! Capitalists! Neo-liberalists!'

'This isn't about politics, Ewan!'

His laughter was a bark. 'Course it bloody is!' He back-handed a beer mat at the table. *'The personal is also the political.'*

I took a breath. 'Look,' I said, 'I asked you to meet me here so we could talk reasonably. You'll still be more qualified, more experienced ...' Ewan regarded me coolly. 'And I promise I won't invest in the business unless you're comfortable with it.'

'How can I be comfortable with earning less money than the fucking apprentice?'

'I won't take any profits till I qualify.'

'Oh!' Ewan laughed bitterly. 'You'll *pretend* to be poor? Thanks very much!' Ewan's glass clinked on his teeth. 'And next time things are tight, who'll be down the road, eh – you or me?'

'Things won't be tight! I have ideas!'

'Oh, save it!' Ewan snapped. The hum of the pub filled my ears. My left shoulder lifted and fell.

'It's a solution.'

'To what?'

'To Stanley losing his house! To you working out of Cribbs estate! To me being stuck with Moneybags Morrison!' The pub pulsed and swam. I swirled my glass. On the next table a blonde child in pigtails was kneeling on her seat, colouring a paper placemat. Her brother was being finger-wagged by their father. Ewan pushed his hands in his hair and they stayed there, they gripped it, then he dragged them down, over his face.

'So,' he said when his face emerged again. 'I get to choose.' I nodded at him. 'I can either feel shit because I make you spend three more years with that freak Morrison, or I can feel shit because the apprentice – the fucking *apprentice* – is paying my wages.' He pressed his thumb knuckles into his eyeballs. I waited.

'So, what do you want me to tell Stanley?'

He took a breath that inflated his whole chest and he held it. It was as if he planned to float to the ceiling. 'I dunno,' he said on his exhale.

'I'm sorry.'

His head rolled back so he was staring at the acanthus in the cornice above him.

'I'm utterly sick of my whole shitty life.' He knocked back the dregs of his drink. I stared at him, this talented blacksmith with DipWCF after his name, two girls chasing him and a steady job.

'I promise I'll make this work,' I said.

He stood up. 'Do what the fuck you want.'

'Ewan ...' but Ewan was already striding for the door. I'd seen it on the films, when someone buys into a business; the champagne corks popping, the cheers, the fist bumps and the cries of *Welcome on board!* I gazed into the dust motes trapped in a light shaft that was slicing through the mullioned window. The door slammed. I sipped at my beer. It was flat.

She got the job. Enfermera registrada!
Now she just needs to tell her face.

Chapter 39

I drove through the mottled valley that divided Eckersley from Loddenden. Heavily leaved trees were splitting and fracturing the sunshine like strobe lights and thoughts of Ewan were flashing under the skin of my skull. All week, they'd unsettled my sleep and wriggled through my wakefulness. They prickled and squirmed like things half-forgotten. They distracted me from conversations and changing traffic lights. When I dragged them into the daylight, they were so heavy I had to lean on anvils and sit on tailgates. I wanted to ring him, but there was nothing new to say. I hoped he would be in The Fleece when I arrived. I hoped Stanley would make him see sense.

I hefted the door of the pub open and its end-of-week hum of hops and voices rained on me. Bob Entwistle had a dog on his knee; a Jack Russell. It wriggled and wagged at the sight of me; I recognised it as Lucky. Though I could see Stanley in conversation at the dartboard, I crossed the sticky carpet and scrubbed Lucky's head. 'How come you've got her?' I asked Bob, though my eyes were on Lucky.

'Doggy day care,' he said. 'Now t'South Africans have gone. She's been no bother – have you Cocker?' Bob didn't own a van and there were no sheep on Hathersage Road, so she'd have every chance to pass herself off as sane.

'So, is this going to be a regular thing then?'

'I'd keep her,' he said, lifting the dog to his nose and nuzzling her in an Inuit kiss. She lapped his face and he kissed her back. He put the happy little dog on his knee again. I looked at Stanley's slab of back as he cheered his opponent's skilful arrow shot. Bob followed my eyes. 'I'd said I'd have had his hens an' all, but he says he's not selling up now.'

I crossed the pub and stood at Stanley's shoulder. 'No Ewan?' Stanley shook his head and a weight of soft sand seemed to sift straight through me. 'Did he say why?' I was pulling out a chair. Stanley patted his opponent on the back and took up the seat opposite mine.

'Aw, he's been sulking all week,' he said, shoving a glass of golden liquid across the nearest table at me. 'I've told him, his *own* job's safer, if there's more capital in the business.' I watched beer bubbles drift upwards in sparkling columns. He took a drink of his beer. '*I don't like it either, Dolloper*, I said to him, *but needs must.*' He placed his glass carefully on the beer mat. 'He wants to grow the fuck up.' Stanley wiped his lips with the back of his hand. 'Daft bastard.'

'What's he said about it?'

'Oh, you know, the subjugation of the proletariat, the on-going privileges of a ruling elite, come the revolution – blah, blah, blah.' I took a gulp of my beer. 'I think he's planning to bury us both on t'moor.'

I chuckled.

'I'm serious! He's borrowed my bloody spade.' Red dust motes were dancing in a shaft of light straining through the stained-glass F in the window over Stanley's head and I was still looking at Stanley when he lowered his pint. Realisation had punched me in the throat. I knew exactly where Ewan would be when darkness dropped.

The tyres of my Land Rover ground on the motorway planings of Mervyn's lane. I drew it against the stock wire fence and pulled the handbrake on. A long-handled shovel was lying across my back seat. If this were a film, it wouldn't end well for me. I peered into the dusk. The last light had leaked from the sky, leaving violets and lilacs layered on the horizon, like a bruise. I looked at my watch. The full moon flashed silver on it. I could be in for a long wait. I flicked on the radio.

A barn owl sailed and dipped against a lavender back light. Had Rochelle just engineered this so she could meet Ewan in a field on a summer's night? That would make me about as welcome as a wasp at a picnic. I was just about to turn the ignition key when the lights of The Old Van floated into sight; one bright, one dim. It rattled on the stones. It stopped. The handbrake creaked on and Ewan dropped out. I reached for my shovel and stepped into the warm night air.

Ewan looked me up and down. 'Have you been sitting up here with your shovel every night?'

'Stanley said you'd borrowed his spade.'

'Get you, Inspector Poirot.'

The starlight flashed on Ewan's eye. 'You'd better not have told him.'

'Give me a bit of credit!'

He turned away. 'Well, with you two being business partners now ...'

'Oh, for fuck's sake, Ewan!' I looked up at the stars. A breeze sifted the leaves of the birch tree. 'Is Rochelle on her way?'

'She was just getting Shaniqua up.'

I turned to him. 'She's fetching the baby?'

'What else can she do?' The silence swelled again and seeped into the corners of our friendship. 'Has Moneybags been busy this week?'

I nodded. 'We're having to work Saturdays. What about you?'

'Same.' Ewan put his hands in his pockets. He had made me laugh from the first morning I'd met him, and here we were, struggling for conversation.

'You know, Ewan, nothing's been signed yet, so if you've got a problem ...'

'I haven't.' He rotated a stone with the sole of his shoe. 'It's just made me think, that's all.'

'About what?'

'Everything: Life, Jade, the Cribbs estate ...' he sighed. 'You've probably done me a favour.' The barn owl floated over the folds of the field, veiling us in its shroud of silence. 'Sometimes, you've to step out of line, haven't you?'

'How do you mean?'

'You did it. You were supposed to go to university and get a fancy job.' I shrugged. 'I'm supposed to work for Stanley, sing in Cribbs Social Club and marry Jade.' Headlights swung from the moor road. Their brightness dazzled. 'Hey up, she's here.' Lurching towards us was Flashman Freddie's battered white Ford Transit van.

Rochelle yanked the handbrake on and jumped from the cab. The smile she flashed at Ewan lit the darkness like stadium floodlights – then she looked at me. 'I didn't know you were coming.'

'Neither did I,' Ewan said, like I was some unwanted kid brother. Rochelle slid back the van's side door and a whimper wavered from the cab. 'Just put her dummy back in,' she shouted over its rumbling. Obediently, Ewan opened the passenger door, followed a trail of a gobbed ribbon through the folds of Shaniqua's blanket and found her dummy. She took it like an unfledged bird and he clicked the passenger door quietly closed.

Flashman Freddie's springer spaniel had snaked from the van, its whole body was a wiggle of welcome. Rochelle shouted thanks to Ewan, picked up a torch and rattled the door into place. Ewan crouched to his haunches, and the dog licked his face. Rochelle shortened its rope and turned towards what could have been the battlefield of The Somme; cratered with shell holes, and piled with blasted earth. 'Come on then!'

I hesitated. 'What about the baby?'

Rochelle flapped her wrist. 'She'll be fine!'

With a backward glance at the van, I opened the gate. Rochelle walked on, the dog wiggle-waggling at her side. She was heading for the moonlit field boundary. We waded behind her, over the mud, between the mounds and past the craters, squelching and paddling. She stopped under the moon-silvered oak tree. The dog was tight to her, gazing up. She tossed a tennis ball vertically, returned it to her pocket, then looking at the dog, she swept her arm in an upward curve. The dog ran. He zig-zagged the hedge line, nose down, tail thrashing. At the end of the field, he turned and worked it back again, sniffing, seeking and searching in the beam of Rochelle's torch. Half way down the second line he stopped. He doubled back.

'Hey up ...' Ewan whispered. I watched, as in the globe of the flashlight, the dog circled then started digging. Clods of filth were flying five feet high. 'He's found it already!' Ewan breathed. The dog's forepaws were thrashing like mixer blades. Fifty yards away Rochelle was bellowing his name. 'I think he's found it!' Ewan shouted into the darkness.

'Has he buggery!' Rochelle answered. She was closing in on the dog. 'Kit!'

When Kit saw her, he snaked an apology and plastered back his ears. At Rochelle's command he continued his methodical traversal of the ruined paddock.

Ewan flashed his phone light in to the dog's half dug hole and sliced his spade into the rasping soil. Meanwhile, Kit was zig-zagging the sludge behind us with methodical enthusiasm. 'I've hit something!' Ewan's voice was a stage whisper. We dug furiously with spade and shovel, widening the hole then caving in the sides with our wellies. Kit was wagging and wiggling on in the distance.

'There!' I hissed at a flash of white. Ewan dropped to his knees in the mud. He was scrambling with his fingers, furiously scooping up fistfuls of earth. Then he sighed. I shone my phone's light into the stillness. Ewan had sagged. He hauled his find to the surface and held it out *Alas, Poor Yorick* style.

'Fuck,' he said.

He dragged himself to his feet, wiped his slutchy hands on his jeans and flung the sheep's skull back in the hole.

Rochelle's voice rang in the darkness. 'Good boy!' My phone light caught the glint of the spaniel's eyes. The dog was stock still, atop one of Mervyn's mountains of muck. He was staring intently at the ground, one paw raised. Rochelle was walking towards him, still praising the dog. She dipped in her pocket, brought out the tennis ball and threw it for him. Even in the darkness, Kit caught it and circled joyously.

Ewan and I joined Rochelle on the pile of earth. Rochelle snatched my shovel from my hands. She was digging where Kit had pierced the soil with his eyes. 'That dog was trained by Her Majesty's Prison Service,' Rochelle said. 'So there's summat here!' Kit dropped his tennis ball at my feet. I lobbed it for him, like a javelin.

Ewan held his phone light over Rochelle's work. It soon caught a flash of something pale. Rochelle dropped the shovel, fell to her knees and reached into the beam of light. When her hand emerged, it was holding a banknote. The whites of her eyes shone up on us. 'A tenner,' she stated flatly. Neither of us had thought to mention the random notes that Mervyn dried over his Aga.

'There's a lot more than that!' Ewan insisted. 'There's a big stash!' but Rochelle was hauling herself to her feet.

'A tenner at a fucking time?' She was shaking her head. 'It'll take us till they've done away with cash!' She pocketed the tenner and whistled for Kit. 'I'll need a fucking pack of sniffer dogs for this job.' She whistled again.

Ewan swung his phone light. It illuminated the dog, stone still again. He was fifty metres away with one paw raised. 'Look!' he pointed. 'He's found some more!'

But Rochelle was not interested. 'I'm not wrecking my gel nails for another fucking tenner.'

'This might be the stash!'

'Or it might be another fucking tenner!' she shouted back. She looped the rope through Kit's collar and turned for the gate. Ewan headed for where the dog had stood. I picked up my shovel and followed him. Ewan thrust the spade in and stood on its lug.

'She's probably right, I told him. 'Mervyn's been turning this field over for months.'

'A tenner's a tenner, though,' Ewan answered as the spade sunk in.

I scraped, he rasped. On the fourth spadeful Ewan's blade clobbered something dense. The light of my phone picked up the curve of a zip.

'It's a bag!' Ewan dropped to the soil. I crouched beside him. Shifting shadows and claggy mud crowded out all sensations but sound. Ewan was armpit deep, grunting and grasping.

'Is there a handle?' Fists full of clay hit the earth at intervals like exclamation marks. Ewan nodded, his head now spasmed skyward as he twisted it to get a grip on the treasure at his fingertips. He drew himself to a kneeling position. One more stretch; one more scramble and starlight touched the edge of Ewan's smile. His arm edged from the bowels of the paddock holding the mud slicked treasure.

Rochelle's dense shadow darkened the blackness above us. Six eyes were plunged downward. We were looking on a Kappa sports bag circa 1996. Ewan pointed to the soil stuffed padlock. 'Have you got something that'll cut that?'

'Mervyn'll have a key,' Rochelle said, holding out her hand for the bag.

'We could take it now,' I suggested. She looked over her shoulder. 'T'lights are all off. It'll be a nice surprise for him in the morning.' Her hand was still outstretched. With his eyes still on hers, Ewan handed her the bag.

Chapter 40

It was five past nine on Monday morning and I was heating a rod of steel in Moneybags' fire when Stanley's name flashed up on my phone. He'd spoken before I could greet him. 'Dolloper's not turned up!'

Why was he telling me? Thoughts thudded on my frontal cortex. Had Ewan crashed the van again? Was he with Rochelle? What came out was, 'Have you rung him?'

'Course I bloody have! He's not answering!'

'Has the van broken down?'

'It's outside his house. I'm parked right next to it.'

Sands of unease were shifting in my stomach. 'He'll have overslept.'

'That bastard Alsatian of his would wake the dead!' The line seethed. 'Did you see him over the weekend?'

'Late, Friday.'

'Did he say owt?'

'About what?'

'Anything! Everything!'

'He said he'd been thinking.'

Stanley groaned.

'Do you want *me* to ring him?' It was the only help I could offer.

'Aye. Ring me back.'

Moneybags had scowled at me twice already and as I swiped the screen of my phone he tapped his imaginary wrist-watch. I turned my back. With my exit door ajar, I cared less and less for his rules.

The rhythmic burr of Ewan's phone pulsed in my ear. I peeled back the skins of Friday's conversation. Had he followed Rochelle after I'd left him? Had he lain awake all night? Moneybags' anvil blows became noisier. Ewan's answering message told me my call could not be taken at this time. I hung up and despite the heat of Moneybags eyes on me, I rang Stanley back.

'Fuck,' he said. His sigh crumpled cellophane in my ear. 'I can't manage at Mervyn's on my own.'

'Should I ask Michael to spare me?' I was careful to use my employer's given name when he was within his earshot.

'What's the bloody point of that? You're still less bastard use than a glass anvil! Is he there?' I handed Moneybags my phone. He put it to his ear, tutted, sympathised and sucked his teeth.

'Aye;' he said at last. 'I were only planning on forging today.' He handed my phone back to me.

'See you at Mervyn's,' Stanley said in my ear.

We approached Mervyn's High Scorthwaite yard from the west. Mirror images of the fells I was familiar with formed through the morning gauze. Moneybags' Discovery scaled them with the silent ease of an escalator. From the bend by Scorthwaite Crag, Mervyn's good-as-new Lambourne Oakley Super Six racehorse wagon was clearly visible, imposing as a monument. 'At last,' I said out loud. Moneybags glanced at me from the driver's seat. Its reappearance meant nothing to him. A trio of partridge glided past us, like a little volley of arrows.

'Thanks for this,' Stanley said to Moneybags as he stepped from The Best Van. It looked fit for the scrapyard next to Moneybags' outfit. 'I know thoroughbreds aren't your bag.'

'Farriers' code of honour,' Moneybags said, and Stanley

wondered out loud why the fucking dolloper he employed had never heard of the farriers' code of honour.

'Sod's law,' he added. 'I've had t'South African Lad here for weeks, but t'Dolloper decides to take off while's he's in Spain.' Mervyn's raised voice rattled the rafters of the American barn. Moneybags flashed a concerned glance but Stanley lifted his eyes to the morning sky and drew a steadying breath.

'We come in peace,' he shouted as we made our way towards the shoeing bay.

There was no horse waiting and no names had been written on the board. Stanley dragged a hand over his face. A stable hand teetered past us with an overflowing wheelbarrow. 'Sorry,' he said to Moneybags. 'It's normally more organised.' Moneybags didn't look convinced.

A flustered Mervyn appeared. 'Bloody Rochelle's gone bloody AWOL,' he said, whipping off his flat cap. My insides turned to congealed ice.

'I've not seen the little beggar since Friday! Left us right up the creek.'

I looked at Stanley and Stanley looked at me. He might have had an image of Rochelle's back, standing before a registrar in Gretna Green. I had an image of her receding into the darkness with Mervyn's muddy sports bag in her hand.

Mervyn saw our look. 'Do you know summat?'

'T'Dolloper's not turned up either,' Stanley confided.

Mervyn stared at us. 'Hey up,' he said and nodded knowingly; except he knew nothing.

My eyes travelled to the giant molehills that had hidden Mervyn's fortune for decades. Our footprints would be marking the spoil heap that had nestled his thousands. I didn't remember filling the hole in. It would still be there. Would the notes even be legal tender? Would the Bank of England ask questions about a sports bag full of old notes? Ewan, though? Ewan, who had despised Flashman Freddie for his criminality and prided himself on his moral escape from Cribbs estate where every other teenager was on bath salts and the good ones just shoplifted.

A bay horse was being led down the centre aisle of the barn. I was reaching for a lead rope when a familiar voice put me in a classic double-take. Grinning from ear to ear, was Jay. 'You're back!' I shouted.

'He were in Tesco,' Mervyn mumbled. 'Bandaged up like Tutankhamun, and I remembered he were marginally better than nowt.' Oblivious to the slur, Jay held up his one dressed hand.

'So, have you got your job back, then?'

'Has he buggery,' Mervyn snapped. 'He's not driving my bloody wagon, he's not touching my bloody tractor and the minute Rochelle rocks up wi' a good excuse, he's on t'muck heap wi t'rest o t'shite.' Mervyn sighed wistfully. 'She were t'best head lad I've ever had.'

'She were t'best head *lass* you ever had,' Jay corrected him.

Mervyn slung him a withering look. 'I know what I said.'

A truck was pulling into the yard. 'That'll be my grass seed,' Mervyn chirped; he was already hurrying away. 'And you want to have a look at my wagon before you go! It's all been done up!'

I watched Mervyn walk out into the sunshine and tried to imagine what had happened after I'd climbed into my Land Rover on Friday night. It was like one of the adventure books I'd liked as a kid, where you could experiment with different endings. In one version, they've always planned to dig the treasure up and scarper with it; in another Rochelle follows Ewan home and persuades him to run away with her, and in another Ewan stands by her van and confesses the worries he'd started to confide in me, and she offers herself and a sports bag full of used notes as his solution.

'Are you planning to do some bastard work, Posh Lad, or have you just come to watch?' I snapped myself back to the corporal world where friends you trust turn out to be thieves and nylon sports bags don't rot away.

Stanley picked up a hoof trimmer and made conversation. 'Did I tell you, Lee's doing my Porsche up?' Or was he bragging for Moneybags' benefit? 'He's found t'same model that's been in a head-on so t'back end of it's like new!'

'You'll be sorry to sell it.'

'I shouldn't have to now, should I?' Stanley shot a glance at Moneybags who was carefully working on a calm grey and dropped his voice, 'Wi' things having changed – you know.'

Half-knowledge lodged in me like a fish bone. Without Ewan, Stanley's business was finished. I told myself I knew nothing – not really; that telling Stanley half a tale wouldn't help. I needed to be sure. I would drive to Flashman Freddie's and see what I could find out. I'd act all innocent.

The sight of Rochelle's yellow Volkswagen Golf parked on the limestone chippings surged warm hope through me. She was here. Ewan might even be with her. I might be able to reason with them. I'd have to get past Flashman Freddie first though. He was repairing the dry-stone wall abutting the lane and beyond him, Belinda was grazing, surrounded by black trotters. At the sight of my car, he stood up from his work and arched backwards to relieve his stiffness. Kit, the spaniel, had been snoozing beside him, but he got to his feet as I drew the Land Rover to a halt.

'Wotcha, Posh Lad,' Freddie said as I lowered the window. That greeting from Freddie always seemed a liberty he wasn't entitled to, but I ignored it.

'Is Rochelle about?'

'I've not seen her.'

'Oh.'

He followed the beam of my eyes to her car. 'She borrowed my van for the weekend, and she's not been back with it.'

'Oh,' I said again, this time looking at the spaniel.

Freddie stooped for a stone slab. 'She's a big girl,' he said, without turning round. 'And it's what we do.' He dropped the slab on to the dry-stone wall.

'What?'

'Travel.'

'You mean she's moved on?'

'Aye.'

'Oh.'

He dropped another lump of millstone grit. It landed with a dull snap.

'It's just that, she's not said anything to Mervyn.' I looked at Belinda who was grazing peacefully in the distance. 'She'll miss her horse too, won't she?'

Freddie turned to me. 'You don't understand our ways, do you, Posh Lad?'

I watched him as he crouched and sought a stone of the right shape in the pile. 'Did she tell you where she was going?'

'Nope,' he answered. 'I dare say she'll ring when she's ready.' I was surprised he wasn't a better liar, given his chosen profession. He settled the slab on the wall.

'Has she gone on her own?'

Suddenly Freddie spun round. His hands gripped the edge of the car window and he leaned in. 'I think it's got fuck all to do with you, Posh Lad.' I pulled my neck back to put some distance between our noses. 'Now turn your wee bumpkin's car round and take your twitching little arse back to where it came from.'

I fired the engine. 'Should I tell Mervyn to advertise her job then?'

'Don't play dumb, Posh Lad,' Freddie scoffed. 'We both know she won't be needing that job.'

I turned the car round and drove back towards the moor road. My tongue was sticking to the roof of my mouth and my grip on the steering wheel felt fluttery. I needed to stop; to compose myself; to drink water, but not where Flashman

Freddie could see me. I let the road swoop me into a dip and pulled the Land Rover onto the wide verge. I took a lungful of oxygen and gripped the wheel. Flashman Freddie probably was a good liar, but a gnat like me wasn't worth his efforts. I groped in the side pocket of the driver's door for a warm half-drunk bottle of Evian. I unscrewed the cap. A car passed me at speed. It whooshed and bumphed the parked Land Rover. My mouth opened with an unexpected click. I gulped the water. The car rocked again as a passing wagon crushed the moor air against its sides and let it go again. I took another drink. Ewan must have said something to his dad, to Lee. I tossed the empty water bottle on the passenger seat and started the engine.

'Our Ewan's not in,' Steve said when he opened the door.

'I know,' I answered. 'Do you know where he is?' Steve swung the door wider so I could step inside and I patted the dog, who'd lolloped up to greet me.

'He's gone down to Jade's, for a few days,' Steve said, walking towards the kitchen.

'And you know that for sure?' I asked from behind him.

Steve blasted water into the kettle. 'Where else would he go?' I shrugged and Steve turned to me. 'Are you trying to tell me summat?'

'No,' I said. 'He just didn't tell us where he was going.'

Steve let the kitchen units take his weight. 'I've been worried about him to be honest, Will. He's seemed ... not himself. Has he said owt to you?'

'He's been a bit distant lately,' I confided. 'And now Stanley's gunning for him for taking off.'

'What? He hasn't booked it as holiday?'

'Nope. He's dropped Stanley right in it.'

Steve threw his head back so vigorously that his Adam's apple was thrust into relief. 'What the blazes is he playing at?'

Lee strolled into the kitchen in his boxer shorts grumbling that he hadn't been offered a brew. 'Never mind that,' his dad said. 'What did our Ewan say to you when he left the house?'

Lee took a mug from the mug tree. 'Nothing. He's a dick-head.'

'Did someone pick him up?' I asked. My eyes were on Lee who was scratching himself absently, but I could feel Steve's eyes on me; he hadn't expected that question.

'Dunno,' Lee answered. 'I didn't see anyone.'

'Did he have a suitcase?'

'He had a rucksack.'

Surely he wasn't going for good, with just a rucksack? But then why would you need more than a rucksack when you've thousands of pounds in used banknotes in a holdall? Had Ewan really wandered so far from himself that he'd steal Mervyn's money and run off? I was still struggling to believe it. Would he really betray Jade and abandon Stanley? But why else would he be so secretive?

I finished my tea and we agreed to keep one another in-formed. Steve was ringing Ewan's mobile number for the third time when I left him.

In South Africa I can stand in our pool and watch dolphins. In Madrid I'll be able to stand in our shower and fry a fucking egg.

Chapter 41

We teamed up for the week, Moneybags and Stanley and me. It was the only way Stanley could keep up with the workload he'd booked in. I watched him struggling to bend, counter-arching his back as often as he could and I saw how much we needed Ewan. The extra work and the attempt to save face in front of Moneybags made Stanley bad tempered. One minute he was raging at his own folly for having employed a lad off Cribbs estate; the next he was raging at me for thinking I was Richard fucking Branson. 'We'd o' done a'reyt, me and t'Dolloper if you hadn't stuck your bastard oar in!' We should have given Ewan an incentive; a share; a pay rise. Something.

I wondered what Moneybags Morrison was making of Stanley's outbursts, but the most challenging questions he ever asked were, 'How do you want the anvil putting back in the van?' and 'Which ones are the antibacterial nails?' Even when Stanley barged him aside for overreacting to a tail swish, Moneybags didn't comment.

We took turns at ringing Ewan. Stanley left him a message saying he could whistle for his bastard wages, and I left him one asking him to ring me.

On Wednesday evening when Stanley walked into the forge, his face was grey and his back was bent. 'We'll have to get another farrier,' he said. 'Moneybags'd shoe 'em from in t'van if he could.' His tool-box hit the concrete with a bash.

'Shouldn't we give it a bit longer?' I suggested.

He leaned heavily on the workbench. 'I can't carry on

like this, Posh Lad.' He walked back-bent and flat-footed up the steps of Bling Manor and crept through the back door. Seconds later he was waving papers he'd found on the door-mat. It was an official noise abatement notice. Lucky had been home alone whilst we'd been working with Moneybags and Stanley had thirty days to cease the pollution deemed to be emanating from 148 Hathersage Road or face a fine of up to five hundred pounds.

'Just let Bob Entwistle have her!' I urged him. 'What's the problem?'

He bounced one forefinger off the other. 'Lynne pisses off! Jonathan pisses off! Katie pisses off!' The names of his family were punctuated by finger strikes. 'And now Ewan pisses off!' He pocketed the letter. 'I'd like to think I could keep my bastard dog!'

'He only wants her during the day!'

'It'll start off wi' day care, then he'll offer the odd over-nighter, and before you know where you are the disloyal little psychopath'll have moved in wi' Bob Entwistle!'

On Thursday, Lucky savaged a kennel maid at Tailwaggers Doggy Day Care and on Friday, Stanley insisted I stayed with her and make half a dozen shoes fit for my exhibition board. 'Dirk and Maria are due back at tea-time,' he said. 'So you can go when they get here.'

'I thought she'd got a job in Madrid.'

'It's a flying visit; they're just picking their stuff up.'

I was sweeping out the grate when Jay's ringtone filled the forge. (Ewan had set all our phones to play 'Everybody Hurts' when Jay rang.)

'What have you done this time?' I groaned, hoping I wasn't going to end the day with another trip to the hospital.

'Nothing!' he laughed. 'I was just seeing if Ewan's back.'

'Nah,' I said, scraping at the stone with a fire rake.

'Well, Rochelle is! She's just been here.' The only sound now was the blood in my ears. 'I thought she'd come for her job back but she never mentioned it. She rocked up bold as brass in a brand new, bright red, Volkswagen Beetle, parked it right next to t'wagon and marched in asking for Mervyn.'

'Did she say where she'd been?'

'Nope! She just stands there and tells him he owes her five hundred quid. She looked a bit rough, if I'm honest.'

'Don't tell me he gave it to her!'

'You're joking! Short arms and deep pockets, that's our Mervyn!'

I let the forge's plastic chair take my weight and mused on the slippery morals, thick skin and sense of entitlement she'd inherited from her father.

As soon as Jay had hung up, I rang Ewan's number. It rang and it rang, and then switched to answerphone.

I was clearing up my work when the chugging of an engine announced Dirk and Maria stepping out of a taxi at the top of Bling Manor's drive. 'Hiya,' I grinned, then pointing at Lucky, 'you're on dog watch!'

Dirk nodded.

I greeted Maria with a kiss and congratulated her on her new job. 'When do you start?'

Dirk snapped round from where he had been paying the taxi driver and made dramatic slashing gestures. Maria rushed past me with the baby.

'What's the matter with her?' I asked.

Dirk's hand smacked his forehead. 'She wants a job – she doesn't want a job. She wants an apartment – she doesn't want an apartment.' I helped him unload a pushchair and a suitcase from the taxi whilst Lucky wagged and circled at his feet. 'I'm at the end of my fucking rope, man!'

'So what now then? Back to South Africa?' Dirk was shaking his head.

'She says she'll take the job.' I trailed him to the door. 'Which means living with the in-laws or in a fucking shoe box.' I followed him into the kitchen. Carlos was still fastened in his car seat, but there was no sign of Maria. Dirk began extricating his tiny son from the padded sausage skins of his outer garments.

'So, you're going to be a Spanish house husband, then?'

'That's been the plan since three o'clock.'

'But what about your diploma? What was the point of coming to the UK to study?'

Dirk's fingers were working on the popper of Carlos' snow suit. 'Don't worry about it, man. Her plans are changing three times a day. I'm just rolling with it.' There had obviously been some hard conversations on the Iberian Peninsula; some dismantling and restacking of priorities, of values and of visions. He squirmed his son's arm free, just as Stanley bowled in.

'*Now* you turn up!' he greeted Dirk. 'We've been a man down all week!'

'Why?' Dirk asked. 'Where's Ewan?'

'That, my lad, is the sixty-four-million-dollar question!' Dirk glanced between us – but what could we say? Ewan's going AWOL only invited more questions. I only knew the answers to some of them and they weren't ripe for talking about. Stanley blew out his cheeks and looked at me. Dirk saw the look but there was nothing I could say that didn't divulge our secret.

'Let's get a takeaway,' Stanley suggested, then he pre-empted the objection he saw forming on my lips. 'Tell your lass to come an' all!' he groaned.

'... so,' Stanley finished off, mopping the rest of his korma sauce with his naan bread. 'We rocks up at Mervyn Slack's, and it's pandemonium.' He fixed Dirk with a stare. 'Rochelle's only gone and done a runner an' all.'

Dirk was staring back. He let the implication settle, then gripped his unshaven chin between thumb and forefinger. 'He was sweet on her – *ja*?' Stanley and I were nodding. 'But why the need to disappear?'

I had some ideas, but I was struggling to believe them. Dirk started counting on his fingers. 'He has a good job, he has his family, he has his gigs ...'

'Jade,' Maria put in. I couldn't tell if she was adding to Dirk's list, or giving him a reason. I could feel Stanley's eyes on me. Wordlessly, we'd agreed to expand.

'There's a bit more to it,' I said. Stanley had cracked open another can of Stella and plonked it at my elbow. I looked at the rounded triangle of its metal mouth. 'When I turned twenty-one, I inherited some money ...' Millie's hand had folded itself over mine under the table. 'So ...' I hesitated, and Stanley took over.

'So t'Posh Lad's putting it in to t'farriery business.' He swigged his lager.

Dirk was staring at us. '*Your* farriery business?'

Stanley nodded, his mouth full of lager. Dirk's brow had furrowed.

'I'll still be t'boss,' Stanley clarified.

'Sixty – forty,' I explained.

Dirk flicked a finger in my direction. 'But you work for Moneybags Morrison.'

I didn't meet his eye. 'There are still loose ends to tie up.'

Dirk sat back in his chair. It creaked with his weight. 'And Ewan was one of the loose ends, *ja*?' Guilt soaked me.

'Did you make it good for him?' Maria asked.

'How?'

'You could offer him a pay rise, or bonus, or a share.' I glanced at Stanley. 'He feels bery betrayed – yes?'

'We didn't really have the chance ...' I began – then felt a puncture of relief when the doorbell rescued me from further explanation.

Stanley looked at his watch. 'Who the fuck's this at half past eight?' He scraped back his chair and ambled through the house whilst Dirk shook his head at our mishandling of my partnership. Millie was collecting the dirty plates and Maria began rocking a restless Carlos. His niggles were overlaid by the susurration of other voices from inside the house. An internal door clicked. The voices swelled louder. Footsteps approached through the kitchen. I looked up.

'Look what the cat's dragged in,' Stanley stated as he emerged, grinning, into the dining room. Walking across the kitchen's chequerboard tiles behind him were Ewan and Jade. Lucky leapt at Ewan, wagging and tail thrashing and dancing on her hind legs. I should have felt like I'd dropped a rucksack of bricks but Ewan wasn't smiling. Lucky's welcome justified his sliding his eyes off my face.

Jade was smiling though. 'Little man!' she exclaimed, at the sight of Carlos. Dirk stood and kissed her cheek, and her vintage dress swung as she swooped on the baby. 'I didn't expect to see this little munchkin!'

Stanley jerked his thumb towards Ewan. 'T'Scarlet Pimpernel's been in London.'

'London?' I couldn't fathom it.

'We've been bustin' a bastard gut, and these two have been sightseeing!'

'*Auditioning*,' Jade corrected him. Her fingers were folding the fleece from Carlos' face. Dirk's brow buckled. Maria's gaze shifted. Ewan had reached for Jade's hand.

'We've been for auditions with Royal Caribbean.' His words seemed to float and spin in my head like trapped feathers.

When no one spoke, Jade looked up from the bundle of baby. 'Cruise ships,' she clarified. It was as if a bubble had floated from the sky and settled over us, sealing Stanley's patio off from the world.

'Fucking Mandy,' Stanley muttered, dragging both hands down his face.

Ewan's gaze was on his own trainers. 'We're sailing to Malta and the Greek islands in three weeks.'

Stanley was rummaging for more words. 'I've invested a lot o' time and effort in you, Dolloper.'

Ewan swallowed.

'What the fuck am I supposed to do while you're playing at Captain Pugwash?' He jerked his thumb at me. 'He can't nail a shoe to a bastard door, and I'm knackered.'

Ewan looked up. 'I'm entitled to change career if I want to.'

Stanley spoke to Jade. 'And what's your boss said? Have you told him?'

'She's been very understanding,' Jade said. And we stood there, the seven of us, in bubbles of guilt, shock, embarrassment and wonder.

'Congratulations!' Maria shouted, suddenly. She even managed a hand clap but the bubble of silence only wobbled. 'Is bery high standard for cruise ships.'

'We've only just got back,' Ewan mumbled. 'So we're putting you in the picture right away.'

'Don't come the gentleman now!' Stanley shot. 'You've been AWOL for a bastard week!'

'Sorry.'

'Sorry?'

'My head's been all over the place.'

'It bloody would have been an' all, if I'd clapped eyes on you with my hammer in my hand!' They looked at one another, master and apprentice, man and boy, mentor and mentee, and I thought my ears would pop with the silence.

Eventually Stanley took a deep draught of the curry infused air. 'So, this is you giving me your notice, is it?'

Ewan swallowed. 'I suppose so.'

'After seven years.'

Maria was still trying to nudge the mood. 'Iss bery exciting!' She illuminated her smile with a fierce glare at Stanley.

Jade faked companionable levity. 'Ewan's never even had a passport, have you, Ewan?'

'Dirk!' Maria barked. 'Fetch Carlos' champagne! Is in blue suitcase!'

Stanley, Ewan and I were inert, but Dirk was lumbering out

of his chair. 'Of course; yeah.' He touched Ewan's shoulder as he passed. 'Congratulations, mate.'

Ewan stopped him with a raised palm. 'It's okay, Dirk, don't bother. I don't think Stanley's in the mood for champagne. We just popped in with the news.'

Stanley was still reckoning the information. 'You'll work your notice though?'

'If you'll let me.'

Stanley nodded. We all knew that we needed Ewan.

'I'll see you on Monday, then,' Ewan said.

It was Maria who saw them out, the baby still cradled in the crook of her left arm. Stanley let the back of his chair take all his weight.

'Well, that's us fucked,' he stated. I'd been thinking the same thing. Without Ewan, Stanley's business was not worth my investment, and without my investment, Stanley was fucked. We could hear Maria's encouraging tones as Ewan and Jade passed through the house.

'We could take another farrier on,' I suggested, but Stanley dismissed the idea. He was right: a useless farrier, or a farrier we couldn't get on with, was as bad as no farrier and whilst we were choosing one, our clients would be going elsewhere. I heard the click of the front door. When Maria re-emerged she was pointing a finger at Stanley.

'You are e-selfish man!'

'Me?' Stanley had slapped both hands on his chest. 'He's just pissed off for a week, leaving me with a book full of his clients, then he's chucked five years of training and a full-time job back in my face – and *I'm* selfish!'

'Listen what you say! *Me, me, me!*' Dirk was looking un-comfortable. 'This is a big adventure for them! Is brave thing to do!'

'It bloody well was,' Stanley muttered. 'In his shoes, I'd have sent me a text message.'

Maria was shaking her head. 'I put Carlos to bed,' she said, and she turned in the doorway. 'Try to remember when *you* were twenty-three.'

'What about your pudding?' Stanley shouted after her, but she ignored him. Stanley stood up. 'You might want to remind your wife that you've been stopping in this selfish man's house rent free for six months.'

Dirk smirked. 'I notice you didn't remind her!' Stanley marched into the kitchen. He reappeared with three choc ices and dropped them on the table. Dirk reached for one and started to peel back the wrapping. 'You know, Madrid to Manchester is two and a half hours,' he said. 'Not even as far as from PE to Jo'berg.'

Stanley filled his lungs then released a long, laboured sigh. 'It's hardly a bastard commute though, is it?'

'Not daily; no.'

Stanley sat motionless. He took a bite of his choc ice. 'She'd never buy that,' he said through ice cream.

'Leave it with me,' Dirk winked.

Chapter 42

'Sorted!' Stanley said, when I picked up the phone on Monday morning.

'What is?'

'Dirk!'

'What? You're taking him on?'

'*We're* taking him on!' I was amazed that Maria had agreed to it. 'Oh, she didn't really want that job in Spain, so she's had to compromise. It's what you've to do in a marriage.' He said it like his wife hadn't just scoured him through the divorce courts. 'Anyway, she has some terms and conditions we've to meet.'

'Which are?'

'Dunno. She wants to talk to us tonight at six.'

I walked into Bling Manor's kitchen that evening to find Stanley and Dirk sitting opposite Maria at the breakfast bar. Maria had a page of notes in front of her and Carlos was asleep in his car seat which was pushed against the cupboards. Lucky was curled in slumber at his side. I stooped for a look at the baby, more to curry favour with Maria than out of interest – and Lucky exploded like a party popper. Her barking, gnashing frenzy was of van-exit ferocity. Stanley bellowed at her and Carlos stirred, but astonishingly, the child didn't waken; it was as if he was used to it.

'That's her latest psychopathy,' Stanley grumbled over Lucky's yapping, 'Nobody's to touch the babby now!'

'She's just guarding him,' Dirk explained. Lucky was on her hind legs like a circus poodle, as Maria swept the car seat up and plonked it on the counter.

'Is not her baby!' Maria snapped. 'And the dog is point four on my list!' Stanley stood up.

'I'll make Posh Lad a brew,' he sighed. 'And then you can start wi' point one.'

I was grateful for a brew after a caffeine-free day with Moneybags Morrison. I settled at the breakfast bar beside Maria with a mug of Yorkshire Tea at my elbow and she picked up her sheet of paper.

'Point one,' she began. 'Dirk is not expected to work at weekends.' There were busy weeks and emergencies that sometimes required it. Stanley opened his mouth to say so, but I booted him under the breakfast bar. 'Point two: Dirk is to be given every second Monday off with no loss of pay.' I saw Stanley's knuckles whiten as he tightened the grip on his mug. So did Maria. 'If he lose money, how can we afford to fly to Espain?' She looked back at her notes. 'Point three: my parents can stay here for visit when they want, for as long as they want.' Stanley was beginning to look resigned. 'Point four: Lucky is never to be left in the house with me when you go work.'

Stanley sat bolt upright. 'Nay, bloody hell, Maria ...'

'Bob Entwistle,' I reminded him, quietly. 'You'll just have to suck it up.' He slumped like a deflated inner tube. 'Point five: you make farewell party for Ewan and Jade.' She folded the paper and looked up. 'You can agree wages and rent with Dirk, but I ask Ewan what he was paid and Dirk is more experienced, so don't take the pees. I will do shopping and cooking.'

'Is that it?' Stanley asked. 'You don't want my kidney, or my first-born child?'

'It is,' she acknowledged. Stanley was silent for a beat.

'Go on, then,' he said. 'So long as Posh Lad's in agreement.'

'Are you all right with me part owning the business?' I asked Dirk.

'Makes no difference to me,' Dirk chuckled. 'I'll do what the fuck I like anyway.' It was true. I looked at the sun-tanned, muscle-bound, six-and-a-half-foot farrier and remembered that he had already felled a tree, trussed up a racehorse and uprooted garden flowers against my advice.

'Right then,' Stanley slapped his hands down on his thighs. 'Looks like we're sorted,' and he held out his hand to Dirk who shook on it. I did the same.

'And now,' Maria said to Stanley, as she slipped down from the high stool. 'You need to start planning a party.' I knocked back the dregs of my brew, and feeling lighter than I had in months, I strode out of Bling Manor.

As I walked up the drive, a red Volkswagen Beetle pulled away from the kerb. It had a new registration. I watched it disappear towards Fowlden. But there must be hundreds of red Volkswagen Beetles in Yorkshire.

The frequency of Stanley's phone calls that week came close to undoing even Moneybags Morrison's contemplative zen. Early in the week Stanley was complaining about Ewan's mood. 'It's like workin' wi' a Cistercian monk!'

'He'll be scared of saying the wrong thing,' I explained.

'What, like, *I'm going to work on a cruise ship*?'

'See! I'd keep my mouth shut in his shoes.' Then he'd wanted to discuss breaking the news of my departure to Moneybags. 'I'll tell him,' I said. 'Face to face, then you can talk to him.'

Moneybags had taken the news very well in the event; he'd not planned on employing another apprentice anyway, he said. He'd only done it as a favour. When he'd finally spoken to Stanley, he'd passed on another dozen clients to give him more time for blacksmithing.

Now, Stanley was in party-planning panic. 'Music' was his first word when I picked up the phone. 'What music does he like?'

'Everything,' I told him. 'He's music mad.' I heard the flapping of Stanley's lips as he let out an exasperated sigh. 'I was hoping to narrow it down a bit.'

'There's a big country music vibe on Cribbs estate, isn't there?'

'Does he like it though?'

'Ask Jade.'

'Surprise party? Duh.'

'Lee then.'

'Good plan. He'll know who to invite off Cribbs an' all.' Moneybags had folded his arms and was glaring at me across the forge. 'Is that it?'

'No! How much do you think I should put behind the bar?'

'You *are* feeling guilty,' I laughed.

'A couple of hundred?'

'Whatever you give, they'll sup it.'

'It wants to be a good do though.' I could feel two circles on my chest where Moneybags' eyes were singeing my polo shirt. 'What do you think about food?'

'Look, Stan, I've got to go. I'll ring you back.'

'You can't. You don't know when Ewan's with me! Is that miserable bugger complaining? Tell him he's invited.' I turned to Moneybags who told me with a wave of his hand that he'd heard.

'Sunday night,' I clarified. 'In The Fleece.' Moneybags was tinkering with the dials on the gas forge.

'I'm not much of a drinker.'

'You'll come though, for Ewan?' The forge boomed.

'I suppose I could pop in for one,' he said. He looked up. 'Remind that business partner of yours, that as of this week, I'm still paying your wages.'

'I heard!' Stanley said in my ear.'

'Ring me tonight,' I told him. 'And don't bother wi' food. Just put plenty o' money behind the bar. Ewan'd prefer that.'

'He's a good lad, Ewan,' Moneybags said, when I'd hung

up. 'Talented an' all.' I knew that Moneybags was talking about Ewan's forging skills. It was another talent entirely that had carried him away from Cribbs estate, and yet Ewan still saw himself as a nobody.

Chapter 43

Millie was on call until seven and Stanley had insisted that he and I should form the advance party, so when I crossed Hathersage Road at ten to seven on Sunday night, I was alone. As I'd looked left, I'd noticed the tail gate of a red Volkswagen Beetle disappearing through the traffic lights; coincidence, surely? I must be attuned to them since Jay had mentioned Rochelle's.

When I walked through the doors of The Fleece, Dirk turned to grin at me. 'Evening, Boss!' I smiled apologetically; the idea still prickled me like a woollen jumper. He sucked more froth off his beer, and headed across the pub. Maria was sitting opposite Stanley on the long window seat; she'd had her nails done and her hair was different. Carlos' carrycot was beside her and Jade was at her elbow, leafing through a Royal Caribbean brochure. I plonked my pint on the table, dragged up a stool and shuffled it next to Ewan's, who thought he was there for a quiet farewell drink.

'I got that for free!' Ewan said, holding his glass up then taking a grateful slurp. Mine had been free too, but I didn't want to arouse Ewan's suspicion by saying so.

Jade turned back a corner of the Royal Caribbean brochure and held up a picture of a blue sea. 'That'll be us next month,' she said, stabbing left-handed at a couple sipping mojitos on the deck of a cruise liner, but Ewan wasn't paying attention. He nudged me and pointed to where Mervyn, Dagmar, Ruudi and Jay had walked in. 'They don't usually sup in here, do they?'

'They must have had a winner.'

Ewan curled his top lip. 'Nah! They didn't come in here when they'd won the bloody National!' Jay turned, waved at him and with a bandage free arm, made the universal drinking gesture. Ewan pointed to his almost brimming glass and declined with a grateful thumbs up. 'What's up wi' him?' he asked me, suspicious of his generosity.

Stanley was suddenly business-like. 'Right,' he said to Ewan. 'What's the actual day you're finishing?'

'Thursday,' Jade answered for him. 'We're back again on the twenty-first and on the twenty-fourth, we set off for the Southern Mediterranean.'

'Ah, try to see Cadiz,' Maria interrupted. 'Cadiz is e-spectacular.' Ewan ignored her sunburst of fingers and turned to Stanley.

'So, are you just getting somebody temporary?'

Stanley smirked. 'Getting cold feet are we?'

'No!' Jade answered for him.

'I'm looking forward to it,' Ewan insisted. 'Only ...'

'Only what?' Stanley asked.

'Only, I might not want to do it forever ...' Jade rolled her eyes, and Stanley sucked on his teeth.

'The thing is, Dolloper, I've got somebody lined up for your job.'

Ewan's head snapped towards me then back towards Stanley. 'What? Already?'

'You're going next bastard week!' Stanley reminded him.

Ewan swallowed. 'I know. I just didn't think it'd be that easy.'

'The right bloke turned up at the right time,' Stanley shrugged. 'I'd have been daft to turn him down.'

'So, have you given him a permanent job?'

Dirk laughed and leant across the table. 'Don't fret, man.' He put his hand on Ewan's arm. 'If you need your job again, I'll go flip burgers in Madrid.' I'd never understood the emoji with crosses for eyes until I saw Ewan's face in that moment.

'You?'

Dirk laughed at him.

'I thought you were moving to Spain!'

'We will,' Maria said, 'when he has learned Espanish.'

'And I've earned enough to buy us a finca outside the city,' Dirk added.

Ewan sighed his relief. He thanked Dirk, he thanked Stanley, he thanked Maria and then he thanked Dirk again.

Behind us, the pub was filling up. The Neanderthal and the Smeg Fridge had walked in, dressed alike as before, but this time in white shirts and bootlace ties. Neanderthal looked across and raised a friendly hand. 'A'reyt, lads?' It was as if we were old pals.

They were followed in by a square bloke in a green sweatshirt. 'A'reyt, Rawhide,' he shouted at Ewan. Ewan raised his hand.

'Cribbs Social must be shut,' he commented. 'I've never seen The Fleece so full on a Sunday.' Next through the door was Millie. She stood on the doormat whilst she scanned for us. I stood to signal to her. 'You never said Millie was coming?'

'Sorry, I'm late,' she told Stanley, as she arrived at our table. 'I was on call until seven.' I stood to kiss her. She still smelt of soap. 'Mandy's just parking her car,' she added, unbuttoning her jacket.

Ewan looked at Stanley and Stanley spread his hands. The thrum and jostle of The Fleece had Trevor as cheerful as when Yorkshire had last won a Roses match. He'd even pandered to the Cribbs country and western vibe by playing Kenny Rogers. There were already more Stetsons and cowboy boots than at a Nashville hoe-down. I noticed Moneybags at the bar. When I pointed him out, I thought Ewan would choke on his beer. He grabbed Stanley's wrist to stop him gesturing Moneybags over but Stanley wrenched it free. 'He doesn't know anybody else!' Stanley said as Moneybags raised his lime and soda in greeting. Ewan's face, when he looked at me, was a dumb show of incredulity.

'What's going on?' he demanded.

'Thanks for asking me,' Moneybags smiled when he arrived at our table.

'Least I could do,' Stanley answered, drawing up a stool. 'You've been very fair.'

'Well, we can't have the lad miserable, can we?' I was suddenly embarrassed. Moneybags had been good to me. He was odd, but he was decent.

'I've not been miserable,' I protested, but Moneybags raised his eyebrows. 'I'm just not that keen on blacksmithing.' Moneybags was shaking his head kindly. 'I've learnt a lot these past few weeks.' His eyes were still on me. 'I just don't like being inside.'

'It's right,' Ewan chipped in. 'The nutter took us on a picnic when it were minus two.' Stanley chortled at the memory and Ewan pointed a finger through the thickening throng. 'Our Lee's here!' There was wonder in his voice. Ewan wasn't just smelling a rat, he was watching it dance on the table. Moneybags' understanding and affability was making me uneasy, so I followed Ewan towards his brother, even though Lee was chatting to Moon Face. 'What are *you* doing here?' Ewan demanded of his brother.

'Supping free ale, like you,' Lee blurted with a cheery glance at his glass.

Ewan's eyes ping-ponged between us. 'Come on! What's going on?'

A tremor of uncertainty flickered Lee's assurance, then he found his script again. 'They're here to watch our dad. He's on at ten.'

'What? Here?'

'No! At Caesar's fucking Palace.' Ewan's head wagged as if it were loose.

'Why did nobody tell me?'

'Nobody's been able to tell you fuck all, have they?' Lee shot back 'You've been like Lord fucking Lucan!' Ewan twisted a wry smile. He was back in role as his brother's adversary where everything made sense.

Over his shoulder I saw his dad walk in carrying a microphone stand. Steve was followed by a rhinestoned couple lugging guitar cases, amps and coils of leads. Trevor bustled from behind the bar with a tea towel over his shoulder and began prodding, bellowing and herding the drinkers away from the dartboard to create a makeshift stage. His action pressed my shoulder against Moon Face's.

'A'reyt, Posh Lad?' Moon Face said. He was wearing jeans and a belt with a bull-head buckle. I nodded, like he was an old pal.

The rhinestoned couple pulled a fiddle and a guitar from two black cases and whilst the pub boomed, they tinkered and plucked. There were perhaps a hundred people in there now but the ping and twangle of their instruments pierced their chatter. Steve plonked a black Stetson on his head and picked up a banjo. I watched, fascinated as he plucked strings, turned keys and cocked his ear to the fiddle and the guitar. Music was in this family's bones. If they'd been to Beaumont College, the Grimshaws would have become record producers or composers. They'd have known the right people; they'd have taken the right routes. I scanned the pub and wondered how many more talents were being squandered on Cribbs estate.

I was still lost in my thoughts when the musical trio started blasting out their first song. *Rollin' ... Rollin' ... Rollin' ..., Keep them doggies rollin' ... Rollin' ... Rollin' ... Rollin', Rawhide!*

Ewan was being manhandled to the bare patch of carpet that was the stage. They nudged him, grabbed his sleeves and shoved on his back until he was between his dad and the woman with the fiddle and the rhinestone belt.

Ewan's dad stepped up to the mic and took up the verse.

'Through rain an' wind an' weather, Hell bent for leather,
Wishin' my gal was by my side!'

Beer bounced in glasses, and drinkers swayed and sang. Only Bob Entwistle and Carlos remained on seats. Ewan was standing with his characteristic cool, but the stretch of his eye sockets registered his puzzlement. At the end of the song the light fittings trembled with the cheer that went up from the crowd. Before Ewan could melt back into the throng, Stanley was beside him at the microphone.

'I don't often throw a party,' he said, circling Ewan's shoulder with his arm to prevent his escape. 'Let alone a surprise one ...' I caught Ewan's look, but I just kept grinning. 'But we've a lot to celebrate tonight.' Stanley gestured towards Dirk. 'There's a welcome back to Dirk Koetzee,' Dirk raised his beer in acknowledgement, and a mild cheer rumbled the pub. Stanley gestured to me. 'And a newly forged business partnership.' I looked at my shoes. 'But tonight is really about Ewan Grimshaw.' He squeezed Ewan's shoulder, shouts bounced the beer glasses behind the bar and the guitar player slapped Ewan on the back. 'I've taught this lad all he knows ...' There were jeers and catcalls from the floor. 'I said all *he* knows, not all *I* know!' Stanley clarified. 'But he's decided to spread his wings. In a few days' time he'll be on a cruise liner in the Mediterranean!' They cheered as if every one of them had a ticket for that cruise liner; as if the whole of Cribbs was sailing away from zero hours contracts, loan sharks and food banks.

'He'll be t'first off Cribbs to work abroad!' Trevor announced from behind the bar, but The Neanderthal put him straight.

'Bullshit!' he shouted. 'Our Chelsea were a cage dancer in Magaluf!'

'And my cousin works in Manchester!' Smeg Fridge added. Over the laughter that followed, Steve started picking the strings of his banjo and Ewan crept from the stage.

'Did you know about this?' he asked me, when he arrived at my elbow.

I nodded. 'Maria gave Stanley a right rollicking for being so miserable with you, so he got your Lee to help him sort it.' Ewan looked to where Maria was quietly nursing Carlos.

'She'll have scared the shit out of him,' he chuckled.

'She must have,' I agreed. 'He's put three hundred quid behind the bar.'

'I don't really deserve it, do I?'

'Course you do. You've taken his abuse for seven years!'

'I've been a shit – to Jade, to Stanley – and to you.'

'You've not been a shit to me.'

'I was jealous.' This was rare self-awareness from a fellow Yorkshireman. 'I saw your life opening up for you, and I thought – what's the fucking point?'

'So, you took off?'

He took a deep in breath. 'I was already cocking it up with Rochelle.' I couldn't disagree with that. 'It was Jade who made me see I could get off the tramlines.'

'She's a good lass.'

'She is. I know.' I watched Steve's fingers blurring on the banjo strings.

'I didn't even know your dad could play the banjo.'

'Banjo, guitar, mandolin …' Ewan said. 'The Von Crap family, that's us.'

Steve had taken the microphone again now. 'Our Ewan'll tell you,' he began, 'that we have a song for every occasion, in our house.' He was still picking on the banjo strings as he spoke. The guitar player joined in a counterpoint. 'So before Ewan sails on the seven seas, I'd like to give him a bit of advice. He took a step back and began to sing: *Promise me, son, not to do what I have done …*' there was applause and laughter as the crowd recognised 'Coward of the County'. Soon the whole room was swaying their pint glasses in time with the melody. I watched Moon Face booming along enthusiastically with absolutely no sense of irony when the song advised him to walk away from trouble.

Ewan shuffled through the crowd and sat beside Maria. I couldn't hear their conversation, but I saw the peck on the cheek and the squeeze of his hands. Maria had been recognisable again this week; she'd berated Stanley, organised Dirk and laughed at my description of Moneybags.

'Time to liven it up, now!' Steve announced. 'I think most of you know what you're doin' wi' this!' He picked the opening bars of 'Achy Breaky Heart' and the Cribbs crowd whooped. 'If you don't know the steps, just follow Shazza and Dogg.' It wasn't hard to work out who they were. They were already side-stepping and heel flicking, hands in front pockets on ten square inches of carpet. Stools were tipped and beer was abandoned as huddles transformed into ranks. Even Lee was swaggering and toe tapping like a cowboy in a gold-rush saloon. Ewan knew the moves too. I watched him guide Jade through some steps.

A fat woman in tight jeans hauled at Dirk's hands. 'Come on!' she shouted. 'You can't sit this out wi' them boots on!' Maria waved her permission and Dirk was crowned with the lass's Stetson and shamed into stumbling and staggering the steps. Jade had the hang of it now; she was twirling and toe-tapping with characteristic grace.

Relieved, Ewan threw himself panting, into Dirk's empty seat. I was smirking at Dirk's stuttering, toe-treading galumphs when I caught sight of a lean figure skirting the ranks of the dancers. Her pink jeans flashed in and out of vision like a broken neon sign. I nudged Ewan sharply. He saw what I saw. His eyes darted towards Jade. She was laughing as she heel-toed on the makeshift dance-floor. He sat up straight. Rochelle emerged on the edge of the crowd. She dodged the unpredictable back-kicks and stumbles of the dancers and stopped right in front of us. Only then did she raise her eyes to Ewan's.

'Why have you been screening my calls?' The desolation of abandonment was hollow in her tone.

Ewan filled his chest with air. 'I needed some space.'

'From me?'

'From everyone.'

Still, she stared.

He fidgeted with a beer mat.

'Can we talk?'

He glanced at Jade. She was attempting to manhandle Dirk through some steps. He looked back at Rochelle. 'There's really nothing to say, Rochelle.' Ewan must have felt the heat of her gaze.

'Come outside.' Her tone had pitched it somewhere between a plea and an order. Ewan's eyes left hers again and he pointed to where Jade was side-stepping with her thumbs in her belt. Her inexperience had caused her a misstep, and she was laughing.

'That's Jade, in the yellow dress.' She was back in rhythm again, swinging and sashaying.

'You were quick enough to forget her at Mervyn's party.'

Ewan dropped his eyes. 'I've been getting a few things wrong lately,' then he stood. 'I hope things work out for you and Shaniqua.' He side-stepped from behind the table and Rochelle watched as he joined the line of dancers and took Jade's hand.

If Rochelle's clothes had been dripping wet, she could not have looked more drenched, more down, more dreary. She stared until the sight of Ewan and Jade had sunk its story into her skull.

She turned to me. 'Will *you* come outside with me?'

'Me?' She must have heard the shock in my voice.

'I wanted to show Ewan something, but I can show you.'

What was she playing at? I followed her through the pressing crowd. She had less swagger, less sass than I remembered. She seemed less than Flashman Freddie's daughter and it showed

281

in the set of her shoulders and the stammer of her walk. She was trodden on and shoulder barged by the crowd.

We stepped onto Hathersage Road in a feathering of summer drizzle. The light was fading. We crossed the road to where her shiny new VW Beetle was gleaming like Snow White's apple under a sodium light. 'If this is what you wanted to show me,' I said. 'I already know.'

'This?' She laughed drily. 'It's on the never-never. I ordered it when I got the job at Mervyn's.' She clicked her keys and the car winked at her; it looked like much needed friendship. She opened the boot and stood back with the gesture of a magician.

There, on the back seat was a black, mud caked, Kappa sports bag, circa 1996. Its broken toothed zip was open by six inches and the elastic band gripping a tight pack of fifties was poking through it. I looked at her. She was staring down at the dirty bag. I looked back at it. I was beginning to see the world through her eyes.

I whispered to her. 'What were you playing at, Rochelle?'

She sat on the tailgate of her new car and sighed. 'I just thought ...' She fished for words; for a new way to spread out the haul of her thoughts and hopes. The whites of her eyes were gleaming in the darkness. 'Shaniqua needs a dad, and he was so good with her ...' A twisting ribbon of water, like molten black glass in the gutter took her attention. 'And I thought he liked me ...' She took a deep breath. 'I'd thought that *that* ...' her eyes had flicked to the booty, 'could give us a fresh start. Somewhere new. Somewhere I'm not a dodgy gypo's daughter and he's not a skank off Cribbs estate.'

I sat beside her on the tailgate. The car wallowed with my weight and soft raindrops spattered on the makeshift roof above our heads. 'He'd have told you to give it back, you know.'

She nodded slowly. 'I know that now – but he'd have known how much ...' Her words trickled away. We sat shoulder to shoulder and listened to the rain. It was swirling in the gutter

now, whirlpooling around my toe. 'I rang him that night –
straight after you'd gone.'

'But he didn't pick up.'

'No.'

I swivelled my head so I was looking at her. 'But, why didn't
you go into work the day after?'

'My dad was all over it by then, wasn't he! Advising me to
scarper before they missed it, telling me how to get it changed
for legal tender, insisting I should go over to Ireland for a bit.'

'But you went back for your wages!' I reminded her.

'Double bluff, dad said. He'd seen them reseeding the
field and thought Mervyn had put two and two together.' The
rain was puddling now; it was dribbling in the down pipes.
'I waited for him on the fell road on Monday morning. I was
going to follow the van and meet him on the car-park – but
he wasn't in it.' The snap and trickle of the raindrops was like
soft discordant music. 'I've blown it now though, haven't I?'
Her laugh was a soft bump. 'I'm an idiot.' We watched little
detonations of rain explode in silver pools floodlit by the street
lamps and I remembered Mervyn's words: *She was the best
head lad I ever had.*

'Why don't you go in there and ask Mervyn for your job
back?' She shifted her weight so a cascade of raindrops show-
ered us from the tailgate. 'You'll have no need to worry about
bumping in to Ewan, week in week out.'

She looked up. 'Why not?'

'He's leaving,' I said. Her lungs filled, then emptied. It was
a gasp of sadness and a rush of relief.

'Because of me?'

'No!' I laughed, drily. 'Because of me.' I felt her curiosity.
'Or maybe a bit of both – I'll tell you some other time. Just go
and give that money to Mervyn.'

'What will I tell him?'

'Anything! He won't care so long as he gets it. Tell him
your dog found it!' She laughed and when my feet were in the

gutter again, she slammed the boot. We hunched against the rain and hurried into The Fleece. The warmth hit me like a wall. The room was stomping, clapping and heel tapping and the press of bodies had been augmented by the smell of beer, rain and sweat. Steve was twangling the opening chords of 'D-I-V-O-R-C-E' and Stanley was being mocked and dragged to his feet. He was belt gripping and side shuffling like a trained gorilla. I slipped onto a seat beside Millie. Her look questioned the raindrops speckling the shoulders of my shirt. I was glad our proximity to an amp made conversation impossible. I answered by pointing through the dancers to where Rochelle was approaching Mervyn. Not even free beer had persuaded him to dance. Jay was dancing inexpertly in front of us. Only his natural exuberance was helping him to wing it. He'd spotted Rochelle's approach. The to-ing and fro-ing of dancers in front of Rochelle and Mervyn cast their conversation as stills from a film.

I saw Mervyn with his arms folded over his belly, then Rochelle with her palms up and her fingers splayed. Jay had seen them too. He was craning round a dancer for a better view and missed a step. Mervyn's finger was outstretched. Rochelle's eyes were on her shoes. Jay was side stepping, trying to see. He crushed Ewan's foot. Ewan screeched and hopped. Behind him, Mervyn was shaking his head. Jay tried to fit back into the line of dancers. Rochelle must have said something funny because Mervyn was laughing. Jay still hadn't slotted back in. He stepped at the wrong time. His leg crossed in front of another leg. Jay was going down. He was grabbing at fresh air. His limbs were tangling with the other dancers, who were staggering and tumbling. The music was stuttering. Lines of dancers were folding to arcs, clotting to clusters then piling onto the carpet. The room clattered to a clanging silence.

A groan droned.

Somewhere near the middle, Jade was clambering to her feet and tugging at her dress to preserve decency. A cowboy-booted man on the edge stooped for his Stetson. A gingham shirted woman held out her hand to another who was clutching her knee. Meanwhile, Jay was lying crumpled on the carpet, his leg at an improbable angle.

Steve put down his banjo. Moon Face had crossed the floor and was crouching beside Jay. He sat Jay up. Jay was white. Lee crossed the carpet and spoke to his dad, Steve. Steve went back to the microphone.

'Right,' he said, the hollowness of his voice bouncing unexpectedly off the watching walls. 'It's looking like this lad needs a trip to A & E.' Mervyn was moving his head from side to side in resigned dismay. 'Is anyone here still under the limit?' Laughter dribbled round the room and gurgled like a hospital sluice.

'Just ring a bloody ambulance,' Stanley grumbled, but Moneybags was parting the crowd like a Superhero.

'I've only had lime and soda,' he announced and Stanley's eyes rolled back in their sockets.

'Harken at bastard Clark Kent,' he muttered. The rest of the pub rumbled a congratulatory cheer – or was it a mocking cheer? One or two even applauded.

Neanderthal and Smeg Fridge hoiked Jay under the arms and staggered him out to Moneybags' car. Behind them, Rochelle slipped out into the rain.

Steve took the microphone again. 'I think we'll slow it down, now,' he smiled as he adjusted his Stetson. 'We don't want any more broken legs.'

The bow of the fiddle drew out long plaintive notes and the crowd started shifting. It was parting for Lee, who handed me his beer as he passed. He stepped up beside his father and stood squarely at the microphone. My mouth fell open when he sang in a pitch perfect tenor:

'The ocean's wide, with many ship afloat,
That'll lead Ewan to who knows where, who knows where.'

As the audience recognised the tune of 'He Ain't Heavy,

He's My Brother', its two hundred eyes drifted to Ewan. I saw his lips disappear inside his mouth, and his teeth drag on his skin. Behind him, Rochelle was skirting the edge of the room; her hair was dripping raindrops and she was carrying a dirty sports bag.

Steve and the other musicians had thrown the force of their voices behind Lee's. *'But we are strong, cos we are all Yorkshiremen.'*

Rochelle was standing in front of Mervyn with the sports bag dangling from her hand.

The singers dropped out for Lee's solo: *'The lad goin' cruising, he's my brother.'* Ewan's eyes were sparkling with tears.

Rochelle was holding out the bag to Mervyn.

Ewan was rising to his feet.

Lee's strong voice was sailing into the second verse. The room was reverent.

Ewan was crossing the pub to, *It's a long, long way.* He was stepping up beside his brother. *But I know he will return, for even in Spain, he'll miss Yorkshire rain.* The brothers' arms were circling each other's shoulders.

Mervyn was taking the bag.

Steve was playing without falter. The brothers were singing with full throated ease. *The ocean's wide, with many a ship afloat.*

Mervyn was shaking Rochelle's hand.

He's goin' cruisin', he's my brother. The last note faded and the Cribbs crowd fumbled pints through coughs and eye brushes. I swallowed a pebble and the three Grimshaw men joined foreheads in a private circle.

The pub door banged open and Smeg and Neanderthal strutted back in. 'Is he a'reyt?' Trevor shouted at them.

'Nah!' Smeg answered, as he brushed raindrops from his shirt. 'It were dangling like Alan Carr's wrist.'

'How did he do it?' Trevor asked.

Shazza pointed at him. 'Hey, if t'carpet were rucked, you'll be liable!'

'He fell over his own feet!' Dogg attested.

'He'll be after t'compo just t'same,' Neanderthal stated. 'I would.'

Trevor looked at Mervyn. 'Is that why you sacked him, Mervyn?' But Mervyn was still staring at the sports bag at his feet, so Stanley answered for him

'That lad'd be a bloody billionaire if he'd claimed t'compo after every accident – wouldn't he, Mervyn?' but Stanley's eyes had also found the sports bag now. 'I'll tell you what though, Trev,' he added. 'If he does come for t'compo, you can always say he tripped o'er that bag o' Mervyn's.' There was a clueless chuckle, during which Mervyn met Stanley's eye and knowledge was exchanged for knowledge of knowledge.

Millie squeezed my hand. 'What's that about?' she whispered, looking at them.

'That,' I answered quietly. 'Is about muck and money.' She looked puzzled. 'You know: *where there's muck there's brass?*'

Her eyes twinkled and she curled a wry smile. 'You'd better hope that's true,' she said. 'Because you've just sunk your entire fortune, into farriery!'

Acknowledgements

Writing a novel is a dogged and often dispiriting task, so I owe an enormous debt of gratitude to Victoria Hobbs, my agent, who persists in colluding in my illusion that I am a proper writer. Thanks are also due to Harriet Bourton at Orion who delivers expert advice with welcome tact.

My husband John has read and re-read experimental versions of this novel until he's nearly cross-eyed and he still blows the trumpet of my limited talent at dinner parties; thank you, John. The late Pippa Taylor's criticism was always kind and intelligent; I was grateful for her kid gloves whenever my confidence waned and I fear the writing process without her gentle encouragement. My son, Joe, is a farrier, a wit, an observer of life, a purveyor of tales and my inspiration; thank you. Neither should I forget my horses, past and present; dead and alive. They have also found life in these pages and I owe to them, not only literary inspiration, but my energy and love for life. Lucky, the dog, is anxious to retain her anonymity.

Credits

Catherine Robinson and Orion Fiction would like to thank everyone at Orion who worked on the publication of *Where There's Muck* in the UK.

Editorial
Harriet Bourton
Olivia Barber

Copy editor
Laura Gerrard

Proof reader
Linda Joyce

Contracts
Anne Goddard
Paul Bulos
Jake Alderson

Design
Rachael Lancaster
Joanna Ridley
Nick May

Editorial Management
Charlie Panayiotou
Jane Hughes

Finance
Jasdip Nandra
Afeera Ahmed
Elizabeth Beaumont
Sue Baker

Audio
Paul Stark
Amber Bates

Production
Ruth Sharvell

Marketing
Tanjiah Islam

Publicity
Patricia Deveer

Sales
Jen Wilson
Esther Waters
Victoria Laws
Rachael Hum
Ellie Kyrke-Smith

Frances Doyle
Georgina Cutler

Operations
Jo Jacobs
Sharon Willis
Lisa Pryde
Lucy Brem

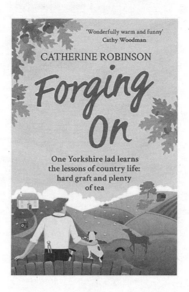